3/18/05 BfT # 23.95

THE MARBLE KITE

David Daniel

Thomas Dunne Books | St. Martin's Minotaur
New York

MYS
DANIE

THOMAS DUNNE BOOKS.
An imprint of St. Martin's Press.

www.minotaurbooks.com

Library of Congress Cataloging-in-Publication Data

Daniel, David, 1945–
    The marble kite : a mystery / David Daniel.—1st ed.
        p.   cm.
    ISBN 0-312-32351-4
    EAN 978-0312-32351-6
    1. Rasmussen, Alex (Fictitious character)—Fiction.   2. Private investigators—Massachusetts—Lowell—Fiction.   3. Women—Crimes against—Fiction.   4. Lowell (Mass.)—Fiction.   5. Carnivals—Fiction.   I. Title.

PS3554.A5383M37   2005
813'.54—dc22
                                                                2004058534

First Edition: April 2005

10 9 8 7 6 5 4 3 2 1

For Stephanie

Acknowledgments

I want to thank the following, who were helpful in various ways: Capt. William Taylor and Deputy Superintendent Dennis Cormier of the Lowell Police Department; Dan MacGilvray at Middlesex County Superior Court; Ken Terrill of Fiesta Shows; John Sampas, literary executor of the Jack Kerouac Estate; Prof. William Roberts and the members of the English Department at the University of Massachusetts, Lowell, who made my term as writer-in-residence such fun; Rick Cooper, for his marksman's eye; Robert Sanchez; Barbara Mellin and Joseph Nardoni, editors of *Middlesex Magazine,* where a portion of this novel first appeared under the title "Carnival"; and finally, as always, my editor, Ruth Cavin.

THE
MARBLE
KITE

Phoebe Kelly jerked away from me with a shriek, and this only our fourth date. I turned to see who or what had spooked her. The clown was several inches over my six-one, broad as a circus barrel, holding a torch that roared softly and lit him in the September dusk. The baggy outfit of red and green stripes, big ruffled collar, cherry red nose—all the standard getup of Emmett Kelly (no relation to Phoebe)—looked harmless enough, but in the torch flare there was something decidedly unsettling in the way he eyed her, his long, crooked teeth yellow against the white greasepaint. It was something that Orson Welles might've tricked up on an overdose of Poe. In the flickering light, everything seemed a little furtive: Phoebe's look of alarm, the clown's leer, people slowing to glance our way as they wandered past. Then he honked a plastic horn, did a little dance step straight from Gene Kelly (no relation to Phoebe or Emmett), tipped his head back in a silent, toothy howl, and shambled away on big flippity-flap shoes, leaving the lingering kerosene scent of his torch. What was there to do but laugh?

"Gah!" Phoebe gave an exaggerated shudder. "Creeps me out. He's crazy."

"What's a carnival without a psycho clown?"

"Not funny, Rasmussen. I'm serious. And he pinched my butt." She rubbed her shapely, denim-clad behind, watching the departing clown, who, judging by other cries—of panic or delight, I couldn't say—was plying his clown trade in the mild twilight of autumn. But Phoebe's shriek had excited something in me, some old pulse from high school days, of taking a girl down to the Rialto on a Friday night to see a scary flick, the girl momentarily frightened, and me comforting, and both of us laughing and feeling the sweet pleasure of closeness, and the promise of something more. "Come on," she said, enthusiastic again. "What should we do next?"

We strolled past a line of children and parents waiting to enter a large semitrailer rigged up as a haunted house. "This?" I asked her.

"Castle Spookula? Uh-uh. I don't like scary things."

Attached to one side of the haunted house was a row of funhouse mirrors. We stepped in front of the first two. She was a squat Humpty Dumpty with a football-shaped head as wide as her shoulders. I was a beanpole with an apple on top.

"Too bad they don't have a mirror maze, like the one in *The Lady from Shanghai*," I said.

"You and your old movies. I assume it's a movie."

"Black and white. Orson Welles and Rita Hayworth."

"Wasn't she that redhead?"

"Yep, only she's platinum blond in this one. Her hair glows white in the dark, like a magnet for suckers."

"I like movies in color." Phoebe was gazing into another mirror now, at the image of a wrinkled crone. "What can we possibly see in each other?" she asked, laughing.

I knew what I saw in her. Auburn hair cut to the collar, dramatic green eyes, and slightly upturned nose. Pretty smile. She still had my private investigator's mind guessing how many sides to her there were—so far, I'd seen several and liked them all. Dressed in ripped-at-the-knees jeans and a sweatshirt, as she'd been on our second date, she gave a hint of mischief; in a white silk blouse and dark skirt, earrings, and a whisper of makeup, the way I'd seen her at work, she was office elegance itself. Tonight, wearing black slacks, a dove gray turtleneck, and a black crushed-velvet jacket, she was all that and more.

Around us carnival rides pinwheeled, dipped, looped, and tilted in the electric dark, shills hailed passersby, air rifles *pop-pop-popped* in the shooting arcades, and a scratchy Michael Jackson record blared out of cheap loudspeakers— *"Why, why? Tell 'em that it's human nature . . ."* From Castle Spookula came the muted shrieks of visitors. "Okay, kid," I said, giving it a Bogart drawl. "How 'bout I win you something?"

"Such as?"

"What do you want?"

"I don't know . . . a rock from Harry Winston?"

"Settle for a stuffed Flintstone from Bedrock?"

"Mmm, not very romantic—but okay. If I get to pick the game."

"Let me count the ways I can make a clown of myself on a carnival midway."

Holding hands, we strolled along under the lights, amid the tents and the little makeshift stalls and the mingling aromas of popcorn, fried dough, and roasting sausage and peppers, the Ferris wheel glittering against the darkening sky. It was the same show that had been coming to Lowell early each autumn for years, setting up for a week in the big field across VFW Highway from the esplanade on the river. It didn't change, any of it. It was childhood and fun and romance and a little tincture of fright, too.

We scuffed through the straw, taking it all in. There were families out, and sailors fresh from boot camp and home on leave, and young people in hooded sweatshirts and jean jackets against the cool drifting out of the river, and a few Lowell cops on detail, roaming. We got fresh-spun pink cotton candy, which, like the carnival itself, was more about allure and promise than about delivery. Though why was I thinking that? We had been out only three times before, the last a week ago, for pizza. I was still looking forward to the delivery (her, not the pizza), but there was already plenty of allure.

Phoebe was a lively thirty-six-year-old who had been widowed for five years and made no bones about wanting to be coupled again—nearly *had* been after venturing into the singles scene for a time and falling for an engineer, but the relationship had collapsed when he got cold feet. I'd been single about half that long, and until recently had been holding on to some hope that Lauren and I would rekindle our flame. But Lauren was remarried now, a new mother, living in Boca Raton. And I was still in Lowell, had in fact bought a house, which is how I'd met Phoebe, during the course of several visits to the Registry of Deeds, where she worked, to clear the title. Things were pretty good, and right now, with a big moon rising, silhouetting the smokestacks of an old textile mill and the spider-work of one of the bridges that spanned the river, and winter still a couple of months beyond worrying about, I was reminded of why I loved (and sometimes hated) this city.

We wandered over to a row of stands at the back, away from the rides and the brighter lights, to the booths of the games of chance—remote chance, if truth were told, but that was okay. Phoebe was holding my hand, and I felt lucky. We bypassed the shooting gallery, the dart toss, the basketball throw, and the stacked wooden milk bottles, and suddenly Phoebe stopped. "This!"

The sign read RING THE BELL. THREE SWINGS FOR TWO TICKETS.

"Hit the thingy with the hammer," she said, "win a prize. I like that teddy bear hanging there. The parti-colored one."

The barker gave us a tentative grin. "The lady knows what she wants."

I moused inside my pocket, tweezed out a string of tickets, tore off two at the perforations, and was about to lay them into his palm when I noted that the hand was deformed, twisted in an odd way and missing the pinkie finger. I gave him the tickets. "Good luck," he murmured.

I took hold of the long wooden handle of the mallet, which was wrapped with friction tape. "The teddy bear, huh? Piece of cake."

"Careful what you wish for." The barker pointed. Halfway up the tall pole, several feet above "Mama's Boy" and "Panty Waist," was the designation "Cake Eater." At the top, at the bell, was "Super Man."

"You're just trying to psych him out," Phoebe told the guy.

I rubbed my palms together and put a chokehold on the thick handle, finding the right spot on the taped-up shaft. I brought the hammer up behind my head, arms cocked, getting my shoulders into it, and swung it down onto the heel of the strike plate. The weight catapulted up a thin wire along the pole, hit the bell, and sent a crisp *ding* into the encircling dusk. "That's one!" Phoebe cried, jumping with childlike excitement.

Keeping the rhythm, I swung the hammer up and around and down. *Ding.*

Phoebe hugged me and gave me a kiss.

The bell was like a dinner gong for passersby. Smelling blood, they closed in like sharks. "Got us a Super Man in the making!" the barker called, waving more people in to watch. "Ain't had a winner all night. Nothing but Mama's Boys. Okay now—three's the charm. Bring home an animal for the little lady."

"Watch it, you!" Phoebe said good-naturedly.

I winked at her, and she clasped her hands together and batted her eyelashes at me, getting into it. "Wouldja? Couldja, Mister Hero?"

Our little gallery laughed.

I did, too. I felt good. It was autumn and I was healthy and had gainful employment. I had a long-term gig with Atlantic Casualty Insurance, running down double-dippers. I had a new home and a new woman in my life. I raised the hammer up behind me, ready to uncoil one final time to knock that little bell right off the top and launch it toward the big rising bell of a moon. I started my swing.

At the scream, I clenched. The hammer hit the fulcrum plate off center. Like a broken-bat hit, the weight wobbled up past Mama's Boy and Panty Waist, limped into Cake Eater country, then fell back with a slack *thunk.* Amid a chorus of *awww*s I turned, half-expecting to see the clown again, but there was no clown there, and Phoebe hadn't been the source of the scream. It had come from farther away, and now another scream followed it, and the flesh on the back of my neck crawled. I dropped the mallet and reached for Phoebe's hand, dimly aware of the barker's pale, frightened face.

She hurried to my side, and we dodged through a flow of people that bumbled along over the trampled straw, away from the midway toward the back, where trailers and campers and carnival trucks sat in an adjacent field.

A cry came again, less a scream now than a call for help. We skirted around Castle Spookula. The commotion was beyond it, in a meadow that ended far back in woods. A short way in, near enough to the carnival midway that the lights cast some fading glow, a small cluster of people stood in shadows, pointing down. I let go of Phoebe's hand and motioned her back. I waded through the knee-deep weeds until I got close enough to see what they were pointing at. A woman, her long dark hair flung in a glossy fan, lay there, face up, her hips turned so that her knees were drawn partway up. She had on tight jeans and a brightly patterned cotton blouse, which was ripped open to her navel.

"Back!" I shouted, more sharply than I'd meant to. It startled the nearest onlookers, who backpedaled hastily, trampling weeds.

"We seen something pale and we come over and she's just laying there," one of the young women was breathlessly telling anyone who'd listen.

Trying my best not to enter the actual space, I bent and looked at the woman's face. She was staring upward with a fixed gaze, her eyes wide, but they were opaque in the moonlight. There seemed to be some kind of bruise or dirt mark on her right cheek, and there was a red or orange silk scarf knotted around her neck. I glanced at Phoebe, who, despite my warning, had followed me. Her face was full of fright. "Oh, my God, is she—?"

"Call nine-one-one," I said.

"Someone already did," said a man standing behind her.

"There's police at the carnival somebody's getting," a woman said.

Careful that I wasn't simply feeling my own pulse, which was fast and hard now, I searched for a beat in the woman's slender wrist.

Phoebe looked ashen.

The wrist was cold. I put my fingers to the woman's throat, below the knotted scarf. Was there a throb there? No. What I did experience was some vestigial impulse, a twitch to take charge, to keep the citizens moving along, to secure the area, to call the ME. But I did none of those. That wasn't my job anymore. I realized, anyway, that the woman was beyond needing my help. I stood and took Phoebe's arm and led her back a respectful distance. In a moment, a pair of cops came hurrying through the high grass.

2

The story was front-page news in the sunrise edition of the paper. CITY WOMAN SLAIN, CARNIVAL WORKER CHARGED. The dead woman, Flora Nuñez, twenty-six, with a Lower Highlands neighborhood address, had been strangled, more details pending. A carnival patron, going to retrieve a thrown Frisbee, had found the body. Within an hour of the discovery, the report continued, Lowell police had arrested a carnival roustabout named Troy Pepper, thirty-four, of Nutley, New Jersey, and charged him with the murder. Witnesses placed him and the victim together several hours before she was found, which he admitted to. Unnamed physical evidence recovered from his trailer at the carnival site linked the man to the crime.

I looked up from the story at the knock on my open office door. Fred Meecham, my attorney neighbor, stuck his head in. "You read about last night?"

I put down the newspaper. "I was there."

He shut the door, not that we needed the privacy; my waiting room was empty. He came in and sat down. "You were at the scene?"

Leaving out my near heroics with the hammer, I told him how I had come to be there when Flora Nuñez's body was found.

"I just came from police headquarters. Nobody mentioned that."

"I wasn't one of the people who found her. The cops talked mostly to them. I hung around in the event they decided to cast their net wider, but they didn't. We stuck till homicide and an ambulance got there, and then cleared out to let them do their job. I was long gone when they busted this—" I broke off. "Fred, am I reading into this that you've got a job to do, too?"

Meecham pushed back his wave of brown hair, which flopped down again at once over his forehead. "I've been retained in the case."

"To represent this—" I scanned the column for the name.

"Troy Pepper. Yes."

"Court appointed?" I knew he did pro bono work.

"Nix, I'm hired. The carnival boss telephoned me first thing this morning and said he wanted legal representation for Pepper. He got my name from someone out there."

"Lucky you. It doesn't sound like you've got much of a case, from what I read here."

"Inculpatory evidence is strong. In fact, the only thing I hear to the contrary is from the person who hired me. He doesn't believe Pepper did it."

"That must be a comfort."

He narrowed his eyes. "Are you angry about something?"

Was I? Last night had been one of those dream dates, until that awful moment of the scream, and the sight of the dead woman had shaken Phoebe badly. I was miffed because the police seemed to have made it a point to ignore me, though that could just be an ex-cop's paranoia. Or perhaps I was upset by yet another act of violence done to a woman by a man, and I was tired of wondering when it would ever stop, sick of men's weakness, bitter at the way it reflected on all of us.

"You sound it, anyway," Meecham added.

I murmured and left it at that.

"Well, if so, that's good, I think. Even the fact that you aren't on record with any statement is a plus."

I set down the newspaper.

"It might serve you well," Fred went on. "That is, if you're willing to take on an assignment. It dropped on me, and time's short. The arraignment is in an hour. I've got that covered, but I'm going to need help pulling details together in order to see what we've got."

In this business that's how it often goes. People in trouble don't comparison shop. When they suddenly need an attorney or a PI—or an undertaker—they're inclined to grab whoever is at hand. Actually, I had enough insurance work to keep me going right through the holidays if I played it right. It was a good, steady gig that I could run mainly from my desktop and telephone, and it didn't require much shoe leather or sweat, many dealings with officialdom, or so much as a whisper of adrenaline. Maybe that's what was wrong with it. Something in me had stirred last night, some old yen for the hunt, an impulse to set things right. I drew myself up sharply. Did I just think that? *An impulse to set things right?* Good Lord deliver us from a PI on a mission. "I don't know, Fred."

"When can you start?"

3

I fired up my two-year-old Cougar and got through downtown traffic. In JFK Plaza a large billboard was currently touting the message PROUDLY SERVING AND PROTECTING YOU under a group picture of various city police personnel of just the right rank, ethnic, racial, and gender mix, all grinning a big "We are the world" grin. All but one. With his mustache and dark, intent eyes, my old partner Ed St. Onge wore a somber gunfighter look. I wheeled out Bridge Street and crossed the river. It was a mild Monday morning, the latest in a stretch of such days, with a fleet of puffy white clouds sailing leisurely northward toward New Hampshire, and midday highs of seventy-two degrees—what some people were referring to as Indian summer, though technically it wasn't because we hadn't had a frost yet, but they meant well.

I made my way west along VFW Highway, past the state university, where the football team was practicing. On an adjacent field, a class of criminal justice grads in uniforms and boots were performing hand-to-hand maneuvers. There was also a cheerleading squad in action. All that sanctioned violence under the blue September sky.

"I'll need some background to start," Fred Meecham had said. "You know what to do." I hadn't needed much convincing. True, I had the work for Atlantic Casualty, but hustling the Internet for credit info on total strangers six hours a day is about as interesting as it sounds. The insurance company wasn't in any big hurry to have it done, and I figured I could manage both.

Any homicide investigation begins with a two-prong approach: find out everything you can about the victim and about the killer. I also needed to find out if there were any witnesses beyond the ones that the police had already identified. Meecham directed me to the carnival boss who had hired him, a man named Sonders.

Regatta Field was several miles out on Pawtucket Boulevard, part of a large fairground and meadow opposite the esplanade and the public boathouse. Like a stranger you pick up in a bar and take home, the carnival site appeared a lot different on the morning after. What lights, music, and excitement had done to beguile you was undone fast. In the distance, a man was prodding at litter with a spiked stick. I parked at the curb and strolled toward a gypsy camp of well-worn vans and small makeshift shacks daubed with colors that tried to look bright but seemed only washed out. I passed among the series of booths for games of chance, souvenirs, and fast food, but I might as well have been in a ghost town. The aromas of popcorn and tobacco smoke and fried foods lingered over the scene, awaiting exorcism. Several diesel generators, the source that had given life to the whirling lights and the rides, and even to Michael Jackson, were silent now, electrical cables trailing from them like rubbery gray tentacles. Castle Spookula had the fright quotient of a Casper cartoon. In the meadow beyond, a large rectangular outline of yellow plastic ribbon marked the place where the body had been found.

In my beige summerweight, which I'd have dry-cleaned one more time before I put it away for the winter, I suppose I could've passed for a cop, though I liked to think my J. Garcia silk tie made me a notch more hip. I was looking for a headquarters trailer when I heard the jingling sound. I turned and saw a young woman struggling to control half a dozen dogs who'd managed to tangle their leashes.

"Can I help?" I asked, going over.

The young woman looked surprised to see someone there. "Oh . . . no. Well, could you maybe take this leash?"

I took one, and then another. None of the dogs was barking, so it all just seemed like good fun. Together we sorted out the pack, though I couldn't imagine them staying untangled for long. "Thank you so much," she said. A few of the dogs took a friendly interest in me.

"Are they all yours?"

"Only the beagle—Otis. The others belong to people here."

"Do you work here?"

"Yes." She was small, and I couldn't tell if she was eighteen or twenty-five. She seemed shy but friendly, and a little childlike.

I stooped and began rubbing the beagle's head. "Otis, huh?" All the dogs, except a greyhound, crowded around, thumping me with their tails.

"This big mutt is Tex. The Pomeranians are Mike and Ike. That one that looks like she should be on a diet is Miss Piggy."

"And this one?" I reached to pet the greyhound, but he drew back.

"He's still timid. He was rescued from the racetrack, so he never got much loving till he got adopted. He's awfully sweet, though. We call him Speedo."

"But his real name is Mr. Earl."

"I'm sorry?"

I grinned. "Before your time. What's your name?"

"Nicole."

"I'm Alex Rasmussen. Do you work with Troy Pepper, Nicole?"

Her eyebrows tensed together above her small dark eyes. "Who are you, sir?"

I showed her my license, not that she paid much attention to it. She suddenly seemed as eager to keep a distance as the greyhound was. "Actually, I'm working with the attorney who's defending Mr. Pepper."

She blinked. "Really and truly? You mean like that'll be *his* lawyer?"

"Yes."

She seemed relieved, actually gave a sigh, but then appeared worried all over again. "The police were here a lot last night," she volunteered. "I didn't get much sleep." She was under five feet tall, with the look of undernourishment, but her feelings were big, most of them visible in her face. She had a warm smile somewhere—I'd glimpsed it—but at the moment her expression was about as cheery as a thundercloud. "I wonder what'll happen to Troy? I'm scared for him. And I feel awful for that poor woman who died." As if the dogs were picking up her agitation, they started to pull at their leashes. She stooped and quieted them.

"I'm looking for Mr. Sonders," I said.

"Pop."

"He's your father?"

Her smile made a partial return, like something she was going to trust me with. "We all just call him that." She rose. "Come on with me."

Contrary to my prediction, the dogs kept themselves straight. She led me over to a motor home, a two-tone green and white affair that had the door propped open with a red sand-filled bucket marked NO IFS OR ANDS, JUST BUTTS that sat on the top step. She leaned in. "Pop? Someone's here to talk to you."

A potbellied man appeared in the doorway. He looked about sixty-five, bald, with tufts of white fluff jutting out on the sides above his ears, and a crinkled face, from which he turned bold blue eyes on me. "Another one?" His jaw worked, as if he were chewing tobacco or wearing badly fitted dentures. "What now? You want me to stay?"

"Stay?"

"Or go? Make up your mind, goddammit. You're either a cop or from the city."

"How do you know I'm not a newshound?"

"Dressed up like that?" He snorted. "Most of them tramp around these days straight from Hemingway, like they'd been posted for Baghdad. I just shook one loose—some wet-behind-the-ears mutt working for a Boston paper. Who're you?"

I handed him my card. He examined it. "Okay. Yup, yup, okay." He looked at the girl. "How they doing, sweetheart?"

She smiled. "The dogs? They're great, Pop."

"Good work, kiddo."

"Bye, Pop." She nodded at me, too. "Nice to meet you, sir." She led the dogs away.

The old man waved me into the motor home. "Thing I like about dogs," he said, "when the world's falling in around our ears, they take us just the same as they did yesterday."

"She has them well trained," I said.

"It's one of the unwritten rules, if folks're going to have pets here. But it's also Nicole, she's got a touch. Give me a sec here." He snatched up a portable phone he'd evidently been using. "Yup, he's here now," I heard him tell someone, and guessed that Fred Meecham was on the line.

I turned away to give him what space the area afforded. The motor home appeared to double as living and working quarters, with the desk and a computer, a three-drawer file cabinet, a vinyl recliner embalmed in duct tape, and, beyond a folding partition, a rumpled cot with drawers underneath for storage. The beige carpeting was coffee-stained, and the walls, which were paneled in ersatz wood, were busy with framed good-citizen awards, a vintage Barnum & Bailey poster, and several plywood cutouts in the shapes of big keys. One said SCHENECTADY. I'd always wondered what a key to a city looked like and what it would unlock. There was also a certificate of recognition from a national parents' association with a splashy signature on it that I recognized as a former U.S. president's. Sonders's first name, I discovered, was Warren.

He cradled the phone and moved some papers aside to make a seat for me in the recliner. "Park your bones. Meecham said you'd be out."

He took a beat-up corncob pipe from his desk, clamped the stem between his teeth, and scrutinized me. Apart from the white tufts sprouting from the sides of his head, the only hair on his face grew in tangles above his eyes, stark against the ruddy forehead and cheeks. He was wearing a weathered brown corduroy shirt and a cranberry knit tie, washed-out denim bell-bottoms, and work boots. There was something vivid and restless about him that reminded me of someone, though I couldn't think of who. "It's evidently an open and shut case," he said around the unlit pipe, drilling me with a look. "Guilty." He sank into a spring chair and drew himself in until the edge of the desk creased his belly. "That how it looks to you?"

The folksy manner had set me up for a softer landing. "It isn't for me to say."

"No? You sure about that?"

If he'd been a fly on the wall in my office a half hour ago, he might've thought he had his answer; but he'd have thought wrong. "I was a cop in this city for a while. My job then was to get information, put it together the best I could, and lay it on the table for others to use. That hasn't changed, though I've got certain freedoms now I didn't have then—some I don't advertise. Your attorney will advise you the best way to use what I come up with."

"Well, yuh, okay. Sounds right."

"What was that, a test of the emergency firing system?"

His reaction was a fleeting grin—though it may have been heartburn; I couldn't miss the jug of Mylanta on the desk. There was also a framed photograph of a younger-looking Sonders with a smiling woman. He plucked the pipe from his mouth. "I know Lowell like I know most towns we pitch camp in—a nice place to come and work our asses off for a few days, then move on. People don't get to know us, that's fine, s'long as they spend money. It works both ways and everyone's happy. But now it seems we got us a situation, and all of the sudden there are jokers in the deck I didn't plan on being there. One thing I disagree with you on is that cops are as fair-minded as you say. In my experience, detectives are just street bulls with bigger noses and smaller feet. They tend to be open about things that make their case strong; otherwise . . . uh-uh. I need to know what I'm holding and make my decisions from that. If along the way I got to shitcan a private eye—or a lawyer, for that matter, or tell a reporter to take a hike—on account of it's not gonna work out, well, it's best we both know it right up front. How's that?"

"I think you've got some mixed metaphors in there, but I get the point." I drew out my notebook. "Outside you were saying something about staying or leaving. Care to translate?"

He swung a hand in a sidewise chopping motion. "First they tell me the show is frozen, that we can't leave—not that I would've. I signed a contract to be here, and my name on paper still means something last I checked. But practically the next minute they're ordering my ass out of here."

"Who's 'they'?"

"City licensing office. Some scrawny little geezer in a Robert Hall suit shows up first thing this morning, along with a patrolman, telling me my permits are frozen. I told him I'd speak with my attorney. He said I could if I wanted to, but it wouldn't matter, I'd still have to vacate the premises as soon as the police investigators are done. 'Vacate.' Hell. I got the feeling if this was a hundred years ago, they'd have had rope in their hands and be looking for a big oak tree. Anyway, like I said, I got a contract, and it goes both ways. If they expect me to play square with them, they better by God do the same. Meecham just now told me to sit tight till I hear from him."

"How did you get Meecham's name?"

"Our fathers knew each other at Yale and sat on the Supreme Court together."

I knew Fred's dad retired after thirty years of climbing poles for Ma Bell and dropped dead a month later bending to pick up the newspaper from his doorstep.

He finally frowned. "I got his name off one of the officers on detail last night, and I don't know a soul here. I'm sure there are plenty of lawyers in town. There always are. Meecham seemed okay when we talked."

"I'm working for him, so I'll spare you the sales pitch, except to say he's honest and productive. Which is what he expects me to be, Mr. Sonders." I clicked my ballpoint.

"Fair enough. Call me Pop, by the way."

"Pop." Belatedly, we shook hands.

"Good to meet you, son."

"Mutual, but I don't want to push the family thing too far. It's Alex Rasmussen, first, last, or something creative, your choice."

"All right, Rasmussen's good. Keep it simple, like they do in the service."

"And prison," I said.

He screwed one eye shut, and I suddenly saw who he reminded me of. Popeye.

4

"Tell me about Troy Pepper," I said.

Pop Sonders uncapped the Mylanta bottle, chugged from it, and put it back, wiping at the pale green chalk on his lips. "Pepper's been with us about five months. He works hard. I haven't had a whisper of trouble with him. Till now, I guess. Some people, you take 'em on, you know day one they won't hack it. This ain't easy work. But Pepper caught on fast, and he pulls his load."

"What did he do before he joined you?"

"Warehouse work, different things, hauled poles and cables for light and power. He was in the service a while before that."

"I'd like to look at his personnel file."

"I'll have to think about that. This is all a big surprise. A murder, and one of our people charged?"

"Were you there when the woman's body was found?"

"Right here. We shut things down quick and got the crowds thinned out. Even so, it wasn't the kind of thing you want folks to have to see."

"Did Pepper say anything when he was arrested?"

He shook his head. "Not really. He had a kind of dazed, sick look.

Sort of rubbery in the knees as they took him away, like a sailor before he's got his land legs. I told him I'd hire a lawyer."

"Have you been over to visit him?"

"Mr. Meecham said it'd probably be a good idea if I didn't. Not yet, anyways."

"That young woman—Nicole. She seemed upset when I mentioned why I was here."

Sonders sighed. "She's most of the time cheerful as a lark, and it rubs off on everyone. I like her around for that alone. She's a sweetheart of a kid, a good scout. But she's like a barometer, picks up on emotional weather real easy. Last night really got to her."

I nodded. It had upset Phoebe badly, too. "She works for you?"

"She looks after things for us when we're on the road, attends to the dogs, sometimes runs the ring toss or does ticket sales." Sonders pursed his lips, as if deciding whether to trust me. "This is between us. Nicole's mom was dying a dozen years back, when the girl was eight, and my wife and me—that's my wife there in the picture—promised we'd take care of the kid. Kind of a deathbed promise, I guess. My wife's gone now, too. Aneurysm."

"Sorry to hear that."

He nodded. "Nicole has fetal alcohol syndrome. It hasn't kept her back much, though I'm not sure what life would be like for her out there." He gestured beyond the paneled wall. "She's never really lived it. Most of her schooling's been right here on the road. I've tutored her myself, and the first five, six years I got her a regular teacher. She gets by."

"Is she a close friend of Pepper's?"

"No more than any of us. We're all close, come to that. Pepper's a little newer is all."

"How are the others taking this?"

"I haven't talked to everyone yet. There wasn't hardly time. I will, though. We'll have a meeting today."

"How many of you are there?"

"Forty-five or thereabouts. That's the gang that travels. I got a booking staff and an accountant back in Jersey, and a safety engineer on a consulting basis. Here I got a full-time ride supervisor and a crew inspects all the rides every day before we open. I got jacks who operate the rides and run the concessions. We add local hands as needed. We do about fifty shows a year, all over the Northeast. Mostly three- or four-day visits, though places like here we'll come in and stay a week or longer. We've got sixty rides, food stands, games of chance, we generally work it with a percentage split between the folks who contract us and the show. If it's a charity benefit or a fund-raiser, we'll slice it accordingly. Everyone's on hourly, with a guarantee of hours per week, and—" He broke off, clapped his hands on his thighs, and stood up. "I'm itchy just sittin' and thinking that we're not operating at all right now. Come on, it'll be easier if I show you around."

Outside we set off among the row of camper trailers, away from the thrill rides and the kiddie amusements, toward the area where the food concessions and games of chance were set up. The aromas of food and defeat lingered in the air. "Are you the owner?" I asked.

"Legally, on paper; but we run it family-like. Everyone gets a say. I make the final call, though. Someone's got to. I give bonuses based on what we take."

"That must create loyalty."

He glanced at me but said nothing. We walked through the big mowed field where the show was laid out, Sonders pointing out things with the stem of the corncob as we went. "We're a small outfit. Independent. A lot of 'em are owned by big operations anymore. They do the big state fairs. I pick up the slack. There're about a hundred and fifty shows like this that move around the country. We generally run full tilt, March through October. We got a few more dates to fill up here, and then we'll start south with the cold coming, wind up in Florida. You've got to pan that stream pretty deep to come up with much, 'cause you're always up against Mickey Mouse, but hey, come December, the weather's nice."

He explained that his father had once owned the show but sold it. Sonders had eventually bought it back. "I made it a profit-sharing operation. No union. I never met a union yet that didn't start off as a good idea and end up feeling like a gun in your ribs."

"Shh—not too loud in this town."

"There may be some, I'm not saying that. But the solution to one problem seems to create new problems. I don't like the idea of shoving a stick into a turning wheel. There's got to be something that works both ways."

Over at Harvard Business School, students were paying plenty to study with people like him. I said, "I'd still like to see Pepper's personnel file."

"I'm not crazy about opening up files to just anyone. It's an unwritten rule."

I gave him a look. "Let me ask a question. Do *you* think Pepper killed that girl?"

Sonders frowned, letting it buy him a moment. "No."

"Then who's going to object to my seeing the file? Pepper?"

"Okay, you're working with us," he said, relenting. "I'll pull his jacket when we go back."

"Did you run a background check when you hired him? Call references?"

"When I need someone, I need them today. Usually, I go on horse sense. Not just anyone can do this work. Remember Edward G. Robinson in *Double Indemnity*? His 'little man'?" He poked his potbelly. "I've got my own little man, right here. Tells me what I need to know. Okay, sure, I suppose I could hire a big fancy search firm, with a bunch of names in the title and letters after the names, and they could run applicants through parlor games, right?"

I let it alone.

"Like I say, I do my own hiring, and I stand by my choices. I can't smoke for real anymore 'cause my wind is shot. Booze is out. My stomach's got more holes than a tin can in a shooting gallery, but goddammit, it tells me when I'm on the right track."

"What's it telling you now?"

Again, he hesitated. "That I ain't wrong to trust Pepper."

We had looped back around to his motor home. Nicole was stepping out of a small adjoining camper, no dogs with her this time. She handed Sonders the morning's edition of the *Sun*. He let his eyes drift across the front page. "You seen this?"

I had. He stuck the paper under his arm. "Nicole, will you go in and pull out Troy's file for me?"

Her small face clenched with concern, and she glanced at me, then back. "Sure thing, Pop."

When she'd gone to get the file, Sonders said, "The bull I talked to is named Cote. Know him?"

"Roland Cote, yeah." The carnival boss was feisty; he wasn't going to let the information exchange only run one way. "He's steady. He'll get the job done," I said. "Is he imaginative? No, but then he doesn't have to be. In this city, the killers aren't very imaginative, either. They get caught."

"Not this time," Sonders said. "Not yet, anyhow. So, where do we go from here?"

"Fred Meecham is quarterbacking. You'll hear from him. Obviously, you should cooperate with the police, but anything you come up with that'll help us, too, let Fred or me know."

Nicole brought out a manila folder, which she handed to Sonders, then went off in the direction of the midway. "You can lamp this in my digs," he said.

"I'd like to take it along with me."

He tugged at an earlobe. "Awright. I sized you up pretty good, I guess."

"And your 'little man' gives me a pass?"

He winced and poked his stomach again. "That, or it's gas." He thrust the folder at me. "Come on, I'll introduce you around."

"I can do that myself. I've got my own horse sense."

The fact was I wanted to keep a small element of surprise.

He regarded me skeptically from under the snowy hedges of his eyebrows, but shrugged. "Be my guest."

"One more thing. The police seem to have their minds made up one way," I said. "I'm going to look at whatever information I can get. But if I don't find anything to contradict their read, I say so."

"Hell's bells, I know that. No one's paying you to kiss ass."

I handed him one of my cards, with the addition of my cellular phone number handwritten on it. Even with the pair of gold-frame specs he hooked on, he had to hold the card at arm's length. "Never seen this spelling of 'Rassmusen' before."

"No one has. It's a printer's error. I'm halfway done with a deck of five hundred."

He put it in his shirt pocket. "I suppose you'll want to be paid." His laugh was the first trace of mirth he'd shown.

"I laugh at it all the time, too. Your lawyer will take care of me. Oh, and just an observation, Pop. You keep saying 'hell's bells' and calling folks 'geezer,' the slickers around here are going to think you're an anachronistic old seadog."

He squinted one eye, and I suddenly felt like Bluto. "Just let 'em try."

As I set off, I realized I liked the guy. If he was a little clattery and overprotective, that was okay. I knew where I stood with him. After freelancing for the past few months for a monolith, where people wore faces like cold coffee—if you got to see anyone at all—I was glad to have a real person, and not to have a sense that my sole purpose was protecting some outfit's Dun and Bradstreet rating. Sonders's rating appeared to be the good regard he held his workers in, including Troy Pepper. I felt inspired to want to prove him right.

5

At midmorning the carnival had a residue of depleted energy and foggy purpose. The jack with the spiked stick was spearing empty popcorn cartons, cigarette packs, and the little paper spindles on which cotton candy was spun. Someone else was stocking cheap stuffed toys onto the shelves of an arcade. In another, a shirtless man with a large spiderweb tattooed on his lean chest was partially inflating tough-skinned little balloons from a compressed-air tank, affixing them to a square of particleboard, where most of the darts that hit them would bounce off. At a booth where for a buck you tossed baseballs to knock over a stack of milk bottles, there was no one around, so I gave in to curiosity. The balls were light and squishy and hit the canvas backdrop with a listless *thwack*. The bottles were made of wood, with weighted bottoms. What did I expect?

I wandered among the tents and booths and food concessions, most of which were shuttered. Farther back, away from the traffic area, was the encampment of vans and small mobile homes where the carnival workers lived. Judging by the number of satellite dishes, they didn't want for much. I made my way in that direction. A woman in pink curlers, several clothespins protruding from her mouth like weird teeth, was hanging ratty stockings and sequined costumes on a line strung between two trailers. I approached a man and a woman who were sitting on the steps of one of the trailers, having a cigarette. The man was making gestures with one hand. I introduced myself and told them why I was there.

"If Pop says y'all are okay, it's fine by me," the woman said. "Me and Red were just talking about it. I'm Penny Bergfors. This here's Red Fogarty, from Bangor." He was a big, rough-complexioned redhead with a hand that felt like lumpy rawhide when we shook. "Red works the Tilt-a-Whirl, and drives truck when we roll."

And apparently didn't speak for himself. Penny looked around forty, with dark roots showing in her blond hair and the Deep South oozing out of her voice. "No, sir, I don't know what-all to think. I mean, you work with a guy, you like to reckon you know him some. Personally, I like him. He keeps to himself, but he's friendly enough, and he works hard. Wouldn't you say so, Red?"

The redhead made some hand gestures again, which I realized were sign language. Penny turned to me. "He says, 'A-yuh.' "

We all smiled. "Was the victim familiar at all?"

"Poor thing." Penny clicked her tongue. "No, she wasn't. Though I gather Troy knew her."

"The police claim that he was here with her yesterday sometime. Did you see or hear anything, arguing maybe, or raised voices?"

"It's pretty noisy around here anyway. With the rides going, you get shrieks and screams all the time. I don't reckon I'd have noticed."

"I did," someone else said.

I turned. A lean man who didn't look much older than twenty, though weathered, drifted over. He wore a red-speckled, tie-dyed T-shirt that made him look like he'd been shotgunned and was bleeding out of many holes. He had small gold earrings. "Heard you askin' about Pepper," he said. I gave him my name and told him what I was up to. He was Tito Alvarez. "You talkin' about the woman," he said. "I seen the two of 'em yesterday, and on Saturday, too. She come over both days. Beats me, man, what was she doing, but I got my ideas."

"You saw them, Tito?" Penny Bergfors asked.

"Oh yeah. They didn't hang around chewing the fat. Went on into his trailer."

"Do you remember what time that was?"

He thought about it. "Morning. Late."

"Did you ever see her before this week?" I was jotting as we spoke.

"Like on the road, you mean?"

"Or anywhere outside of Lowell?"

"No. I think I'd remember her. She was a *bonita muchacha.* Pepper, man, he's a little strange. Quiet. He don't mix much. In the time he's been with the show, I can count on two fingers the times he's ever drunk a brew with us. Wouldn't you say so, Red?"

Red Fogarty pinched the stub of his cigarette, dropped it into a red can, and nodded.

"And that's only when someone buys a case and we sit around here," Tito added. "I don't think he's never gone to no bar with us."

"Maybe he's on the wagon," Penny said.

"No, c'mon, you've seen him havin' a brew."

"So maybe he just doesn't enjoy the company," she teased.

"Yeah, right. No, I'm thinking some of the bars we find are pretty rough. I wonder maybe he's got a glass jaw?"

"He certainly looks like he can handle himself if he had to," Penny said.

"No lie, I've seen rugged guys couldn't take a punch."

"Which trailer is Pepper's?" I asked.

Penny indicated a cream-colored camper with a chrome strip along the side. "That's it yonder." It was hooked onto the bed of a gray pickup truck with a New Jersey tag. I copied the number into my notebook.

"Do any of you think Troy Pepper killed that girl?" I asked.

Penny Bergfors's brow crinkled. "I don't think he did," she said tentatively; then, with more certitude, " 'Cause we ain't like that." The two men agreed, though with something less than firm conviction. I made sure I had their names in my notebook and thanked them for talking with me.

Pepper's camper trailer was half the size of Sonders's motor home. There was a set of metal stairs in the down position, and police tape on the door. The department techs would already have examined it but hadn't released it yet. Meecham would likely request permission for us to look it over, too, but we'd have to wait our turn. I did peer through a little louvered window in the back door, but it was dark in there and I couldn't see anything. I wandered around the carnival site some more. As I did, I had the sensation of being watched. It was one of those feelings you sometimes get, but when I stopped and did a slow 360 I didn't see anyone. I walked toward the haunted house.

By daylight, Castle Spookula was about as macabre as a plastic jack-o'lantern. A few hundred feet beyond it, though, there had been real horror. I kept outside the yellow crime scene tape and tried to see it as I'd seen it last night—and as I was likely to go on seeing it for some time to come. Phoebe had been so shaken by the experience that she had phoned a girlfriend and asked me to drop her there to spend the night. I hadn't suggested that she come to my place. We hadn't gotten that far yet, and anyhow, since my move, I still hadn't unpacked much beyond clothes and my day-to-day needs. My living room was stacked with cardboard cartons, and going to remain so for now.

Birds sang in the autumn-tall grass, telling me nothing. A large dead pine tree stood about fifty feet back, and far beyond that, woods. I thought of the torn-open blouse, the knotted scarf. According to the *Sun,* the police believed the woman had been strangled in Pepper's trailer. I judged the distance from here to there to be a hundred yards, give or take. A fair distance to carry a body—though she was small, and he was strong. The area was too trampled by the activities of last night to make much of it. I'd leave evidence gathering to the police. I'd stick with looking for answers—though at the moment I didn't have any of those, either, only the challenge of finding some.

As I headed for my car, jotting a final question in my pad, I had the perception again that I was being watched. I stopped. When I glanced about, I noticed a shimmer of reflection on one of the crazy mirrors on the side of Castle Spookula and turned to look behind me. In an alleyway between trailers, some distance away, a large bald man wearing green work clothes was looking my way. I couldn't tell his age. Seeing me notice him, he turned abruptly and went into a stubby Airstream trailer parked apart from the others. On the door, painted in a gaudy red and gold circus script, was a sign: ROGO THE KLOWN.

6

Back at the Fairburn Building, at Ten Kearney Square, I unlocked my
waiting room, dumped my sunglasses and Troy Pepper's employment file
on my desk in the inner office, and went down the hall to Fred
Meecham's suite. I sometimes did this anyway, to deliver his mail if I'd
been the first to fetch it from the crate in the main lobby where the postal
carrier had taken to leaving it after the elevator died (and kept on after it
was fixed, the way I kept using the three flights of stairs). Occasionally, I
went down the hall just to chat up Meecham's paralegal, a bright beauty
named Courtney, whom he'd hired straight out of Mount Holyoke. She
had done a senior project on the women's labor movement and come to
Lowell for research, then fallen in love and decided to stay. "She must've
left a lot of heartbroken college men in her wake," I'd told Meecham.

"And college women, too," he confided. "Courtney is gay. And very
up-front about it. Not in any militant way, just a friendly midwestern FYI
kind of thing, the way she'll also let you know she's from Duluth."

"Hi, Alex," she greeted me with her glowing smile.

There was no resisting her. I grinned back. "Is Himself in?"
Meecham was my quarry today.

He was sitting at his law library table in his shirtsleeves, his face in a tome, which he clumped shut as he waved me in. I took one of the two vacant chairs facing his desk, each marked with the logo of Suffolk Law, his alma mater. "How'd the—" we began simultaneously, and both backed off.

"After you," he insisted.

"How did the arraignment go?" I asked.

"Martin Travani was on the bench, which is probably good for us. He's levelheaded. I got Pepper to plead not guilty, though his preference was to say nothing at all."

"Just keep his mouth shut? What's that mean?"

"I'm not sure. He seemed a little removed from the proceedings. It could be shock, which might be read either way. He admitted to the police that he had been with the victim yesterday morning, and that the scratch on his chin is from her nails, and that he'd just bought her the silk scarf that was found around her throat. But he won't say he did or didn't do it. For the time being, I'll just have to work around him. As for bail, the DA argued that Pepper's transient lifestyle and lack of community roots make him a risk to flee. Travani set a status date, at which time we can offer a case for bail. For charges, we've got murder, destroying evidence—oh, and possession of an unlicensed firearm. Police found a handgun hidden in his trailer."

"Great," I said.

"It appears not to have been fired, but they're running it through ballistics now. There may be another problem, too. It seems that the victim had filed a 209-A against him."

It was a restraining order. "Filed it here in the city?"

"No one was quite clear about where or when. If true, it clearly establishes a prior relationship—which Pepper doesn't deny. He told me they were in love."

"Aren't they all."

He went on. The police had two witnesses who saw Pepper with the victim outside his living quarters Saturday afternoon. " 'Speaking with raised voices' is how the report put it. It sounded domestic, but the witnesses said they couldn't hear the conversation very well and they didn't linger to eavesdrop. The coroner places the time of death yesterday between noon and early evening. There were signs of a struggle in Pepper's trailer."

"Has he got an alibi?"

"He was working—or supposed to be—during the time. He was on duty when he was arrested. A detective, along with one of the patrol officers pulling a detail at the carnival last night, went to the trailer and knocked but got no answer. On the strength of their witness reports, they felt they had probable cause. When they went inside they realized it was most likely the crime scene. They found him working and charged him."

"Did he say where he'd been earlier?"

"He's been pretty vague so far, but he hasn't denied anything. My turn now. How did things go on your end?"

I gave him a replay of my visit to the carnival. "Warren Sonders is called Pop by everyone out there, claims they're like a family. Sonders is definitely in Pepper's corner. I sensed a little ambivalence in some of the others, but it's more like they don't want to believe it happened. They're pretty subdued. They seem like a close-knit bunch, and now trouble has invaded their world."

"Courtney pulled together some basic background from what I had and what the police have got." He slid a neatly typed double-spaced sheet across the glossy table. "For you."

When I reached the law library door, Meecham said, "By the way, did I mention who's prosecuting?"

He didn't have to; his forced grin told me.

Down the hall in my own modest shop I checked the morning's mail and then phone messages. I'd been nominated for a national leadership award; all I needed to do was call an 800 number with my credit card to talk about the press release. I decided to hold out for the Nobel. I scanned the notes Meecham had prepared. Troy Samuel Pepper, born Paterson, New Jersey, grew up in Nutley, New Jersey, as a ward of the state and sometime foster child. He didn't finish high school and joined the service at eighteen. Stayed in six years, discharged nine years ago, worked for a power company—which is where he got the injury that had mangled his left hand. He worked in a warehouse, made foreman. He left that a year ago, did odd jobs for several months, and started with the carnival as a roustabout last April.

It would give me a few places to stick a pry bar. With that and the file Sonders had loaned me, maybe I could conjure something that Fred could use. I hadn't missed his oblique mention of the prosecutor. On the job, I'd worked with Gus Deemys. With Ed St. Onge and Roland Cote, too, but at least with them the feelings had ranged from friendship to tolerance. I'd known Deemys as a well-dressed and aggressive little rooster who'd seemed to get off on needling people, friend and foe alike, but it was a mean-spirited needling, never the bonding kind. He'd probably lost his hero when Robert Blake went up on murder charges. Deemys had always been ambitious; I'd give him that. For years he'd attended night school to earn a law degree. Now he was an assistant county DA, and with an audience other than corpses to parade his five-foot-four-inch, well-draped form in front of, he'd proven a winner. His conviction rate was one of the best in the state.

Ambitious wasn't a word that leapt to mind when Roland Cote's name came up. Brilliant wasn't, either. Dogged worked. Unimaginative (as I'd told Pop Sonders). Loyal. And now large. I'd glimpsed him last night when the detectives showed up, and I almost hadn't recognized him. His somber, vaguely handsome bachelor's face was intact, but free donuts and the big meals at his mother's house, where he still lived at forty-five, had undone him. He was heavy now in a way that no tricks of clothing could disguise. At some point he must have shown promise of *some*thing to be punched up to detective in the first place. In a typical career arc, he would've made sergeant or lieutenant by now, or been busted back to patrol duty for having screwed up somehow—but he hadn't gone either way, and that was telling. As a cop you got pigeonholed, and if you accepted it and didn't fight it, you got to stay. As with mediocre schoolteachers (or doctors or judges, for that matter), your peers didn't have the stomach to kick you out, so they let you dangle at the point of least hassle. Unless you'd done something truly vile—like get caught with a bag full of money and leave a state trooper in a coma—in which case you were gone.

I took out the sheet that Courtney had typed and hoisted the phone. I didn't bother with the U.S. military—getting a date with Cameron Diaz would've been easier, though I didn't try that, either. I dialed 411 and got the listing for the New Jersey department of human services. It took several more calls and some waiting through taped menus before finally I reached the division of youth and family services and got hold of a Ms. Alice Parigian, who confirmed that she was the person who had handled Pepper's foster care case in Nutley sixteen years before. "Who is this again, please?" she asked.

I told her, making it clear that I was on Pepper's side, at least in terms of the law. From her questions, I got the sense that someone, probably Cote, had already been in contact with her. "I don't want to seem rude or impolite, Mr. Rasmussen, but is there somebody who can vouch for you?"

I gave her Fred Meecham's number, and she said she'd get back to me as soon as she'd vetted me. I wasn't holding my breath when the phone rang three minutes later. "What do you need to know about this individual?" Alice Parigian asked.

"Anything that you can tell me, ma'am."

That was a long while ago, she said; I agreed that it was. In a profession where people tended to get used up, burned out, and shuffled to other agencies like tattered office furniture, it was a stretch of time to be a social service worker (or a sofa, for that matter). Was she another Roland Cote? Of course, some people had a particularly strong sense of mission—or a stoic sense of delayed gratification that enabled them to envision a Florida condominium for the golden years. I couldn't tell from her voice what drove her but she sounded dedicated. "As a matter of fact, he was one of my very first cases. And I did take out his file when a policeman called me this morning. I can tell you exactly what I told him. The boy's mother got struck and killed by a commuter train when he was just five, a freak thing. The father was pretty much a nonentity, so the boy was picked up and put into DHS care. He was an only child, healthy, and seemingly well adjusted. For the first few years after he came into our custody, he was in foster situations and moved around from family to family. He was a shy, respectful boy. Tested average on IQ. He liked sports. He left our official custody when he turned seventeen. I know he didn't finish high school, but I believe he went into the marines. That's about all I can tell you. This office had no further contact with him after that."

That was the formal end of our conversation. I took a chance. "Ms.

Parigian, you said he was quiet and polite, and yet he never ended up being adopted?"

There was a silence, and I wondered if she'd already hung up; then she said, "No, he never did," in a kind of wistful voice, as if it were a mystery she still hadn't fathomed. "His early childhood wasn't any picnic, but he was a survivor. He had no physical or severe emotional handicaps. Though that isn't necessarily a factor in adoption. Families choose for reasons of their own. Some people, God bless them, are willing to take on even the most challenged children."

"But no one took him," I said. "No one adopted Troy Pepper."

"Mr. Rasmussen, it would break your heart to know the children who never find a loving home. Troy was one of my very first cases, as I said. I really believed he'd do just fine. I worked hard to place him."

"I'm sure you did. You said he had no 'severe' emotional problems—were there some other kind?"

"That's not anything I'm able to address. In our system, each child receives a periodic professional evaluation, but I don't have any of that data here. It's medical information, so it's classified."

"You knew him, Ms. Parigian. You're a professional. Would you venture an opinion?"

"Well . . . if I had to guess, I'd say his big problem might have been temper. He could get very angry sometimes. I think it was especially noticeable because he was so quiet most of the time. Possibly he was depressed, though I just considered him to be deep . . . you know, still waters?"

"Do you happen to know what would set him off?"

"No, I don't."

"Does his file show any kind of disciplinary record?"

In the silence, she drew a long breath, and I had an image of her: a somewhat formal middle-aged woman, sitting in an office no bigger than mine, at a desk with papers and folders stacked high on it; perhaps with a window overlooking a city street, but I saw her looking inward. Hell, maybe I was way wrong, and she was sitting in her bra and panties on the lap of the boss, who was blowing in her ear as she tried to stifle giggles, but I didn't think so. She let the breath out as slowly as she'd drawn it.

"Each time he would get placed in a foster setting—and he did during the ages of about five through nine—he was hopeful that this would be the one, the family that wanted to hang on to him and cherish him as their own. I remember he had a pennant that he showed me one time. One of those felt souvenir pennants that said 'Welcome to Asbury Park.' He loved that. I think one of his foster families had taken him to the beach. He'd bring that with him wherever he was living and tack it on the wall. One day somebody—it may have been a foster sibling—tore it down, and Troy got very upset. Physically."

"A fight?"

"I don't think it went very far, but I do know the family didn't keep him for long after that. He was crushed. He'd been hoping it would work out." A sigh escaped her, like some energy going out of her, out of all the kids who'd dreamed the same thing and never had it happen. "There's a term . . . the 'foster home bounce'—but there comes a point when a child sees the way it'll be, and I wonder if maybe they give up a little."

"What finally happened with Troy?"

"When he stopped bouncing around? What happens to all of us, I suppose. We . . . *he* grew up. He was pretty much a loner by the time he got to school. And, in time, he left us, as he was legally bound to do."

"After the service," I said, "he evidently worked at a food warehouse in the area. Would you happen to know anything about that?"

"The big outfit here is Garden State Foods, out on Ethyl Turnpike. That'd be the likely one."

I asked if she could get a telephone number, and in a matter of seconds she had one for me. I shifted the phone against my cheek. "Do you think he could have done what he's charged with?"

"Killed that young woman? I wish I could say categorically no, that it wasn't in him. That the core values we instilled in him, reinforced by his military discipline, would make that impossible." She gave a small joyless laugh. "But I can't say that. I *hope* he didn't do it. And I thank you for asking. I think the policeman I spoke with—Officer . . ."

"Roland Cote?"

"I've got it right here. Duross, that was his name. Anyway, I think Officer Duross just automatically assumed Troy had done it. My earnest prayer is that he's innocent. Sometimes, though," she added softly, "it's those standoffish ones you find can be the most destructive later on."

I pressed the phone tighter, to hear better. "Was he destructive?"

The line was silent a moment. "Well . . . there was one time. In junior high school. Someone broke a bunch of windows in the school, and some classmates of Troy's put the blame on him, said they'd seen him do it. He wasn't involved at all, actually, but it was his word against theirs, and I think the police believed them—they were from the *good* side of town." I didn't miss her emphasis. "But there wasn't any hard evidence, so he was let go with a firm reprimand."

"How do you know he didn't do it?"

"Why, he told me. He knew those other boys had done it. So one by one he caught up to them, and he whaled them pretty good. The parents of one of the boys pressed to have Troy arrested, and that led to his bout with real trouble. This isn't in his file, of course."

"No, ma'am."

There was a storyteller in Ms. Parigian. I could almost see her peeling away layers of memory, opening the storage banks, and now she didn't care to seal them up again. I didn't have to push hard to get her to tell the rest of it.

7

The person in human resources I'd spoken to at Garden State Foods was a temp, taking care of the day-to-day, but after some waiting on my part, and some trial and error on hers, she was able to confirm that a Troy Pepper had once been employed there in the warehouse. The one I should really talk to, though, she said, the person who had the history of the company in her head, was the woman she was filling in for. That person was out on family leave, but the temp promised she would get a message to her, along with my number. I didn't sit around waiting to strike oil twice in one day. I headed for my wheels.

Fred Meecham had suggested that my talking with Troy Pepper might be useful, so he had faxed a request to the warden of the Middlesex County House of Correction to grant me permission to visit. Traffic eastbound toward Billerica on Route 3 wasn't heavy, but a crew blasting granite ledge as part of a highway-widening project slowed it. Portions of shoulder had already been hydro-seeded, and in the September sun, the grass was sprouting as green as Easter basket excelsior.

Time was when Route 3 was a swift and a scenic route across the Merrimack Valley, especially beautiful this time of year, as the red maples, birches, and alders grew flush with colors. But the attractions of the area, north of Boston, had drawn people looking for a place to settle, so traffic was heavy, many of the cars bearing tax-free New Hampshire plates, with the "Live Free or Die" motto—which, of course, worked better as a motto than reality: The jobs were in Massachusetts, where there were taxes aplenty. As I waited for a flagman to wave us on, I replayed what several of the carnival workers had told me.

The men remarked that Pepper never went out to socialize with them, citing theories that ranged from his being on the wagon to not liking company, but I weighed another possibility. Suppose he stayed away from bars because they sometimes brought trouble—and for reasons of his own, Pepper wanted to avoid trouble. Why? The most logical reason was that he'd been in trouble before. Flora Nuñez had apparently taken out a restraining order against him some while back. Another "Why?" These were questions that I hoped to get answers to.

From the front, Bihoco, as the Billerica House of Correction was known among the state's prison population, had a forbidding look, an odd mingling of old and new, like a fortress that had been upgraded for modern warfare. In reception I showed a copy of the request that Meecham had sent to the warden. A guard with a buzz cut, whose uniform fit him like shrink-wrap, gave it a few seconds' interest, then had me empty my pockets into a small basket: keys, an assortment of coins, a pack of gum, and my notebook and pen. He looked at me expectantly, his fingers moving in a "gimme" gesture.

"I'm not carrying, if that's what you're thinking," I said. "So sorry."

He seemed disappointed. If I'd been packing a hog-leg the size of Dirty Harry Callahan's, I'd have been a made man. He gave the wand a perfunctory pass over my torso, front and back, and then down my legs, quipping, as he probably did forty times a day, that it wouldn't ruin my love life. I pocketed my belongings. "Through there," he said, nodding at a steel door, which he buzzed open.

The inside guard was tall and gray-haired and not nearly so jolly. He scoped my paperwork carefully, eyeing me with suspicion, but I didn't take it personally; it wasn't. In the legal system's game, we were just on opposing teams. Off the clock we could drink a beer together as civilly as any two guys. Jangling keys, he unlocked the holding area and ushered me into a room the size of a three-car garage.

The walls were a washed-out brown that gave the impression that they'd be sticky to the touch. A tired-looking, heavyset woman was talking through a circular screen to a hard-eyed young man on the other side of the long plate glass window that divided the room. Otherwise, the place was empty. "Sit anywheres," the guard told me, and went to a black wall phone. I took a seat as far from the chatting pair as I could, to give everyone some privacy. The only real color in the room was the red sweep hand of a wall clock, ticking off the seconds. Somehow it didn't seem an adequate measure of time in a place like this. I leafed through a little pamphlet called the *Inmate Handbook,* which began with a message from the sheriff and, according to the table of contents, addressed everything from inmate property and leisure time activities to work assignments and discipline. It was written in a clear, direct fashion that showed no hand of attorney or tech writer. Several minutes later, a wiry man of medium height in a loose-fitting orange jumpsuit and manacles was led through a door in the back of the room on the other side of the glass, and my look at Troy Pepper was one of sudden recognition. Last night I'd given him two tickets in exchange for the privilege of being publicly identified as a Cake Eater. He walked slowly to the place opposite me and sat.

A person in a cage is an interesting animal. Sometimes there's one little moment, when you first come face-to-face, without history, and you get this flash of his truth. From the set of his shoulders, or from his eyes, or his soul, it speaks to you, and you know his guilt or his innocence, his capacity for violence, or the kind of threat he poses. Then, in another blink, the balance shifts, gates come down, walls go up, and as cleanly as you might snap a cracker in two, there's an understanding that one of you is free and the other one isn't. I looked for something else in Pepper beyond my flicker of recognition that I'd seen him the night before, something murderous or craven, resentful or remorseful, anything, but I didn't see it. I honestly could not tell a thing more about the man.

He was a lean package, with straw-colored hair, worn short, and a muscular neck and forearms (a faded tattoo of a rose on the left one), physically intimidating, even in the county jumpsuit; yet his shoulders slumped, and there was something contrastingly soft about his eyes, which were a bright blue, like gas flames turned down low. He had a broad nose, a cleft in his chin, and, of course, the ruined left hand, which lay with his other hand on the small table between us, and which I avoided glancing at. His overall manner, I realized, was resignation, as though he'd been on the lookout for something bad, and it had finally come. I told him who I was, pushing one of my cards through the small slot into the tray on his side to back up my self-introduction. He didn't show much interest.

"I'm working for your lawyer," I said. "I'd like to ask you a few questions."

"He already did."

"I know. I've got some additional things to ask you."

"Nothing else to say."

"You haven't heard the questions yet."

When he didn't respond, I said, "Okay, the first thing—"

"First, last . . . I got nothing for you."

I hitched in closer. "The way it looks right now, Mr. Pepper, there's a strong case against you. You deny it, and some of that case is circumstantial, but there's crime scene evidence, eyewitness testimony—and you better believe the police are beating the bushes for anything else they can find. The DA will show that you knew the victim, that you argued with her. I think you know where he's going to go from there."

Pepper looked miserable, but he said nothing. I still wasn't sure whether he knew I'd worked his game last night. I doubted it, and I wondered if it was because he saw so many people come through the carnival, or if possibly he'd been distracted by what he'd done to Flora Nuñez earlier in the day. Maybe I just wasn't that memorable. I said, "The thing about the so-called wheels of justice is they can move slower than almost anything—until they don't. Then they can turn so fast you get dizzy, and sometimes they roll right over you." Boy, did I know that. "What we've got to try to do is get the wheels turning in the right direction at the right speed. You pled not guilty this morning. Now your lawyer needs to make your case to prove it. I can help. I want to. But I'm going to need your help."

He went on saying nothing. I slid even closer. If there hadn't been a wall between us, our knees would have touched. "I talked with some of your coworkers. They seem to be on your side. Warren Sonders is. You've got allies."

He stirred slightly, his eyes coming up to meet mine—and I saw again that they weren't eyes that went with the rest of him. There was a quality of appeal in them, a softness, a woundedness, if that was the word. I could imagine some women going for it. "Where did you first meet Flora Nuñez?"

His eyes stayed on mine for a moment, then slid away, gazing beyond me. It occurred to me that his face was the exact opposite of Nicole's face, in that his showed almost nothing.

"Were you in love with her?"

He sat motionless.

"Did she love you?"

He blinked.

"I need something here."

Same response. I did a bit of business with my notebook, turning pages, not looking for anything, really. I felt angry at being ignored. "I'm putting together some background on you, because you know the police are doing the same," I said. "You have whatever story you told them. If it's straight, okay. If not, if it's just something you latched on to, or if you've remembered more, we need to sort it out and get the facts straight. We can take the upper hand if you give me proof you didn't kill Flora Nuñez. Anything. It'll all be confidential."

The silence went on, like something being woven by long-legged spiders.

"She took out a restraining order against you, didn't she?"

Nothing.

"Can you tell me why?"

More nothing.

I sat back. I slapped my notepad softly against the palm of my hand. Tap tap tap. "Okay, if the cop case adds up, if the woman is in the morgue because you put her there, then my job is easy. I won't help some weak, uncompetitive bastard who feels the only way he can get a woman is by force." I paused expectantly but was disappointed. "But if it's *not* true, if someone else killed Flora Nuñez and is walking around out there right now . . . think about it. And if you're sitting here imagining that the police are going to come to their senses and realize they've caged the wrong bird and you're going to fly away home, think even more."

I tore out several pages of my handwritten notes, fanned through the rest of the notebook, which was blank, tucked my card inside, and pushed it under the screen. He cast a quick look my way, a little more white showing around the blue eyes, but he didn't grow talkative. "If you think of anything you want to share and that might help your case—anything at all—jot it down and get word to your lawyer." I left.

"I told you the guy is a clam. Which doesn't bode well for his defense." Meecham's voice on my cell phone didn't seem to, either; he sounded far away. "What a defendant doesn't say can work against him even more than what he does say."

I realized what I was hearing was frustration. I briefed him on my earlier telephone conversations.

"So, according to this Ms. Parigian, Pepper was facing jail for going after his classmates after the window-breaking incident?"

"The father of the one kid was ready to put him away for life. The judge gave Pepper a choice, jail or a uniform."

"Why hasn't he told us any of this?"

"Would you, Fred?"

"If I thought it would be extenuating. Though extenuating to what? I guess if you're charged with something you didn't do, why offer excuses as to why you did it? Okay. And the warehouse he was employed at?"

I told him I was waiting for a callback and that I'd keep him posted. In the meantime, I had questions of my own: chief among them, a motive. Based upon my brief exchange with Troy Pepper at the carnival last night, I had to wonder: Would the barker have worked as calmly as he had, knowing a woman was lying dead in his trailer? Would he have looked me in the eye, wished me good luck the way he had? Was he that calculating and cold? He'd shown me nothing to assure me otherwise. I found myself thinking of the souvenir pennant that Alice Parigian had told me about. Would a person who'd fight for a scrap of cloth kill for his sense of honor?

8

Like the rest of us, cops develop habits that provide them a little order in the chaos. Even beyond the rote of drill and the paperwork, they find something: a watering hole for after-shift whiskey, a floating card game, a pew at the back of a church. One cop I used to know would go to the shooting range once a week and blast away at man-sized targets, because, as he said, "it keeps me from shooting people." Ed St. Onge had a place, especially when the city crime rate was up, and his blood pressure along with it. Blindfold me and I'd still know the smells: liniment and cigar smoke, b.o. and tired canvas.

The West Side Gym had a history as colorful as the city's, including gunfights, gaming rings, and more characters than Damon Runyon. Mostly, however, it was dedicated to the manly art of pugilism. Outside of Brockton, where Hagler had come from, and Marciano before him, Lowell had produced some of the best prizefighters in the country, a lot of them developed in the West Side Gym, under the tutelage of Christy Speronis. These days there were still prospects, title contenders, and even a champion or two who trained there, but working at the front counter was a moon-faced fellow who should've served as fair warning to anyone considering taking up gloves. Joe Doyle had worked up through the amateur ranks and had a stretch as a pro, fighting as a mid-heavy under the name Kid Sligo. He'd never topped any big card or come within hailing distance of a title belt, and yet he'd lasted a lot of years, many of them taking it on the chin, and the last few of them, it was rumored, refusing to hit the canvas for the New England mob, which some would claim was more a testimony to stupidity than anything else: Better-wired men than him had ended up as landfill. He'd wound up mumbling his words out of a face that looked like an Edsel's hubcap that had rolled all the way from Palookaville.

"Hey, Kid," I greeted him.

He dropped into a crouch and did a one-two with his shoulders. "Hiya, gooda seeya." He recognized me, though I don't think he could have picked my name off a list of one.

"Last I knew, you were the gate over at Matty Silver's lounge."

"Still am. This is supplemental. Christy says he likes to keep me around to add class to this joint." His grin showed more gums than teeth. We chewed life for a moment, then I asked for St. Onge, making it sound as if Ed was expecting me, and Kid motioned with his head. "Steam room. Want a towel?"

St. Onge was standing in front of a locker mirror, unbuttoning a brown cardigan. He didn't see me, and I paused, struck with an image of a much younger cop, standing before a squad room mirror, trimming the corners of his dark mustache. He caught sight of me and turned. "Rasmussen, what the hell?"

"I know, it's your naptime. I won't take much of it."

He dropped his arms. "You won't take any of it. When I come here I'm off-limits."

"The billboard over City Hall Square neglected to mention that."

"Spare me. That's part of the new approach: Cops are your friends, you should trust them. The idea was old when Pat O'Brien played it in the movies and the crime was kids swiping fruit off the apple cart. These days I figure anybody who's got to worry about me coming after them, I don't want to be friends with. All right, you got two minutes, then we're done here. There's no way I'm letting you climb into the steam bath with me."

"Good thinking."

He hung his sweater on a hook in a locker. "By the way," he said, "congratulations."

"For working the other side?"

"What side? I heard you bought a house. Out in the Ivies, I heard."

It was on the west side, off Princeton Boulevard, in a section where streets were named Harvard, Columbia, and Cornell, don't ask me why. It was where I probably ought to have been right then, sanding floors, scraping wallpaper, buying new accessories with income from my good steady unglamorous insurance gig. "I like the peace and quiet."

"What's this about the other side?" he asked.

I told him Troy Pepper's attorney had hired me.

"Makes sense." He loosened his pink necktie and let it hang, like the tongue of an exhausted bloodhound. "You and Meecham are both right there in the same rat hole, you can huddle together and nibble the cheese."

"That's mice, not rats. They don't live together. Anyway, I want to get some details on the police investigation."

"I like peace and quiet, too. It's why I come here." He began unknotting his tie.

"Maybe you can preview what'll be in the *Sun,* save me from reading between the lines."

He looked at me, his lips pursed under his mustache. "That's *all* you'll get from here."

I nodded.

He motioned me to a bench, and we sat. He began untying his shoes. "We got the squeal about eight forty last night. There was a uniform detail at the location already, doing security. We sent detectives, and they're handling it. I might've caught the case ordinarily, but I'm doing this task force on gangs, I'm spread thin. I just came from Lowell General. Southeast Asian kid, fourteen years old, he's critical after a beating. You'll read *that* tomorrow."

I sensed he wanted to talk about it, so I kept quiet.

"There's this ritual to join a gang—a 'jump-in,' where members get to beat on you for a while. To see how well you defend your manhood. They're too young, too dumb to figure out yet that being tough isn't about being violent. Jumping *out*, though . . . that's a bitch. This kid wanted to quit, go back to school, reconnect with his family. A dozen of his so-called crew beat him senseless. When he wouldn't wake up, somebody with a shred of brains took him to the emergency room, and then split. So he's down there, fourteen years old, his family heartsick, and it's touch and go, all because he wanted out. We had a seventeen-year-old shot the day before yesterday. We picked up the shooter because he was bragging about it. The sad part? A lot of these kids aren't stupid and could make something of themselves. But they're all twisted up in this machismo crap, like it's about honor or something. They're violent because they're weak, and way down inside they know it, but no one's ever showed them another way to express it." His face was damp and grim, and I tried to think of some appropriate words, but I knew that words wouldn't help, any more than the steam bath would, that maybe only time had any chance. "Anyway," he went on, clearing his throat, "the carnival killing. I hear there are some people working out there who are worth taking a close look at their backgrounds. But that's Cote's case." He glanced around and added in a lowered voice, "Though you know who's riding herd on it personally, right?"

I hadn't until that moment. "Frank Droney?"

His silence was his answer.

"Is it just one of Mother Nature's tricks, or has his face been carved Mount Rushmore–fashion into the granite ledges along Route Three?"

"Did you hear what I said?"

"Yeah." It was interesting; and it added up. Strangers come to town and one of them kills a citizen, dumps her in a field. It was simple. This was election season, and Droney's man Cavanaugh was up for another term. They were hands washing each other, crime and punishment. "Rumor has it there are a few people around who still think being a crook doesn't pay, but none of them are politicians."

"It's just as well. If they weren't sitting in office, half of them would be sitting in jail for exposing themselves in public." He flung off a shoe. "The point is, it's not for you to decide whether this carnival character is innocent or not. That's for the law. You know where I'm going to land."

"Where you can huddle and nibble cheese."

"Hit the bricks, pal."

"Good luck. I hope that kid in the hospital makes it."

Walking back through the gym, listless in the aftermath of cheap victory and loss, I caught sight of a young woman in a corner, kickboxing at a heavy bag. Something in the energy of her attack—let alone the very unlikelihood of her presence there in that temple of testosterone—drew me over. Her dark hair was in a tortoise-shell clip, high on her head. Her Everlast sweatshirt was form-fitted and ended below her ribs, baring her muscular midriff and a small gold belly ring. She had a good rhythm going, and a vicious kick. She may have been vaguely familiar, but I wasn't sure and I wasn't going to lay that old line on her. I listened to the steady *whap* of canvas for a minute, then she stopped, took a towel that was draped nearby, and mopped her face. She saw me looking. "Don't step on your eyeballs, Jack."

I gave it an embarrassed smile. She reared back on one leg and drove her other foot into the bag with a *whump* that set the bag swinging like a hanged man.

Driving along the river toward the fairgrounds, through the slowly changing trees, I reflected on the changes I'd been living. Finally letting go of the fantasy I'd clung to for too long concerning getting Lauren back was the big one. Buying my own place was part of it, too. Now I realized in a way I hadn't looked at it before that my relationship with the cops was changing as well. For a time after I left, I maintained some profile there. Cops knew me as having once been one of them, though to be honest, with many of them it wasn't a benign knowledge; I was the guy who'd dirtied them all by getting caught taking a bribe. Frank Droney had been the one to demand my shield. With others, people who knew me and knew the truth, there was a sense that my fall possessed a kind of grudging honor. Ed St. Onge had stuck his neck out for me and had gone on record as saying I was an innovative and gifted investigator. (I'm only quoting him.) Then, his good opinion cut ice with others. Now, only St. Onge really remembered. My relationship with the department had devolved into a dispiriting war of attrition. In the daily world at JFK Plaza, Droney ran the detective bureau. While St. Onge would still help me in ways he could, he could foresee a time when he would ride into the sunset—literally, probably, heading to the Southwest, where he and his wife could be with their only daughter, who practiced medicine near

Albuquerque. There was no reason to risk his reputation or his pension by being anything more than courteous to me. Still, he'd been there when I needed him, ready to risk a lot more. I liked to think it went both ways.

9

At the meadow where the carnival was set up, I parked behind a cruiser and an unmarked city car and walked over to where I found Pop Sonders standing outside his motor home, hands cocked on his hips. Nicole squatted nearby, petting the greyhound. Seeing me, she hopped up. "Hello, Mr. Rasmussen." I winked at her.

"I see the city hasn't run you off yet," I said to Sonders. There was no sign of the cops.

"They might as well have. I can't open tonight, and unless I can get a whaddyacallit—injunction—lifted, not any night soon, either."

"Have you spoken with Fred Meecham?"

"He was gonna make some calls. For now . . ." He put his hands up, in a palms-open gesture. "Meanwhile, somebody shot Speedo here."

I glanced at the dog, then at Nicole. "I took a BB out of his side," she said.

"Is he all right?"

"I think so—aren't you, fella?" She scrubbed the dog's long, narrow head. "Maybe it was kids playing in the woods and it was an accident. I don't think anyone would do it on purpose, do you?"

Pop caught my eye, and his expression made it clear he thought otherwise.

"Do you want to take him to a vet? The city animal clinic is just across the river."

"No, thank you. The BB came out, and I can take care of him good. He hardly notices. He just wants to go back into the woods." She patted him. "Did you speak with Troy, Mr. Rasmussen?"

"I saw him, but I didn't get much."

Sonders frowned. "He isn't denying the charges?"

"Denying, confirming . . . he's not saying much of anything."

Nicole's small face clouded with uncertainty. "He's always pretty quiet," she said meekly.

"Except now ain't the time for it," Pop grunted.

The girl seemed nervous at such talk, and her dog was eager to run. She said good-bye, and they went off. I turned to Pop. "The city won't even let you leave?"

"Oh, we can leave, all right, if we want to go without the show. But I get the idea that if we do leave, it'll be for good. Someone'll say we broke our agreement and put a lien on all this stuff. But I'll be damned if I'm going to let them railroad me. Or railroad Pepper, either." He glanced in the direction of Pepper's camper trailer, and I noticed that the door was partway open. "Guess who's back?" Pop said.

"I saw the cars. What are they after?"

"You're the ex-fuzz. You tell me."

I said I'd catch up with him later and wandered over to the trailer that belonged to Troy Pepper. The door was ajar, but I knocked anyway. A rugged young officer pulled the door open wider. He had a brutal battering ram of a face and close-cropped hair a few shades darker brown than his eyes. He was one of the patrol officers who'd been on detail the night before, the male half of the pair I'd seen. He wore short sleeves, fade-washed jeans, and short boots, his weapon and handcuffs on his belt, his badge on a lanyard around his neck. He lifted his head in inquiry, and I gave him my name and asked if one of the detectives was around. "What's it about?"

Roland Cote appeared behind him in the doorway of the camper. Neither of the cops was wearing latex gloves, which seemed to confirm that that the forensic heavy lifting had already been done. "It's okay, Paul," Cote said in a slow voice. "Rasmussen here used to wear a badge. He misses it sometimes and tries to compensate by carrying a piece of paper. Or have you sprung for a shiny star out of one of those rent-a-cop catalogs?"

I let it alone. The patrolman's jaw clenched for a moment, as if he were chewing marbles, then he stepped aside to let Cote emerge.

The detective had thickened with time, like stew. The aluminum steps creaked with his weight, which I pegged at near 220, most of it on the torso of his five-ten frame. His thinning brown hair was scraped back across his head like wires on a faulty electrical coil. He was wearing a forest green blazer with brass buttons over a shirt and tie, both the color of beef gravy. He shifted a Dunkin' Donuts coffee cup to his left hand. The extended right hand was perfunctory, but I took it.

"Carnival doesn't open till nighttime," he said.

"Not even then, I gather."

"Oh?"

"The city shut it down."

"I didn't know that." And didn't much seem to care, judging by his tone. "So what brings you?"

"Work."

Cote stepped back and raised his brows, which gave his face a momentary curiosity before it settled back into its bland cast. "For the lawyer representing the perp? Seems kind of a waste. This one's going to be convict-by-the-numbers, from what I see. We got our man."

"Fred Meecham's old-fashioned that way. He still has this idea about innocent until proven guilty."

"And you bill by the hour." Cote's grin looked like it had been snipped into his bland face with garden shears.

"Idle curiosity," I said, "what brings you back today?"

"Just dotting *i*'s and crossing *t*'s."

"Do you mind if I have a peek inside?"

"Yeah, right."

"Why not? You've broomed it."

"Because I said so." He raised his hand in a slow gesture to indicate the pointlessness of further entreaties. I didn't push. He was on firm ground; until the police released it, it was still a crime scene, and until Meecham directed me, I had no formal clearance for access. From what little I could see through the open door, the trailer was eight by twelve, with a couple of folding chairs, a small dressing table, and a day bed, which had been stripped of sheets. The floor looked to be carpeted with Astroturf. The patrolman was jotting on a steno pad. Taking a different tack, I asked Cote, "So how do you read it?"

We'd never been friends, but we weren't enemies, either. I hoped he wouldn't mind talking, cop to ex-cop. He took a sip of his coffee. "Pepper and the victim had a past. She came here to see him yesterday morning. She'd been here Saturday, too. We've got eyewitnesses that put her with Pepper that afternoon and early evening. On Sunday, she apparently got herself prettied up and came over. There was some sort of argument, it got physical, and she got dead."

"Why'd she show if she had a restraining order against Pepper?"

Cote showed no surprise that I knew about it. "Why does any woman? I could spend all my time on domestic relationships that go bad but where the partners can't let go. Plenty of shrinks do. Anyhow, that went back more than a year, and when it lapsed, she didn't renew it."

"Had Pepper ever violated the restraint?"

He tried to read whether it was rhetorical or a genuine question. Finally he just said, "I haven't seen anything about that."

"Have you talked to her friends and found out if he'd made any threats to her?"

"You looking for something special?"

"It seems to me part of the job for both of us is to get some back story."

"Back story? What is this, Hollywood? Okay, sure, there're always things in anyone's life that are interesting to dig up—but where are you going to begin that story? 'Your Honor, I'd like to start on a blustery March morning, when the moon was on the wane. My client's mother gave birth to him . . . ' I mean, the way I see it, we may be interested in entirely different things. So the best policy right now is we don't talk anymore. That okay with you?"

I let it go. Beyond, the meadow was bright with goldenrod and purple loosestrife and the little stark-white tufts of burst milkweed pods, and farther back still, the woods were aflame with scarlet sumac and yellow and orange maples, the colors a vivid backdrop to Cote's drab presence. I gestured in that direction. "Why there?" He turned. "You guys obviously have your evidence," I pursued, "but wouldn't it have made more sense to wait till he could get her out of here for good?"

"What did I just tell you?"

"This is just me spitballing. Pretend I'm not here. Why not stick her in the river down in Lawrence or Haverhill or put her in the New Hampshire woods? No body, no crime, and maybe next spring, or five years from now, some hiker comes across decomposed remains, and Pepper and the carnival have been in a hundred other cities and no one remembers."

Cote's interest didn't stir. "You think too much, Rasmussen," he said.

"No one's ever told me that before." I shrugged. "The spot where he allegedly carried her is a hundred yards from here. Does that make any sense?" Saying it, I realized I was working through it for the first time for myself, too.

He gave his shoulders a vague twitch. "Dumping the body somewhere else is maybe what he'd like to have done, but he didn't get a chance, the dumb shit. He had to be on the job. So he left her in the trailer, waited till later, and hauled her straight out. We estimate that to be around seven, seven-thirty, when he took a short break from working the midway. It's going dark then. He didn't even take time to clean up the evidence. She was found at eight-forty. Her pocketbook was under the bunk in his camper."

The officer came out now, glancing at Cote for instructions. "Seal it up," Cote said.

The cop set to affixing crisscrossing strands of yellow tape to the door, pressing the ends in place with thick-fingered hands. He seemed to have a relish for the job.

I asked, "Do you figure Pepper carried the victim out of the trailer by himself?"

"Why not? She weighed all of a hundred pounds. Plus we caught a break. There were officers on detail, and their quick thinking helped us ID Pepper as a suspect right away. Officer Duross here was one of them."

Duross. He was the one who had talked with Alice Parigian in child services in New Jersey.

Cote looked around, then underhanded his coffee cup toward a clump of weeds. It spun through the air, spraying coffee in a golden pinwheel. "Probably just as well the city is shutting this place down," he said. "They ought to rethink the whole idea of carnivals coming to town, you ask me. If you ran criminal checks on some of these shitbuckets who work here, you'd be amazed how many got sheets. Well, I guess I'll see you in due time." He started off, then stopped and turned. "Hey, speaking of . . . how about our boy, huh?"

He read my blank expression.

"Deemys is prosecuting. I used to rib him about how he wore clothes they have to unlock cables before you can buy them—Mr. Fancy Pants. But he's the man now." He gave it his crinkled grin. "You, me, Gus . . . gonna be like old times."

Pop Sonders was in his motor home, talking on the phone. Nicole sat at the computer. She cut a timid glance my way and went back to the keyboard. Pop sounded angry at whomever he was speaking to, his occasional words strained, his face ribbed with deep, disapproving lines. With a grunt of good-bye, he hung up and jabbed his chin my way. "How's it look?"

"The police investigation? Like a noose tightening." Nicole had turned now, listening. "They've got the coroner's report and evidence from Pepper's trailer. I don't suppose you can alibi him between noon and around six last evening?"

"Already told you. That was a busy stretch. It got pretty hectic and noisy around here."

"Are you wondering if anybody saw him then, Mr. Rasmussen?" Nicole spoke up.

I looked her way. "Did anyone?"

She thought for a moment, then her small face darkened. "I seen him for some of the time. But everyone's got jobs to do and we do 'em. Plus, part of the time he'd have been inside his trailer."

"How about the woman—Flora Nuñez? Did you see her?"

"I didn't think so. But people saw him here in the morning, and I definitely saw them together on Saturday."

"That's the afternoon you opened?"

"Yeah . . . she was here," Pop said. "Troy took her around. Won her a stuffed doggie sinking baskets or something. Women like that kind of thing."

Yeah, I thought, *they do.* "Did you know he kept a handgun?"

He pulled a morose face and shook his head.

"Does Pepper use drugs?"

"What are you getting at?" His bushy eyebrows tensed together.

"Just fishing. Is that a no?"

"It better be. We got a policy about that."

"Do you go into each other's trailers?"

"Only if invited. A person's home is his castle here, same as anywhere. Going in would violate one of our unwritten rules."

"You seem to have a lot of rules, written and unwritten."

"Show me a place that doesn't." He nodded with obscure meaning. "Another one of ours is no go, no dough. Right now I'm sitting here on my duff, so if it's all the same with you, I've got some things I've got to do to deal with this shutdown." I wondered if this had something to do with his just-completed phone conversation, but I didn't ask. He was already feeling a little harried, and I had things to do, too. As I got to the door, he said, "Why don't you fall by this evening?"

"What have you got in mind?"

"I'm calling a meeting of my staff to talk about what we should do next. You could meet some of the others, maybe get a few answers to all those questions you got."

I told him I would, and we agreed on a time. Outside, I saw that the police had gone. As I opened my car, Nicole called me, and I turned and saw her hurrying toward me.

"Are things going to be okay, Mr. Rasmussen?"

"Call me Alex," I said. She nodded. I had the feeling she wanted me to assure her that God was in his heaven and all was right with the world. I turned the question around.

She clenched her hands together at her chest and sent a furtive glance around, though we were the only ones there. "I wonder if people are going to be angry with us . . . on account of what happened. I mean, not that we caused it—I don't think that—but that it, you know . . . happened here."

Her face was a transparent screen where I watched her emotions come and go. "Nicole," I said gently, "are you thinking that someone shot your dog on purpose?"

She lowered her eyes. "Well, only that I know sometimes people get angry and . . . scared over things they don't understand."

"True. Anything else?"

"When I was walking just before I saw you, a car went by and someone yelled out the window. I won't repeat what they said. It wasn't nice."

"For some people life is so boring, they feel they have to bother other people just so they know they're alive. Don't mind them. Just be careful, all right?"

"Okay."

"Good," I said, keeping my own sudden worry to myself.

"Thank you. I feel better."

"Maybe the city will change its mind, and Pop will decide it's a good idea for the show to get back on the road and let the legal system take care of things here."

She forced a smile through an expression of pain. "I can tell you don't know Pop very well, Mr.—Alex. He don't quit easy. But I will do like you said and be careful. You be, too."

I watched her go back to her carnival, and I turned and headed for my car to go to mine.

10

Courtney approached me in the hallway as I unlocked my office. "Mr. Meecham just sat down with a woman who knew the murder victim. Can you join them?"

Flora Nuñez's acquaintance was perched on one of the client chairs in Fred Meecham's inner sanctum, looking edgy. She was a tan-skinned woman in horn-rim glasses and wearing a dark sweater with an autumn leaf pattern on it and black jeans. "Ms. Colón," Fred said, "this is Alex Rasmussen. He's working as my investigator. Alex, Lucinda Colón."

"Lucy, please," she said. "It is nice to meet you." Her fingers were cool, her grip soft.

She wasn't pretty by conventional standards—her mouth was too wide, her dark coppery hair cropped very short—but there was a fashionable glamour about her. I took a chair, and Meecham said, "Ms. Colón was just telling me that both she and Flora Nuñez came from the same town in Puerto Rico. Patillas, wasn't it?"

"Yes, but we only met when we were here. We went in a class at the community college together, and we became friends."

"How long did you know each other?"

"For more than two years."

"Did Ms. Nuñez ever mention Troy Pepper?" I let Meecham pose the questions.

"They knew each other in New Jersey, before Flora came to Lowell. They were in contact with each other and were planning to get together when the carnival came to town."

"When did she tell you this, Lucy?"

"In May, I think. She said this guy that she used to date and was sometimes in love with, he was going to be in Lowell in September. They dated before, but it never got too serious." She had a charming accent and a lively manner, though I read sadness for her friend in it, too.

"Did you ever meet Troy Pepper, or see a photograph?"

"Yes, she showed me a snapshot she had of him. But I never saw him with my own eyes."

"When did you see Flora last?"

"Oh, not for a while. She was working at the Hilton downtown. A chambermaid. But on the telephone, we spoke often. Is very sad what happened."

"When you talked with her the last few times, did she mention Troy Pepper?"

"She just said that she was going to tell him something. But I don't know what it was. She seemed pretty excited to see somebody, but I don't know for sure. I think it was him."

"Were they lovers?" Meecham asked.

Her hesitation was either modesty or surprise. "I think so, you know. Once upon a time. Back in New Jersey. But since then? *Quién sabe?* Flora didn't tell me too much of her life. I think she seen other men sometimes."

"Here in the city?"

"Maybe here, yes. But I don't know who."

"Did you ever see her with bruises, maybe, or a swollen eye?"

"No, never."

"Did she ever seem . . . frightened, or afraid?"

She hesitated. "Maybe yes. I think so."

"Recently?"

She nodded.

"Do you know why?" Meecham asked.

"No. I don't."

"Have you any idea?"

"No. But what I think . . . I think maybe it was of Troy Pepper she was afraid."

Meecham sent a glance my way but didn't lose his rhythm. "Because of things she said, or . . . ?"

"Is just what I think. I don't know very much." That was the theme she stayed with for the rest of our questions. When she finished, he thanked her for coming in and saw her out.

"What do you think, Alex?" he asked when he came back in.

"If Pepper and the victim had a history, it could be motive, especially depending on what she was planning to tell him—if she was breaking something off, that could be motive. It could also be that she was going to tell him she wanted them to be together. Hell, it could be any number of things, some of which would support Pepper's innocence, others that would damn him."

He pushed fingers across his forehead, as if to erase the deep creases there now. I said, "The cops seem pretty sure they've got the case on ice, but I don't know enough yet."

He nodded. The accused hadn't given us much to form an opinion on. I'd have liked to insist that I was simply an information gatherer, as impartial as a machine, as wise as Solomon, but the reality was that believing a client was innocent, or that he'd been wronged in some way, was valuable. If it was the other way, and I was comfortably convinced that he was guilty, I had decisions to make. With Pepper, I wasn't close to anything like assuredness yet. And I realized that the only person who could help me decide was the person who seemed not to want to.

Back in my office, I had a phone message to call Phoebe Kelly at her office in the Registry of Deeds, which I was happy to do. "What are you doing?" I asked when she answered.

"Hey, it's you. I thought I heard bells ringing. I'm reading the latest issue of *People*. Don't worry, I'm not on county time."

"You'd be getting more done than a lot of people who are. What's the deal?"

"Coffee break. What are *you* doing?"

"Sniffing out clues."

"I'm sniffing mocha latte."

"So much for a fascinating probing of each other about our life's work."

"I'm sorry. I thought you were kidding. Were you finished?"

"I am kidding."

"Okay. I'm not. The boss is taking all of us out to dinner tonight. Jennifer, the office manager—do you remember her? The older woman who has the cubicle by the window? Anyway, she's retiring. Guess who might get her desk?"

"No kidding?"

"It's not a sure thing yet. Anyway, we'll be at Cobblestones. Do you want to meet me there after, or are you going to be glued to the Pats game?"

"The TVs there are bigger than mine." We agreed on a time.

"And now I really am on the clock, so I've got to run. Bye."

We were a new item, and part of the fun was learning each other's little moves: on the phone and in person . . . maybe, in time, in a life. I tried on that scenario. Phoebe had declared herself a team player, a born lifer in whatever situation she found herself. She had married her junior high school boyfriend and insisted it would've been a forever thing if he hadn't died in a car crash. She liked plugging away at the steady job, putting in the time and making grade, a cubicle by the window, maybe even retiring in it someday, with handshakes and good wishes, and the prospect of a financial pillow for the rest of her days. Not a bad trade, I suppose, for some people. It's what Roland Cote was doing, and Ed St. Onge: one an inveterate bachelor, the other contentedly wed for years, both devoted to the job. But not yours truly. I'd once been married and had once been on the job. I told Phoebe this, going into the whole ignominy of my fall, admitting to her that it wasn't something I liked to dwell on, and she listened and said that time was often enough to get beyond things, but not always, that occasionally it was necessary to go back and try to work through something. Was that what I needed to do? I glanced at the bottom drawer of my desk, where I kept the fat yellow file of all that had gone down, beginning with that fateful night in the courtyard behind the old hosiery mill. I started to pull open the drawer . . .

I yanked the galloping horse of soul-searching to a halt midstride. I shut the drawer. I hung up my jacket and settled in to give a couple of hours to Atlantic Casualty, but the hoofbeats echoed on for a time before they faded completely.

11

Later that afternoon I drove over to the courthouse. Superior court for Middlesex County was a complex of large granite and limestone buildings, in the oldest of which Daniel Webster had argued cases. They were in the neoclassical style that in an earlier century gave dignity and formality to the proceedings that went on there. Now—who knew? In the late afternoon sunlight, though, they still possessed a kind of majesty. I passed through the metal detectors and let a sloe-eyed county employee massage me with an electronic wand. No bells went off, so I guessed it wasn't love. It was after 4:00 P.M. and formal sessions were done for the day, giving the vast lobby an echoey emptiness. There was an office locator on the wall beside the large center staircase, and I looked for and found Judge Martin Travani's hearing room on the second floor. Outside the room, I whispered to a uniformed court officer that I was there to see Attorney Meecham. He opened the door for me and motioned me in. Meecham and the prosecutor, Gus Deemys, were at the front of the room, talking with the judge. They all glanced my way as I entered, and I tiptoed forward and slid in on an oak bench four rows back. Deemys, who had been speaking, frowned, cleared his throat, and resumed.

"My argument, Your Honor, is based on the hard fact that the man has no known ties to the city—or to much else that I can determine. By the very nature of his work and personal life, he's a vagabond. With due respect to Attorney Meecham, I would suggest that Mr. Pepper poses a high risk to flee."

Travani, who was a sober-looking, vaguely boyish man in his early sixties, with a round head of close-cropped gray hair, had his steel-framed glasses in his hand, twirling them by one of the bow pieces. He didn't look impressed with anything he'd been hearing. "Come on, Mr. Deemys, a vagabond? He's held steady employment with the carnival for some time, hasn't he?"

"Less than six months, Your Honor. But you're right, not a vagabond. I misspoke. It's fair to say, however, that his work and life have been itinerant." It wasn't the way I remembered Deemys talking on the job.

The judge turned to Meecham. "Counselor?"

"May I confer with my investigator?"

Travani looked at me, regarding me a moment; Deemys did, too, as if I were an interloper into their cozy fraternity of Juris Doctors. I gave a little wave and went forward, where Fred Meecham drew me aside.

"Good timing," he whispered. "I'm not going to get bail, or at least not anything anyone is going to be able to afford. But I want to get some things on the record. Have you got anything I should add?"

I told him what I picked up from some of Pepper's coworkers, especially from Warren Sonders, and he went back while I resumed my seat. "We believe that Mr. Pepper is very unlikely to flee, and that the carnival staff are like a large extended family, wherein certain social sanctions obtain, and that flight would put them all in legal jeopardy."

"Oh, bull!" Deemys exploded with exasperation. "You're talking about a group of carnies. Social sanctions? How about social diseases? It's in their nature to rove, for Christ's sake." That was the Gus Deemys I remembered.

Meecham and Deemys duked on awhile, raising additional points, each trying to buttress his own side of the argument while battering his opponent's. It was fun to watch, but the clock was running. I raised my hand. "May I say something, Your Honor?"

Travani put on his glasses and motioned me to stand. "What is it?"

"The city licensing office has decided that the carnival shouldn't be allowed to leave."

The judge glanced at the DA, who shook his head, and at Meecham, who did the same. "I hadn't heard that," Travani said.

"Evidently the discussion is ongoing, but that was the word when I spoke with the carnival boss a few hours ago."

The judge glanced at his watch. "If there's nothing more, I'm going to rule. Owing to the serious nature of the crime, and granting Mr. Deemys's point that there is a risk of flight, I am going to deny bail at this time. However, as I said at the arraignment this morning, I want to move forward with the case quickly. I want no needless delays on either side. Understood?"

And that was that.

Outside, as Meecham and I walked together to our cars, he told me how things stood. It seemed the killing had struck a nerve with a lot of people, and the cries for swift justice were loud. The court was responding to that. We agreed to huddle in the morning. At the rapid march-step of feet, I turned and saw Gus Deemys coming our way, carrying a bloated briefcase, his tasseled lifts tapping the pavement. He pretended not to see us, but as he neared he murmured from the side of his mouth, "I tot I taw a pwivate eye."

I looked at Meecham. "Who's Tweety Bird?"

Deemys stopped and gave me a slow grin. "You know what? Holding this guy without bail is just the start. His sorry ass is grass. I'm going to eat you and your jailbird up. See you in court." He pressed a little car alarm deactivator, which answered with a chirp, and he marched over to a smoke gray Lincoln Navigator and pulled himself up onto the running board and in. All five-foot-four of him in a two-and-a-half-ton truck.

Back at my house, I gave some thought to unpacking a few more of the boxes that were still piled in the front room and in the kitchen, but I let it remain thought, untainted by action. The house was small but big enough, the way the place Lauren and I had on Paige Street downtown had been, our first apartment together. We listened to the Beatles and Erik Satie and drank wine and made love. We'd have been happy in a packing crate. But I was here now, I reminded myself. I'd finally gotten off memory lane.

I put on water for pasta. I poured a premixed salad out of one of those cellophane bags—the Mediterranean special—and heated marinara sauce out of a jar. I switched on the TV for the local news, which carried a clip on Troy Pepper's arraignment earlier that day, including footage of him being led out of court in handcuffs and looking hangdog. There was also coverage of a conviction in a gang killing in the city, with the teenage defendant, tried as an adult, being whisked off to begin the rest of his life at Cedar Junction. The pairing of the stories bothered me. As had Gus Deemys's righteous anger. When I tried to analyze why, I didn't have a good answer. A community's outrage at a killing was justified, even welcome, but wasn't it part of the legal system's duty to put the brakes on a little? To give reason a chance to prevail? Or was I just being oversensitive because of where my checks were coming from?

I popped a can of beer. The weather radar showed a whirling tropical storm, Francine, which had heated up the Caribbean for a few days but was now just a lot of wind. The meteorologist went on at length about hurricane season and the prospects for anything making its way north. Meanwhile, kudos to a tropical depression that got upgraded to storm. They were calling it Gus. I shut off the tube and raised my beer. Gus. I had to love it.

Fortunately I was able to locate a colander in one of the boxes before I found a tennis racket, so didn't have to drain the pasta the way Jack Lemmon had in *The Apartment*. The meal wasn't Jacques Pepin, but it ate just fine.

12

The first time I heard Phoebe Kelly's name I told her that it had a happy sound. That had been in the Registry of Deeds office, where she worked. She laughed. At Cobblestones, Phoebe was sitting at a table over drinks with three other women as they chattered away beneath a hanging Tiffany lamp. *Monday Night Football* wasn't on yet; the big TVs were tuned to some kind of music awards show. Seeing me, Phoebe waved, and I joined them. "Alex, you know my coworkers—Kathy, Janelle, Roxanne."

We exchanged hellos. I'd met them all briefly before, in the busy office pool. There was a close-knit group of half a dozen or so who socialized together. Jennifer, the woman whose retirement dinner it had been, was gone. I saw no sign of the boss. On one of the TVs behind the horseshoe bar, a relic of the seventies glam rock scene was reading a teleprompter, trying to balance on six-inch platform soles and not put too many wrinkles in his latest face job as he presented a lifetime achievement prize to someone half his age. "I thought the music awards were on last month," I said.

"And next month," Kathy said, "and the one after that. Everybody gives them these days."

"Yeah, you're up for one in the running-your-mouth category," Roxanne gibed.

Kathy made a cat hiss and clawed the air. Even money said the boss had picked up the tab and beat a retreat for home, eager to escape the estrogen wars.

"Do you want the game?" Phoebe asked me. "We can get the bartender to switch channels."

"I can wait till nine," I said.

"I thought maybe you'd want the pregame stuff."

"Jock foreplay," Roxanne said. "Guys are wham bam in the bedroom, but they sure can delay pleasure when it comes to sports. You notice that?"

"The Super Bowl," said Kathy, "my boyfriend starts watching the day before."

"Same here, and believe me, it isn't because he's hoping to catch some witch flashing her titty."

All eyes went to me, as if I were being asked for a rebuttal. I shrugged. "What can I say? It's the NFL Kama Sutra."

Topics changed, and pretty soon one of the women asked, "Are you really working for that killer from the carnival?"

"Well, he's the suspect."

"I guess it's a job, huh?" Kathy said sympathetically. "Boy, I don't envy you."

"They should throw away the key."

"Why don't we have the death penalty anymore?"

"Because it's 'inhumane,'" Roxanne said and rolled her eyes.

"*Life* is inhumane," said Janelle, speaking for the first time. "Our job is to make the best of it." She was the spiritual one in the office, Phoebe had told me, always reading books by the guru of the month and going on meditation retreats. ("For her, going to 'club med' means sitting in a full lotus for six hours at a whack.")

"Forget that. People like this guy they caught aren't human. I say fry him."

When the others had left, Phoebe looked chagrined. "I didn't plan on that. I'd told them about our date last night, how nice it had been and everything, and then . . . that. They had a million questions. I mentioned you'd been hired. Was that okay?"

"I didn't take it personally. And I wasn't really planning to watch the game. I just wasn't man enough to admit it publicly."

She took my hand. "Is it tough on you, though? Working for a lawyer who wants to get that guy out of jail?"

"Let me put it in perspective. At the Registry of Deeds, you charge a filing fee, right? When someone closes on a property?"

"Sure. A hundred seventy-five dollars. To record the deed. The state requires it."

I nodded. "And some of the people are going to run into difficulty at some point—maybe for reasons they can't help—and when they miss payments, the bank can foreclose."

"Well, yeah, but that's the system."

"Yep. Like the right to representation and a fair trial. No?"

She nodded slowly. "I guess."

"Anyway," I said, "he won't be getting out on bail. But enough shop talk. We're both off the clock. How about dessert?"

"You go ahead, I'm stuffed."

I ordered Black Forest cake, which came in a piece the size of a cuckoo clock, and the waitress was savvy enough to bring two forks, though Phoebe resisted until there was only one bite left on the plate. "Waste not, want not," she said and speared it. "Appearing soon on a panty line near you."

"How soon? How near?"

"Shut up, you. I've got a black-and-blue on my ass where that crazy clown pinched me. Maybe *he* should be in jail."

Afterward, we sat in my car in the parking lot, sharing tidbits about our respective days. "That really freaked me out last night, Alex. Seeing that woman. I mean, being there and . . . I just never . . ." She pushed down the door lock.

"It was upsetting," I agreed. "Are you okay now?"

She snuggled into the curve of my arm. "It set all kinds of things running through my head. Who was she? How did she get herself in a situation where that could happen? And the weird, silly stuff, too. How my mother always used to tell us to be sure we were wearing clean underwear and nylons, because you never know . . . Not that it matters, I suppose. The clean underwear. I don't guess there's a sign in the morgue that says, 'Your failure to plan ahead is not our responsibility.' "

"I've never seen one."

"And then I got remembering Todd and how he had just phoned me from the airport and said he was on his way home, a drive he'd made so many times, and then . . . It was probably the one in a thousand cases where wearing a seat belt might've cost a life instead of saving one. If he'd been able to get himself out—though the doctor said the heart attack probably had taken him before he even hit the tree." She broke off. In the reflected gleam of the vapor lamps, her eyes were suddenly very bright. I turned my face into her hair and stroked her shoulder.

She had told me about it on our first date—just to let me know, she said. Wanting me to see where she'd been and what she came with. The one other man she'd dated and had begun to like, she had not told right away. They'd dated a handful of times, and then she'd told him. "In two flips of a fish's fin, he was history. I never heard from him again. Maybe he thought I was a black widow." So she'd learned she needed to be right up front about her marriage. When I called her a second time, she sounded surprised, and then explained. Maybe as some show of good faith, I'd told her about Lauren, and that had led to telling about how I'd come to lose my police job—which reminded me why I tended to avoid going into any of it. It was like digging in the ground and reaching to pull up a small root only to discover it was part of a whole underground network of roots that resisted being tugged up but then came, spreading out, stirring up even the ground beneath your feet, which had seemed so solid just a moment before.

Phoebe cleared her throat and went on. "We'd had this life plan. After we both got through college, I'd work, and Todd would study and take the exams—those endless exams—and he'd become an actuary and get a really good job. And we did. We were real penny-saved-penny-earned types. Our house here was a starter. The plan called for Concord or Lincoln, and a family . . ." She shook her head slowly and blinked, and several tears overflowed. I brushed her cheek with my thumb. "It didn't work out the way it was supposed to. But mostly . . ." She cleared her throat again and drew back to look at me. "Mostly, you know what last night has had me thinking, Alex? About us."

"You and me?"

"How we're pretty different. Oh, you're really hardworking too, I don't mean that."

"Let's not be *too* hasty."

"I was thinking that we're both really dedicated to our jobs, but your work involves you sometimes with bad things that happen, and with the . . . well—"

"The bad people who do them?"

"I was thinking that, yeah."

"My job can be dull as dirt. Most of the time, in fact. Don't tell Atlantic Casualty Insurance I said that, but it is. The people are the thing that makes it worthwhile. The rest is just . . . work."

She dabbed at her eyes again. "Well, I'm trying to keep the blinders off and see that all those other plans and dreams were only that—plans. That other lives, other dreams are possible. I've just got to get to where I believe it."

Her cell phone began to sing Beethoven's Fifth. She answered and listened. "I'm with Alex," she said, giving me a glance. One of her girl-friends, I gathered. She had the phone programmed to play different songs for different friends. I don't think I'd been with her yet when someone wasn't calling. "Yes," Phoebe said. And "Okay." And "Yes. Okay. I'll call you soon."

Outside, we made plans to see each other on Thursday, three nights away. "The moon will be full that night," she said. "The corn moon. You know about that? The full moon closest to the autumnal equinox is the harvest moon, but if that moon occurs in October, the September moon is called the corn moon. I think I got that right."

"It'll be nice. I'll turn off my phone if you turn off yours."

"Deal."

"No interruptions, it'll be just us and the corn moon."

As if to seal a bargain, I kissed her. Her mouth tasted of coconut and chocolate. I tried to make the kiss linger awhile. She drew back first, her eyes finding mine. "Be patient with me, Alex. I'm trying."

I squeezed her hand. "There isn't any rush. You be patient with me. I'm trying, too."

I walked her to her car and watched her drive off; then I went back on the clock.

13

There were about thirty people gathered by the gleam of a kerosene lantern outside Pop Sonders's motor home. Some had set up folding lawn chairs and canvas camp stools, but most stood, their cigarettes glowing here and there in the mild dark. Nicole was perched on the step of a nearby trailer with a notebook and pencil. Seeing me, she waved hello. Pop introduced me to several of the nearer people, and I said hi again to Penny Bergfors, Red Fogarty, and Tito Alvarez, whom I had met that morning. Pop hadn't heard anything more from the city, so he wasn't optimistic that the show was going to be allowed to reopen anytime soon. He said he had sent home some of his people who lived in the area. The others would stay, on salary. Even so, the group seemed restless as he addressed them.

Most of the talk focused on practical issues that didn't much concern me, but he gave them opportunity to weigh in, too, and the exercise increased my admiration of Sonders. They were a motley crew for sure, ranging in age from about eighteen on up to forty and more, with men far outnumbering women, but he gave everyone who cared to a chance to speak. Their language was a kind of American plain-speak, flavored with slang and profanity, and undercurrents of the shared knowledge that they were all part of a group that excluded me, an awareness I couldn't miss in the occasional glances I got—not hostile, exactly, but curious and excluding. When the meeting had about run its course, someone said, "What's the story on the dog?"

"Speedo's just fine, Pete," Nicole said.

"You think it was done on purpose?"

"Kind of hard to shoot a greyhound if you're not aiming to," Sonders said. "But let's give it the benefit of the doubt and say it was bad aim. Kids are kids. But just so's we're clear, let's keep our eyes peeled and our noses clean. I don't want nobody hurt, or any incidents that put us in trouble with the law."

"Seems like we're already there, ain't we?"

Sonders used it as his segue. He waved me over. "This here is Alex Rasmussen, the investigator who's working with the attorney. You'll see him around. Some of you already talked to him. If he's got questions, give him what he needs."

"What if *we* got questions?" The voice came from the shadows, and then the speaker stepped into the glow of the lantern.

"Well?" Pop said.

He was the large bald man whom I had seen watching me that morning. "What the hell do we need with some gumshoe? Aren't the cops enough? Christ, the way they were clanking around here last night you'd think it was a goddamn brass band."

"The cops have Troy Pepper in jail and are convinced he's their man," said Pop. "I don't see any incentive for them to change that."

"Well, goddammit, if Pepper did it, screw him. Let him rot there. As for this bird, I'd prefer our meetings be like usual, without no outsiders hanging around."

I looked at Pop. "I can fade."

He ignored it. "Anybody else?"

When no one spoke up, he said, "All right, we're done here. Go on, then, and everyone get some shut-eye. I'll let you all know soon as I hear anything."

When the carnies had drifted off to their living quarters, Pop waved Nicole and me into his motor home and motioned me to have a seat. Nicole sat at the computer. He grabbed his corncob pipe and took the patched recliner. "It ain't personal," he said. "Or widespread. Every group's got its resident grump."

"Who is he?"

"Ray Embry. He's our funnyman."

"Rogo the Klown?"

"That's him."

"No wonder I was laughing so hard on the inside."

"Really, he can be very funny," Nicole said earnestly. "When he's in a good mood, he can have you in stitches."

Just then there was a soft knock and the door opened and a thin old black man wearing a gray suit coat and a porkpie hat came in. He handed Pop a brown envelope, then turned and saw me. He looked to be about Pop's age, or even more, but he had an erect, dignified bearing. He lifted off his hat. "Sorry, I didn't know they was company."

"Alex Rasmussen," Pop said, "this piece of work here is my spiritual advisor, Moses Maxwell."

"Delighted to make your acquaintance, Mr. Rasmussen." The old man's fingers had a brittle, bony feel when we shook hands, but his smile put warm creases in the freckled skin around his eyes. Under the suit coat he had on a maroon V-neck sweater over a pale blue shirt and a tie, clothes that appeared well worn but neat. A little soul patch of whiskers sprouted beneath his lower lip.

Nicole said, "Pop, I just wanted to say something else about Ray, so Mr. Rasmussen knows. He really is a good clown. Or anyway he was. He used to work in a big circus."

Pop rolled his head toward her. "She's sensitive. Overly. When the little paper clip icon comes up on the computer screen with suggestions, she feels bad ignoring him."

"He's got those expressive eyes," Nicole said in her own defense.

"Nicky, he's a paper clip, for God's sake. And not even a *real* one."

"I know that."

"But thanks for your input. Your testimonial for Rogo the Klown is noted."

She blushed, smiling. "You're welcome."

She printed the page she'd been working on and put the sheet into a manila folder. "There's the notes, Pop. I'll be on my way now. G'night, Mr. Maxwell. G'night, Mr. Rasmussen. See you in the morning, Pop."

"Don't let the bedbugs bite." Pop tapped her lightly on the arm with the folder, and she went out.

Maxwell took the vacated seat to form the third point of a triangle. Pop said he wasn't kidding about Maxwell being his advisor and that we could talk candidly. I caught them up to date on my doings, including speaking with the murder victim's friend and attending the bail hearing. "The court sees Pepper as a risk to skip. Do either of you see that?"

Pop Sonders shook his head. "His life belongings are in that trailer parked back there, and there's no way he'd get that out of here. Anyway, no, I don't think he'd even try." He explained again the close-knit community, and having seen tonight's meeting, I was inclined to agree.

I said, "The police detail last night—what time did it start?"

"Started at five for a six-hour detail."

"You paid for it?"

"Yep, my dime. City requires it, but I'd do it even if they didn't."

"I understand you got Fred Meecham's name from one of the detail cops. Do you remember which one?"

"The one who was in on the bust with those dicks from homicide."

"Officer Duross was his name," the black man said quietly, emphasizing the first syllable. "Paul *Du*ross."

"Moses does the *New York Times* crossword puzzle every day," said Sonders, as if it explained everything.

I looked at him, recalling something. "*The* Moses Maxwell?"

"Well now, that all depends."

"You played with the Count Basie band."

The old man looked impressed. "Shoot, you got you some ears on you, Mr. Rasmussen."

"If they were a few years longer, I'd tell you I filled them with your sound at the old Commodore Ballroom, but that'd be more wishful than truthful. I do have you on a record somewhere at home. But not with Basie."

"My quintet, prob'ly. Count needed another piano player like Valentino needed lady friends. 'Sides, he had that smooth sound. When I played, I had this left hand that liked to sneak away and boogie-woogie. The record must be a seventy-eight—it *feels* that long ago."

"It's an LP, and you've got Oscar Santos on tenor and Stanley Reade on bass," I said, hauling out the lineup from memory, the way you could name the infield of a ball team from twenty years ago if you didn't stop to try. Which I did with the other musicians and couldn't grab handles.

"Kenny James on skins and Scott Kendall, vocals," said the old man. He looked at Sonders. "Gen'leman's definitely got him some memory."

"Of course, I could never remember my wedding anniversary," I said. "You still play?"

"You still married?"

I grinned. "Got it."

He raised his hands and twiddled long fingers that were bent like crabapple twigs. "Arthritis. I push a pencil now."

"And remembers stuff," said Pop.

Maxwell admitted that he was an unofficial historian for the show. "Emphasis on 'unofficial.' And that 'spiritual advisor' riff you got to take loosely." He drew a pewter flask from his coat pocket and held it up. "I brought the spirits. You, sir? Brandy?" He didn't offer it to Pop. I figured it would keep the Black Forest cake company in my stomach. He filled the pewter cap, and I took it. He lifted the flask. "To the Count."

It wasn't five-star, or French, but the heat warmed all the way down.

"I'll leave you two to bullyrag awhile," Pop said. "I want to walk a quick rounds, make sure there's no lingering grudges among the crew."

"He works hard," I said when Sonders had gone.

"Basie used to say, 'They don't pay me for playing.' The bread was for the travelin', sittin' on the bus for long miles, the hotels and lost suitcases and bad food. He always said the playing was a gas, he did that for free. Pop's like that with the show. Shoot, he'd *give* that part away. But the hassles, the cash worries . . . and this shuckin' and jivin' with city hall? Nuh-uh."

"That envelope you slipped him—cash?"

"He asked me to go withdraw some from the bank. He's got expenses mountin' up. Pop's drink these days is *ant*-acid, case you noticed. And this here, too." He leaned and slid open the top drawer of the desk and took out a small plastic pharmacy bottle, which he handed me. It was Prilosec, prescribed for peptic ulcers. He put the bottle back and shut the drawer. "And now this poor dead girl being found here . . . that sure ain't any too cool."

"You say 'found' here—not killed here?"

"Did I?"

"What's your take on that?"

"Well, I've never had much truck with Mr. Pepper, one way or another. He tends to blow solo. But he always did his job. I hope he didn't do it, for his sake and Pop's, but I'm gonna reserve judgment till I know more."

It seemed like good policy. After a pause, he said, "This your hometown, Mr. Rasmussen?"

"It's home, though I've gotten away once or twice. Compliments of Uncle Sam."

"Touring with the band is how I come to see this city for the first time. We had a gig in a hotel downtown, but we couldn't flop there on account of . . . you know. We ended up at a place called the Venice."

"Jim Crow died hard," I said.

"Didn't he though? Some white folks didn't like it much, either, but it took a lot of people of both colors to do something about it. Still does, just more colors now. Anyway, in spite of that, this town's always had a certain vibe to it that I like. There were some good rooms to play, too. The Hi-Hat was one, the Moulin Rouge, the Laurier Club. I heard Billie Holiday played her last date here 'fore she got sick and passed. I remember I got me a pearl gray Borsalino here one time. Used to be a good hatter's over on Middlesex Street."

"There used to be a dozen of them. And millinery shops, too."

"Ha, there's a word no one knows anymore. A crossword puzzle word. In a way, a carnival is in tune with this kind of town. Like you seem to be, too. A private op who actually drives out and asks questions and doesn't just set poking keys?"

It had taken me a while, but I realized that in his oblique, courteous way, Maxwell was checking me out. I smiled. "You've got me confused with a 'security consultant.' No, I'm old enough to take that the way you mean it. I've got two fedoras sitting on cedar blocks in my coat closet, waiting for the season. And I'm going to give this job the best I've got."

When he'd poured me another little nip, I asked him how long he'd known Pop Sonders.

"I knew his daddy, so we go back. But traveling with the show? Six, seven years. When my wife died, and it got boring sitting around an apartment in St. Pete watching *Wheel of Fortune,* I decided. So when the show came south one winter, I asked could I tag along. That spiritual advisor line's a good one, but truth is, Pop can't drink anymore, account of his stomach. What I do to earn my keep is to have an eye on small expenses, things like that."

Pop returned and declared things were quiet. Moses Maxwell said he reckoned he would turn in. "Nice to meet you, Mr. Rasmussen."

I said the pleasure was mine. "He's pretty circumspect," I said to Sonders when the old jazzman had left to navigate back to his digs.

"A true gentleman," Pop said.

"Are all your people?"

His gaze sharpened. "What's that supposed to mean?"

I shrugged. "I came over here tonight to learn things. I'm trying to do the job."

He let the bold eye linger a moment, then sat down. "What's to tell? I've got a lot of people work for me, okay? Are you asking if any of *them* could've killed that girl?"

"Or been accomplices before or after the fact? If the girl was killed back there in Pepper's trailer, as the police say, she had to be carried out to the field. Maybe someone heard or saw something."

"Look, everyone here's got a story. Police, lawyers—even you being here—it's got people jumpy. But I'll tell you this: I know these folks. I'll vouch for 'em."

"Let's concentrate on Troy Pepper, then. He hasn't been with the show long. He doesn't say much, isn't especially close to anyone. Is that about right?"

"It don't make him a criminal."

"It makes him more of an unknown, though. I'm going to be asking questions, digging into his past, his habits. It'll be helpful if you can keep your eyes and ears open, too."

"I intend to."

"Okay. The outspoken one tonight, the clown. What's his scene?"

"Embry's generally burned about something or other. He's been in the business as long as I have, though not with me all that time. He knows all the old tricks of the trade. Like he does a walkaround, the way he used to do with the circus—stroll the crowd, interacting with folks. He's good at working a slow crowd. Gets them loosened up and spending money."

I didn't mention that he'd pinched Phoebe's butt, or that I'd caught him watching me earlier; if curiosity were a crime, I'd be on death row. "A cop I know says you've got some people here who might raise suspicion."

"Seems you got cops on your mind."

"I know a lot of them. Cops who'll give me the time of day, that's a different story. This one is to be trusted."

"Who the hell you working for, anyway?"

"You want to tell me categorically that none of your people have ever been collared, so we can put that to rest?"

He frowned. "Okay, sure. Moses had a couple pops, way back in his music days, when whiffing weed was common as chewing gum, but the public protectors of everyone else's morals put the rap on it like it was the devil's work. Big deal."

"I didn't mean him. And I'm hip about reefer. When Robert Mitchum got set up in the late forties, the tabloids made him out to be a wild-eyed dope fiend."

He nodded, obviously remembering. "Mitchum was cool. Okay, some have got rap sheets—and jailhouse body art, and three-pack-a-day smoke joneses. So what? In my book, I trust most of them a lot farther than I do these clucks running Fortune Five Hundred companies. Besides, where the hell you think I get my people? At job recruiting fairs? We travel ten months a year—*hard* travel. You see any first class accommodations out there? This is the best it gets," he said, nodding around at the flimsy paneling with its good-citizen awards and city keys and the rumpled cot beyond the folding partition. "I need people with few attachments and lots of loyalty, who can take the pay, which, frankly, stinks. Who can work outdoors, and survive on food that'll give you indigestion now and probably heart disease later. I need someone who can deal with tedium and disrespect, with bum weather and cop suspicion and equipment that busts down just before showtime and sometimes breaks a jack's leg in the bargain. You know what it costs for insurance premiums? Am I getting through? Oh yeah, and private dicks who expect there to be problems and damn sure look hard to find 'em." His face blazed so red I thought the tufts of white hair would ignite. "Let's see, am I leaving any of the perks out?"

I grinned. "I get the idea."

"A crack like you made, I'm not sure you do. We're the only ones we got, so we depend on each other. We're each other's family."

"I apologize."

"I'll put my jacks alongside any state or city workers you want, and I'll bet mine can outwork 'em two to one. Hell, a lot of these people have been with me for years—and you been here for about ten minutes. I hope I've hurt your feelings."

"If my hide was that thin I'd have lasted in this *racket* ten minutes."

He harrumphed. "All right, we understand each other."

"Yup, so back to my questions. You said that you've got people with you who have some history. Not Pepper, though."

"Is that a question?"

"Poorly worded."

He glanced at the low curved ceiling of the motor home, then sighed. "One time. In Jersey, when he was young. Long before he came to work for me. But he wrote it right on the application form the first day. He paid for it. It was in the past, he said. And I said all right, keep it there."

It was the incident that Ms. Parigian at youth and family services in New Jersey had told me about, when Troy Pepper had been given an option of jail or the service. It made me feel a bit better that he had owned up, and that Pop had now, too. I got more comfortable in the chair. "Where you from, Pop?"

"Me? Newport News, Biloxi, San Diego—here and there."

"Navy towns."

"The old man was an anchor-clanker, swore if he didn't make chief petty officer he'd muster out. Twelve years later, he was still swabbing decks. My mother told him get out or she was going to run off and take us kids. He got used to dry land eventually, but he couldn't sit still. He strayed into carnivals because it was a chance to move around but keep his family. Eventually he bought a piece of the action. Summers I traveled with the show. Those were good days."

"Is this the same show?"

"More or less. I don't know for how much longer, though." He hesitated, then said, "I've been getting some pressure to sell."

"Who from?"

"There's an outfit called Rag Tyme Shows, with a *y*—a better name no one's ever thought of. All they talk is trash. They're medium sized, but they seem to want to become the Microsoft of carnivals. They don't got the manners, or the nice suits, but they got the same shark values. It's run by a couple of sharpies named Louie Hackett and Bud Spritzer."

"I can hear their sport coats already."

"As New York as an egg cream, the pair of 'em. Few years back, they offered to buy the show—which right away means someone should be comin' after them with a net. You got to have a screw loose to want to be in this business."

"You're in it."

"Case in point. Anyway, I told 'em forget it. A year later, I had to make some equipment upgrades to meet new safety regs—goddamn Democrats in the statehouse. Well, dough was hard to come by. It always is. But I got a lender and borrowed against equity. Come to find out later, the lender sold the note. Guess who to?"

"Rag Tyme, with a *y*."

He shook his head in disgust. "The juice went up ten percent. I go to Hackett—he's the business guy—I say, 'What the hell is this?' Very calmly, he shows me spreadsheets, and according to that, he says, with revenues flat and yadda yadda . . . I told him his math was bogus, and so then he hauls out the signed contract, which says that he can use his firm's own accounting methods, and I realized he had me. I said, 'I'll pay you back, every dime. But don't horse with me. I don't want you talking to anyone, my wife'—my wife was alive at the time—'friends, workers, *no* one. If I don't give you your money by the fifteenth of each month, you can chop this off!' And I showed 'em this."

He showed it to me, too. "You've still got the finger," I said.

"And a gut you could strain coffee through, not to mention four payments still due on the loan."

"Four months isn't so bad. I just put on a thirty-year straitjacket."

"Good luck, but the way this note is written, if I miss a bounce, just one, the remaining comes due all at once."

"Is that legal?"

"The whole donut. Or I forfeit the show. My lawyer said it was legal. Stupid but legal." He sighed bleakly. "Now I don't know if I'll make it."

"Could you borrow?"

"How the hell you think I got into this fix?"

"How much are you talking?"

"You don't want to know. A lot more than I can afford."

"Sometimes selling to a hungry buyer can mean money in your pocket."

"Not these guys. Hungry, sure. They call it mergers and acquisitions, happens all the time, right? Supposed to be good for everyone? Horse manure. The strong eat the weak, and crap out the bones of workers. Good for who?" He twisted his lips. "Fuckin' Republicans."

"What are you, a Whig?"

"A thinker. I'd have been lucky to get fifty cents on the dollar. And what they'd do if they bought me out, they'd put in people they already got on their payroll, and my workers would be on the bricks. This show maybe ain't much in the big scheme—it ain't Cirque du Soleil—but I put years and sweat into it. Rag Tyme is strictly a bottom feeder, looking to wipe out competition. There's a tired show that comes through these parts in late spring—maybe you've seen them. Moths fly out of their equipment when they open it up, and you can hear the gears creaking in Boston. That's one of theirs. It's a wonder no one ends up killed on the rides, or gets ptomaine off the food. But Louie Hackett don't seem too concerned, as long as the bottom line is in his wallet."

"You mentioned another name, too."

"Bud Spritzer. The Squisher. He used to pro wrestle."

I knew it had sounded like more than a fizzy drink. "He goes back. Wasn't there some controversy about him?"

"That's a way to put it. He kept some kind of choke hold on an opponent too long one time, guy ended up with scrambled eggs for a brain. Spritzer had to give up the ring. He knocked around the rackets for a while. He's a businessman now."

"With a knuckle-crusher handshake and a specialty in hostile takeovers, I'll bet."

"Hackett is the so-called brains of the outfit, Spritzer is the ball buster."

"Have they been around lately?"

He tugged an earlobe. "I get your drift. The answer is no."

"No they haven't been around? Or no to my drift?"

"Both. I ain't heard from them since May, which is jake with me. But I don't figure them in this. Do you?"

I shook my head. "I can't see how."

"Any luck, they won't get wind of it. The carny world's a small one. If they do hear, you can bet your britches they'll come sniffing around, chipper as popcorn, checkbook in hand, and it'll be two bits on the dollar now. Judas H. Priest. Listen to me. I got to get off the pity pot. Take a walk with me."

Outside, the moon that had shone the other night was fatter now in the indigo sky, hanging imperiously above the river, oblivious to the follies and travails of the people on the little blue planet it looked down upon. Traffic streamed by on the boulevard in long parallel glows of red and white lights, duplicated on the other side of the river and doubled by reflection in the water.

"Look at that," Sonders said morosely. "Nice evening, a lot of them folks could be here, walking around with their families, their sweethearts, eating fried dough and corn on the cob . . . winning Kewpie dolls. Having fun. That's it in a nutshell, ain't it? Giving people a break from their lives, something a little different from what they get elsewhere. *And*—I'm not gonna snow you with a Mother Teresa riff—we could be doing twenty-five, thirty grand tonight . . . instead of sitting here dark and the season growing long." He ran a palm across his head and looked at the moon. I half expected him to howl. "But then I think, what kind of shallow guy am I? I've got one of my people sittin' in stir, could be facing hard time." He dropped his arm. "It's a changed world from the one I used to know."

"Back in the good old days, when a dollar was still worth forty cents, and risqué was couples sitting around the living room listening to Rusty Warren records."

"Hold the jokes, will you?"

"You hold the straight lines."

"I wish I could."

I felt for him; a good old guy who was trying to do right by his people. Sonders saw a mission in what he did, and it wasn't all about profit. The question was, had others done right by him? As though he'd read my thoughts, he called after me as I made for my car. "Hey, Rasmussen. Find out, will you?" His gruffness was gone, and for the first time, standing there in the gleam of light from the parkway, he looked older than his years, tired and stooped and a little lost. "Find out what really happened?"

14

My phone was ringing when I unlocked the door to my house. I put on a light. On the floor, among the cardboard packing crates, I found the handset.

"Mr. Rasmussen?" a woman asked.

I said it was.

"This is Maddie Hartley, director of human resources at Garden State Foods. I hope it's not too late to be calling." It sounded as if it might be too late for her; I thought I heard her yawn.

"It's fine, Ms. Hartley. Thank you for getting back to me." I fished my notebook out of my jacket pocket.

"You had a question about a former employee?"

I told her the reason for my earlier call and gave her Troy Pepper's name.

She made a little hiss of indrawn air. "Oh dear. I'm sorry. This happened up there in Massachusetts?"

"Last night. He was arraigned today. His attorney is gathering information for a defense." I shoved some clutter aside and sat on the couch and switched on a table lamp.

"Well, I do remember him. He started with us four years ago. He worked second shift, as a picker—that involves filling orders, getting items off the warehouse shelves, and putting them on pallets for delivery to supermarkets. To be honest, I wasn't sure he was going to be able to cut it. He has a disfigured hand. Well, I was wrong. He never missed a shift—all in all, a reliable worker. He did have one difficulty, I recall." She sighed, and I heard the weariness for certain this time. "A group of others on the shift, who'd been there longer, approached him one night at break and asked if maybe he was working too hard, if maybe he should take it easier. Evidently he thanked them for their concern, but he decided he didn't like the suggestion, so he worked even faster."

"And the others saw the light, increased productivity, and set a plant record," I said.

"Yeah, exactly." There was a hint of zest in her voice that seemed to want to bubble up through the weariness. "No, they decided that telling gets more results than asking. They met him in the parking lot one night. It got physical, and he took the worst of it, but he fought them until security broke it up. The other men could've been terminated, but Mr. Pepper insisted it had been a misunderstanding. They worked it out, and life went on—with probably some middle course hashed out on the workpace issue." She sighed. "Why can't world leaders resolve differences that smoothly? Anyway, Mr. Pepper was fine for about three years, worked his way up to forklift operator. And then he resigned. That's the last I knew."

"Do you know why he left?"

"We didn't have a formal exit interview process in place then, but he did come in, and he was polite and all, thanked us for the opportunity, and assured me it wasn't because he was unhappy there. But that's about all he had to say."

"Would you happen to have the file right there with you?"

"No, I'm at home. It's in my head, though."

"You remember that?"

"It's this problem I've had for years. I can't seem to forget a darn thing."

"That's not a bad problem to have."

"It is when you can't shake the name of every schoolteacher you ever had, every classmate you shared Valentine's Day cards with from grade one on. If I could lose all that rummage it might free up some space on the hard drive."

"To do what?"

"Good point. Anyhow, I do recall one other thing about Troy Pepper . . . he had this nervous way of looking at you—or avoiding looking, maybe. I got the feeling that he had things to say but couldn't quite bring himself to say them. Well, I wish you the best, Mr. Rasmussen. Now, I've got another clock to punch. I'm caring for my mother, who's in the last stages of Alzheimer's. She can't remember a blessed thing, including who I am. And I can't *stop* remembering—and realizing that eventually each of us ends up in the cemetery, flying the marble kite. Of course, if I'd known that back in the day, when I was a camp follower with Springsteen's band, I'd have done things a lot differently."

"Put your nose to the grindstone and started saving kite string?"

The zest welled up finally in an honest laugh. "It only takes six feet of string to fly that puppy. No, I'd have enjoyed myself even more. Good luck to you."

A minute after I hung up, the phone rang again. It was Sonders. "You've been yapping a while," he said. He sounded agitated. "I'm getting jerked around here. Who makes up all these chickenshit rules, anyhow?"

I asked him to take a breath and explain. He'd spoken with Fred Meecham about resuming business, he said, but Meecham told him there wasn't much legally he could do. "I'm allowed to keep the equipment where it is, because I've contracted for the field, but will they let me operate? Negatory. And if I'm not operating, no residency permit. Deal is we can flop here tonight, but that's it. Starting tomorrow we need to find someplace else to live. I had Nicole phone up some hotels, but at those prices we'll go bust before they have to change the linen. There's got to be someplace cheaper, and I figured you might know where."

I tried to picture forty bodies camped in my four rooms but couldn't see it. "I'll snoop around and call you tomorrow," I said. "Get some sleep."

15

On Tuesday the Boston papers were waiting in the lobby, and I scanned the front pages of both as I climbed the three flights to my office. Courtney was putting the finishing touches on an autumn display in the hallway across from the elevator. She had on a salmon silk blouse and a navy skirt, her honey brown hair done up in a French twist. It was an ability she had of looking either her actual twenty-one or like an older sophisticate—something of a young Grace Kelly, or Phoebe Kelly, for that matter. She'd fashioned a scarecrow for her display. "Like it?" she asked.

"If he's looking for a brain, the hunt is over."

"Oh, you." I couldn't tell whether the incandescent smile was something they learned at Mount Holyoke or if she'd brought it with her from Duluth. Either way, it worked; there was more behind her expression than the headline of any newspaper.

"Is your boss in?" I asked.

Meecham, in a dark gray pinstripe with suspenders and a gold bow tie, waved me in. "I just got off the phone with the DA. He's sounding more and more confident. He says he's going to show a pattern of threat and intimidation going back over time. He's got Pepper's run-in with the law and that 209-A the victim filed when she got here."

"But didn't bother to refile when it lapsed," I said.

"Deemys claims that's because Pepper didn't know her whereabouts and she felt safe. Evidently he's spoken with the woman we talked with yesterday—Lucinda Colón—and I think she's going to be a prosecution witness. The idea is Pepper planned the murder in advance, that he'd finally located where the victim was living, and when the carnival came to town, he got in touch, lulled her with a visit on Saturday, and then strangled her on Sunday afternoon. The unlicensed handgun figures in there as a backup plan."

"So he kills her with a scarf he's given her and puts her in the field, where he'd be the instant suspect. Where's the premeditation in that?"

"Stupidity doesn't rule out a plan, Alex."

"Or prove one."

"If I can anticipate the prosecution's case, they'll claim expediency. The field rather than just leaving her in his trailer. Later he was going to dump her somewhere. Put her in the river, maybe. Or drive her up to the New Hampshire woods."

"How was he going to get her there? His camper is set up in an encampment."

"Bury her there behind the site, then. I don't know. I'm just trying to think like the DA."

"That could be a strain."

He grinned. I mentioned Pop Sonders's claim that the carnival people wouldn't enter a trailer uninvited. Meecham said he'd have to think more about that. Courtney came in with a legal pad and took a seat. We talked through what we knew about the case so far, and then went to what our strategy ought to be. Meecham said that he was going to concentrate on getting Troy Pepper to provide answers to key questions that remained. I suggested that we also look into Flora Nuñez's life in the days and hours before her death, to see if any suggestion of a motive other than what the DA was promoting might exist. Meecham assigned me the task.

Courtney lowered her reading glasses. "Won't the police do that anyway?"

"They'll get around to it," I said, "but at the moment, where's their incentive? They're too focused on slamming the cell door on Pepper."

At Courtney's look of dismay, Meecham said, "Alex's years as a police detective in this fair city have given him a certain hardening of the attitude."

"Or dose of reality," I said. "Drive by a road repair project. The cop's been there for hours, waving traffic past. He's bored. He's drinking a coffee, jawing with the job boss, yet he looks at your vehicle, then at you. Cops are alert, they see things. Sometimes they're wrong, but once they've got the idea you did something, they don't let it go easily. They've got Pepper in their sights."

Meecham said, "I see our defense growing out of shaking the DA's contention of premeditation. Absent Pepper giving us something clear, I'm looking at a crime of passion. Pepper in a sudden rage strangles her, panics, and dumps her in the field. That's what you might find out, Alex. Was there something Flora Nuñez might have done to provoke him? Was she seeing somebody else? Let's learn more."

"I'd like to get a look at her apartment," I said.

"I don't think we'll be able to. I broached it with Deemys. It's not considered a crime scene. The police don't have to let us in."

"If you can get the charge dropped to second degree," Courtney said, "and he's convicted, he'd still get a long sentence, wouldn't he?"

"Better than life without parole. First we've got to find the evidence to support it, or no one's going to buy it. Even so, whatever we come up with will have to convince a jury, and you can never predict how a jury will react. But the fact that the victim lived here and he doesn't—and there's his occupation—" He let out a small breath of frustration. "Even the most fair-minded jurors have notions about things, biases that can run deep."

"Like the old idea of carnies as suspect," Courtney said, thin lines of worry marring her brow, like the tiniest cracks in a bone china plate.

"At best," I agreed. "At worst, they're viewed as a clear and present danger to decent folks everywhere. That's sure to rear its head. I see it already starting."

"So it'll be best if we can come up with something strong," Fred Meecham declared. "Very strong."

From my office, I called some of the motels in the area, as I'd promised Pop last night I'd do, but if the places had any vacancies at all, the rooms were scattered and few. There was some kind of trade show at the civic auditorium, I was told, and foliage was promising to be prime this year, so the leaf peeper bus tours were already starting. I called Pop back to tell him no luck so far, but his line was busy. Then, on my way to the car, I remembered a conversation I'd had with Moses Maxwell.

16

The Venice Hotel sat on the ragged fringe of another age. Constructed in the 1880s, drawing its name from its location along one of the canals that ran for six miles through the city, it had ridden economic boom-and-bust cycles and natural catastrophes, narrowly missed being pulled down in half a dozen urban renewal campaigns, and survived more or less intact. Even in its heyday, it had never possessed the elegance of some of the city's other hotels, and yet it had its charm. In the late 1920s a prominent Boston bootlegger had been shot to death, along with his two mistresses, in one of the suites; in 1956, Joseph Kennedy, upon the eve of his son's winning a U.S. congressional seat, had publicly declared that someday, one way or another, Jack would be president. But the hotel's charms had grown frowsy with time. Then, in the 1980s, the city caught renaissance fever and, buoyed by state and federal money, set up commissions to preserve this and that. The Venice wasn't in the Historical Register, and it wouldn't make any of the chamber of commerce's four-color puff pieces, but there it was. In Vegas the developers would have run a grand canal through the lobby, with gondolas to carry the rubes from casino to casino, last stop debtor's prison.

These days the hotel was mostly residential, though even with its low rates, it didn't run near to capacity. It had the faded splendor of an era when beauty was its own reward. The other thing in its favor was what Moses Maxwell had reminded me of: its tradition of being color-blind. In the days when bands like Maxwell's came through town, a black performer's money spent just as good as the next guy's. My guess was that a gaggle of displaced carnival workers would find the same hospitality.

The carpet and drapes and the lobby furniture were saturated with the effluvia of tired salesmen and behatted conventioneers and glamorous women in black dresses, and some women in red dresses, too. It wasn't hard to conjure up women with cigarette trays, and bellhops still calling for Philip Morris, and gangsters and their molls, and musicians, but all that was as gone as hip flasks and hipsters. The ventilation system seemed to wheeze with emphysema, and cancer was eating at the ceiling molding. Still, the place whispered of a tarnished grandeur you weren't going to see the likes of again outside of a Disney theme park. At the timeworn registration desk, a black man with faded rust-colored hair sat reading the *Christian Science Monitor* through half-moon glasses. He wore his black beret with panache and had warm brown eyes, even if the mouth beneath his thin gray mustache barely moved to say, "Good day, sir. May I he'p you?"

I said that I was looking for information.

"If you're with the blues, I got a instant dislike. Sorry, but it's personal."

"Save it for someone deserving," I came back. "I'm private." I showed him my license.

He studied it, moving a pink-nailed finger along the words. "Right here in the city, I see."

"I've got an office that overlooks Kearney Square, in a building nearly as old as this, but not as suave."

"The Fairburn?"

"You know it?"

"I used to go to the reading room there on the street floor."

Quicker than you could say Mary Baker Eddy, we understood each other. I told him that that space was a pawnshop these days. Then I told him I was looking for rooms for a group of carnival employees.

If he had a reaction, I didn't see it. "Want to look at one of the rooms, sir?"

It was what you'd expect of a place that still used actual door keys: two double beds with nubbled cotton spreads, dinged furniture, sturdy green carpet, beige-and-green flocked wallpaper, reasonably clean. The water tumblers didn't have little paper jackets on them, but at least they were real glass, and not everything movable was attached with a chain. As I was returning to the elevator, I passed a door that stood partway open, and I caught a glimpse of an old man in his underwear sitting on a bed, his lifeless white hair streaked with yellow, like snow around a city hydrant, staring at nothing. It was stuffy and warm in the corridor, but I felt a chill along my backbone. Outside I welcomed the sunlight and took a deep breath of air. From my car I phoned Sonders. An answering tape as tattered as a big-top tent came on, and after the moths fluttered off I left word that the rooms would seem to do, and his people could come over anytime.

I was on my way over to Bihoco when I saw blue and white flashers light up behind me. I drew to the right to allow a city cruiser to pass, but it stayed Velcroed to my rear bumper. I shut down the mill and waited. In the side mirror I watched the cop do his thing with the onboard computer before he climbed out. He didn't don a cap (had I actually seen a city cop wear one in recent years?). He came up, adjusting his belt. He wasn't going to quip, "Going to a fire?" and I wasn't going to be able to volley back, "No, to jail," because I hadn't been speeding, and we'd get this sorted out in a minute and both be on our way.

He bent toward my window. He was young, with a narrow face and a wedge of crisp auburn hair. "Do you know why I stopped you, sir?"

I said I sure didn't.

"Your automobile registration has lapsed."

"It has?" The surprise was genuine.

"May I see your operator's license and registration?"

I dug them out. The license was in a clear plastic foldout alongside my PI ticket. It didn't make much impression. He scoped the paperwork, then pointed out that my auto registration had expired as of the last day of August. I'd been riding around in a fool's cocoon for two weeks. "My mistake. I'll drive over to the registry right now," I promised.

"I'm sorry, sir. The car will have to be towed."

"Towed?"

"Once I punch you in and the registration comes up as expired, the car can't be driven."

May not be driven, is what he meant; it ran fine. But what was I going to say? *I was on the job once; cut me some slack?* That and five bucks would buy me a cab ride to the Registry of Motor Vehicles. I didn't have a paper bag to put over my head as law-abiding gawkers crept past, lamping us with paparazzi eyes, so I sat in the cruiser with the officer while he called for a tow and then I listened to him Tuesday-morning quarterback last night's Pats game. The fatal error, he said, was Brady throwing an interception early in the fourth quarter when he had a man long and free. He said Brady needed to learn to stretch a defense more. The wrecker arrived in minutes, the way it never does when you really need it. The tow driver introduced himself—Eddie, truck number nine—and handed me a smudged card that told me the name of the company and where I could reclaim my car once I had the proper paperwork. He ducked under the back bumper of my car with the nonchalance of a man who'd lifted more rear ends than Cher's lipo doctor and got the chain hooked. The cop even apologized again.

Figuring I might be able to get a courtesy ride through my insurance agent, I phoned there but only got a recording saying that business hours were Monday through Friday, 9:00 A.M. to 5:00 P.M. I looked at my watch. It was 10:05. I called a cab.

If you want to see the changing face of the American city, visit the RMV. I quit guessing countries of origin at about twenty and just melted into the pot, which included one gray-haired woman who held her yellow sari very tight around herself, as if she were in the midst of the underworld. But there wasn't anything to be afraid of that I could see, if you didn't count the thief of time. Everyone there was just eager to enjoy America's biggest freedom: mobility. An hour later, equipped with my new registration, I took a cab over to the tow company, which was housed in a tin-sided shed tucked away behind several nondescript industrial ventures. The fleet of wreckers was evidently out and around the city, winching away people's money, which left one guy behind to run the op center. I gave him the registration, and he pulled the pink invoice from a stack as thick as a rare Porterhouse. "That'll be a hundred and eight dollars," he said.

"How much?" I croaked.

He repeated it.

"To tow the car a half mile?"

He put a grimy forefinger on the bill. "This is the seventy-five fifty the state authorizes us to charge," he said patiently. "This twenty's for storage. Plus a city fee."

"You could stash a chinchilla coat for less."

"And you got state tax on top."

"Why don't you just tow the bank away?" I hauled Visa from my wallet.

"I'm sorry, sir. Cash only."

"What?"

"I know," he sympathized. "The owner's been burned too many times."

I looked at him. "Aren't you the owner?"

He sighed. "All right, then, *I've* been burned too many times. People cancel a credit transaction or bounce a check, and I'm hanging in the wind."

And cash is easier to hide from the taxman. "I don't carry that much on me."

"There's an ATM down at the corner in the drugstore. Sorry. I don't make all the rules, sir."

No, he was just chiseling along like the rest, a little here, a little there. Still, *he* hadn't allowed my registration to lapse; I'd managed that all by myself. It stinks when there's no one to blame but you. I hooked a ride with the Portuguese tow truck driver, paid an extra dollar fifty for the privilege of having a machine give me my money, and had an amiable conversation with the driver going back. He was as nice as the cop had been, and with thank-yous all around, I picked up my car and was back in business. Forgetfulness had cost me half the morning.

17

I didn't stew long; sunshine and blue sky wouldn't allow it. I got over to the house of correction, and after a short wait Troy Pepper was led into the interview area in his orange jumpsuit. He sat across the screen from me and pushed something under it. My notebook. I fanned the virgin pages. I put it in my pocket and looked at him questioningly. I drew a breath. "You don't have to convince Fred Meecham. He's working for you regardless. Hell, you don't even need to convince me. I get paid one way or the other. But everyone else—cops, the judge, jurors—you need to sell them, and sell them good, because the way things are stacked up, you're going down for murder."

"They can't do that."

"Who's 'they'? I believe 'they' can and will. And you won't end up back at this place. It'll be Walpole, which makes life here seem like day camp."

His face tightened, but he said nothing.

"I spoke with Lucy Colón," I said. "Do you know her?"

He shook his head.

"She told me that Flora had been planning to tell you something. What was it?"

He didn't answer.

"Did Flora tell you something when you saw her?"

He went on not answering. When he spoke at all he bit off his words, not letting anything like emotion creep into them. It was the way that prisoners talked; even their language was in jail. I had to find a way to bust it out, just to feel I was earning what I was being paid. If the man was guilty—or a fool—I still owed him my best shot.

"Well," I answered myself, "I'm sorry you asked that, Mr. Rasmussen. Because it stirs up a painful reminder. Flora told me that she didn't want anything to do with me anymore. Didn't say why, but I think she found someone else. But you see, my sense of manhood couldn't take that." His eyes were on me, narrowed and dark. "A tiny little woman like that telling me she didn't want me?" I went on. "Well, the hell with that. Be told off by some chippie? Me? I showed her. I *made* her love me. And afterward, I put a scarf around—"

Pepper got to the wire fast, grabbing at it the way I imagined he'd like to grab my throat, his fingers hooked through the mesh. I was glad for the barrier. I sat back down, letting my heart slow. He backed off, too, his face losing its tension again. We shared a new knowledge now, one that we probably each would rather have done without, but there it was. The man had the potential for sudden violent action. He let out a long, heavy sigh.

"Look," I said, "I was pushing you, but I'm done listening to myself talk. If you want help on this, you've got to speak up, because we're running out of time. The clock is ticking." I hesitated, then said, "If Sonders can't make a loan payment in a few days, he stands to lose the show."

Some of the resistance left his face. I saw uncertainty in it now. "Lose it?"

"To a couple of sharpies who think they're the General Motors of carnivals. They hold a loan on the show, and if he can't make the nut, it's all going to come due at once. It'll break him. His problem is the show's shut down, and he can't—excuse me, *won't* take it on the road. He's got some crazy notion he has to stay here to show solidarity with you."

His brows drew together. "That's dumb," he murmured.

"You're telling me? If I were Pop, I'd toss you over just on general principles."

"Hey—"

"You 'hey.' What the hell have you done to earn anyone's loyalty? Why should anybody give a rip about what happens to you, when you obviously don't care enough about it to make a case for yourself?" I drilled him with a stare. "Or to confess?"

He put his good hand across his mouth and blew a breath against it, making a sound like steam escaping from a pressure cylinder. He lowered his hand and sat still.

"You should be singing like a bird, filling me up with more details than I can ever use, instead of me having to pull them out of you one by one. Fred Meecham has got to build a case, and from what I'm seeing, he doesn't have anything to go on."

He scowled at the floor, a restless man in a situation that gave no room to move. His eyes flicked up and met mine. "Flora and me were going to get together. Permanent. We talked about it. The show had a layover in Hartford. I took a bus up, and she met me. We walked along the river."

"Wait." I had the notebook out again. "When was that?"

"May, it must've been. All the trees were blooming, and there were birds. We walked and we talked and we set all the old stuff between us to rest." With the telling, his voice had softened a little, and his body lost some of its tension. He looked at me only once in a while, and briefly, but he talked as though the events he was describing were happening right now. "We knew we wanted to be together. The idea was, when I came up this time, we'd do it and then she'd come on the road with me. She was going to ask this priest she knew. We'd get married and maybe travel with the show. Or that was the idea anyways."

"She was willing to do that?"

"She wanted to try it. I said I could give Mr. Sonders notice and quit the show, get other work. She didn't want that."

"Did you tell anyone else about your plans?"

"You mean like Pop, or people in the show?"

"Anyone." I almost said "relatives" but I remembered he didn't have any. "Or did Flora?"

"I don't know that. I would've, when the time came. I didn't want to jinx it."

"It'd be helpful if there were someone else who knows about this."

"Maybe . . . maybe she told the priest."

"Do you know his name?"

"No."

"What about the restraining order?" I dropped it on him. His expression grew dark. "You had to figure I'd find out. It'd have been better if you'd told me about it."

He furrowed his brow and looked away. "It was a mistake," he said softly.

"The court system didn't think so."

"My mistake, I mean. I shouldn't have got so mad. When she told me about the baby, and . . . I didn't even know. And anyways, it was too late, she'd already taken care of it. I didn't know she didn't want a baby. I gave her some money, said it was okay, we could talk when she was ready. She threw the money at me. I guess I got mad—but it was like I was mad at everything, you know? Not her. But . . . things." His shoulders drooped. "She left. Didn't tell nobody where. I didn't even know she was up here till a month after. She got a court order for me to stay away, probably 'cause someone down there told her I was asking. But I wouldn't have hurt her, not ever. I loved her."

I wondered how many maggots doing life terms had fed themselves that line. I wanted to think he was telling the truth, but wanting isn't the same as believing, and I wasn't able to decipher any subtextual meanings in his silences and body language. I still had plenty of questions and blank pages in my notebooks when the guard came in and said our time was up.

18

Okay, I'd gotten Troy Pepper to open up a little, maybe more than he had to anyone else so far, and yet I couldn't shake the image of him lunging at the barrier when I'd prodded him. That outburst hinted at the possibility that he had done what he was accused of. No one can push our buttons like someone we love, or believe we do. It was time to find out more about Flora Nuñez.

I drove over to the Lower Highlands and found the address where Flora Nuñez had lived. It was a triple-decker with gray asbestos siding and a sagging porch. I paused just to look, then headed back downtown.

At my office I shuffled among the papers in the file folder and found the photocopy of the restraining order again. A mistake, Pepper had called it . . . *his* mistake. The form was filled in and witnessed. There was Pepper's name, written in the proper space. And the reason Flora Nuñez had given for filing the request: "He's angry with me on account I don't want his babey." She hadn't bothered to file for an extension of the order when, after six months, the term had lapsed. Significant? Perhaps, though not uncommon. Men and women fooled themselves all the time, about all sorts of things. Or maybe it was just a case of out of sight, out of mind. The signature of the witness to the document was Carly Ouellette.

I got the work number that Lucinda Colón had left and dialed it.

She sounded surprised to hear from me, and a bit cool when I said I had a few follow-up questions for her. I asked, "Did she tell you that she might get married?"

"I already told you everything what I know."

"Okay. You said that Flora seemed frightened or nervous when you spoke with her. Did you wonder why?"

"Maybe I did, but she didn't splain nothing. I just thought she was a-scared, but maybe I was wrong. We wasn't really *close* friends, you know? We just knew each other from night classes at the community college."

"Did you get the idea that it was Pepper she was scared of?"

"Who else? He was her boyfriend, no? But I got to go now. The boss he don't like us taking personal calls here."

I thanked her and hung up wondering if Flora Nuñez was the only one who was a-scared.

Courtney had commented on my investigative "method," as though it were a protocol of careful steps and procedures. In truth, it was pretty scattershot. You thought about what you wanted to know, imagined ways you might find out, and then you made your approach. A lot of the time, I felt as if I were climbing tall, rickety ladders in the pitch dark.

There was still the option of trying to track Pepper's military service record, but in strict time-value terms, it didn't add up. I hunted in my Rolodex for a name, which I found, but there was no phone number. Only an e-mail address.

19

I hauled down the overhead cage door of the ancient freight elevator and began a slow and clanking ascent, each deserted floor floating spectrally past. If you looked very closely into the murk of the elevator shaft, you might notice the insulated ductwork and the heavy duty electrical conduit snaking upward, but you'd have no reason to look, really; no reason to have come through the rusty portcullis into the courtyard in the first place, and certainly no reason to be headed for the roof of a dilapidated old mill.

The building was formerly part of Lamson Woolens, which had been one of the companies whose vast holdings stretched along the Merrimack River for a full mile. Prior to the Civil War, this was the epicenter of American manufacturing. Along with the Lamson, there were a dozen others, built by the city's movers and shakers.

The fortresslike design wasn't for aesthetics: Inner courtyards surrounded by high walls, coupled with the canals on the outer side, like moats, gave the image of castles, removed from the outside world, protected. Typically there was but one way in, over a footbridge and through iron gates. The gates would be locked right after the time when the original workers—the mill girls—were due to report for their twelve-hour shifts, so that if they were late they were forced to enter through the mill agent's office. In this way, tardiness could be noted and pay docked. Repeated offenses and you were on the bricks. But that was lifetimes ago. The flesh and sinew were gone, and the Lamson mill, and what remained of most of the others, was back to bones now. The only hints of life I could detect were pigeons cooing in the upper dimness of the elevator shaft, and vague scurrying sounds beyond the walls, which made me think of rats.

When the elevator stopped and I lifted the slatted door, Randy Nguyen was standing inside an enclosed entryway, waiting. He slid a heavy insulated door shut behind me. I felt an instant bath of cooled air surround me, and I had the sensation of docking at a lonely space colony on the far reaches of the solar system. The rooftop shed I walked into fit the setup, too. Despite the surrounding landscape of decaying brick, the shed's interior was modern, with an electrostatic tile floor, thermal windows, and halogen lighting. He gave my extended hand a blank, red-eyed look before apparently remembering the ancient custom and shook it. His palm was as dry as a circuit board.

"Hey," he said by way of greeting.

Nguyen would be in his midtwenties now, I guessed, though he had the unkempt look of a college freshman coming off finals week. He wore a loose white sweatshirt with a large bar code printed across the front, and crinkled cargo pants that bloused over the tops of his Timberlands like virulent elephantiasis. On a computer screen behind him I saw that he'd been playing solitaire.

"You actually send that e-mail yourself?" he asked. "Or do you got a ghost writer does your tech work?"

"I've traded in the Underwood for a PC since I saw you last."

"*Pffft.* Ancient technology. Might as well carve symbols on stone tablets. Anyway, you could've saved yourself fifty cents."

"That's what it cost to e-mail you?"

"To park. There hasn't been a meter maid on that street since July." He nodded toward a bank of video screens built into a console along one wall. "Courtyard," he said. "Scan left." On one of the screens, my car appeared, sitting alone on a stretch of empty street. "Four—replay." The vista grayed a moment and then there I was, five minutes younger, plugging coins into the meter. "Voice-rec tech," he said. "These keep a continuous scan of over a million square feet of empty mill space."

"And you sit and play solitaire."

He shrugged, gesturing for me to look around.

The room had been designed to take advantage of the rooftop height, with thermal glass panes that gave views of the river and the city. The rooftop surrounding Randy's shed sprouted sumac and small trees, the result of airborne seeds that found root in the humus of decaying wood and decades of soot, though there was purpose there, too. The random saplings camouflaged a thicket of antennas. There was nothing random, however, about the equipment Nguyen had. The bank of monitors gave crisp black-and-white images of various sectors of the mill complex, though the only movement in the landscape of broken bricks and shadowy cloisters and occasional quick glimpses of my car was the shifting of the images themselves. There wasn't a human to be seen. Lines squiggled across a set of smaller screens—oscilloscopes, I realized—which I guessed meant Nguyen had set up listening posts as well.

Why? I thought. For what purpose? Who cared? But I said, "Any luck with what I asked you?"

With a smirk he drew me over to a pair of comfortable swivel chairs in his workstation.

I'd first met Randy Nguyen when I was a cop and he was a high school detention rat who'd been awarded a police department grant, ostensibly to keep him off the street and out of whatever trouble kids with a 140 IQ got into. Fast access and connectivity weren't a given in those days, and Nguyen, who was a graduate of every video arcade in town, had soon made himself indispensable. Over the year and a half he spent with the department, he got the city hooked into national crime registries and fingerprint databases and had organized police files going back decades, all of it accomplished with a minimal human interface. Digital machines were his world. Unfortunately, he also dropped out of school during that time, and his grant was canceled. I'd heard he'd gone on to get a GED. He now worked for the outfit that oversaw security for a number of the abandoned mills that stretched along the eastern shore of the river like the ruined palisades of an ancient city-state. He swung into his padded spring chair. "Some ex-jarhead's service rec, right?"

"Never ex."

"*Semper.* I'm hip. I'm surprised you couldn't locate it yourself."

"I didn't have the hours to play Ping-Pong with forty different voices on a telephone—some of them even human."

"Yeah, must be rough being analog these days."

He made it sound like not being toilet trained. He said it without irony or malice—or an ounce of understanding for a world that was other than his neat on/off binary world. Guilty or innocent, black or white: It was a zone that had none of the grays of complexity that bedevil the rest of us poor souls. He turned to a computer and began commanding his minions.

"Your bosses know you pull all this juice?" I asked.

"They see the bills and don't squawk. With what they pay me, they're still way ahead of what they'd have to lay out for a fleet of rent-a-cops walking rounds."

"Yeah, their shoes alone would add up to more than your mouse pad. But why not just do it from home? Then you wouldn't have to get out of bed."

"I like to be out in the world. Besides, where else would I get the penthouse views and the roof garden?" He shrugged. "Print," he said, and rolled his chair sideways, the casters moving swiftly on the Lucite carpet protector. A sheet of paper slid crisply out of a printer. Nguyen handed it to me with a "Voilà!" flourish. Before I read a word, a second sheet came out.

It was the military service file of Troy S. Pepper. I didn't bother to ask Randy how he'd done it. His answer would've been from a 1930s movie, von Stroheim going, "Ve haf our vays"—if he knew any films that weren't by Tartantino. I hoisted my wallet and gave him a questioning look. He scraped at his sparse black whiskers. "How does fifty sound?"

"A lot better than 'One Is the Loneliest Number,' which is what I'd still be listening to on the telephone without you." I forked over a twenty and three tens, which he tucked into the pocket of his cargo pants.

"Seriously," he said, "I'm the only heart beating in this desolation, and the owners know it. You know how in a winter pond, there'll be one little patch of water that the ducks keep open by moving around, keeping the ice from forming? That's me in this gothic labyrinth. I'm not here to protect against crime. Even the taggers don't waste paint on these walls—no one to see their work. Rats rule here."

"And you're the last line of defense before total entropy."

"I'm not kidding you. Someday, everything's going to be run by people like me sitting alone in towers, ringed by security, because, after silicon, we're going to be the most valuable resource on the planet. Wait and see."

In his world we'd all be overwired and disconnected. I spooked a few pigeons on my way through the alcove to the elevator, which made a good old-fashioned mechanical rattling as it took me back to my world. In that world, when I phoned Pop Sonders from my office, he told me that the carnival crew had finished gathering their personal belongings and had made the move over to the Venice Hotel. He thanked me for arranging it.

"What about you?" I asked.

"I'm gonna squat here, for tonight at least."

"Is that legal?"

"It don't feel right just leaving. Besides, I want to keep an eye on things."

I told him I'd call him there later if I learned anything new. At my house, as I fixed dinner, I put on the TV and caught the tail end of the six o'clock news. Francine had fizzled, but tropical storm Gus seemed hot to trot, the weatherman promised, grinning like a maniac, and *this* one was the real deal. When I had my food on the table, I laid out the pages of Troy Pepper's service record. I felt my appetite die.

20

The carnival looked forlorn in the fading afternoon, the colored lights unlit, loudspeakers mute, the amusement rides inert. I didn't spot another soul. As I walked past the haunted house, I caught a distorted flicker in one of the old crazy mirrors. I moved closer, watching my image metamorphose as I approached. On the night I'd come with Phoebe, she had laughed looking at herself, dragging me into it, too. "You know what I like?" she asked. "We get to see ourselves as a little absurd."

Looking for a new perspective now—or perhaps chasing absurdity—I walked to where Troy Pepper's camper was parked. The police seal was gone, but when I tried the door, it was locked. Someone had been here since, however. On the wall beside the steps was painted the word KILLER in drippy red letters.

To satisfy curiosity, I paced off the distance from the camper to the spot where the body had been discovered. It was a pretty straight shot, but it was close to a hundred yards, and part of it passed close to the vans and trailers of other carnival workers. Carrying a body such a distance, even that of a small person, would have been a feat.

A scattered flow of traffic went by on the boulevard, but it seemed very far away. At the edge of the field, where the unmowed grass began, I paused. The police had taken away the crime scene tape. Or perhaps kids had, and it streamed from the handlebars of their bikes. Either way, I was glad. A birch stood at the edge of the clearing. In the fading light, its leaves darkening, it looked as if it were full of blackbirds waiting to swoop. A soft wind prowled through the high grass and stirred the trees beyond, like the passing of an uneasy spirit. I shut my eyes and tried to think myself back to Sunday night.

In darkness I'm walking the midway with Phoebe, Michael Jackson singing . . . "Tell 'em that it's human nature" . . . Phoebe pointing at a parti-colored teddy bear asking me to win it for her. Swing the hammer and be a hero. Troy Pepper is there, just a face in the crowd at this point. He says something to us. "The lady knows what she wants." Okay, I remember that. Anything else?

A drop of sweat crept down my temple. I let it roll and drop. My eyes still shut.

I tear off two tickets at the perforation and put them in his hand. His deformed hand. I grip the friction-taped shaft of the mallet, feeling my arms and shoulders swinging the hammer down onto the strike plate . . . "careful what you wish for—" That's what he has said. Swinging the hammer again . . . A scream. The weight wobbling up . . .

No. Rewind further.

I pick up Phoebe at her house 5:30 P.M. Is Flora Nuñez dead in the trailer? Already in the field?

Further.

In my office, maybe three o'clock, doing a background check for Atlantic Casualty . . . dull, routine stuff . . . The ME's time span for death was between noon and five. Meaning Flora Nuñez could still be alive. It's Sunday. Has she gone to church? And taken the afternoon to go to speak with Troy Pepper?

No one I'd spoken with could place her here that day alive. Where had she been? With whom?

Fast forward.

Careful what you wish for . . .

The woman dead. Cops arriving, first one—the woman officer, then Duross . . . moving the crowd back, securing the scene for the detectives to take it over. A little later they pick up Pepper.

Killer . . .

"Sir? What are you doing here?"

The female voice startled me, and I snapped open my eyes.

I turned and saw a patrol officer stepping through the grass toward me. I hadn't heard the cruiser, but there it sat, parked near my car. "Just looking," I said.

"For what?" Her gaze was steady and probing.

I realized I'd just been thinking about her. She was the female half of the detail that had been here Sunday night, but I'd seen her one other time since then—seen more of her, too—and I suddenly remembered where.

"Trying to find my eyeballs, so I don't trip over them." I grinned. "It was a better line when you used it at the West Side Gym yesterday." I couldn't see the gold ring in her navel, but she was the kickboxer.

"Who are you?"

I told her. "I'm a private investigator. I'm working with the lawyer representing Troy Pepper." I took another step toward her, reaching for ID.

"Hold it right there."

I stayed put, and she reached to take my offered wallet.

She had a no-nonsense face, attractive in a hard-edged way. I tried to read her name tag, but I couldn't. She handed back my ID. "And you're doing what, Mr. Rasmussen?"

"I'm just a cat, mousing in the field." I nodded toward where the body had been found. "Flora Nuñez wasn't very big, but still it would have required some effort to carry her out there from the suspect's camper."

The cop appeared to give it some thought.

"Unless there were two people to carry her," I went on, "which seems unlikely. Another possibility is that the suspect's camper wasn't the crime scene after all, which would mean she was killed somewhere else and brought here. That could also suggest that Pepper wasn't her killer."

I thought she might get interested or angry or resistant to my ideas, but she just lifted a shoulder. "That's not for me to say. I'm on patrol and saw your vehicle. You really shouldn't be here. There've been incidents of vandalism."

We started back toward the cars. Walking alongside her, I was finally able to read her tag. Her name was Loftis.

"You were here the other night when the victim was found," I said. She seemed surprised to learn that I had been here, too.

"That must've been rough," I said. "Not your everyday paid detail."

She raised a hand to cut me off. She had a call on her walkie-talkie and said something into it, listened, said something else, and signed off. "I've got to go."

"I happened to notice the other officer from the detail—Duross—is working with Detective Cote."

She gave me a sideways glance. "You seem to be well informed."

"I was on the job for a number of years."

"What's your name again?"

It didn't seem to ring any bells. "Paul Duross has a goal to make detective," she said. "He's very motivated."

"What about you?"

"I like what I do now."

I nodded. "Investigation isn't all it's cracked up to be. The paperwork can be more of a killer than the bad guys with guns and knives." We got to our cars. "Can I ask you one more thing? If Pepper did kill her, why leave the body so close to the carnival?"

She hesitated, and I sensed she was going to shut me down, but after a moment she said, "Maybe he panicked. Or possibly he wanted it to be found. But that's not my area of expertise. I wish you well."

The officer trailed me in her cruiser out to the boulevard and then took off, with her own sector to patrol. I drove away considering the implications of what she'd said. I'd thought of both possibilities, and yet they ran counter to Roland Cote's idea of premeditation. Now a new idea came to me. Had the police investigators read the crime as they had because it had been set up to be read? Was that why Pepper was so passive in his own defense? Had he wanted discovery as part of a plan?

I didn't like it. As an explanation it worked in a Poe story better than in reality. A killer's instincts, like most everyone else's, were toward self-preservation.

So why not just leave the body in the trailer until he had a chance to dispose of it farther away, where it wouldn't so clearly be tied to him? Sonders had said the people here didn't go into each other's quarters uninvited, which made it unlikely that Pepper would have feared accidental discovery. Still it made no sense . . . unless someone else had killed Flora Nuñez and brought the body there, wanting to make it *seem* as though Pepper had done it. But how? And who?

Go ahead, Rasmussen, keep asking questions. That's your job.

I drove along the boulevard to Bedford Avenue, turned right, and took the next right, which put me on a course behind where the fairgrounds and the woods were. There were houses in there, and a city playground. A group of Southeast Asian kids were shooting hoops. None of them would be able to dunk the ball from a stepladder, but they had a good fast game going. I went past until I found a turnout and drew in and got out.

The adjoining area was overgrown with bushes and small trees. Several old telephone poles had been laid down to keep motor vehicles off the paths. Judging by the litter of empty malt liquor bottles, cigarette butts, and nasal inhalers, the place was a hangout for youths. There was a crude fire ring, fashioned from blackened stones. I kicked a toe through the nuggets of burnt wood. In movies there is often a moment when someone finds a tiny clue and gets a flash of insight that makes everything else snap into place. I only got ashes on my shoe.

I wandered the rest of the way into the woods, another thirty feet or so, until I came to the back edge of the meadow behind where the carnival was set up about fifty yards away. I stood concealed in shade, hearing the errant buzz of insects around me, smelling the fragrance of Concord grapes ripening somewhere nearby, watching a hatch of flying insects twirling manic figure eights in the quiet air, thinking. If the dead woman had not been taken from Pepper's trailer, suppose someone had driven her in here and transported her through the woods to the meadow? This would still have meant carrying the body, though the distance was shorter by half, and the cover much better. As a theory, it had possibilities, but it didn't provide me with any knowledge. As I reached my car, I saw three boys moving along a branching path. They looked to be nine or ten, two of them carrying air rifles. I called to them, and they saw me and stopped.

"Hi," I said amiably. "I'm a detective." More as a bit of actor's business than anything else, I showed them my license. It bought some attention.

"We didn't do nothing bad," the taller of the two riflemen said at once.

"No, I know that."

"These are only just BB guns."

"I'm only just looking around. Maybe you can help me."

Shrugs. "Okay . . . sure."

"Do you kids play here a lot?"

"Sometimes. After school and stuff."

"Do cars ever come in here?"

"Sometimes, yeah. There's a gap between the logs."

"Yeah, big kids drink in here sometimes," the second rifleman said.

"Have you seen any cars in here the last few days?"

"No. Only just a police car. 'Cause of what happened at the carnival, I bet."

Cote had the bases covered; I had to give him that.

"I seen one other car."

We all turned to the smallest of the boys, who had spoken.

"A green one," he said. "Small."

"Do you remember what kind?"

"Mmm . . . Wait. TV."

"You've seen it advertised on TV?""

"No, it *is* a TV." His friends looked at him as if he were joking. "I mean the same brand, only I can't remember it."

"Yeah, right, Sully. Car and TV."

"A Mitsubishi?" I said.

"That's it. I seen it here on . . . Sunday. Around suppertime."

Suppertime, Sully guessed, was around six or maybe seven. He didn't know much more, but I was interested in what he'd given me. I thanked them. "What are you hunting for?" I asked.

"Nothin' really, we're only just pretendin'."

"You didn't happen to shoot at a dog, did you?"

They exchanged a nervous glance, then chorused, "No."

I nodded. "Okay, just be careful."

They raised their hands, as though swearing to it.

For the record, when I got to my office, I checked with a friend at the registry. Flora Nuñez drove a dark green Mitsubishi.

21

I waited until near dark, which was coming sooner each day—7:40 by the clock on my dashboard—and drove over to the Lower Highlands again. Like most cities, Lowell was a collection of neighborhoods, and "lower" was literal, suggestive of a district where downhill was the directional flow of most things, from wealth to municipal services and, too often, to trouble. I'd dug up a telephone number for the property owner, a Boston attorney, and had asked her if it would be possible to have a look at an apartment recently occupied by Flora Nuñez. I told her I was working for a lawyer, thinking she might be sympathetic. She cut me short. "Let me put it to you this way. No." I was left to supply my own reasons. Possibly she was hypersensitive to litigation and wanted to avoid even the remotest possibility that the fact that her tenant had been a crime victim might come back to haunt her. Maybe she just didn't want the address to become notorious, a stop on the Mill City Gore Tour: "Y'see that apartment up there? That was where . . ." She probably just didn't want to return the security deposit.

I parked on Westford near Dover Square and sat in the car. The block was an amalgam of multiunit apartment houses and small shops. Branch

Street ran down toward Little Phnom Penh, a half mile away, and lighted billboards saturated area traffic with ads for cable TV shows, cheap liquor, and the names of personal injury lawyers. As I'd hoped, there was little activity on the street. The only place open was a quick mart–liquor store combo. Streetlamps mounted on every third or fourth telephone pole cast just enough light to read a scratch ticket by.

I locked the Cougar and walked briskly down the block, like a man on a mission, which I was. I reconned the block and circled around, and when I came back along the original stretch, I was moving more slowly and alertly. I went up to the building where Flora Nuñez had lived.

NO TRESPASSING, warned a sign on one corner of the house. No one had taken off the asbestos siding in favor of vinyl, and the trim had not been painted since they took the lead out of paint. I suppose just being there constituted a health hazard, but I had no plan to make the stay a lengthy one. I didn't envision a security door, either, and wasn't disappointed. In the foyer, a strip of Astroturf that had been worn to the nub scratched at the soles of my shoes. If the single weak bulb in the ceiling fixture threw twenty watts, I was Tom Edison. I used a small flashlight on the names below the mailboxes. They were the names you'd expect in a melting pot. Some aspirant for school committee trolling for votes had delivered a hopeful stack of campaign fliers delineating her position on key educational issues, but no one had bothered to take off the elastic band. In that precinct I think some of the voting machines were still steam powered. F. NUÑEZ was the name on mailbox number five.

The stairwell smelled of roach spray and last Friday's fish, even three flights up, at the end of a short hallway. I knocked softly, more for form than from expectation, and waited, listening for sounds. There was a key plate for a dead bolt, though if I understood right, it wouldn't be locked because there was no one inside. The lower lock was a basic spring catch. It offered as much resistance as a building inspector did to palm grease. I clicked it shut behind me.

There were no lights on in the unit, which could confirm that Flora Nuñez had left during the day on Sunday or could mean nothing at all. I left it that way and switched on my flashlight. I got an impression of scuffed linoleum and worn furnishings, lots of colors in the wall coverings and drapes. In the short inside hallway, someone, presumably Flora

Nuñez since she lived alone, had set up a small tabletop shrine, with a statuette of the Blessed Virgin, ringed with candles, prayer cards, and other religious trappings. I offered it a quick glance and moved on. Somewhere in the building, a water pipe coughed.

Barring total randomness, murder usually led you to the life of the victim: patterns of behavior, known associates, finances, love life, habits, affiliations, predilections, perversions, and possessions. What might Flora Nuñez's have been?

I didn't spend a lot of time on the obvious; it was unlikely there'd be anyplace the police hadn't laid trail ahead of me. Still, I had to wonder: Because they were so sure they already had their man, was it possible they had overlooked something? In the kitchen there were several shelves in front of a window, holding potted herbs. I thought of Pepper's idea of marrying the woman and taking her on the road. Would she cook big meals for him? The plants were beginning to wilt. Someone dies and other things die with her.

I opened cupboards, counter drawers, the refrigerator. I looked under the sink and in the wastebasket. There was a calendar tacked to the wall, Diego Rivera murals, and I paged forward and back, looking at the scarce notes she'd jotted there: a dentist appointment for early September, three days of last July inked in as vacation . . . nothing I needed to know. In the bathroom I checked the medicine cabinet and the linen closet. I even lifted the toilet tank cover—other people weren't that imaginative, why should I be? The living room didn't take long. I saved the bedroom for last.

I was hoping there'd be a hidden diary with entries up to the time she'd been killed and it would all be laid out in a neat hand—a dangerous liaison gone wrong—and you could stamp another case "solved" and add it to the Rasmussen files. There wasn't. She kept a neat house: bed made, no clothes lying around. I found some CDs, a few back issues of *Latina,* some college textbooks on paralegal studies. In a bureau drawer, among neatly folded panties and nylons, I came across a Polaroid snapshot. I held it close to the light. Taken at a table in what appeared to be a nightclub, it showed a group of four women and two men. Two of the women were Flora Nuñez and Lucy Colón. A third looked vaguely familiar, though she was holding a drink up in a toast, so that part of her face was hidden.

The other woman and the two men were strangers. To have a working photograph of Flora Nuñez, I slipped the Polaroid into my jacket pocket.

In the hallway, the statue of the Virgin watched from its shrine. I examined it more closely than I had before. There was a strand of rosary beads wound around the base, along with several votives and a book of matches. The matches were from Viva!, a strip club out by the city limits, and I had a sudden recognition. I took out the Polaroid and tentatively identified the third woman as Danielle Frampton, who danced at the club, and whom I had helped out of a jam once. So? No bolt of lightning hit me. But a thought did.

I picked up the statuette, which was twelve inches high, made of ceramic, painted blue with a white shawl and headscarf and halo. I turned it over and saw a small hole in the base. I gave the figure a shake. Something made a papery movement inside.

I hesitated, then banged the statuette against the front edge of the altar and broke the head off. With my forefinger, I did a body cavity search and felt a curl of stiff paper, but I couldn't get another finger in to tweeze it out. I banged the headless figure, and the torso shattered. I picked up the curled paper from among the shards and discovered that it was an index card. I straightened it out and held it to the flashlight. It was actually a ballot card, the kind they pass out to prospective jurors at the district courthouse. On the blank side, handwritten in ballpoint, was a list of letters and numbers.

None of it made any particular sense to me, though there was also a row of what looked to be dates: 4/18; 6/7; 7/14; 7/26; 8/26. Alongside several of them was the letter T. I looked at them a moment, feeling a sudden tingly paranoia. T for Troy?

For "Trouble," I knew, if I got caught there. I put the juror card in my pocket. I picked up the bigger shards of broken statue with my handkerchief and dropped them into the kitchen trash bag. On an impulse I filled a glass from the sink tap and poured water on the potted herbs. I was at the door when I heard footsteps climbing the stairs.

One person? Two? I listened for voices but heard none. Then the steps started along the landing, coming toward the door. I slipped into the bedroom and got down and crawled under the bed. A key scratched at the lock. The door opened, and someone came into the apartment and shut the door. I heard footsteps move along the hall. My heart was drumming hard. Peering out past a dust ruffle, I looked for light but didn't see any. Then I heard a sound that prickled the hairs on my nape: the soft crackle of a belt radio, with the gain turned low. Police?

I lay on my stomach in the dark, hoping that whoever was out there wasn't responding to a report of someone seen entering the apartment. The person went down the hall to the kitchen. I heard more walking, and the belt radio again. The person retraced a route along the hallway and left. I waited until the descending tread of footsteps faded before I crawled out. From the living room, I peered past curtains and after a moment saw a man move along the street to a patrol car and get in behind the wheel. I saw him for only a moment, but I recognized him. Duross.

22

The carnival had a few safety lights burning here and there, but the over-all effect was of a ghost encampment. I'd stayed in Flora Nuñez's apartment just a few minutes longer, wondering what Officer Duross had been there for, giving the place a quick scan, but I didn't see anything that struck me. When I knocked on the door of Pop Sonders's motor home, he opened it a crack, saw me, and quickly waved me in.

"You see the watchers out there on the boulevard?"

I had seen several cars parked there, seen the glow of cigarettes in the dim interiors. "Who are they?"

"Citizens, near as I can tell. Keeping vigil. Somebody painted graffiti on Pepper's trailer. Red Fogarty scrubbed it off this afternoon."

"Maybe you should be over at the Venice."

"Fat chance. I'm sticking here."

I thought of Randy Nguyen in his lonely aerie.

"Have you got that schedule?" I asked, getting to why I had come.

From his desk drawer he produced a large accounting ledger. He opened it, and we sat down. "This here's our itinerary for the year, date by date. What are you after?"

I looked for the days corresponding to those on the juror ballot card

I'd found inside the statuette at Flora Nuñez's apartment. On two of the days the show was en route to places; on one of the others they were set up outside Hartford, and on the final date there was no listing in the ledger.

"What's that supposed to mean?" Sonders asked.

"Could Pepper have slipped away from the carnival on these days and come up here?"

"To Lowell?" He frowned. "I don't see how. He'd have to have requested it—or just walked off the job, and I don't buy it."

"But it's possible?"

"I can't say one hundred percent no, but damn close. You mind telling me what this all means?"

I told him, leaving out the part about illegally entering the woman's apartment. "Beyond that," I said, "I don't know what it means. Maybe nothing." I put the card away. "Okay, next question. Did you know that Pepper was busted another time?"

"Old news, Rasmussen. We've been there, remember? The cops know all about that."

"I'm not talking about the broken school windows incident."

His eyes deepened under the snowy ledge of brow.

"He did a month in the stockade at Camp Lejune for assaulting an officer—who happened to be a woman. You familiar with that?"

"Of course I am!" he blustered. But after a pause, he frowned. "No," he said. "I wasn't aware of that."

At least someone was being honest with me. "The point is, it happened, and we didn't know about it. The woman was a lieutenant who was riding him hard. They threw insubordination and verbal assault charges at him, but there were extenuating circumstances. The officer had a rep for hassles. In fact, she got a reprimand in a similar incident, so he was released with time served. I guess I can see reasons for him not to bring it up. A boyhood incident—that's one thing, but maybe he figured two arrests would kill any chance of you hiring him."

Pop Sonders's face looked like a boiled potato. He puffed his lips and sank back in the chair, and for a while he kept silent. Finally he waved a hand in the direction of the boulevard. "We're a reflection of them," he said. "Those people out there in the cars. A reflection of what's inside them. Most folks just want a good time, and that's where we're at. We're happy to give it. But some people, not many, but some . . . they see ugliness. They want to win easy, no work involved. To some, we're the traveling cheap thrills show. There's people still come out to a carnival expecting bearded ladies and a guy who'll bang nails into his head, or a hermaphrodite who'll swing both ways. Get a life. We don't bite the heads off chickens. But we've got a . . . a mystique, and it excites people in some way. You can bet your boots and mittens on it. The mirrors—lot of truth in them mirrors. It's all there. The venality, the cheap thrills . . . a chance to look down on somebody else. And next day, we're thankfully gone, no reminders, and you can all forget and get back to being who you were. Until next year, when those acids start to bubble up and they need to be released again."

"You're saying I'm with them?"

"You tell me."

I met his stare, and after a moment he withered. "I'm no judge. Forget it. The fact is, we're in a leper colony. A Gypsy camp. A reminder that things could always be worse."

"They could be worse for you, too."

"Meaning?"

I was thinking about the cars keeping vigil out there, about the messages there between the lines in the newspaper, the politicians who saw an issue to exploit, and I wondered, *How long before the vigil becomes vigilantes?* "You've left a town early before, haven't you?"

"Not often, but it happens. If something can't be worked out. We blew a generator once and had to fold early. Outside Springfield a year or so ago, the promoter switched sites on us last minute, put us near a chemical plant, the smell was strong enough to peel paint. Got so bad no one was coming out, we sat there twiddling our thumbs. I was losing money the whole time."

"Did you stick and fight city hall?"

"It was more hassle than it was worth."

"Go now," I said, suddenly sensing that was the wise thing to do. "Leave before the smell gets worse here. I think it will."

"Not this time," he said stubbornly. "That last time it was only money. This is about one of my people."

"*And* money. You're not making any sticking here. You're going deeper in the hole."

"The hell with that."

"What makes you think your staying is helping?"

"I go on my own terms, dammit! We won't run."

I'd been leaning back, but I sat forward now and rose. I drew back the small curtain and glanced out the window on the side of the motor home facing the boulevard. The cars were still there. I turned. "How bad is your stomach?"

His gaze darted up at me from under the unruly brows. "I don't know what you're driving at."

"Yeah, you do, unless that line about the tin can in the shooting gallery is left over from P. T. Barnum. If Mylanta was the remedy, you wouldn't need whatever's in that brown bottle I've seen in your desk."

He scowled and crossed his arms, drawing them in tight across his chest. "It's just a sometimes thing. Anyways, look, my health ain't any of your concern. I hired you to investigate, not play Florence Nightingale. Besides, I go on my own terms."

"Since we're avoiding medical topics, maybe you can not tell me what really happened to Moses Maxwell's fingers."

"What'd he tell you?"

"Arthritis."

"He would."

"Well?"

He puffed air into his cheeks. "This doesn't get back to him, right?" I nodded.

"He was a damn good piano player, Moses. I heard you say you'd listened to his records. He'd have gone on playing a lot longer. The drummer in his band had a major habit and ran afoul of a dealer. It was the guy's monkey, it should've been his hassle, but Moses was the headman of the group; he felt a responsibility. He paid for the musician to go away to kick. Only trouble is the bad guys don't care about that. When they didn't get their money, they came looking for Moses, figured to get it out of him." Pop shook his head slowly. "They might as well have just shot him."

"They broke his fingers?"

"Did it slow and methodical, is the way I heard it. 'This little piggy went . . . *snap!*'" I winced. "That was it for him as a musician. Pride won't let him tell you, so the arthritis story covers it. There's some truth there. I don't know what's worse—the pain in my gut or in his fingers. He knocks back a lot of aspirin."

"He's loyal to you."

Sonders exhaled slowly. "Moses and my old man had known each other in the navy, so the old man hired him on. One night someone burned a tire outside the show. Moses got wondering if it'd be a cross burning next, or maybe the whole show, so he told my dad maybe he thought it best to skedaddle. Moses left, and the show got pushed out anyhow. 'Creating a disturbance' or some such nickel 'n' dime ordinance the local authorities can always cook up. My old man sold the outfit a year or so later, and died not too long after that."

"How did you come by it?"

"The people who'd took it on near to ran it aground. It was a sorry-ass pile of junk rusting in an Alabama field when I bought it off them. I knew I was going to have to put up my life savings to salvage it, but my wife said, if that's what you want to do, let's do it. First thing I did was look up whatever of my dad's crew that were still around. I said if they wanted to work, I'd hire them. Once we got rolling again, I told 'em we'd done it together and they were part of the show for as long as they wanted to be. I guess that's why I don't worry too much about people's pasts, and didn't worry when Troy Pepper showed up with that bad hand." He let a breath out through his nose. "So if that's what folks mean by a freak show, here we are."

A sound outside startled me. Somewhere, one of the dogs took up barking. I looked out the porthole window. I saw that a tent-fly line had come undone, causing the rope to blow against the side of a trailer. We walked outside and retied it. The cars were gone now, but I said, "I can still drive you over to the hotel tonight if you want."

"No thanks."

"I guess I don't have to remind you about the villagers with pitch-forks and torches."

"No. But I've got to figure that out myself. *I'm* not going, and the others decided to stick, too. Look, I throw 'we' around—but my folks here know they're their own people. They got no ropes on them. That goes for you, too, you know." He paused. "I'm real glad that you're working with us—you're good at finding things out—but if it comes to it, and you say you have to bail, I'll understand."

"Will you?"

"Absolutely."

I liked it about Sonders, I reflected as I drove home, that he thought of his group as a family, that it was always "we," but when it was the prospect of trouble, he didn't expect others to have to put their necks on the line and was willing to stand alone. I half considered trying to haul the city council down and have them meet him, but what would that prove? They'd just organize a subcommittee and hold hearings, and then pass the buck back to anyone foolish enough to take it, like me. And it still didn't mean Troy Pepper wasn't guilty.

At my house, I got ready for bed. On top of a long day and all that talk about places to sleep (never mind taking the big sleep), I didn't need much prompting to do likewise. As I shut off the kitchen light, the window over my table exploded.

I dove among the cardboard cartons, my face to the floor, as a second pane blew out. Shatters of glass rained onto me. The shower seemed to go on a long time, though it couldn't have been more than a couple seconds—just long enough for two more shots. I lay there among my life's possessions, things I hadn't really cared enough about to unpack, and about which I cared even less right now. My prized possession was my life.

Heart beating fast, driving my blood in a hot river, I low-crawled to the counter. Some of the shards were stiletto sharp, and I avoided them as best I could. I stretched a hand up, felt around on the countertop, and got my revolver. I drew the .38 from the holster.

I got outside on wobbly legs. Beyond the property line, which was marked with a dilapidated picket fence, there was an alley that ran behind the houses on this and on the next block. There wasn't much light other than what was cast from the windows of adjacent houses, a number of which, dark only moments ago, were lit now. I used the illumination to look around. Already some of the neighbors were drifting cautiously out, dressed in robes and slippers. The old woman who lived directly across the alley from my property came to me as I was bending over, examining the ground. "What the hell are you doing, young man?" she demanded.

I told her it was my house that had been shot up.

"Well, if you're looking for evidence," she sniffed, "whoever did the shooting already policed up the spent ordnance."

I gawked at her. She had on a housecoat and limp white hair. If she was less than eighty, I was pimple-faced teen. "I was a WAC," she said, as if it explained everything. "I thought what I heard was the television at first. *Murder, She Wrote* is on A&E at this time."

"And I suppose you're Jessica Fletcher."

"I know what I saw. There was a car—came cruising down here bold as you please. I happened to look out and saw it. A small car, dark. Just a driver inside. It stopped right there by those bushes, and the person inside opened fire on your house. Four or five shots or more. Then he got out, which is how I figure he policed up the casings."

I was impressed. "Do you remember anything else?"

She gave me a look.

"Actually, you saw and heard plenty," I backpedaled. "Thank you."

We were hearing sirens then. A patrol car blitzed past the end of the alley, heading for my address. A moment later, a second cruiser came up the alley, lights winking in my neighbor's eyeglasses. She looked thrilled. In another minute we were standing amid enough heat to open a neighborhood precinct. As several officers began asking questions of my neighbors, I headed for the house with several others to show them the damage. "What'd you do to your ear?" one asked.

Inside I put on lights. Shattered glass lay all over the kitchen floor, like large jigsaw pieces. It was a wonder I had only the one cut. Some of the officers got busy looking around as I tended to my ear, which had a small glass cut on the lobe. I was finishing describing events for one of the cops when Ed St. Onge knocked on the open door and came in. He was in flared gray slacks, polyester short sleeves, and a bargain-bin tie, red with gold polka dots the size of beer coasters; I suppose two decades on the job was enough to make anyone lose sartorial perspective. The interviewing officer said he had what he needed and went off to join the others, closing the door behind them.

"Surprised to see you," I told St. Onge.

"I caught the address on the dispatch. So this is chez Rasmussen? You really know how to live large." He looked around. There wasn't much to see. The uniforms had already done the bullet thing; now there were only the unpacked boxes and the shattered window to deal with. He nodded at the pair of bright, unframed paintings that leaned against the wall, awaiting hanging. "Still have those?"

"There's the proof."

He looked at me. "Sorry," I said. "I'm a little shaken up."

He went over, small bits of glass and plaster popping under his shoes, and squatted for a closer look at the paintings. They'd been done by a painter named Gregorio Montejo, when he was a struggling art student and my neighbor in a roach shelter in the Acre. When he was evicted for being delinquent on the rent, he stacked a bunch of canvases out with the rubbish. I asked if I could have a few and he said help yourself. For twenty-five bucks I took the lot. These days you see his work in the Guggenheim, and he could afford to buy the block we'd once lived in, not that he'd want to. He was in Maui last I heard.

"Had them appraised?" St. Onge asked, rising.

I hadn't and wouldn't. Call me sentimental: Lauren and I had hung them in our first apartment, apprenticeship work over an apprentice husband and wife. We split the haul when she went south. Someday a distant cousin, generations down the gene line, might lay claim to them and swipe away the dust and be like the poor country parson who finds the Andrea del Sarto in the church belfry and it fetches seven figures at Christie's and saves the parish; but to be real, the paintings were more an indicator of where the painter might go rather than where he'd gone. No matter, I liked the look of them. They had color and flair and could break up the tedium of the drabbest walls. The way the blue ink splotch on Ed's wash-and-wear shirt did.

"I don't object to short sleeves and a tie," I said, "but at least get the pocket protector to go with it. You're leaking." He plucked the pen from his pocket and clicked it shut, but he was bulletproof where my quips about his wardrobe were concerned. "Okay, the shooting could be random, and you could've just heard the squeal and showed up out of brotherly concern, but what's the other reason?" I asked.

"Someone observed a car roaming this part of town, like the driver was checking things out. The vehicle and driver description sort of match someone we're interested in."

"You're talking about your gang task force?"

He nodded. "Generally that's the Community Response Unit's turf—intervention, a more compassionate approach . . . try to understand what's got these kids running with the wolves."

"Yeah, I saw *Rebel Without a Cause.*"

"A lot of the time it works. But there are always a few guys that're just bad to the bone. Vanthan Sok, for instance. Heard of him?"

"No."

"The shooting idea fits, but I'm not sure about a motive. And you'd more likely be under refrigeration downtown if it was Sok."

"A good one, huh?"

"Eighteen years old and he's got a body count. But I'm guessing whoever did this saw you here and decided to spook you. Maybe somebody wants you out of the scene," he said, only half joking. "But it's extreme. In Chandler, weren't people always trying to get rid of Philip Marlowe by throwing money at him?"

"I'm not Philip Marlowe, and what peppered that wall wasn't dimes. Thanks for coming out."

"We'll check the ballistics. If anything turns up, I'll let you know. For now, you may want to sleep with a night-light. Congratulations again on the new place." He didn't say the rest: that it showed I was finally moving on with my life. He didn't have to. Back when I was facing dismissal from the job, Ed St. Onge had talked about resigning in support, but I'd quickly made him see reason. The matter never came up again, neither his gesture nor my rebuttal, but it meant that things between us had a new complexity, and it was never again a simple matter of who owed whom.

Alone, I shooed out several big moths that had bumbled in to flirt with the kitchen lamp and tacked some plastic sheeting over the broken window. Vanthan Sok was the name St. Onge had mentioned. I floated it back over the sluggish pool of my brain, but nothing rose. I locked the doors. As for the night-light, I made sure it had a full load in the cylinder when I carried the .38 upstairs, put it on the nightstand, and went to bed.

23

On Wednesday I lifted the shade at 6:00 A.M. and looked out. No fusil-
lade of gunfire crashed through the glass. Daylight wasn't full yet, grayed
by a light rain, but the morning walkers and runners were stroking past
undeterred. I envied them their discipline and dedication to routine, their
clinging to this fragile balloon of life, as if by clutching tightly to its
string they could keep it from floating away. I turned over and burrowed
back to sleep. The phone woke me at eight.

"My God, I just heard. Are you all right?" It was Phoebe.

"Catch a breath. I slept like a baby." I gave her the story as I knew it,
which she said was about what the morning paper had.

"Do the police think it has to do with the carnival murder?"

I said it was unlikely, mostly to calm her; the truth was I had no idea.
"Probably just somebody worried about property values," I said. "You let
in one and before you know it the neighborhood is all PIs. Ought to be a
law."

When we'd signed off, I retrieved the city newspaper from the
bushes, shucked off its plastic raincoat, and skimmed the front section
with my coffee. The carnival murder continued to occupy page one, with

a related story about the growing tension in the city over the case. A side-bar noted that Flora Nuñez's funeral would be held that morning at Señora Nuestra del Carmen church. The shooting at my place had made page four. Showered, I peered into my cupboards, but the Welcome Wagon hadn't come by in my absence and filled them. I made a mental note (again) to pick up some provisions. For garb, I pulled a dark suit out of its dry-cleaners' wrap and chose a solid charcoal silk tie over a white shirt. I took along a raincoat. On my way out I gave the unpacked boxes on my living room floor a parting glance.

The parking lot at the Owl Diner was full, as usual. Rodrigo was at his usual place by the short order grill, the band of his chef's hat sodden with perspiration. He gave me only the briefest nod when I said hello, then went straight back to cracking eggs, pouring batter, and slapping down rashers of bacon. I headed for an open booth, where the waitress brought me coffee. On the TV mounted high in a corner, a cocky-looking Gus Deemys was talking. "Turn it up, hey," a counter patron called. Without even a glance at the set, Rodrigo reached a hairy arm and raised the volume.

". . . invite potential trouble to our community," the DA was saying, "by bringing in these shows. With no reasonable way of doing background checks on the workers, we put ourselves at the mercy of a flawed system. Would any sane individual invite known criminals into their home? Bullies, thieves, and sex offenders?"

"Is he talking about the Boston Archdiocese, Matt?"

"Shh."

"Murderers? No!" Deemys was saying. "This shocking crime has made one thing tragically clear. We have no choice but to protect ourselves, and if that means banning these archaic, renegade shows, then that's a price well paid. Therefore, when I—"

"Give him the hook," said the patron named Matt. "We heard enough."

Again without a glance, Rodrigo lowered the volume, leaving Gus Deemys jawing away determinedly, in pantomime.

"'Renegade shows,'" Matt said. "Did he really say that?"

"But he's making a point, isn't he? Over the top, sure, but still . . ."

"No, I know what you're saying."

"I mean, there's crime that *is* ours—"

"—and there's crime that shouldn't be here. I hear you."

"It's a question of balance."

"My kids are grown, so we don't go to the carnival no more anyways."

"Am I right?"

"Seems we ought to do *some*thing."

"Besides talk."

But I didn't see it happen. I was mopping up egg yolk with a crust of rye toast when Rodrigo came over. "Sorry," he said, "I didn't want to break my rhythm." He sank into the seat opposite me, blotting his shiny face on the hem of his apron. "In this racket, lose your groove and you're toast, no pun intended. You wind up with egg on your shoes, pissed-off waitresses, and thirty customers who won't be back."

"I hate when that happens."

"You're all dressed up. How can I help you, my friend?"

In my work you took your information where you found it. I told him I was headed for a funeral and explained what I was doing here. He was nodding before I finished. "I can tell you how it looks from back there." He hooked a thumb toward the griddle. "The guy the cops arrested is as good as guilty—but it doesn't rest there. Mood around town is turning ugly. You heard it just now. And that was mild. Some of the talk, you've got people ready to go over there to the carnival with ball bats. And the thing is, what makes it sort of surreal—how often is a woman with a *z* on the end of her name going to be the center of sympathy?" I asked a few more questions, probing him about anything specific he might have overheard about the killing, but he didn't have a thing. With a new round of short order slips starting to dangle from the carousel over the grill, he rose and went back to work. I left a sizable tip: whatever the opposite of hush money was.

As I got to the car, my cell phone rang.

"Mr. Rasmussen?" said a hesitant-sounding female voice. "This is Nicky."

I drew a blank.

"Nicole. Mr. Rasmussen . . . it's Pop. He's sick."

What I got from her was that he'd had a "stomach attack," which I took to mean his ulcer had started to bleed. An ambulance had come for him. She and Moses Maxwell were at All Saints now, waiting to learn more. He was conscious when they admitted him, but he was obviously in pain. I looked at my watch. "Do you want me to come over?"

"I don't think there's anything you can do. No visitors allowed right now. I just wanted to let you know. Say a prayer for him if you can. And . . . something else. Um . . . we're gonna have a meeting tonight at the hotel, at nine o'clock. Mr. Rasmussen, some of the people here are scared and . . . nervous. I know I shouldn't be troubling you with our problems, but I was wondering . . . Mr. Maxwell and I were wondering. Do you think you could come, too?"

"Are you expecting trouble?"

"With Pop in the hospital, I guess I don't know what's going to happen. I just thought . . . maybe you could talk to us?"

Wonderful. I should have followed up on that leadership award. I had absolutely nothing to tell them, zero, and yet I'd heard how awkward it had been for Nicole to ask. "I'll come and listen," I said, "and if I've got two cents to add, I'll toss them into the pot. Nine o'clock. If there's any news about Pop, call me."

She promised.

24

Death always wends its way to the graveyard, which was where I found myself sitting at a little before 11:00 A.M., a magnetic FUNERAL sign stuck to my hood. I watched people get out of the cars in the line ahead of me and, following the efficient guidance of the undertakers, file toward a freshly dug grave with Flora Nuñez's flower-draped casket poised over it in a sling. The drizzle had cleared for the time being, but I buttoned my forty-dollar raincoat and followed the flow. I felt like one of those freelance mourners who still operate in old New Orleans, bringing up the rear at the funerals of strangers, for that's what Flora Nuñez and I were to each other: strangers, whose journeys had intersected only on the final leg of hers.

She evidently had made friends in her few years in the city, though; about twenty cars with their headlights on had trekked out from Nuestra Señora del Carmen for the burial, which had inevitably forced the thought: How many carloads would come to mine? I abandoned speculation and drew in among the people clustering at the grave as the priest began some final remarks.

The sleuth in me was ever curious. My ex-mother-in-law had once remarked that if I had brought that kind of attention and focus to bear on the stock pages of the *Wall Street Journal,* I'd be a wealthy man. I judged myself to be that anyway, I told her; after all, I was married to her daughter.

In the small quadrant where Flora Nuñez was to be interred, laid out in neat rows beneath the spread of large maple trees were stones bearing family names representing a dozen or more ethnicities. Discrimination didn't exist six feet down where dust mingled with dust and worms were the ultimate egalitarians.

Among the people at the fringes of the small crowd, I picked out Lucinda Colón, and after the brief ceremony ended, I moved over and said hello. She was teary, but she remembered me. I offered my condolences, and we made a minute's worth of small talk. Perhaps it was just her grief, but she seemed a little unsteady, and I wondered if she was medicated. She turned to go. I took out the Polaroid I'd found in Flora Nuñez's apartment. "Do you happen to remember when this was taken?" I asked.

She looked at it, and her brow clenched quizzically. "I'm sorry?"

I rephrased it, though I was convinced she'd understood the question the first time. "This is you and Ms. Nuñez, isn't it?"

"We was in the same night class together, a paralegal class. Sometimes we used to go out after class. Just for a drink or food."

"Are these other people from your class, also?"

She avoided my gaze, dabbing at her eyes with the corner of a lace handkerchief. "Yes, some, I think. I'm not sure," she said quickly, and seemed nervous again. "But that has nothing to do with this sadness about my friend. The cause of this is Troy Pepper, and he is a son of a bitch for making us so sad. Now, I am going." And she walked away steadily, despite her heels and the soft grass.

I put the Polaroid away and caught up with the priest. He was a youthful forty, with dark hair just starting to thread with gray and thick black eyebrows. He had delivered his funeral remarks in a fond, even exuberant way. I knew from the funeral program that he was Father José Marrero. I waited as he spoke with an older woman dressed in black, nodding thoughtfully as she spoke to him. When she went off, he saw me and offered his hand, which I took.

"I liked what you had to say today, Father," I told him. "Too many times I get the feeling the clergy folk are talking about strangers. Your words were personal and heartfelt."

He smiled gently. "I was fortunate that Flora often came to mass, so I got to know her. It's sad that she died. You were a friend?"

"No, I never met her. But based on what I've been hearing about her, I'd like to have." I explained who I was. His manner cooled a little, but he didn't dismiss me.

"If you're looking to learn anything that Flora might've confided in me, Mr. Rasmussen, naturally you will be disappointed."

"I understand. I'm not going to ask you to betray confidences, but I wonder if you had any personal sense of what her relationship with Troy Pepper might have been?"

"He's the one the police are holding?"

"Yes. He indicated to me that they were thinking of getting married. Did she say anything about that?"

"No, she didn't."

"Father, did Flora ever hint that she felt threatened by Troy Pepper? Or afraid?"

He seemed to consider the question, or whether to answer it; then he shook his head. "By answering what you're asking me, Mr. Rasmussen, I might be aiding the person who took Flora's life. Wouldn't that be a betrayal of her?"

"Perhaps. Though you might also be allowing her to reach out and show mercy to a man whom she may have loved. That could be a charitable act, too, couldn't it?"

He gave me a patient look. "She didn't come often for pastoral counseling. Still, I did have a sense from our occasional conversations that there was someone she cared for. I don't know his name or anything else about him. Do you think it's this man the police have arrested?"

I admitted I didn't know. There was a lot about Flora Nuñez and Troy Pepper I didn't know. A small jet passed overhead, descending: some kind of corporate flight, heading for Hanscom Field. I asked, "Did you have any sense of whether he was someone living here in the city or elsewhere?"

"No idea. But now that I think of it, I recall something she asked me, oh, eight or ten months ago, that got me wondering if she'd made some decision to seek a different life." We were mostly alone now, the bulk of the mourners having returned to their cars and driven off. Colored leaves shimmered in the maple trees and made a soft rustling, like the bright, eager gossip of schoolgirls. "She asked about making sacrifices for love. And then she asked . . . this is what struck me—she asked what taking holy vows might be like."

"Vows for becoming a nun?"

"That's the thing. She didn't say she wanted to take orders or anything, but she did seem curious, especially about wearing the habit. Where one got the costume, what the various parts of clothing meant. When I tried to open her up about it, she told me it was just something she wondered about."

We had come to a deeply polished black Marquis. Father Marrero turned and shook my hand. "I wish you well. Each in our own way, we're all searching for answers."

"One more thing. Do you know if she was in church Sunday morning?"

He thought a moment, then shook his head, the thick brows coming together. "Not then, no."

I watched the Marquis move slowly toward the cemetery exit, the trees and sky mirrored in its sheen. As I headed for my car, I noticed that one other vehicle remained, a maroon Chevy. It had drawn farther around the loop road and was parked, partially obscured by a line of tombstones. It wasn't on the way to my car, but I turned and went toward it. Before I could get there, the driver started up and drove off, but I recognized him as Paul Duross.

25

One of the maxims I'd heard Phoebe use—Lincoln this time—was that a lie stands on one leg, the truth on two. There seemed to be a lot of wobbling going on, and, if not outright lies, at least half-truths that had me scratching my head in confusion. Like why was Frank Droney overseeing the case? Was it really about political careers? Had Flora Nuñez loved Troy Pepper or feared him? Was there another man in her life? Was Pepper a killer or simply a man incapable of convincing anyone otherwise? I hadn't forgotten what Ms. Parigian had said about the quiet ones. I set the questions aside and drove over to All Saints Hospital. Roland Cote was walking across the visitors' lot as I was getting out of the car. Seeing me, he came my way, frowning. "What are you doing here, Rasmussen?"

"My bank account's on life support. I visit when I can." I nodded toward the entrance. "I'm going to try to visit Warren Sonders. You heard he landed here?"

"I was just up there. He blew out an ulcer. Stress'll do that. He should've just gotten out of town and left Pepper to face his punishment alone."

I wasn't going to mix it up with him, but as I started past, I thought of something. "I saw Patrolman Duross at the victim's funeral earlier.

Was he hoping the real killer would return to the scene of the crime?"

Like any cop, Cote was much happier asking questions than answering them, and adept at bleeding the emotion out of his reactions. He showed nothing.

"Then it must've been for the purest of reasons—like you coming over to wish Sonders well."

He gave it a quarter inch of grin.

I bought some flowers in the lobby shop and took an elevator upstairs. A male nurse at the nurses' station had me identify myself, then called down to intensive care and directed me there. A middle-aged woman with the manner of friendly reassurance you wanted in a place like that met me. She had a little glass-enclosed office with views of the patient rooms. "He's resting comfortably now," she said in response to my question. "We've got him on antibiotics and some other things."

"What's the outlook?"

"It's a peptic ulcer that perforated. With abdominal bleeding, we don't take any chances, but at least it didn't bleed into the peritoneum. That would be real serious. For now, he's stable and his signs are good. He's known of it for some time, I think, but he hasn't been very careful about treating it. He reminds me of someone in the comic strips. You know, stubborn but likable."

"Popeye?"

"Crankshaft. You know that one? You can go in and sit if you like. If he wants water, it's okay for him to have it."

With the blinds drawn, the room was dim and cool. Sonders lay asleep, tethered with IV tubes and sensor wires. In repose, his face was a wrinkled, half-deflated balloon. He had lost his color since I'd seen him last; there was little contrast between his hair and his skin and the pillowcase. I set the flowers on the windowsill and moved across the rubber tile on soft feet and took a chair by the bed. Pop didn't stir except for the rise and fall of his breathing. In the semidarkness, with the delicate sounds of the machinery, I felt as if I were on vigil in a submarine. I half-closed my eyes, settling into the rhythms of the place.

At the sounds of movement I looked up. Pop was awake, gazing at me with an odd, unfocused gaze. As I stirred, he tried to pull away, but there wasn't anyplace for him to go. "So you're with them?" he croaked. He sounded as if someone had dumped a spade full of dirt into his throat. I got out of the chair and poured a cup of water from a plastic pitcher and offered it, but he ignored it and went on staring at me peculiarly. "You're one of 'em, aren't you?"

"Come again?"

"A cop, right? You're a cop."

I realized he was dazed, possibly from whatever they were pumping into him. "Drink this." He took the flex-straw between his dried lips and sipped. I told him who I was and why I was there. Had to tell him more than once. He finally seemed to get it and relaxed a little, and I did, too. "How are you feeling, old timer?"

"More rested than I have in weeks."

"Good."

"I'm going to see if I can get them to move one of these beds into my motor home."

"I think the deal is if you stay in the bed, you've got to do it here."

He grunted. "That bull working the murder case—whatshisname?"

"Cote. I saw him. What did he want?"

"Probably thought he'd grill me one more time before I took the last chariot to glory."

I drew the chair closer to the bed. "It's not like that, though, right?"

"Him with the questions?"

"The other part."

"An old sinner like me? I've got to hang on for spite. Actually, I was half asleep, and I think Cote gave up any idea I'd have answers. Sorry I didn't recognize you for a minute there." He arched his bushy eyebrows. "You here to grill me, too?"

"Only if you're up to it."

He rolled his head sideways on the pillow and sighed. But some of his color had returned. "Feature it, all these years working my butt to the bone, I finally get a break from the grind by blowing a gut gasket. How is everyone?"

"Concerned about you."

"Mutual. I don't suppose anyone told you when they're gonna spring me?"

"I'm not in that loop. Nicole and Moses are walking point there."

"Don't get me wrong, I'm glad to be here if that's what the docs say I need. But I prefer my own machines and their big winking lights to these contraptions. *That's* what keeps me going, not all these tubes and wires and . . ." He trailed off. "Why *are* you here?"

I told him I'd been to Flora Nuñez's funeral. His eyes locked on mine with some of their familiar force for a moment before he sank back into his pillows with a grimace. "I've thought about her. I had Nicole send flowers. That can't have been much fun for you. Any more than seeing Troy Pepper in the joint. He still there?"

"Nothing's changed, but right now you don't need to worry about any of it."

"I'm determined as ever. We run now, they're right about us. And Pepper is standing under the gallows, as good as hanged."

I didn't point out to him that Massachusetts didn't have a death penalty. There was an electric chair around somewhere, but no one had fired it up in close to sixty years as far as I knew. Of course, no one had died of rabies in that state in that long, either, but it didn't keep people from worrying about strange-acting skunks and raccoons. Or clowns, for that matter. "About the chat," I said, "maybe it can keep for another time."

"No. Now."

Insisting that he make it brief, I asked him what he could tell me about Ray Embry. Pop shut his eyes and gave his gray-whiskered mouth a pucker. Words came slowly, and I got it that Embry had once been with a circus, one of the biggest, and had traveled with them all over the country and Canada. "Then he got involved with a young woman who ran off from home to travel with him. Well, someone worked up some sort of Mann Act rap against him. It never went nowhere, but it must've shook up the management, or wised them up, because he was out of a job the next season. When I met him, a few years later, he was a department store Santa Claus. Funny thing was, he used to be a damn good clown, had trained under some of the best. Good juggler, too. He did this bit with half a dozen flaming torches. He still practices it sometimes. Anyways, I hired him."

"So what ax is he grinding?"

He craned a questioning look my way. I hadn't gotten into my plans to meet with the crew that night. Pop said, "He's like a ballplayer who's sent down from the majors. Attitude out to here. When he came to work with us, he acted like he should run the whole shootin' match. He's smart enough. Hell, I was ready to make him a manager, but he . . . he rubs people wrong. Somewhere in there, though, is a decent guy. Or was once. But he's meaned up over the years."

The nurse came in and saw her patient was awake. "How are we doing this afternoon?" she crooned.

His face crinkled into crabby lines. "We?"

"Good," she said. She checked the IV drip and gave him some pills to swallow, which he did obediently. When she'd gone, I told him I was going to let him get some sleep. My other questions could wait.

As I moved to the door, he said, "Thanks for the flowers."

I nodded.

"And sorry for that crack about you being a cop."

"You're welcome. You should hear what the cops call me. Rest."

My cell phone rang ten minutes later. "Are you sitting down?" Ed St. Onge asked.

"I better be. I'm doing forty on the VFW."

"I just got the ballistics back on your exterior decorator. It's the same nine-millimeter that was used in a drive-by in the Acre in June. No one killed that time, but not for lack of trying. We think it was tied to one of the bangers we're interested in."

"That Vanthan character you asked me about?"

"Vanthan Sok. He runs around with a pair of nickel-finish SIG-Sauers, like some cowboy, and loves to light them up. You see any connection to what you're working on?"

"I can't see one."

"Neither can I. Well, I thought you'd like to know, another name to add to your fan club. But seriously, if he crosses your path, don't go up against him."

"Part of that's up to him."

"I'm not kidding, Raz. He's a stone killer. You see him, you dime him. The sooner we take him off the street, the easier I'll breathe."

26

"Eyewitnesses place my client and the victim at the carnival on Saturday afternoon and evening, and again on Sunday morning, and report them having an argument. Pepper and the victim have a past. And he did time in a military stockade," Fred Meecham said, acknowledging me with a nod.

I picked it up. "When they were in New Jersey, Flora Nuñez had an abortion, apparently, and told Pepper after the fact. He got angry and upset. He admits it. That's why she left and why she applied for the restraining order once she got here."

Meecham was rubbing at a spot on the arm of his desk chair. "That's going to be a tough hurdle to get over," he said.

"He told me he'd never have hurt her."

"Do you believe him?"

"I believe he means it. Which isn't the same thing."

"No, and not a distinction that's likely to be worth much in court."

Courtney glanced up from taking notes on a legal pad. "Don't sell your feelings short, Alex. I think they're important to how you work." I gave her a tired grin.

"All right," Meecham resumed, "for the sake of argument, let's suppose a different killer. If someone else did it and planned it to coincide with Troy Pepper's being in town, it raises questions. Like how did the killer know Pepper was in Lowell? Or was it just an opportunity that had presented itself? 'Let's blame it on the former boyfriend? Tie him up for the murder.' No—it's a stretch, and no jury is going to buy it. Not unless we can come up with an identity for this phantom killer and establish a clear MOM."

Courtney frowned. "A what?"

"Motive, opportunity, and means," said Meecham.

Here the latter two were mostly clear, but motive wasn't. The police theory was that the pair had some past history and had acted on that— that Pepper had drawn Flora Nuñez to the carnival and killed her. As Meecham was growing inclined to argue, it had not been a premeditated act; the woman had gone there, and while she was there, something— which was still unclear—had set him off, and in a fit of anger he'd strangled her.

I thought about bringing up Vanthan Sok, the badass St. Onge had warned me about, and tossing him into the mix. Would someone have paid him to shake me up? To scare me off? What for? Why not just shoot me? And what did any of it have to do with Flora Nuñez's murder? Nothing as far as I could see, and we had enough of nothing to deal with without it. The one thing I did bring up was what the young hunters had told me about seeing a green car, possibly a Mitsubishi, on the day of the murder, in the woods behind the meadow where the body had been found. Flora Nuñez drove a green Mitsubishi. Could someone have used it to drive her, perhaps already dead, from somewhere else to dump her and then park the car where it was later found? We kicked that around inconclusively for a while and then quit. Flapping your gums only got you so far; then you had to lay down some feet.

27

Nicole and Moses Maxwell were assembling the carnival crew in one corner of the Venice Hotel lobby when I arrived shortly before nine o'clock. Seeing me, Nicole hurried over with greetings. Pop had told her of my hospital visit, and she plied me with questions about what I thought of his progress, as though somehow my opinions mattered. I told her that the nurse had said she thought he was on the mend. Nicole seemed relieved.

"How's your other patient doing?" I asked. "Speedo."

"He's fine. But his real name is Mr. Earl." She gave a delighted grin, and I had to laugh. "It's an old song, right? I asked him." She gripped Moses Maxwell's arm as he joined us.

"Mr. Maxwell knows his stuff."

The jazzman smiled. "That's a myth I have perpetuated by sprinkling my talk with crossword trivia, and otherwise lyin' my fool head off. How are you, Mr. Rasmussen?" We shook hands. I was conscious of his bad fingers and adjusted my grip accordingly. "Thank you for booking this hotel for us," he said. He wasn't being facetious.

"It isn't much."

"If the beds sleep good, I'm satisfied. You ready to mingle with the restless natives?"

I followed them over to the corner of the lobby as people drifted in from smoking outside, and soon about twenty-five people were assembled in couches and overstuffed chairs, others standing nearby. Moses opened the meeting with an update on Pop Sonders's condition and a report on where things stood with the city on letting the carnival operate; then he opened the floor to discussion.

Penny Bergfors spoke up. "Bad enough we cain't work," she drawled, "but without Pop, I got to wonder how long the show can survive."

"Hold on." Ray Embry shouldered forward. "That's the trouble with this whole damned outfit. Pop's been living in the past. High time we got our act together, get into the present."

"What kind of present you got in mind, Ray?" Tito Alvarez asked from a wing chair in the corner.

"I say we get moving again, for one thing. Screw this fool city! Sitting around here waiting for something to happen . . . This is a road show. It's time we got back on the road."

There were murmurs of agreement and dissent. I watched Moses Maxwell, trying to read the mood through him. He stood listening, pinching at his little soul patch, not overreacting to the hubbub. Finally he said quietly, "What about Troy Pepper?"

"What about him?" Embry challenged. "He's got to take his own chances. We're not doing him any good sitting here. Or ourselves, either."

"The dude is right," said a lanky roustabout with tattoos covering both his arms. "If Pepper was level in the first place, maybe Pop never would've hired him and none of this would've happened."

"Whoa, whoa." Penny held up her hands. "Let's get real, folks. Even if we wanted to go, how can we with Pop in the hospital? He's our helmsman . . . our anchor."

The implications of the metaphor were a little too frightening to work through, but I knew what she meant. She was confused and uncertain; they all were.

"Then maybe we need to put someone else in charge," Embry said. "The show ain't about any one person."

"What? Replace Pop?" Nicole looked aghast.

"No one's irreplaceable. Besides, I don't think *he's* been level with us, either."

"That's a dirty filthy lie!" Nicole cried.

"Is it?" Embry's grin was like a joke only he knew the punch line to. "Come on, girl. Did Sonders ever tell you about the offer he got from an outfit that wanted to buy him out? He ever tell any of you?"

Tito Alvarez pushed up from the chair, his ponytail swaying. "The hell you sayin', man?"

"This outfit wanted to invest some money in the show. Wanted to upgrade it."

I caught Moses Maxwell's eye as he stepped forward, one hand raised in a calming gesture. "I can tell you all about that, and put your minds to rest." His hand looked like a spider with broken legs. "First place, it wasn't no genuine offer—just mostly talk. And the people talkin' wanted to buy the show for chicken feed. If that deal went down, a lot of us would've been out of a job long since."

"That what Sonders told you?" said Embry.

"It's what I seen and heard for myself."

"*You'd* be out of a job, maybe. What are you doing here anyway, Moses? I mean, you were a musician, right? A piano man. What've you got to do with a carnival? Want to tell us that? I never figured that one out." The words came rapidly, like coal clattering down a chute.

Maxwell maintained his dignity, but he was shaken. He licked his lips but said nothing. No one else spoke up, either. Perceiving his advantage, Embry pressed. "Sonders has got reasons why he doesn't tell us things. Sure, he talks that all-for-one, one-for-all shit, but I think that's all it is is talk. I mean, hell, bottom line, it's his show. He's going to do what's best for *him*." Nicole fidgeted and looked lost, unable to keep up with the caustic flow of words. "Truth is, I don't think he's been level with us at all."

I cleared my throat. "Who here is?" I said.

People turned to where I'd been standing by the wall, out of the way. Embry looked flummoxed for a moment, but he recovered fast. "What's any of this got to do with you, pal?"

I saw the question rise on the faces of some of the other people, too. I stepped forward. "Who here is level?" I said again.

"What are you, crazy? Everyone here is," Embry cried.

"Completely level? Right out front about everything?" It bought a silence. To plug it before it grew too loud, I said, "Okay, form a line over there." I pointed. "Every one of you who doesn't have some secret, something to hide, that he'd rather not share with anyone, step over there. Come on, I'll go first."

I stood right where I was.

The know-it-all, Embry, marched over. He was a tall man, big in a way that spoke of power underneath the heaviness. For a sticky second, I thought he intended to attack me, but he stopped, laced his arms across his chest, and turned to the others. "Let's go. Show him."

In the stillness, the old hotel went on with its life: A desk phone rang, music tinkled faintly from the bar, an elevator hummed.

Penny Bergfors laughed. "Ray, you're a finer person than I had y'all figured for. Yes, indeed."

Embry's face blazed crimson right up to his bare scalp. "Don't let this two-bit rent-a-cop push us around." But whatever momentum he had faltered; although there was some muttering in the group, no one else moved to join him. Embry searched their faces. "Alvarez," he said. "Come on."

His badgering flickered on for a time, the way a fire will after the fuel source has burned low, but no one joined him, and soon Moses Maxwell and Penny, and even silent Red Fogarty, prevailed on their coworkers to forgo any big decisions for now. Moses promised to keep them updated on Pop Sonders's condition and got me to agree to speak with Fred Meecham about the city's cease-operations order. "Now," Moses said, "it's late. We'll talk again when we're not all running on empty. If anyone's of a mind to have a nightcap, I'll buy."

About half the crew took him up on the offer. I joined him and Nicole and we repaired to the hotel bar, but I imagined that I could feel Embry's angry eyes drilling me the whole way.

"I betcha this bar hasn't moved this much juice since Repeal," Moses Maxwell said over a glass of Hennessy five-star. "What do you think, Mr. Rasmussen?"

"It probably moved more *before* Repeal," I said.

We were standing by the door with our glasses—brandy for

Maxwell, bourbon for me. The carnies were hunkered around tables and the ancient oak bar, keeping a bartender busy with drink orders. The tensions of earlier hadn't been resolved, but for now they seemed to have been set aside. Maybe it was just the prospect of a hotel bed for a change, or the idea that Pop Sonders was going to be okay. I saw Nicole table-hopping, a Shirley Temple in hand, and I realized that everyone liked her and she them. Her function was more complex than I'd first imagined. She was the social glue of the group, a tuning fork that brought cadence, a softener of some of the rough edges of these people. Nicole would have tossed a maraschino cherry at me if I'd tried to say this, but it was there. These people were a family; this fact had been lost on me till now. Although there almost certainly was a hierarchy, with its own pecking order, it wasn't obvious. Men and women seemed to be equals, as did young and old, and there was energy here that it felt good to be near. Nicole caught my eye and waved. I smiled back.

Moses Maxwell was saying, "There's always a little . . . *contretemps.* Just like in my days playing music. We'd be in some town—shoot, this is fancy compared to most—and hear a train goin' by, you know, hootin' out there in the night and, like as not, one of us would say, 'I believe I hear the old Lackawanna.' And we'd laugh. That's what it is, too, y'know? It's about wanting something bad enough you're willing to deal with what you got to deal with. I guess Pop's dream is that little six-letter word for a just-right society."

"Utopia?"

He chuckled. "I think he knows there ain't really no way you can do it in the *big* world, but maybe, if you're lucky, you can make it turn out in a small way. Only it's hard work. When you're just a sideman, you get spared some of that. But when you're the headman . . . whew. I know that from when I had my band."

"But you made some good music," I said.

"Could've made more. We had a contract to record some more, but my fingers didn't work so good then. I urged the others to carry on, said finding a piano player wouldn't be hard, but they said no. So that record you got—hang on to it, it's all there is." He grew a little somber, though maybe it was just the nostalgia of remembering. I couldn't imagine anyone being sentimental about having his fingers broken. He mustered a smile. "Sometimes I see one or two of the old cats, and it don't go by without someone mentions hearing the old Lackawanna."

"Is that where you people are now—you folks here?"

"You meanin' should Pop sell the show?"

"He's got a lot on his plate. It would be a way of dealing with some of it."

He sucked his mouth in, as if he were getting ready to blow a lick. The little tuft beneath his lower lip stuck out. "It's Pop's call. What he says, I go with."

Tito Alvarez came over, grinning. He'd taken his hair out of the ponytail and it hung dark and thick to his shoulders. He gestured to us with a beer bottle. "What you distinguished gentlemen drinking? I hate to see grown-up dudes with empty glasses."

"I'm not crazy about it myself," I said, "but, alas, I have some things to do. Buy a *cerveza* for you and whatever Mr. Maxwell wants." Over his protest I gave Tito a twenty. The three of us shook hands and said good night. As I got outside, Nicole caught up to me.

Her eyes shone. "I said my prayers for Pop, and for all of us. For you, too, Mr. Rasmussen."

"Thank you."

Her face clouded. "You think it's true that God knows the names of every star in the sky?"

"Well . . . you know the names of all those dogs, don't you?"

"Do you believe that prayers get answered?"

When I hesitated, she shook her head. "I'm sorry, I shouldn't ask that. I'm too nosy sometimes."

"No, it's fine. I think they probably are answered, but not always in the ways we want them to be."

Her face unclouded slowly, and she smiled. "Good night, Mr. Rasmussen."

I got my car, and as I drove past the hotel, I noticed someone emerge from a lighted side exit and start along the sidewalk, peering about as though looking for a taxi. It was Ray Embry. I pulled up, opened the window, and leaned across the seat. "Need a lift someplace?"

He bent to peer in, then straightened at seeing me. "I was hoping to get a cab."

"Unless you phone ahead, you're not likely to catch one cruising over here. Get in, I'll save you a fare."

He hesitated a moment but then got in. "I'm going back to the carnival if it's not out of your way. I want to get some things from my trailer."

Neither of us brought up our earlier differences of opinion. "How'd you get to be a clown?" I asked.

He looked over. "How'd you get to be a private cop?"

"Fair point."

He grunted. "Being a professional clown isn't something you fall into. It calls for skills—it's part mime, part dance. There's juggling. It's got a tradition, a time-honored one. The royal courts had clowns, jesters, fools. It was something rulers considered important. I used to believe that making people laugh helped them, made them healthy, made society stronger. Now . . ." He shook his head. "Clowns aren't in the mix anymore. People sink themselves in front of the TV night after night and get canned laugh tracks." He waved a hand at the passing night, where in darkened houses television sets glowed. "I think people are numb to any real joy."

"Yet you still have a job," I said.

His expression held sour. "Call it that. Carnivals are a throwback. That hotel's a run-down rat fest, but my coworkers seem to be delighted to be there. Compared to living on the road, it's the Ritz."

There wasn't anyplace to take it. I stopped for a traffic signal. When we were rolling again, I said, "What about the killing? You don't seem to be Pepper's biggest ally."

He looked at me. "Why should I be? I have no proof, obviously, but it's certainly a possibility he did it. People in their tawdry sexual relationships and passions are capable of most anything. Still, I suppose it's passion that keeps someone like you in business."

We were silent the rest of the way to the fairgrounds. I pulled to the curb and he climbed out. "Thanks for the ride," he said. He seemed eager to be gone.

"If you like, I can drive you back. I'm in no rush."

"No. I appreciate it, but I'm going to stay here tonight."

"All right, then."

He shut the door.

I drove off and a short distance up the boulevard pulled over and parked. I waited a few minutes, peering back at the mostly darkened cluster of trailers in the big field. I picked out Embry's Airstream by its rounded contour and a light on inside and kept an eye on it. When I saw the trailer go dark a few minutes later, I wasn't surprised. Embry emerged, looked around furtively, as if satisfying himself that he was alone, and set off on foot toward the highway. In a moment a cab slowed and drew over, and he got in.

28

Fifteen minutes later I had followed the cab across the state line into New Hampshire, and I found myself hoping he wasn't headed for a clown convention in Montreal. But the cab got off at Exit 1 and we got over onto Daniel Webster Highway. We cruised along with the endless traffic lights of Nashua, past the tax-free mishegas of malls, discount furniture showrooms, auto dealers, muffler replacement shops, and every chain restaurant you could think of and a lot you couldn't, all the crap that the city had zoned into one area, like a postmodern paean to the free market. As the cab got beyond most of that, it slowed, then slowed some more, and I sensed that the driver was looking for an address. I kept back a distance, and soon the cab drew into a motel entry drive. The blue-and-yellow-lighted sign identified it as the Bamboo Court Inn. It was a two-story set of units that sat perpendicular to the highway, with a drop-off and reception loop in front and guest parking in the rear.

I let the taxi have the loop, and I watched Embry get out before I pulled up into the drive and went past and stopped. I killed my lights and used the rearview mirror. Embry paid his fare and went into the lobby. The cabbie paused, looked around hopefully, then flicked off the IN SERVICE light and headed back to Massachusetts empty.

I waited another minute, then got out and went into the tall, glass-fronted lobby. Embry was nowhere to be seen. To my left, opposite the front desk, was a fieldstone wall with a small waterfall running down among tropical plants and Polynesian tiki heads. It was an impressive design and probably would have been a success in a hotel in Cambridge circa 1960, but here, now, with a transient, motorized population who didn't care squat about *feng shui,* it seemed an extravagance—a conclusion that upper management had evidently reached, too; the waterfall had been choked back to a trickle that ran over the stones in a rusty drizzle and gave the impression of a leaky roof more than an island Eden. On the wall behind the registration counter, a copper starburst clock showed the time to be 10:21. Beyond the desk, on the right, was the entrance to a lounge, with the sounds of Kenny G issuing forth. I hipped in close to the stone-topped counter, stealthily slipping my wallet from my back pocket as I did. The clerk, a sharp-featured youth in a tan blazer, looked up expectantly.

"The gentleman who just came in," I said, "he left this in my cab." I held up my wallet for a quick view.

"Oh . . . well, I can get it to him if you—"

"I'm hoping there might be a little reward in it if I can take it to him myself. Hacking is no ticket to Easy Street." The youth looked sympathetic. "If the reward's more than a sawbuck," I said, "I'll cut you in for half."

He checked the ledger. "He went up to room two-oh-two."

"Is that his room?"

"It's registered to Mr. Lou Hackett."

Before I could compute that, Embry emerged from a stairwell near the lobby entrance, accompanied by a second man. One look at the man's madras plaid sport coat over a pink shirt told me who he was. I asked the clerk to be sure.

Embry and Hackett went through a door and disappeared. "How about another fellow?" I pressed the clerk. "A guy with funny ears and a neck like a nail keg? Is he here?"

The kid grew suspicious. "The old wrestler—how'd you know that?"

"I'm a huge fan." I took a single from my wallet and slapped it on the counter. "Better luck next time."

151

Embry and the man I'd tagged as one half of Rag Tyme Entertainment had gone outside together. Keeping a row of potted trees between us, I followed. They walked away from the lighted entrance area and stood in the glow of the motel's marquee. With a show of ceremony Hackett took something from his inside jacket pocket. I saw the brief, bright green of money as he handed several bills to Embry, who pocketed them. I couldn't make out the denominations, but I was pretty sure he wasn't cheaping Embry the way I had the desk clerk.

The pair chatted a moment more, then shook hands. Hackett raised his arm, and a set of headlights came on. I faded back into shadows. A black SUV with tinted glass eased up a short distance away from the men. Hackett made a broad "here's your ride" gesture, and Embry waved and opened the passenger door and got in. He rolled down the window and said something more to Hackett, who waved.

I didn't get a look at the driver until the SUV—a Toyota 4Runner, I noted—drew past, and then it was only for a second as it passed beneath the marquee light and Embry's window went up. It wasn't a face I'd ever seen before, but I wouldn't mistake it in a million years.

Conventional wisdom said follow the money, but this time I thought it might be more productive to backtrack it. I'd seen enough of Embry for one night, and I knew where I could probably find him if I needed to. As for trailing, and perhaps encountering Bud "the Squisher" Spritzer— that was a pleasure I'd forgo for this night.

As Hackett passed me on his way back to the entrance to the Bamboo Court Inn, evidently in deep thought, I stepped from the shadows. "Mr. Hackett?"

He did a quick half-turn, his high brow furrowing, one hand moving to his side pocket, leaving me to guess whether he was carrying or not. "Who the hell are you?" he demanded.

"My name's Alex Rasmussen."

"So?"

"If you're handing out green, can I get in line after the clown?"

He gave me the full frontal posture, which I took to mean that either I had his attention or he was going to shoot me. He wasn't as big as his business partner—an inch or two shorter than I am—but he was my width again by half. Muscular or fat or both, it was hard to tell in the madras plaid. The ridges in his face certainly didn't look pillowy soft. "What's the deal?" he demanded. "And you better make it good."

I showed him my PI license. He looked at it, measured me a long moment, then said, "Let's get a drink."

The Bamboo Court Inn's cocktail lounge was small, though something short of cozy, more like an airport bar, a place for people on the move. At the moment, we were the only patrons. We sat at a corner table where an eager-faced young waitress appeared and started to recite a litany of exotic drinks. Hackett cut her off: "Bacardi and Coke." I told her bourbon. Hackett put his elbows on the table, his palms flat, stubby fingers facing each other. There was some kind of blue stone in a gold setting on his left pinkie. Thick shoulders strained at the bright cotton fabric of his coat. In the glow of the mood lights strung through several indoor palm trees, Hackett appeared to be in his early sixties, his hair an improbable shade of brown and combed back from a pronounced widow's peak. Bright dentures and rough-cut handsome features made him a cross between an aging soap actor and a ward heeler no longer content just to work behind the ballot. "Well?" he said.

I explained how I had come to be there, starting with why I'd been hired in the first place. The waitress brought our drinks and stood there for a second, as though hoping for approval or a tip. Hackett gave her neither; I said thanks.

"So when Embry got cute with you and called a cab," Hackett recapped, "you got curious, that it?"

"That's it. I'm still curious, you laying green on him like that."

He tossed aside the swizzle stick, took a healthy knock of his drink and dabbed his lips with the cocktail napkin. "You got a beef with rewarding initiative?"

"I guess dropping a dime for your outfit's competitor is a kind of initiative."

"Call it a finder's fee. We'd have heard about Warren Sonders's troubles anyway. Soon as he missed the payment, bells would've been ringing. Embry letting us know just streamlines things, positions us maybe to be of help."

"By getting Sonders to sell you his show?"

"Call it wiping out his debt."

"Will he see it that way?"

"Probably not. He'll just smell conspiracy . . . big bad collective out to backdoor the little guy. But some of Embry's beefs are legit. The way Sonders has been running things is a crime."

"Why should that concern you, if he's been making his payments?"

He shrugged. "It doesn't. Until he can't. A democracy, for Christ's sake. People with know-how ought to be calling the shots."

"Like Rogo the Klown?"

"He knows his way around."

"As I understand it, he was a department store Santa when Pop hired him."

"Why don't we get down to the situation at hand, Mr. Rasmussen? The show's got a problem. It can't operate. Sonders can't pay his bills, and I hear his health isn't too good. The outfit I represent is in a position to liquidate his debt, eliminate his liability."

"And then what? Shut the show down?"

"Where'd you get that idea?"

"I think Pop gave it to me."

"We'd scrap sentiment and make an impartial business decision, I can tell you that. The carny market has been dying for years. Nowadays small owners are lying around with their feet in the air."

"Sonders seems to be making a go of it. At the very least, he's got a crew of workers who are willing to pitch in and work hard."

"It's more complicated than that. And my heart goes out. Hell, I'm in the business, too. But someone wants a guarantee, I tell 'em buy a savings bond. I'm not the government, not even close."

"You hold the note. Why not just extend his credit?"

"Give him some grace?"

"He's good for it."

"You aren't a businessman, are you?"

My silence was his answer.

"Then let's not have this conversation," he said. "Okay?"

I guess from one point of view he was right. Anyway, I told him, I was there strictly because curiosity had led me, and now that it didn't appear to be anything I was officially involved in, I was ready to go. Now Hackett had questions.

"This guy they arrested for the murder," he said, "you're looking to find ways to save his sorry ass because he may be innocent?"

"If he is, it'd be a shame for him to go up for it. And for Pop to lose his show over it."

Hackett's face darkened. "And if he killed that broad? I'm sick of stories about people wrongly accused, wrongly convicted." He gave the words a mocking twist. "Okay, I got tears for 'em. But what about all the assholes *rightly* accused?"

"It happens," I said.

"You're damn tootin'." He bared his teeth, but I didn't offer him anything to sink them into. "Either way, it's none of my concern. That's for justice to deal with. My interest is strictly business. Now," he said, more equably, "I can see how you strayed in here tonight. It's under-standable, and now that we've huddled, I'm not even sore that you nosed into my business. *One* time." He rapped his pinkie ring on the lacquered bamboo arm of his chair for emphasis. "It shows initiative and gave us a chance to have this talk. But understand, we've got different concerns. I don't care to have you straying over into mine again. Because when I get momentum, I don't always look at the little things in front of me. I'm liable to roll right over them."

"And vice versa," I said. I wasn't sure what I meant, but neither was he, and I made it my exit line. He'd promised to buy the round, but I cov-ered it. It was the second time that night someone had offered me a drink and I'd picked up the tab. A hotshot businessman I wasn't.

On the way back along Daniel Webster Highway, I looked for something interesting to catch my eye—a lavender neon martini glass or a knotty pine roadhouse facade, something besides the Japanese noodle shops, dis-cotheques, and sports bars, each no doubt licensed to serve whiskey, though it always seemed like an afterthought at such places, a sideline to the more important business of pushing food, sports, or romantic encoun-ters, so I drove back to Lowell, to turf that I knew. I considered my usual spots—Evos Arts, the Copper Kettle, and the Old Worthen, where Poe is said to have watered on his visits to the city and been inspired to pen "The Raven"—but I wasn't in a mood for history or company. There were joints to choose from along Gorham Street and on Middlesex, but I wanted a drink, not the lush life. I settled for a pub on Jackson near Central, a quiet cave with few customers and an impressive array of bottles on the back-bar, not that I planned to sample them all. "George Dickel, neat," I told the high-colored brunette who put down a cocktail napkin.

She poured it full. "Are you and Mr. Dickel old drinking buddies?"

"Thinking buddies."

I commented on her brogue, which she said was Galway. "D'you hear the one about the Dublin lawyer who passed the bar?" She leaned close to give me the punch line. "No one has."

When she went off to dish with one of her regulars, I thought of my new house, where I could go and it would certainly be quiet. But it wasn't the same. Too quiet, maybe; with a different timbre of solitude. I had a desire to telephone Phoebe, see what she was up to, but it was almost eleven. Where had the evening gone? I envisioned her asleep; she was an early to bed, early to rise, makes a girl healthy, wealthy, and wise type. Benjamin Franklin was her guru. We were different, as she reminded me on occasion. She'd also said that she was trying, and I respected it.

The TV news came on with a story about the carnival murder case, a windblown junior varsity reporter floodlit against JFK Plaza, remarking that threats against the members of a carnival troupe had been reported to police, who were assuring the public that the threats were probably from cranks but nevertheless were taking them seriously and putting on extra patrols. My glass was empty for the videotape of the Pats prepping for Sunday's game, and a look back to Monday night, the clip of Brady getting intercepted late in the fourth, with a man deep and all alone, yoo-hooing in the end zone. The sportscaster couldn't let it go, anymore than the meteorologist could the tropical storm. Gus was in the alley between the Bahamas and the U.S. mainland, evidently trying to make up his spiraling mind as to where and when to come ashore. "Should we have quit giving them women's names?" the fifty-something white male anchor joked to his twenty-something Eurasian black female co-anchor. I refocused.

I thought about Rag Tyme's sudden appearance on the scene. Pop Sonders had hinted it could happen, though he'd hoped his problems wouldn't be noticed before they could be resolved. Now they *had* been noticed. Was it a case of a disgruntled employee dropping a dime, a competitor paying off Embry for the information, as Louis Hackett said? Or was the payment for something else? Had Embry killed the girl in order to make trouble for Pop, and soften the beachhead for Rag Tyme, and set it up for Pepper to take the fall? It was too over-the-top for me. There were too many uncertainties that couldn't be controlled, and Hackett had struck me as someone who liked control. Besides, I didn't make Embry for a killer; a whiner, a hassler, maybe, but not a killer. I supposed I should tell Sonders that Rag Tyme was here, but I worried that his reaction might set off another ulcer attack. I'd wait and see what else I could learn. Meanwhile I needed something that would help Pepper. I felt like the deep receiver: They'd sent me long, but I wasn't catching much. I thought of Pop, lying there in All Saints, probably asleep, too. I wished him well.

When I got outside, the night had grown misty. At my back, a neon shamrock fizzed insistently, like a bee behind glass. On the other side of Jackson, half a block down, a factory in its graveyard shift hummed. For some reason I thought of Flora Nuñez. Some streets away, the lights of an ambulance splashed jittery colors on the nocturnal facades of buildings. A late bus floated past on Central, bearing a cargo of weary souls. A city created an illusion that beyond the avenues and the buildings, the bridges, power lines, highways, and rivers, the lives in it were connected somehow, too. A death broke a connection, set other forces in motion. I stood on the sidewalk, trying for a moment to imagine what those forces might be, but the inner fog of weariness wouldn't lift. Drifting from a distance came the sound of a clock-tower bell. Midnight. Another day tipping toward dawn. I waited for the tolling to fade, then drove home as cautiously as a judge.

29

I slept for eight straight hours, interrupted once by the dog barking to go out and the cat scratching to be let in, but since I have no pets it was obviously a dream, from which I awoke with a final distillation of last night's whiskey throbbing in my brain. A shower and a pot of coffee had me feeling halfway real again, until I fetched the morning newspaper and caught the front page. Sometime overnight one of the amusements at the carnival had burned to the ground, possibly the result of faulty wiring, though the fire inspector wasn't ruling out arson. The story carried a photo of firefighters hosing down the scorched ruin of Castle Spookula.

I called Fred Meecham's office, and Courtney told me that Meecham was over at superior court, at a hearing in a different case, but that he wanted to speak with me. He expected to break around noon. I said I'd try to meet him at the courthouse, or phone him at least, and Courtney said she'd get a message to him.

Although last night hadn't brought any "Aha!" moments, the appearance on the scene of Rag Tyme Shows had opened a new front for exploration. I wasn't optimistic that another visit with Troy Pepper would be fruitful; still, it was a logical place to start. As I'd tried to explain to

Courtney, when you didn't have a road map, often the only approach was to go in whatever direction drew you, eliminating destinations as you went, and hope that eventually you got somewhere. If Pepper was being set up for the killing as part of some weird takeover attempt by Hackett and Spritzer—although frankly, the concept seemed weak—he might have some idea why.

The trees were spangled with yellows and oranges and arterial reds, though in six weeks' time, with wind and one good drenching rain—a real October reaper—the leaves would be sopped all over the streets like the tears of autumn, where car tires and pedestrian feet would beat them to a brown paste. For now, however, September was in her glory. At Bihoco I was too early for the swarms of lovers and families, so I had the waiting area to myself. I wasn't sure that Pepper would even agree to see me, but after a few minutes he came in, his cheeks stubbled and wan against the bright jumpsuit, his red-rimmed eyes evasive, and I wondered if it was the sleepless look of a man tormented by guilt. He sat across from me, and I asked if he had seen the news.

He nodded. "On the TV in the mess hall."

I mentioned Rag Tyme, and he professed to know very little about the outfit beyond the fact that people had brought up the name on occasion. "So who are they?" he asked.

"There have been some feeble attempts at explaining them," I said, "but they're all variations on a theme that spells 'loan sharks.' They'd bristle at the idea, of course. Their contracts apparently pass legal muster. Did Flora ever mention them?"

"No. What are you saying?"

"Tell me about Ray Embry."

He blinked. "Rogo the Klown works for them?"

"Have you had any problems with him?"

"I hardly know the guy."

"Can you see him having any reason to get you in trouble?"

"What?" He frowned. "I can't say I'm crazy about him—I think he's a pain in the ass . . . but no."

If true, it confirmed my feeling that Rag Tyme's appearance wasn't connected with the killing. I was fishing, plain and simple, but my questions had thrown Pepper off balance; they'd chipped his stony silence and gotten him speaking more than monosyllables. I didn't spend time wondering why. "I spoke with Flora's friend Lucy Colón. She said that she thought Flora seemed nervous about something the last time they talked. She seems to think that the cause was you," I said.

"Me?" He licked his lips anxiously.

"It's not an unreasonable idea."

His brow knit. "I don't even know the woman. Anyways, I told you. I'd never hurt Flora."

"Yet she took out a restraining order."

"That was in the past, a mistake."

Now I was the one to keep silent, waiting for him to go on. Which, after a pause, he did. "I don't know . . . nervous. Well . . ." He sighed. "When I saw Flora on Sunday morning, she seemed a little scared."

"Did you ask her about it? Or tell anyone else?"

"I was waiting for her to tell me, if she wanted to. But I don't think it was about me."

"Why's that?"

"We'd talked a little about that time in New Jersey—the restraining order, how I was supposed to keep away from her. Though I didn't even know where she was then. But she said it was a mistake."

"A mistake. The restraining order? Or coming here to Lowell?"

"Both, I guess. I don't know if she said it, but I think she meant because it caused her more trouble."

"In what way?"

"I don't know."

I stared at him. "You didn't ask her?"

"I guess I was a little scared, too."

"What about?"

He lowered his eyes, and I waited for them to come back, but they didn't. He went on staring down. "Thinking . . . maybe she was seeing someone else, and she was scared to tell me. Or maybe she was worried because she was going to break something else off."

"Why would she fear that?" I looked at him, but he wouldn't look up. "Was she seeing someone else?"

Now he did look at me, and his voice was a murmur. "I don't know."

I thought about that. If there were another person, would that person hurt her? Would he have killed her? I let out a breath. "Come on, Troy. I need something here if you've got it."

He looked away. I thought of what Fred Meecham had said about Pepper not being a very persuasive witness. He seemed to lack energy, and I couldn't see him convincing a jury that the case against him was wrong. We sat there in a sluggish little pool of silence, and then from my shirt pocket I took a juror ballot card and laid it on the ledge between us. Pepper stared at it a moment. "What's this?"

"The fruit of Mary's womb. It was in a statue on an altar in Flora's apartment."

"How'd you—" He broke off. "What's it supposed to mean?"

"I was hoping you'd explain it to me."

He looked at the card again, examining it as intently as Moses Maxwell did the *Times* crossword puzzle, then shook his head blankly. "I don't know."

"These places with the *T* beside them—were you with her on those dates?"

"Huh? I don't know. No."

"You don't sound sure."

"What's going on?"

"I talked to Sonders already. The show was in Connecticut on two of those dates, en route elsewhere on the other. You were traveling, right?"

He shrugged.

"Possibly you called Flora and talked by telephone."

"I don't know. Maybe."

"Definitely maybe!" I wanted to reach through the barrier and grab him and drag him forward and bang his head. I actually felt my hands twitch with the impulse. Controlling it, I said, "Give it to me straight. What happened on those days? What's *this* mean? *T* is you, right?" My voice had risen. The guard glanced our way.

Pepper looked at the card, but he only frowned. I put the card away. He didn't move, thinking maybe, then said, "Pop's in bad trouble, isn't he?"

"Pop?" His response surprised me. "What about you?"

"But Pop . . . tell me."

"Yeah, he's in trouble. Maybe worse than he knows."

Deep lines etched themselves in his face. The guard signaled that our time was up. Pepper rose obediently. As he started to turn away, he stopped. He leaned toward me. "Pop's got other stuff to worry about. Make him forget about me."

I rose, too. Was he telling me something? But he turned and went out with the guard.

30

It was almost noon by the time I got parked and through security at the superior courthouse. Some of the proceedings were in recess, and people scurried through the lobby, a few looking relieved, others resigned, some beating it outside for a quick cigarette. There was no sign of Meecham.

"Alex?"

A woman in a flowered blue dress with padded shoulders set a book down on the bench beside her and rose. I went over. The calm oval face framed by brown hair pulled back in a braid was familiar, though she had to remind me. "Janelle. Phoebe's friend from the office."

"Of course." Cobblestones the other night. The quiet one. "You have jury duty."

She smiled. "I got impaneled. I can't say any more about it." She zipped her fingers across her lips.

"Your secret's safe with me. What're you reading?"

She held up the book, which was by some Indian yogi whose name I didn't have enough time to try to say. "I'm practicing being a center of stillness," she said, "letting things remain in the realm of pure thought and not become action, which is where trouble starts. I like to just sit."

"It seems to be working. You're the only thing here not gyrating."

"All crime grows from desire. Enlightenment means we can get beyond crime. If we could manifest that, it'd be a new world. This whole structure—the courts and juries and bail bondsmen—would become totally superfluous."

"I'd get lonely."

"No, because you'd be unnecessary, too. *This* you, anyway. A new you could devote your time to love relationships and just being."

"Of course. What was I thinking?"

She smiled. "I know—where's the airy music? It sounds painful, but it's not. It would just free us all to become who we really and truly are. I've come to believe that well-being is a lack of consciousness about ourselves, or about anything at all. But believing is one thing, becoming it . . ." She rolled her eyes.

I spotted Fred Meecham descending the broad stairway, and I told Janelle I had to go.

"Glad you could make it," Meecham said. "I'd suggest we go grab lunch, but I'm due back upstairs before you can say habeas corpus. Let me just duck in here a moment."

When he came out of the men's room, we went down to a basement-level snack shop and got coffee in paper cups. Fred explained that he had tried to get the desist order lifted so at least the carnival could begin working again, or be released to go elsewhere, but no dice. I told him about Louis Hackett and his paean to the common man. Meecham grimaced. "Is there a chance that Sonders could really lose the carnival?"

"Rag Tyme makes their point the way sentimental heavies always do," I said. "They hit you over the heart. If that doesn't work, they break your legs. This time I think they're just going to wait until Sonders can't pay his bill."

"And then it's theirs." Meecham sighed. "Well, it's the criminal case we've got to concern ourselves with. That's what's pressing right now."

When he'd headed back upstairs to tilt with the windmills of the system, I checked to see how Janelle was coming with being the calm center, but she was gone. I found the building locator in its glass case and checked the names. On the restraining order that Flora Nuñez had filed at the court, a Carly Ouellette had signed as a witness to the signature.

According to the courthouse directory, she was an assistant to Judge Martin Travani, with an office on the third floor.

A white-haired custodian was swinging a wet mop, leaving gleaming swooshes on the worn terrazzo. He nodded me past a set of double oak doors to the first door on the left. A sign on the pebbled glass read JUDGES' LOBBY, and I went in and asked the matronly-looking woman seated there at a desk for Ms. Ouellette. Carly wasn't in, she said; she was in Cambridge, where the county's other superior courthouse was located. "Is there something I can help you with?"

"On a request for a 209-A, is the witness verifying the reported events or just vouching for the signature?"

"No, the witness is vouching for the signature. Or sometimes, with people who can't speak English too good, the witness might help them translate to fill out the form. And then the police get a copy and . . ."

She walked me through it. It was mostly as I'd understood it. I thanked her for her help. "I do have one further question for Ms. Ouellette. Could I leave a number for her to call?"

She took my card and said she'd pass it along.

In my car on the way back to the office, I phoned Phoebe, who generally took her lunch break out of the office, but she was there today. Getting settled into her new cubicle, she said.

"The one by the window?"

"Someone else got that." I heard momentary disappointment, but her enthusiasm bobbed to the surface again almost at once. "I jumped one desk closer, though. And thank you for the flowers. I've got them right here."

I beamed. "You're welcome. Are we on for tonight?"

"I'm counting on it. But, hey—is it okay if we stay in?"

"You don't want to try that new restaurant?"

"I'm just feeling a little wimpy. I'm not sure I want to be out."

"With me, you mean?"

"No, silly. But the mood in town . . . this carnival case has made things crazy. I hear they're now convinced that fire was arson." I'd missed that but it wasn't surprising news. "So I was thinking—dinner at my place? I grill a mean Rock Cornish hen. I could invite some friends."

"Yes to the mean hen, but you're the only company I want."

Sociability was a theme we'd discussed before. She said therapy had helped her discover that with the pain of her sudden widowhood, she'd filled the hole with friends but also developed a fear of trying new romantic relationships. She was trying to change that. I asked what I should bring, and she said, "Surprise me."

"On the topic of people . . ." I told her about Lucy Colón's turnabout, without mentioning names. I valued her insights. "What would keep someone from talking?"

"She's not suspected of being guilty of anything, is she?"

"No."

"Then it sounds as if she's scared."

"Of what?"

"What women are often scared of. That kind of scared, anyway. A man."

A gaggle of elderly people were milling around on the sidewalk in front of the city library, showing each other their large-print book selections, happy as kindergartners as they prepared to trundle aboard a bright yellow school bus. They'd gone full cycle and looked as if they were enjoying it. *I* enjoyed just seeing them there.

In the reference room I dug up a Dun and Bradstreet report on Rag Tyme Shows, and a profile piece that had appeared in the *Wall Street Journal* eighteen months ago, under the title "Talking 'Rag Tyme.'" In it, Louis Hackett was quoted as saying that his business was "like trying to knock over the milk bottles in an arcade—not easy, but if you succeed, you get the prize." They'd started out operating a small show. In the past four years they had bought out half a dozen competitors, not with any desire to operate them but to absorb their assets and shut them down. Rag Tyme was a privately held outfit, with Hackett and Spritzer listed as the principals, backed by something called the East River Trust. There was a New York City address and a phone number.

I went out to the library lobby to use my cell phone. I got an answering machine that told me the number I had just called and said I could leave a message. I left my name and number and asked to have someone get back to me. As I was pocketing my phone, a woman backed into my arms. I caught her and she turned, sputtering apologies. It was fine with me, I told her. She'd been stepping back from a big glass display case. Inside it I saw an assortment of papier-mâché, ceramic, and old cloth jack-o'-lanterns interspersed with an array of books about Halloween.

"Did you do this?" I asked. "It's good."

She beamed. "Halloween is over two thousand years old, did you know that? I just learned it. The ancient Celts held a ceremony to mark the end of summer—and the start of the long, cold winter."

"Thanks for reminding me."

She smiled. "They believed that the boundaries between the worlds of the living and the dead become blurred. They celebrated Samhain, when they believed the ghosts of the dead returned to earth. In Mexico, it's *El Día de los Muertos*. Oh, it goes on . . . it's fascinating. You can read it for yourself—we've got a lot more books inside, for all ages. Enjoy the day."

Outside the library, which sat just around the corner from city hall and police headquarters, I saw a runner come to a stop, glance at the big sports watch on her wrist, then put her hands on her hips and continue to jog in place for a moment. With her brown ponytail bobbing in the sunlight, she looked a bit like a schoolgirl, though I hadn't forgotten the six-pack abs I'd seen at the West Side Gym. She quit bouncing and did a few side bends, then leaned against a concrete parking barrier to stretch. I went over. "You *are* ambitious."

She looked up and straightened, recognizing me. "It's an alternative to heavy lunches. You were a cop, you know how we eat."

I rubbed my stomach. "The memory lingers on. How about a light lunch? On me."

"Thanks anyway. I've got to go shower and get back to work."

"Another time, maybe. Have you got time for a couple of quick questions?"

She shielded her eyes with her hand and regarded me. "Come on, I want to walk this off. Then I have to get back to work."

We set off toward Post Office Square. I wondered aloud, "At the carnival site, the distance from the suspect's trailer to the place where Flora Nuñez was found is close to a hundred yards. I keep wondering how the suspect could have gotten her out there without anyone seeing it."

"No one claims to have seen anything?"

"Evidently not. Which leads to my real question. Could someone else have dumped the body—maybe having driven it over and left it?"

She looked up at me curiously, her lips pursed.

"I checked, and there's an area on the other side where a vehicle could get partway back. There'd be cover from the trees, and the distance to the drop spot would be less by half. Of course, it raises other questions," I admitted. "If that happened, who did it? Because Pepper seems to have been on site all afternoon and evening. So did he have an accomplice? Or—"

"Did someone else kill that woman?" Officer Loftis finished my question. "Look, I wish I had answers. I'd love to be the one who broke the case. But I don't. Officer Duross and I were on detail that night. I think we'd have seen or heard about anything like that. But this is stuff for the detectives."

"Sure, agreed. I'm just jamming here, trying to open up possibilities that may not have been considered."

"Well, that's your job, I suppose. But I really have nothing for you."

"Maybe just your listening is helpful. How about Officer Duross? He seems to still be on the case."

Abruptly, she stopped walking and faced me. The runner's flush was fading, and she had a lean, weathered look, just a little too drawn from relentless exercise. "You need to realize that I've got a job, too."

"I know."

"I'm not sure you do. What are you really doing here? You weren't just passing by."

"I was at the library."

She glanced away, as if weighing something, then back, her gaze firm. "When you had a badge, the department was a boys' club. Things have changed, but in a lot of ways, it's still that. The other women officers and I have a mantra—'twice as hard for half the respect.' I've got to be smarter and better qualified and tougher just to be even. That's why I'm really out here pounding the pavement, if you want to know. I'd rather be over at the Blue Shamrock like the others, having a burger and fries, swapping stories. There are days I'd rather be getting a pedicure than be in a smelly gym kicking a heavy bag—but if you're thinking *The sister is the weak link, I'll go at her for inside information,* then you can take a flying leap." She spun on her Nikes and loped back toward the station house. So much for the idea of endorphins making people mellow.

31

I drove over to the neighborhood known as the Acre and parked. It was the district that had been the first home for successive waves of immigrants who'd come to work the mills—Irish to Greek to French Canadian and on, each group supplanting its predecessor as people got their feet under them and moved out to better districts. With the dying of the mills, the Acre had become a catch basin, hanging onto whomever and whatever washed there. Grady Stinson, for instance.

A city police department could usually carry a few roughnecks on the rolls, the way a sports team could, as long as they didn't become too visible. When one did, he was like the football player who tries to rip the opposing player's head off: He was a liability. Grady Stinson was that guy. He and I had overlapped several years on the job, had even been partnered together for a short time, to no great effect on the city's crime rate. A year or so back, he had lost his badge on a repeat brutality rap, though to this day, as far I knew, he had never seen it like that. In his view roughing the opponent was a part of the job.

Stinson's world was encompassed by the rooming house where he stayed and a small orbit of local bars. The sun had well transited the meridian, so I didn't bother with the rooming house. The circuit included the Mill Stone, the Goalie Cage, and two or three other joints strung along Moody Street, which was an irony I'd come to appreciate. That's where I started to look.

His sustaining myth was that one day he would be reinstated and given back his badge. But it had been a while now. He occasionally said that he might get into my racket someday, maybe as an associate. I always let it pass without comment. Mostly, he'd resigned himself to being an informant. It wasn't any sort of formal arrangement; it rarely is. When he had something that he thought might be useful to me, he passed it along. I'd give him a few dollars, depending on the usefulness of what he had, but I don't believe he did it because he liked me, or cared one way or the other especially. I think it was a way for him to flip a bird at the system that had taken him down.

I found him at the Goalie Cage.

I hadn't seen Stinson in several months. It was as if someone had turned his timer to a faster setting; he looked older, paler, thinner. His voice was the same rusty wheeze, though, when he bellowed my name from a corner, where he sat alone at a table. "C'mon the hell over."

I got us each a cup of coffee at the bar, plus a shot of Black Jack for him, and took them over to the table he occupied in the corner, underneath a large photo of Bobby Orr, airborne in the Stanley Cup final of too long ago to remember. "Why don't you yell it a little louder?" I said. "I don't think they heard you in Tyngsboro."

He blinked at me, openmouthed, then got it and laughed. "Ah. Sid-down."

Grady has a face like one of those character actors you recognize in a hundred movies without ever knowing their names. I think he saw me as some kind of affirmation that he still moved, roughly speaking, in law enforcement circles, though this seemed a bit like an LAX cabbie giving Spielberg a ride, then going around telling people he was in "the industry." I got to the point.

He didn't rush at it. Why should he? I was buying. He tipped some of the whiskey into his coffee, took a sip, and smacked his lips. "The carnival killing? Who hasn't? It's big news. And the city seems ready to bust out in war. But you're looking for more than a man-in-the-street angle, right? Well, I got one word for you. C-o-p-s."

At times, what Stinson had to sell was of use, but mostly I'd come to consider him something of a Johnny One-Note, and the note was always cops. For a roughneck, it was an odd revisionism, but to his mind, the police were the ones who pulled all the strings, from the drug dealing and illegal gambling to the garden-variety crime and corruption. Whether they actually perpetrated it or not, he claimed, didn't matter; they were gatekeepers, involved by the degree to which they did or didn't prevent it. The city's crime, he insisted, was a joint effort. It was a convoluted argument, but I suppose that like many an argument advanced in this world—that one god was somehow three beings, or that war was really in the best interests of humanity—it could be made to seem plausible.

"Keep spelling," I said.

"What is this? I give you good information, I've got to figure it out for you, too?"

I drank some coffee, then set the cup down carefully. "Indulge me."

"Jesus, Rasmussen. People pay you to be an investigator? Start with the obvious. Who else controls the crime scene? Who holds the chain of evidence, and can yank it whatever way they want? Who writes the reports? Who can intimidate—excuse me, *interview*—witnesses? You mean to tell me at a carnival, with several thousand people strolling around, nobody saw nothing? Yeah, right."

"Go on."

"And who else is required to carry deadly force at all times?"

"The woman wasn't shot to death," I pointed out.

He didn't waste any more of the Jack in his coffee; he took it neat. "Who said she was? I'm explaining how things work, 'cause evidently you've forgotten."

Actually, I hadn't forgotten. I was my own shining example of how things could go very wrong inside a large and complex city police department. But I also knew that, even with the flaws inherent in any bureaucracy, most of the time it operated efficiently and even fairly. I knew, too, that Grady Stinson kept his favorite ax well ground. Still, if only to write him off, I listened.

"This isn't your run-of-the-mill junkie pop or gang drive-by. No way. Here you've got all the elements—a good-looking babe, from the picture in the paper, sex, a mysterious outsider, a carnival and all that means. I mean, shit, if Hitchcock were alive, he'd be all over this."

"With you as story consultant."

"Wait. Okay, the case is getting news, and I don't need to tell you what time of year this is. A solid conviction makes the cops look good, which makes the candidates happy."

"It's pretty thin gruel," I said.

"Wait, it thickens. On top of that, I hear there's some beef in the department that a patrolman is gonna make detective."

"What's to beef? That's the normal path."

"After just a few years?"

"You're talking about a cop named Duross?"

"I was beginning to wonder there, man." Grinning, Stinson shook his head. "Duross shares a collar on the perp and gets a letter in his file for heads-up police work. Okay, fine, but you know where his juice is, too, right?"

Stinson looked pleased that I didn't. "His mother is Frank Droney's sister."

It was an interesting detail. While there was a rank structure, and a system of qualifications, detective jobs were generally posted and an officer could bid for one, but it was commonly known that the superintendent made the call. "Maybe Duross is a very good cop," I said. He'd seemed sharp enough, if not overly friendly.

"Maybe, but Uncle Frank in your corner can't hurt. I heard this Duross was a wild hair when he got out of the academy." Stinson's grin widened. "My kind of cop. Maybe when I get my badge back, I'll show him a few things."

"You know how to bring out the best in people."

"Hey, why not?" Irony passed through him like X-rays. "There's always room on the street for a hardcase." I probed his line with a few more questions, trying to make something useful of his scattered information, but beyond my sense that it linked in vague ways to things Officer Loftis had said—or not said—I didn't find it. When I took out my wallet, he gave it a halfhearted wave. "I'm just doing my public service."

I grinned. "That angel on your shoulder has to eat, too."

He palmed the fifty bucks and said he'd give me a call if he heard anything. "And hey, don't forget what I said about you ever need a hand with an op. Have gun, will travel. Remember that show? With Richard Boone? You're old enough."

"The good old days. Thanks," I said, nudging his train into a siding, "I'll get in touch soon and we'll go on a nostalgia binge."

Driving back to the office, I thought about how when I'd told Phoebe that I was going to see an informant, no name mentioned, she said, "He's only going to drink anything you pay him." She was probably right. Every person who worked the street, for information or for anything else, ran an account for small sins. Would I have preferred that Stinson think about counseling, or a rehab program? Maybe, but that wasn't for me to determine. He earned the money by providing data, not by submitting to my demands for self-help. Tough love might have called for an intervention, pulling his family and friends together in a tight bond and compelling him with unconditional support to seek help. Beyond a coterie of determined drinkers, though, I doubted that Stinson had many friends or family, so I reserved some sympathy for him and credited him with a degree of cop honesty. Besides, fifty dollars wasn't likely to corrupt either of us any more or less. It would purchase a round for the house and fade into another lost afternoon, and that would be put to my account, too.

Since All Saints Hospital wasn't far away, I decided to pay another visit to the ICU. After a short wait, a nurse came whispering along on foam soles to tell me that Pop Sonders was resting at the moment. As for prognosis, she was a bearer of happy tidings. "He's a tough customer, in the good and bad senses of the term. If he takes care of himself, he should live a long time." Pending a visit from his doctor, she said, he could be discharged as early as that afternoon.

As I parked in the lot behind my building and headed for the rear door, someone called, "Hey, hawkshaw."

How many people this side of sixty knew that term? I turned. There was the pair of them, walking my way with a clip-clop of shiny shoes. Hackett was the front man. Just behind him and over his left shoulder loomed a large bald head, as if Hackett were towing a balloon wearing sunglasses. Parked behind them at the curb was the black 4Runner with tinted glass I'd seen at the Bamboo Court Inn. "What is it with you?" Hackett said. "You don't remember our talk?"

His sport coat this time was a rust-and-black houndstooth over a lime green silk shirt. It made my eyes hurt. Stepping out from behind him, his partner took off a pair of Wayfarers, and I didn't pay any attention to his garb. I got my first close look at Bud "the Squisher" Spritzer. My notion of a fizzy drink evaporated right there. Hackett wasn't a small man, but the former wrestler was constructed on a whole other scale of large. His chest was like a corn silo, and he had a neck I couldn't have buckled my belt around. His ears stuck out from his naked head like baked pork rinds, and he had a jaw like the prow of a navy icebreaker; his pallid skin was pocked with old scars. I put him at around sixty, but even in this day of steroid-built freaks, he'd have been a specimen.

"I thought we reached an understanding last night, Rasmussen." I dragged my eyes back to Hackett. "You weren't going to mess in my business."

"You said that, not me. And what makes you think I've been in your affairs?"

"You called, right? I got the message. Plus I've been in touch with Sonders's office. It seems you've been advising him not to sell."

"Not true, but the man's in the hospital. Why hassle him now?"

"You don't got a clue, do you?"

"Enlighten me."

"That old coot isn't in the pink of health. Payment comes due Friday, and I need to know I'm gonna get it."

"That's two days away."

"Tough. What's that got to do with you?"

Spritzer shuffled a step closer. "Maybe this chooch needs a demonstration of what you told'm, Lou," he said, opening his mouth for the first time. His teeth were studded in his jaw like yellow fence pickets.

"Might have to," Hackett agreed. "He doesn't look very bright today."

"I'll betcha he ain't ever."

"Though I'll bet he's loaded with emotional IQ. Aren't you, shamus?"

I had to grin. "Okay, not bad. But Hollywood already did that two old hard-guys number. Burt Lancaster and Kirk Douglas, wasn't it? I saw it on TV. It wasn't much."

"Oh, you're a comedian, you are. Okay, here's the skinny. When I—"

"Wait, wait—" I stopped him. "I'm going to try to say that without smiling. The *skinny?* Hawkshaw? Do you know what year this is?"

"Forget year—you're about two minutes from fucking flatlining, you asshole."

I assessed the situation and shut up.

"Now here's the deal. I don't give a good goddamn what you think of the contract I've got with Sonders. And I'm not going to waste any more time explaining it to you. Bottom line is this. Sonders has got one of his jacks up on charges he offed some chick. He's got a city injunction that says he can't operate, and someone torched one of his amusements. Rate that's going, the whole show's gonna blow up like cheap fireworks, and it won't be worth a nickel. I'm not even gonna bother to hondle with Sonders now. Too late. He either comes up with my money, or he sells me the show and gets the hell out of the racket. So, final warning, mister—you tell him that, and I let you off easy this time."

"What's hard?"

"You don't want to know. Come on, Bud."

They headed for the black 4Runner.

32

An osprey soared above the river on wings that would stretch across my living room. For years they'd been absent, pushed out by urban and suburban sprawl, poisoned; now they were back, fishing upriver from the coast. Not a lot of them, but when you start from zero, every one is something. I watched the bird from my car, drifting high and higher, until it had soared out of sight, and then I put my attention back on the mirrors, which I had positioned to watch the apartment building halfway down the block to the rear. I was snugged in behind an old VW van that looked as if it had been boosted off a street corner in Haight-Ashbury and beamed here in a time tunnel. A bumper sticker on the rear declared I MISS JERRY.

I hadn't received a callback from Carly Ouellette, so I tried her again, and the woman I'd spoken to earlier assured me that she had given Ms. Ouellette my card. "I'm sure she'll get back to you, Mr. Rasmussen. She always does. She just tends to be rushing around with a million things. We kid her it's why she needs that little gold sports car she drives. To keep up with all she's got going on."

I'd mentioned her to Fred Meecham. "Carly Ouellette," he said, nodding recognition.

"It's a nice name," Courtney said. "Musical."

"Don't be fooled," Meecham said. "There're men bleeding up and down the halls of superior court."

"For love?" I said.

"For getting on her wrong side. She's armor-clad, with machine guns for eyes."

Her address was in the phone book. "Careful, Alex," Courtney said with a warning smile.

A knock on my window startled me. I rolled it down. A lean man in a sweat-soaked Olympic Gym T-shirt and cotton shorts, and still sporting a boot camp haircut at forty, eyed me suspiciously. "Can I help you?" he asked gruffly.

I gathered he didn't belong with the VW van. "Who are you, homeland security?"

"You were here when I went out to run. You're still here."

"And it's still a public street, last I checked. But if you must know, I'm waiting for a friend."

He frowned but seemed to buy it and marched off to fight other battles. I saw occasional cars whisk past on Tenth: red Toyota, gray Ford, Market Basket van. I watched a squirrel salting away winter provisions and thought I should be doing the same. The dashboard clock showed 4:23 P.M. I'd been there since three, when I'd been told Carly Ouellette's job ended for the day. Earlier, I'd knocked at her unit in a small apartment complex and got no answer. A gold Mazda with a black vinyl bra stretched over the front end rolled up and parked, and I grew alert. In my side mirror I watched a woman get out. She had a bush of hair the color of her car and was wearing a striped beige knee-length suit, with a little flare to the jacket over her chunky hips. She moved along on swift feet in squat heels, heading toward her building.

I got out and started after her. I sent a quick glance into the Mazda, which had one of those studded rubber steering wheel covers that looked like it came from someplace called Auto Erotica. I crossed the street. "Ms. Ouellette."

I had to call twice before she turned. Beneath the froth of hair, her round face crinkled skeptically as I explained who I was and showed her ID. "Yeah, what is it?" she snapped.

"Can I ask you a few questions about Flora Nuñez?"

"Like I know who that is. I don't have time for this." She spun away.

"You may want to make time. Flora Nuñez is a woman you once helped fill out a request for a restraining order. If you read the paper, you know she was murdered."

She turned; her frown deepened to a scowl. "Who the hell are you?"

"You weren't even listening." I told her again. "I left a card at your office."

"How long have you been spying on me?"

That was a surprise, but I used it. "It could be for days. I like that steering wheel cover you have." It was just what had come to mind.

Her eyes narrowed to those little slits that German soldiers used to fire Mausers out of. "I could have someone come and fix your nose," she hissed.

"Thanks, but it's too late for that. Besides, you can't say for sure I don't have everything I need already, tucked someplace safe and ready to roll. Or a tape recording I made just now of what even a Quaker would construe as a threat." I patted my chest.

"You son of a fu—" She dropped it quick.

"Look, I don't have a tape and I haven't been spying. I just want to talk. How about a cup of coffee?"

But she was a seasoned civil servant, dodgy to the last. She raised a fist and, quick as popping a switchblade, snapped up a middle finger. She about-faced on the squat heels and stomped to her building, looking as if she wanted to go kick the teeth out of a spider.

Downtown I parked near the cabstand behind my building and was heading for the back entrance when someone called me. No "hawkshaw" this time, or "shamus"; he had my name. I turned to see a young man coming my way. If he was from Carly Ouellette, she had cast against type. In his jeans and tan bush jacket, a haymow of sandy hair piled on his head, he looked like a model from Abercrombie & Fitch. "My name's Jed Piazza, Mr. Rasmussen. From the *Herald*."

"I already subscribe."

"Well, no . . . I write for the paper."

"Reporter?"

"A stringer, actually. Correspondent." He had a steno pad at the ready, his close-set blue eyes hopeful. "I'd like to ask you a few questions about your client, and what you think about the stir his case is causing."

"I'm not the one to talk to. The police and his attorney are better bets."

"Got them covered. And the DA, too," he said proudly. "Mr. Deemys was glad to talk. You're the last link in the chain."

It occurred to me that he was probably the reporter Pop Sonders had shaken loose the morning after the killing. Evidently he hadn't given up. Was this an assignment, or was he just trolling? I didn't ask. It didn't matter. "I'm sure they've given you anything I could, Jed, and more. I'm not the person to talk to."

"Well, according to my sources, you are."

"What sources?"

His expression got foxy. "I can't reveal that."

"Fair enough. We'll both keep quiet."

Under the epaulettes of his bush coat, his shoulders squared. "Are you using the old 'I've got a responsibility to my client' dodge? Because I've heard that one."

"Nope, I just don't have anything to tell you."

"And truthfully, that's largely a myth, right? I doubt there's any such thing as client privilege for private investigators. I think Dashiell Hammett invented that."

"The way Woodward and Bernstein invented you? Why is it when the court squeezes you guys to reveal a source, you act like you've sworn a pact with God himself? Can't I keep quiet, too? All I said is that I don't want to talk. There's enough information and rumor floating around without me adding my two cents—and believe me, that's all it'd be. But for the record, I'm working for an attorney, and his privilege extends to me."

His ears reddened, but he kept his smile. It looked starched on his face. "Every former cop either opens a bar or goes private. Since a criminal record rules out owning a bar, I guess you chose door number two."

"And every news writer has the great American novel tucked away in a sock drawer, just waiting." His grin wobbled, and I knew I'd pitched a ringer. "How many have you got, Jed?"

He hunched his shoulders and let them drop. "One. About thirty pages along. And it's only taken me four years. I'll have it done before I'm seventy."

I had to smile, too. He was likable in his way, like the puppy that's *almost* house-trained. "Maybe you'll do it," I said. "It happens." And maybe I'd walk out of this case like Sam Spade. It was good to stay hopeful. "All right, you get three questions—but one of them's got to be a Moon Pie, so I go out looking smart."

After that session of Meet the Press, I walked up Bridge Street to the front of my building on Merrimack, intending to check the mail. A car went past, slowed, and a man in the passenger seat shouted at me. With sunlight glaring off the chrome, I couldn't see a face before the car gunned off, but I could hear just fine. The novel epithet was "Geek lover."

I fumbled the mail and had to pluck envelopes off the stairs as I climbed. Louis Hackett was sitting in my waiting room. "Hiya, pal," he said, both hands raised, palms out. He rose. "I came to apologize. Let's forget last time. Deal?" He swept a hand through the air. "Wiped out. Forget about it. Let's start fresh."

I unlocked the inner office. "Why do we need to bother? As I remember it, you wanted quits."

"True, but I didn't want it to be on a bad note."

"Okay, you convinced me."

He followed me inside. "Let's swap stories. I bet you've got a fascinating life story."

I dropped the mail on the desk. "Compared to what?" I didn't want to encourage him, but it was obvious he had something on his mind. Reluctantly, I waved him into a seat.

"I dunno. Compared to I could tell you about the old days," he said. "Like my partner, Bud, for instance. Catch this. Killer Kowalski—remember him? His shtick was this Claw Hold, he called it. Supposed to paralyze the opponent right there in the ring, then Killer would whomp him. Well, Bud had this bit *he'd* do where he'd lock his legs around the other guy—had these tremendous strong legs on him, still does—and he'd squeeze, y'know? Squeeze the air out of a guy. Dramatic as hell, like a balloon goin' soft. He called it the Squisher. If he really put the press on, and the other guy wasn't trained proper, his guts would come out his mouth like bad spaghetti. Actually happened to this one guy one time. Sonofabitch promoter had no business putting him in the ring with Squisher—and unfortunately it queered Squisher's career on account of the guy practically died. Check with Hogan—Hulk'll tell you, the Squisher was one rough customer."

"I'll ask him the next time we sit down for a bucket of blood."

"He was a name in his day, Squisher. He put the hold on me once, no kidding around. I had to walk around in a brace for months. But let me tell you about this one time when—"

"Look, maybe you can save it for the Biography Channel. I've got things to—"

"Hold on." He waved a hand again. "I think you owe it to yourself to hear me."

I humored him and shut up.

"First job I had, I was a waiter at this restaurant in Red Hook, okay? Which was a legit business for some not so legit other stuff the owner was into. We don't gotta go there. But this restaurant, place called Santana's . . . linen tablecloths, different glasses for different color wines, nice—only, it seems someone was skimming the take. The manager's going bananas, doesn't know what the fuck. It's the goddamnedest thing. You earn the cash, but it don't end up in the drawer. Word is, he tells this to the owner, only the owner don't do anything. We never even see the owner. Time goes by, it's summer. The manager rents a boat, has a party for the staff, guys only, okay? I'm excited. Twenty-two years old, I'm thinking I'm a hotshot. We go out from the Battery with a locker full of booze, a hi-fi with some Tony Bennett, Vic Damone, a nice day, y'know? We cruise the harbor, people gettin' pretty loose. Then we start up the East River and after a while this motorboat pulls alongside, three people come aboard. The manager introduces the owner. None of us never seen him before that—he comes aboard, no hello or nothin'—just him and a couple of tree-swingers with him. First time I ever laid eyes on Squisher, too. He was still in wrestling then, but he did some strong-arm on the side."

"This story's got a point, right?" I said. "I have a date this month."

"Right off, the owner says he knows someone's been skakin' the till.

But it'll be hard to find out who, he goes on. Hell, maybe it's *all* of you, he says. But he must figure no one's gonna cop, so what's he do? He whispers something to one of the muscle guys—to Squisher, who's got these big long arms—and Squisher goes into the motorboat and hauls aboard this old junkyard john. Just sets it there on the deck, okay? A toilet. Then the owner picks one guy. 'You,' he says. Points to the guy wears the nicest clothes—Italian silk suit, two-tone shoes, y'know? On the *boat* the guy's wearing this. Squisher and the other muscle guy grab him, strip him to his undershorts—hell, even his shorts are silk—and they put him onto the old toilet, okay? Tie him on with rope. By now the poor bastard practically *needs* a toilet. He's yelling how he didn't do anything wrong, he's been loyal . . . Me, I'm so scared my heart's goin' like a Teletype. I keep thinking, just say you did it, man; take your chances. But no, guy kept on denying, begging now. *Crying.* The rest of us are cringing, okay? No place to go. We're all the way up by the Harlem River now, no other boats around."

Hackett cleared his throat. I fidgeted in my chair. "And the owner—cool as ice—never said a word about anyone shitting on him or on the operation, he just gives a signal." Hackett brought his palms together with a sharp *clop.* "And Squisher and the other guy pick up the toilet and drop it over the side. Ker*splash.* Right into the fuckin' river, the poor sonofabitch lashed to it! I couldn't believe it. I just looked at the stream of bubbles coming up—kept coming up for about five minutes, it seemed like, and then they stopped."

My head was light. Hackett cleared his throat again. " 'Drink up,' the owner tells the rest of us. 'Everybody relax, enjoy the cruise. You got a confession, tell a priest. The operation's looking for loyalty.' And he and Bud Spritzer and the other guy get in the motorboat and split. I drank all afternoon, musta had twenty beers—but you think I could unbuckle my thoughts? No way. My brain stayed cold sober." He blew out a breath and fell silent.

I was the one suddenly wanting to move around, to talk. "Maybe the guy was guilty," I said. "He could've been the one stealing and the owner knew it."

"That'd be a nice piece of justice."

"The owner might've just been psyching out the rest of you. It's sick stuff, but if you mess with someone like that . . . The guy should've confessed and taken his chances."

Hackett smiled faintly and shook his head. "But he wasn't guilty. Okay? The one skimming the dough was me."

I looked at him, feeling sick to my stomach.

"But I'll tell you what. I never did nothing like that again. Never took so much as a fuckin' dime. So you see? I learned. It *is* about psychology." He leaned forward and brought his hand down softly on my desk. "Now you take this carny that supposedly killed the girl, and you working for his lawyer, trying to prove he didn't do it. Maybe you're right, maybe you're wrong, but it's like I learned on that boat. Sometimes it don't matter what side you're standing on. It comes down to being the wrong guy, wrong time, wrong place."

I swallowed at my rising gorge and rose.

I didn't want to be with people like him. I walked over and opened the door, turning to usher him out, but before I could tell him to go, something heavy struck the base of my skull. White light flashed and I cried out, or vice versa.

33

I stood in an unfamiliar room, the walls moodily lighted with wall-washers that revealed a series of Gregorio Montejo paintings. It was a reception of some kind, and people were milling about. One was Squisher Spritzer, in a blue blazer with brass buttons and wearing a cream silk ascot. On him it looked like a yellow ribbon round the old oak tree. Officer Loftis was working out in spandex tights over by an hors d'oeuvres table. Seeing me, she flashed a seductive smile. Grady Stinson was examining the paintings with a lorgnette, though he needn't have bothered; these canvases were strictly from hunger. Oblivious to it all, Maxwell Moses was sitting in a corner, chewing the end of a pencil. He said, "I need a word for 'fool.' "

"You're looking at him," I said.

But he wasn't. He had his attention on the *Times* crossword puzzle. "Seven letters."

"Buffoon," said someone else, who stepped from the throng. It was a young Ed St. Onge in a tasteful suit. "Or dead man," he added.

I swam back up to the air and daylight of a world I seemed to remember, though when I blinked it into sharper focus, I saw that it wasn't the world I'd been in. I was inside a nasty-smelling vehicle, a panel van. If well-being was unconsciousness about the self, as Phoebe's coworker Janelle believed, I definitely wasn't well. There were enough aches in my head to make five masochists smile; unfortunately there weren't any around to share with. I recognized the smell as vomit. I was alone, my hands shackled to the steering wheel. Through the van's dusty windows I saw that I was in an industrial yard, behind a stack of what looked like large boilers, bleeding rust at the rivets. Beyond them I could make out a smokestack and trees, and a field fading off into junked cars. It might've been the east end of town, though that was a guess; I could've been in Delaware. A wire fence, overgrown with dying vines, blocked any view beyond.

At a scrape of metal behind me I turned my throbbing head to see one of the van's rear doors open and Spritzer appear. He reached inside and took hold of a large tank of bottled gas that was lying on the bed. It grated over the floor as he pulled it out. A label on the tank said it was from Acme Rental. Spritzer noticed me and ducked his head to peer in. "Oh, you're feeling better," he said.

"Says you."

He shouldered the tank and slammed the door. In a moment he came around to the driver's side, where I sat. He wasn't wearing an ascot. "You were breathing okay when we waltzed you outta your place, so I wasn't too worried, but you got sick on yourself. You got a headache, I betcha."

"When you're done throwing bouquets, maybe you can get me the hell out of these shackles, and out of here. Where are we?"

"It's your town, you tell me."

Which I took to mean he didn't know. Hackett would've picked the place, and I didn't waste time asking for a road map. Up close to Spritzer, I could feel heat and smell the wintergreen tang of old liniment coming from him. It smelled better than my shirt. He unlocked the handcuffs. I climbed out, wobbling only slightly. I rubbed circulation back into my wrists. Piled on the ground nearby were a second tank of bottled gas and the hoses and nozzles for several acetylene torches. There was an egg on the back of my head that belonged in a museum.

"I had to tag you and let you sit out a couple dances, so Louie could go talk to Sonders in peace."

"In the hospital?"

"Wherever. With you hounding around, that ain't easy."

"I was sitting in my office. You came to me." I realized it was point-less arguing with him. "Anyway, you wasted time if it's about getting Pop to sell. He won't."

He showed yellow picket-fence teeth. "You figure he's got much choice?"

It caught me off guard. Then I remembered the article in the *Wall Street Journal*, and I felt a ripple of anxiety. "What's this stuff for?"

"Once we get the show, we keep what's good and dismantle and sell the rest for scrap."

"What about the people who work for Pop?"

"Tough shit, wouldn't you say?"

My lips felt cracked and dry. "So Gordon Gekko was right."

"Who's he?"

"Someone you and your partner would understand."

His flat black eyes worked me over for a moment. "Yeah, well, wish I had the time, but we gotta get back. Your shitbox is over there." I saw my car parked near the rusty boilers, saw a man get out of it, and recognized Ray Embry.

"Keys are in it," Embry said as he approached. "No funny stuff."

"That coming from you?"

"This wasn't my idea," he murmured, and got into the van, with Squisher Spritzer at the wheel.

As I followed their lingering dust trail, I briefly tried to find sense in things, but they weren't any clearer than my dream had been.

34

I got home, and surprisingly I felt better than I had any right to. To keep it that way, I took three ibuprofen tablets and then phoned Phoebe. Tonight was my night to see her, and having that to look forward to had kept me going all day. She wasn't home yet, so I left a message to say I might be a tad late but would be along. I showered until the bathroom was thick with warm steam, then shaved and put on fresh clothes. I called the hospital and learned that Pop Sonders had been discharged. I tried his trailer office but got no answer. Next I phoned Fred Meecham but got his answering service. I didn't leave a message. Where was Randy Nguyen's wired world when I needed it?

I stopped at a wine shop and picked out a Louis Jadot Chardonnay that the merchant said would be a good complement to grilled fowl; it had a crisper finish than its California counterpart—a "French finish," he said. I took his word; my two rules about wine were go with a corked brand if you can't find a vintage date on a screw top, and don't chug it straight from the bottle.

Phoebe had a small house off Stevens in the Highlands, the remnant of her brief marriage. She greeted me at the door smiling and vivid in a green sweater with an autumn-leaves design and faded blue jeans. As she stood tiptoe for a kiss, she stopped and her eyes popped wide. "Alex, what happened? You look awful."

"Always nice to hear from my fans." I hadn't intended to say much about my day, but I told her the story, wrapping up with my visit from Rag Tyme's controlling partners. It did nothing to calm her. Her face didn't unfrown for a long moment.

"Have you told this to anyone else?"

"Not the last part. The earlier stuff, Fred Meecham. And Lieutenant St. Onge, too. I figured I owed him."

"Are you sure you want to do this tonight? We could make it another time."

"I've been looking forward to it."

Her enthusiasm made a tentative return. She hugged me and softly fingered the knot on the back of my head. She clicked her tongue. "Do you want anything for that?"

"A drink would be a step in the right direction."

"Okay. I was just about to light the charcoal. Why don't you come out back with me, and you just sit while I fix us one."

"I'm not an invalid. What can I do to help?"

But she was insistent, so on the little backyard patio, with wind chimes tinkling softly and plants still blooming in their border beds, I sat and let her be domestic. To lighten the mood, I told her about seeing a Southeast Asian fisherman land a huge carp from the Concord River earlier that day. "Maybe somewhere in the city right now," I said, "there's a family of seven sitting around that big old fish, their mouths watering."

There were clay pots with mint and basil growing in them, and Phoebe plucked a few leaves and tore them and put into the marinade, the way I'd seen chefs do on television. I thought about the little herb garden in Flora Nuñez's apartment, about people cooking for other people whom they cared about. It seemed such a basic form of affection, and when Phoebe was finished, I pulled her onto my lap. "A spontaneous gesture," she cooed. "Todd was a plan-way-ahead guy. I sometimes thought he had every move on a little list in his pocket."

I didn't confess to the dark thought that had prompted my hug. I kissed her and she kissed me back. She squirmed around so she was sitting facing me, her legs straddling my hips. Our lips pressed hard against each other's and soon our breath came fast. I slid my hands up her back and sides, felt her nipples rise hard to my fingertips through the fabric of her bra, and suddenly I knew—as she had to know, too—that tonight would be the night when we would make love for the first time. Not here, not now; there'd be drinks first, and dinner, and intimate unhurried conversation—but a deal had been struck. It was all unspoken, but we knew.

We drew ourselves apart, and Phoebe handed me the chilled Louis Jadot. I uncorked it and made ready to pour.

"Wait. You have to let it breathe."

"Couldn't we just give it mouth-to-mouth?"

"It won't take long."

We went inside, and she took out a jug wine she had in the refrigerator, already open, and poured us each a glass of that. We settled on a couch on her screened porch and watched the news. The case (which the media were calling the "Carnival Murder," or, in one of the more colorful Boston papers, the "Carny Slay," happy to turn the verb to a noun) got another mention; they were keeping it alive. The phone rang, and Phoebe went into another room to get it. I heard her make some brief conversation, and after a moment she came back in. "Kathy, from work. You met her. Just checking in."

On the national news, Hurricane Gus was the story, having opted on a run back at the Bahamas. The broadcast showed fishing boats bashed to matchwood against a jetty, a coastal village being leveled. The days of kidding about storm names and indecision were over. We watched the footage of collapse and fragmentation, the ground of people's lives being swept away. "Dear God," Phoebe murmured several times, and I knew what she meant. The news anchors tried for a light counternote at the end of the broadcast with a story about early snow in Montana and pictures of the first snowman of the season. It was a good try.

We went out on the patio again. The sun had set, leaving only lingering splashes of gold on the tall pines at the back of the small yard, moving now with a cooling breeze. I held my hands above the grill, savoring the warmth. As Phoebe got ready to put the Rock hens on, her expression was troubled. "What?" I said.

"I think you should get out of this."

" 'This' meaning . . . ?"

"It's more complicated than what you took on. And dangerous. Can't you call someone and say you're resigning?" Color had risen in two patches on her cheeks, like daubs of rouge.

"What's wrong?" I asked, taking her hands. "Was it your friend's call? The newscast?"

"This is no good, Alex. A policeman? Maybe others? Do you have any idea what could happen? What if they come after you?"

"I don't think that's likely." I thought about the guy yelling at me from the car on Merrimack Street. Random harassment was more likely.

"But it's possible. Or something else that's bad. Don't ask me what. I don't know." Her voice was taking on an edgier, more manic note. "I just know that I like my drama on TV, where it's safe, and I can turn it off when I want to. I don't want it in my life."

I liked it at a distance, too, but it had this bad habit of not staying there. I picked up trouble like gum on my shoe, and it tended to stick.

"I'm serious, Alex. I think you're being blind about this." She gripped my hands and fixed me with a soft, questing gaze. "Is a woman still the way to a man's heart?"

"She can be."

"How about to his senses? To reason? Darling, do you understand what could happen?"

I could play stupid; it never came hard to me, but this wasn't the time for it. I said, "Not all of it, no. Some, though."

She was looking steadily at me, her green eyes bright and concerned and slightly desperate. "Tell me."

I glanced at the bottle of wine and had to restrain myself from reaching and pouring our glasses full and raising mine in toast to clink against hers and to hell with the wine breathing, let's *us* breathe, let's dance, let's . . .

I said, "If I go for the cops, I'm challenging the system. It can be done, *has* to be sometimes, but usually as part of long-term investigations, blue ribbon commissions, with lots of Beacon Hill backbone and federal probes and more time than anyone's got. This is too uncertain. If I stick with Sonders and the carnival"—*assuming I stayed healthy,* I thought but didn't say—"there'll be people in the city who'll never forget it. Influential folks, some of them. They'll call it betrayal."

Her look stayed worried, but at least I was talking some sense. "So let the carnival guy find someone other than you," she said, an undisguised plea in her tone. "Couldn't you do that?"

"Phoebe. Who? No one's lining up to get in on this."

"There must be somebody that . . . who's . . ." She drew a breath and let it out in a gust.

"Dumb enough?"

"Idealistic enough."

"Jimmy Stewart is dead."

"Just stop, then. Resign!" Her abruptly chopping hand hit a wine-glass and knocked it onto the patio, where it broke. She ignored it. "You've got that in your contract, don't you? That you can terminate a client?" I picked up the biggest piece of broken glass and set it on the table. "Aren't you afraid?" she went on.

"A little," I admitted.

"I am. I'm really afraid."

I reached for her, but she stepped back. "Talk to me," I said.

"No, I just did. It didn't work."

I lowered my arms. I paced a little. A shard of glass crunched under my shoe, and I stopped. "I can see it play out. Pepper comes to trial, with evidence and testimony from you-know-which cops. He'll be tagged for the murder so fast his bunk will still be warm when he gets back to jail. Except he won't be in county. Even if Meecham can get the charge reduced, he'll be on the yard at Walpole. He'll do fifteen to twenty hard."

"Maybe he *is* guilty." She shook her hands dramatically. "Have you forgotten that?"

I hadn't. It was the thing I couldn't entirely let go of.

"Isn't that card in the deck somewhere?" she asked.

"It's there."

"Okay. You were a cop. Did you often arrest a wrong person?"

"Almost never," I admitted. But all at once I was thinking of the man on the junkyard toilet, and the stream of bubbles rising in the mouth of the Harlem River.

"Suppose he did do it, and you risk all this and the verdict comes out the same? If you don't quit, how's that going to affect your work? You're your own boss, aren't you? You don't owe those carnival people anything you haven't already given them. They'll forget."

She was probably right; people do forget—but the point was, *I* wouldn't. If I walked, I'd have to live with their faces—Pop and Nicole, Moses Maxwell, Penny, Tito, Red Fogarty—and I'd always know that when . . .

I let the thoughts go. "Oh, hell's bells. I'll deal with all this later. Let's eat."

She lifted her shoulders in a forlorn shrug. "I don't have any appetite."

Suddenly I didn't, either. "Some wine, then." I picked up the bottle. It was plenty cold. "It's supposed to have a French finish, not the kind of thing you get hammered on, but it's a start. You like Ben Franklin—didn't he compile a long list of synonyms for getting drunk? Let's add a few. The hell with all this. Let's put a package on, let's get snookered, let's paint the town."

Phoebe shook her head slowly. "I wish I could. I'm not in the mood." I set the bottle back. I took her hands. They felt warm. She looked me in the eye. "I've been to all those singles events, the mixers and the soirees at the art museum . . . I told you all that. And do you know what single people think about most?"

"Is it a three-letter word that is often mistaken for a four-letter word?"

"Wait. When you and I went out that first time, you told me you thought my name was a happy one."

"Phoebe. It is."

"Names are just names. I have my dark moods, too; believe me. But being on my own these past few years . . . I've come to know what it is that most of the single people I've met really think about deep down. They don't want to die alone. How would that work for us? Just supposing we got together? Would I end up alone anyhow? A widow?"

"Those all sound rhetorical."

"When I first met you, you came by the office, dressed in a nice suit, and I thought your job was sitting at a desk, like most people, and filling out your share of paper, moving it around, making phone calls."

"I do all of that."

"But it doesn't end there," she said with gentle insistence. "You've also got that scar on your leg you told me about, and the lump on your head today."

"I imagine most people have got scars. They come from living."

Smiling wanly, she shook her head, and I shut up. "I'm no different than those other people I mentioned. I don't want to be alone, either. But if I have to, I'd rather stay alone than go through that loss again. I think you need to decide, and then act. When you do, and if all of this craziness is behind us, call me. We'll have a nice time together."

As though she were sealing a bargain, she kissed me gently on the mouth and then turned and went quickly into the house.

35

A few dry leaves skittered across the road in my headlights, urged by the rising wind, as I drove back across the city. Cold was coming, but I left my window open, letting the air blow in on me. With some vague notion of making up for the missed meal with simple fare at home, I stopped at a supermarket and bought a bag of provisions, though I wasn't very hungry. I put the bag in the trunk and crossed the river and went out the VFW, my mind finding focus on nothing in particular. I twitched the radio on, then twitched it off again. As I passed Regatta Field, I noticed several vehicles in the field, ringed in a semicircle, facing inward, their headlights aimed in a converging V and illuminating a group of people. That was odd; the carnival crew was still holed up at the Venice as far as I knew. There wasn't supposed to be anyone at the fairgrounds. Curious, I parked along the street and got out. For a moment, I stood there, uncertain, then I unlocked my trunk and got my .38 out of the hidden compartment by the wheel well. I snapped the holster onto my belt. As I started across the big field, an old plastic bag came whipping along, wrapped around my ankle for a moment, then danced on past. The air had a damp ash smell from the burnt-out haunted house.

When I got to where I could make out details, though no one had seen me yet, I realized the group consisted of ten or twelve people. Some had their backs to the headlights, and others stood slightly farther away, so I couldn't make out any faces; they were just shapes and shadows in the night—a shaved head here, a baseball cap there. Carnival people, gathered for an informal meeting?

Then, over the sigh of wind, a voice said, "Since you birds shut down the show, we figured we'd come out and get our own show. Lucky we found you."

My hackles rose. I edged closer, and that's when I saw that the two people facing the light were Moses Maxwell and Nicole. Moses was wearing his porkpie hat, and his face was shiny with sweat. The others, whoever they were, had the two surrounded.

"Hey, you're a pinhead, aren't you, girl?" the man who had spoken before said. He was a tall, lanky party with a beak that could etch glass.

"There's no call for that," Moses said. "No call for you to be here. Let's just let it alone, shall we, gentlemen? And all go home peaceably." He said it in his calm way, but I heard a thread of worry in his voice.

"Say what, dude?" the tall man said. "And what would be your role?"

"Maybe he's the bearded lady. Ain't you the bearded lady?" said another, a shaved-head, dressed in shorts and a football jersey with the inevitable number 69.

"Quit it, you!" Nicole said. "Go away."

Hoots of laughter. "Ooohhh . . . 'Quit it, you,'" Shaved Head mocked. He gripped her arm and gave her a shake.

"Stop it!" Nicole cried. There was an ice-skim of hysteria on her voice.

I looked around, hoping someone else was nearby to even the numbers a little, but there were only the scattered trailers and the shutdown rides. Something had brought Nicole and Moses here, but I didn't waste time trying to figure out what it had been. I needed an angle, something more inspired than simply turning up and saying, "Hi, guys."

Alongside Ray Embry's trailer, I noticed one of the torches that he used for his juggling stuffed in an open can, and it gave me an idea. One sniff of the wick told me there was still kerosene in it. I hoped it would be enough. Holding the unlit torch, I walked over to the ring of headlights.

At my approach, heads turned. Most of the strangers appeared to be in their twenties, a few slightly older. The tall party looked forty. I stepped just to the edge of the light, and with my free hand I drew my gun. It took a few seconds for the effect to register, then I saw people stiffen.

"Mr. Rasmussen!" cried Nicole.

"What the fu—" began the tall guy.

I held the torch wick down, put the gun barrel next to it, aimed at the ground. If my idea flopped, it was going to be hard to find another entrance line. I squeezed the trigger.

People jumped at the explosion. The snout of flame sparked the torch, which instantly caught fire. The effect was riveting. No one said a word. Hiding my own amazement, I lowered my gun, raised the torch, and walked into the center of the lighted ring.

"You want to play with fire?" I swung the torch in a half circle. In the after-silence of the gunshot, the flames made a suitably dramatic roar. I swung it back again, and people edged away, gawking at me as if I were some madman, or a wraith of vengeance. Even Moses Maxwell and Nicole seemed suddenly not quite sure what to make of me.

"You're shit-crazy, dude," the tall one said. He had on a green surgical smock and a pair of baggy canvas pants.

"Stick around and see how crazy. I just pushed nine-one-one."

Several of them traded worried looks, but the tall guy just stared. "We gonna shit our pants over one guy? I think he's bluffing."

I noticed that the torch flame had dwindled slightly and had given up its throaty sound. I shook it a bit, for effect.

"We could fuckin' take you down right now," the tall guy said.

I brought the .38 up. My finger was well away from the trigger, but he wouldn't know that. "Grin big, brother," I said.

"Come on," said one of the others, "let's split."

The leader had other words for me, but no one seemed ready to back him up. After a few more seconds of standoff, even he must've agreed that discretion was the better part of valor. They got into the cars and gunned off across the field, headlights stabbing the dark, dust rising in their wake. I holstered the .38.

"Good to see you, Mr. Rasmussen," Moses said, using his hat to fan himself. "And that's a fact."

I held the torch out to the side, so we could see one another more clearly in its florid light. "Sorry for the cheesy special effects. Are you two okay?"

Nicole was hugging herself, shivering. Emotions were coming and going on her face like the restless flicker and shadow of the torchlight. "They had me really scared. We didn't hurt them. Why did they do that?"

There was a note of hysteria in her voice, but she seemed to be calming down. Moses put a comforting arm around her. "For some folks it seems to be a labor walking upright all the time. They want to get down on all fours sometimes and howl. Tomorrow, they'll be sobered up and maybe feel ashamed. They ought to, anyway." He sent me a look. "You suppose they the ones burnt up the trailer?"

I said they could be, though something told me they had been a ragtag group. I could imagine them parked in a local juice mill, corking up a head of steam, until finally someone mentioned the carnies, and they'd tumbled out into cars and come looking for mischief. I snuffed the torch and set it back in the can where I'd found it, although the kerosene smell stayed on me like a taint.

"That true about you calling the police?" Moses asked.

"A bluff. Though I doubt any of that crew is going to report it."

"Not till they change their shorts, leastways." Moses chuckled. "Cats were some spooked for a while there."

"They weren't the only ones," Nicole said.

I didn't doubt that they'd be back; probably not tonight, and maybe not the same ones, but when people did come again it would be with bigger numbers and more determination. I detected a crusade growing in the city, a need to repulse the invaders, fanned by lamebrain candidates trolling for votes and at least one opinion columnist willing to exploit the issue. "What are you two doing here?" I asked. "Shouldn't you be at the hotel?"

"We came with Pop," Nicole said.

That surprised me. "He's here?"

"He got let out of the hospital earlier. He insisted on comin' over here."

As we approached Sonders's darkened motor home, through the little porthole window I could see that the computer monitor was alight inside, like an eye that refused to close. "What's all the ruckus?" Pop demanded when we went in. "Was that a gunshot?"

"Nothing to worry about," I told him.

"Jesus," he groaned. He was sunk in the patched vinyl recliner. In the curved rim of light cast by the computer screen, I made out some little scraps of toilet paper on his cheeks and chin, where he'd plastered over a bad shaving job.

"What you doin' here practically in the dark?" Moses Maxwell said. He switched on a lamp, and I saw Pop's dismal expression, his eyes sunken and lusterless. With a weak gesture he waved us into chairs. Nicole retreated to the little corner desk, with the computer, and sat. I'd been in the motor home only a couple of times before, but something was different. I couldn't put a finger on what it was. "How you doing, Rasmussen?" Pop asked.

"I'm glad you're out of bed. How do you feel?"

"About like somebody put me on the Rocket Whip and spun me around a thousand turns. I feel like crap," he said morosely.

I glanced at the others for elaboration but got none. The mood in there was as cheery as the Red Sox dugout after dropping a doubleheader to the Yankees, and there were a lot of evasive looks racketing around the walls. The *walls*—that's what was different. They were bare. A cardboard carton was pushed into one corner, with the framed citations and awards heaped inside. I nodded at it. "No pawnshop will give you much for those," I said, pointing at the carton. "There's a glut on keys to cities. I just picked up Bangor and Boise for peanuts."

Moses Maxwell offered his flask. I waved it away.

"What brought you, Mr. Rasmussen?" he asked politely. "Cold night to be out just cruising, though don't get me wrong, I was some happy to see you."

I looked from him to Nicole to Sonders, wondering what I was missing. And then something dawned. Squisher had told me. "Hackett visited you at the hospital this afternoon."

Sonders frowned. "What the hell's that to you?" His voice was scratchy, but it had a note of its former ferocity, and I was beginning to fathom the gloom in the trailer.

"It's done?"

"Already sent word to my accountant to get the paper together. Right, Nicole? You sent them the e-mail?"

"It's gone out, Pop."

He nodded. "Rag Tyme wants to take possession tomorrow. Any objections?"

I didn't have words for my sudden swarm of thoughts, but my face must've conveyed them. "I needed the reality," Sonders said. "World don't stop spinnin' just 'cause some old duffer's stomach goes south. Right now I'm feeling the way I ought to be feeling. Lucky, maybe. Who knows?"

"Windy this evenin'," Moses said, tipping his head to listen as a gust whined in the jalousie panes. "The hawk is talkin' out there. Better night for a fellow to be sitting by his home fire with his squeeze." He held out the flask again. I ignored it.

"Shoot, Moses," said Sonders. "You're being too damned subtle with your St. Bernard routine. Rasmussen here's something of an idealist. You got to club him over his fool head. If I were you," he went on, meaning me, "I'd see this as a lucky thing, too. A way out. This ain't the fight you signed on for. You've got cops breathing heat on you. You've got hoodlums—and a guy in jail who won't give you the time of day. Hell, your lawyer friend evidently got wise."

I frowned a questioning look at the others, then at Pop. "Fred Meecham?"

"Where the hell you been? Don't you two share scuttlebutt? He quit."

"Is that true, Pop?" Nicole thrust forward, making the chair creak. "I didn't know that."

"I only told Moses. Meecham called me just a short while ago, said he was sorry but he had to withdraw."

I was still trying to muster words. Nicole got to them first. "You mean he isn't Troy's lawyer anymore?"

"Professional reasons is how he explained it. I didn't even ask. I heard the first part plain enough." He blew a slow, disheartened breath. "He said he wouldn't charge me, and he'd find someone else to recommend."

"Did you tell him about Rag Tyme?" I said, finding my tongue.

"I didn't say anything."

I asked to use his phone. I wasn't surprised that Fred Meecham was still in his office; an honest lawyer works hard for his money. He knew from my voice that I'd heard. "Alex, I tried to reach you earlier. I'm just about to go home. Look—" He cleared his throat. "It's complicated. I'll try to explain in the morning, first thing."

"What is it, Fred?"

"I just can't do it. I had to let the case go."

"Does it concern Rag Tyme?"

"Huh? What's that?" His mystification was genuine.

"Is it what's going on in the city right now?"

"It's many things. *Too* many. They're churning around in my head right now. That's why I want to take time when I explain it to you. I'll recommend other representation. Pepper's case will go to a jury, and who knows? *I* don't." I heard him sigh. "Jurors think they come to weigh guilt or innocence, to determine truth, but mostly they're wrestling with their own demons of crime and punishment, outrage and righteousness. And there seem to be plenty of both right now." I wondered if Fred had been drinking, though I'd never known him to, not at the office. "Somebody left a note on my car," he said, "implying I was no different than a killer."

"You can't let that get to you," I said.

"No . . . I know. That isn't the reason." But he vented a long breath, and I heard exhaustion in it. "I'll speak with you tomorrow, Alex. I've got to get home to my family."

Sure, I understood. I told him I'd see him in the morning. Pop was watching me as I put the phone down, his chin quirked up so that in the lamplight I could see a piece of tissue on his chin, like a tiny white flag of surrender. He roused himself. "Anyway, you should get out, too. The good news is you have friends here in town."

Did I? I was no longer sure. The wind pulsed against the motor home, making it tremble like a subway car moving through a tunnel. "You ought to get over to the hotel," I said. "Those jokers could come back. I don't think they will tonight, but just in case."

He ignored it. "Remember you one time asked me where I come from, and I rattled off a list of places? It's true for these folks, too. Moses,

Nicole, the rest. Most of us ain't from any one hometown, a place you know folks and folks know you and your birth certificate's on file in the town hall. You're *from* here. That means something. You've got history. You can pick up that phone and call folks and they know you. Your high school math teacher recognizes you in the supermarket."

"Make that truant officer," I said, "but I get your point."

"Roots is what I'm talking. My roots I can pull up with one hand and shove in a five-dollar suitcase. No, you're well off, and you know it. Or if you don't, you ought to. Christ, you'd do better to step down there in the shooting gallery with a bull's-eye target on your head than to stand in the way of the police and public opinion and all the rest. Am I right, Moses?"

"Amen," the old jazzman agreed. "There ain't much difference that I can see."

"You'd be best off keeping warm in your own bed on a cold night," Pop insisted.

"While you lie in a smutty hotel room, trying to get to sleep with the water pipes coughing? What'd you do, find religion in the ICU?"

"Too soon old, too late smart. It's a bitch, but at least I'm ahead of my dad. He never did wise up before they rolled him away in a shroud."

I shook my head. "It doesn't feel right."

"That was *my* line," he snapped. "You set me straight. Deal with facts, you said. Situations. Well, I am. The situation is this—I can't pay my bills, and the fact is I got to get out from under. So the show is going to the syndicate. Contract says so. I signed it myself." A dab of tissue had come off of his chin and a shaving cut was beginning to bleed, but he paid it no attention. "I'm meeting with Hackett tomorrow at noon to sign the papers."

"Can't you hold off?"

"For what? They'll call for an audit. Some bean counter will sieve every scrap of paper I've got, and you can bet your bottom dollar he'll find something."

"You're clean, though. You said your accountant is honest."

"Honest schmonest. There's always something to find. Even if it ends up being nothing. It's the auditor's job. Hell, if he doesn't find *some*-thing, the G's take his abacus away."

"Chew on this, then. You sell the show to Rag Tyme, and that's the end of it."

"That's what I'm saying. I'm done."

"Literally. Your legacy is scrap iron." I told him about the cutting torches and the equipment auction.

His eyes sparked momentarily with outrage, but there was no place for it to go. "It's their call," he said dejectedly. "We'll be hauling stakes after that. Time to move on. I'm out of choices." He glanced at the bare walls, as if confirming it. "And I don't want no date with that sicko wrestler. Selling will give me some cash. I'll take care of people as I can."

"And Troy Pepper?"

"It ain't about him now. He doesn't have sense enough to put up a fight."

"You do, though. Or did."

"I'm tired out, I tell you. I've got a stomach that could blow for good any time."

"Pop—" Nicole cried.

"Not according to your nurse," I said. "She thinks you'll outlive Mount Rushmore."

"Is it *her* stomach? Anyway, we talked it over and we're in agreement, each and all. Don't none of us like it, of course, but there's nothing to fight anymore. Deals are deals." I glanced at the other two, who didn't meet my gaze. "Plus there is one other thing that decided me."

I waited.

"Lying there in that bed, all those tubes crawling into me and the little screens going beep-beep, I had time to think. Didn't want to necessarily, but there it was." He sighed. "Now I figure he may have done it."

"Pepper?"

"Hell, yes, Pepper. Who do you think I'm talking about?"

"Pop's right, Mr. Rasmussen," Moses said quietly.

I turned to him, his lean dark face half shadowed by the lamplight, a little arc of dusty freckles on one cheek. "You think he did it, too?"

"I don't know about that. I was referring to cuttin' losses. Like those old days touring with the band and not being able to stay at some hotels, or eat at restaurants on account of being the wrong shade. Sure, it made a person angry, but you decided when there wasn't no point fightin' it and you went along, because goin' along kept the world spinning at thirty-three and a third, and that's what mattered most. You got to sit up on a bandstand and play, and to eat, and have some clear space all your own between your ears. In that regard, I guess, I felt like a mostly free man."

"Do I hear the old Lackawanna?" I asked.

For a moment I thought I observed anger glitter in the jazzman's eyes, like sparks from night fire, and I thought, *Go for it, man. Let's put it all out where we can get at it and learn what's really going down*—but evidently I was wrong. Maxwell pinched at the little soul patch under his lower lip. His voice, when he spoke, was calm. "Nossir, just sayin' you already done what you could, and now maybe you want to let it be."

"So you're free to go, too," Pop said. "While you still got a place in this town."

Nicole had been sitting in the corner through most of this, staring at her knitted fingers in her lap. "What about you?" I asked her.

"Me?" She flicked her glance away, but her face was as transparent as ever. I saw confusion and worry. Still, she managed a woeful smile. "I don't do so good with these kind of things. Pop and Mr. Maxwell are most likely right."

Pop's shrug said, *You see?*

Why was I so stubborn as to be arguing with people who had my own best interests at heart? Hadn't Phoebe been for me, too? And even St. Onge? And Meecham would've advised the same. "What'll you do?" I asked the old man.

"I'll celebrate is what. I'll pay off creditors. I'll call in a few favors I still got and try to land jobs for some of my people. I'll go on relief, if there's any left after these robbers in Washington give it all away in blue-blood welfare. And there's you. Four days' work at your rate per day sound right?"

"You don't owe me."

"The hell I don't. You earned it."

"Save it for—" I'd been about to say for Pepper's defense fund, but I remembered he didn't have a defense anymore. I shut up. I had worked for them, and my time was worth something. "You have my address." I got up and took the two paces to the door.

" 'Rasmussen,' with one *s* and then two," Sonders called after me. "I'll mail it."

The wind yanked the door wide when I turned the knob, and I nearly lost it; then I went down the steps.

"Good night, Mr. Rasmussen," Nicole said quietly from the doorway. "Thank you for all your help." She meant it, too; poor sweet simple girl. She actually thought I'd helped the situation somehow. As I closed the door I wished I'd had the presence of mind to ask her to explain it to me.

I stood there on the matted grass, my mind full of incoherent thoughts. An eddy of night wind twirled dead leaves past. Somewhere a dog *bark-bark*ed. When I got into my car, I slammed the door. I gunned the motor a few times. Someplace I found maturity enough not to lay down smoking tracks of Goodyear. I jerked into the flow of traffic on Pawtucket Boulevard, three lanes of unimportant little people, pushing their big gas-guzzlers hard to get nowhere and do nothing.

Motion helped. Definitely. If Warren Sonders and Co. wanted piano for blues and brandy, what was that to me? They were adults; they could make their own damn decisions. And in one regard they were absolutely right. My intentions had been good; that's what mattered. If my judgment was faulty, Pop had straightened me out. It wasn't my fight. Where the hell did I ever get the idea that it was? I was strictly a day-jobber. A private shadow would be a fool to get between the cops and the courts and wannabe gangsters over a man who was most likely guilty— especially when said shadow didn't even have a client. He was fool enough to have practically insisted on turning down the fair wage he had coming. He'd be a bigger fool to turn down a good woman who was waiting. Moses had it right: a night to sit with a lover by a cozy fire, tally the costs tomorrow. All at once, I felt a strong desire for Phoebe. I drove off, praising myself for finally coming to my senses, lauding my good luck . . .

Are you afraid? Phoebe had asked me.

I stopped for the red light at the intersection before the Rourke Bridge and waited for a green arrow. On the skyline, a moon was just beginning to shine, fat and full and yellow as—the corn moon! We'd forgotten all about it. Well, there it was. A left turn and I'd be crossing the river, heading for Phoebe's house, ten minutes away, to announce my wise decision, and to cash the one chip I still seemed to hold. Her arms would be warm, the wine chilled. We'd raise a glass to good sense and *vive la différence,* and then a second to *auld lang syne*, and a final giddy glass to something more sweetly carnal. It was our time. The traffic signal glowed ruby red and teetered in the wind. Green-eyed Phoebe was going to be glad to see me, and vice versa.

Across the river, a train hooted, a long, lonely sound in the night, and for some reason I thought of Pepper, sitting in his dark cell, in his solitude. Was he waiting for something from me? I thought of him last Sunday evening when he'd handed me the big wooden hammer and murmured, "Good luck," like somehow I'd been given the one chance, a long shot to ring the bell, but I got stuck in Cake Eater land, and I'd fallen away, *clunk.* I sat there. The train hooted again, farther-away-sounding now. Bound south for Boston? North to Nashua? If the signal told the answer, I couldn't translate it.

Damn.

I hammered the steering wheel with the heel of my hand.

Double damn.

A horn beeped behind me. I looked up and the arrow was green. I pulled over to the right and waved on the VW bug behind me, which blew a testy little blat that didn't need translation. When the road was clear, I hung a U-turn and started back.

The cell phone chirped.

36

"I've drunk so much coffee I'm humming."

Courtney accompanied me to my car, double-parked outside the Dunkin' Donuts shop on Merrimack. She shivered and drew up the collar of her jacket. "I kept watching the office," she said, "waiting for Mr. Meecham to go home. I could see the windows from that corner booth."

Our offices across the square were dark now except for reflected moonlight.

We took the back stairs up to the third floor. She unlocked Meecham's suite and ushered me in. We went into his law library, and she turned on a table lamp. "Judge Travani called, and Mr. Meecham called him back. Afterward, he spent time in here, but he wasn't studying. He was brooding about something. I heard him pacing. I stayed for a while, in case he needed me, and I had some typing to get caught up on, but finally he told me I should go home."

"How did he seem?"

"Preoccupied for sure. If I had to guess? Depressed."

The lamp had a deep-green glass shade, and it cast a glow on the rich mahogany of the table. A legal pad lay there. On it were some doodles and scribbled notes and a phone number. One of the drawings was a gallows. I wondered if he liked to play Hangman or if it meant something else. "Did he make any calls after he talked with the judge?" I asked.

"Not while I was here."

I pressed redial on his phone, and it rang through. A machine answered, and a voice that I knew from only a brief encounter identified the line as the courthouse office of Carly Ouellette. I hung up.

Courtney turned off the lights and locked up, and we went back down the corridor to my office. I put on my desk lamp. She took the client chair, and I sat at my desk. I brought out the bottle of Wild Turkey and held it up inquiringly. "I shouldn't," she said. "But maybe it'll settle the coffee. With a little water, please."

I poured two, adding water from a carafe. I drank mine off. She took hers in a more refined fashion, but she didn't grimace.

"Did you learn anything just now?" she asked.

"From the bourbon?"

She smiled. "From your phone call."

I scooched my chair in closer to the desk. "Fred apparently called Judge Travani's office assistant."

"That Ouellette person?"

"Uh-huh—who also happens to be the person who witnessed Flora Nuñez's signature on her request for a restraining order. And whenever I've tried to talk to her, she runs away. Apparently she's a one-woman flying wedge around the judge. All of which may mean nothing at all."

Courtney drew a pad from her purse and clicked her pen. "On the other hand?"

"I don't think you can bill Fred for any of this," I said.

"I haven't felt this wired since my last No-Doz binge, cramming for finals. Talk."

"Okay, question number one. If Pepper isn't guilty, why doesn't he squawk?"

"An innocent person usually protests his innocence loudly," she agreed.

"That's the puzzler, isn't it? But there might be an explanation."

I reminded her of Pepper's childhood as an orphan and foster child, always looking for a family. I told her about the Asbury Park pennant.

"And now, with the carnival, it's like he's been on a trial basis again," Courtney said, a little breathlessly, connecting dots that I thought only I saw. "He didn't want to screw up. So now he doesn't know what to do." She leaned closer, her smooth brow crinkling, and I had an image of her as she must've been in school, sitting in the front row, interested and eager and as smart as they come. "He's learned not to speak up because it's always tended to go bad for him. Right from childhood."

"It adds up. Behavioral patterns run deep. We keep making the same mistakes, 'round and around. Sometimes therapy, or a life-changing event, can help us see, but it's tough. And it isn't something a defense attorney could take to court with much hope of selling it."

"I know Mr. Meecham was struggling with that." Courtney's blue eyes clouded. "Do . . . do you think Troy Pepper killed that Flora Nuñez?"

I hesitated, then said, "Do you want to go further with this?"

Her turn for hesitation; then, "Yes."

"Hold on to that question for a bit. We'll get there." I gestured with the bottle. She shook her head. I poured mine again.

"Do you drink a lot when you're working on a case?"

"What's a lot?" I didn't go into my woes. "All right—your question. I've grappled with that day and night since Monday morning, and I finally have my answer. I haven't seen anything that proves it one way or the other, so it gets down to what I understand about people. That past experiences can help us predict what we might do. Pepper is an extremely sensitive person—a loner who nevertheless is looking for connection."

"But even a sensitive person can do something really bad," Courtney said.

"I know—and therein lies the key. He's taciturn to a fault. He has a hard time even going out with his fellow workers for a beer. But if he'd done something like what he's accused of, he'd have felt a strong need to talk about it, because it would bother him so much. A psychopath or a hardened criminal can deal—for different reasons—but they won't crack. He would. So he'd have talked with somebody. Fred, Pop Sonders, the cops. Even me. But he hasn't. So that's your answer. That's why I don't believe he did it."

"But rather than protest that he's innocent," Courtney said, "he went even deeper inside . . . and he's trapped there."

"I think so. But try to prove it. It's a tall order."

"Was Fred right to drop this one?"

I was slow to answer. "I'm not judging Fred. I'm sure he's got reasons, good ones. But I don't."

"You're staying on, then."

Through the window, riding above the illuminated sign for the *Sun* building across the square, was the moon, small now and bleached white as a bone. "For now," I said.

She nodded.

"And for now we're done," I said. "You, girl, did good. Very good. But you need to be on your merry way and get some rest."

"I think I'll sleep fine." She capped her pen and put her notes away. She reached for the phone. "I'll call for a cab."

"I'm going that way. Let me just make one more call."

Her apartment was in the stretch of artists' lofts on the lower end of Middle Street, in the block beyond Palmer. As I double-parked in front of the building that she indicated, a woman came to a tall third-floor window and looked down. Beyond the glass, she appeared to be some years older than Courtney, dark hair to her shoulders and wearing a green robe. She saw Courtney and me get out of the car and waved vaguely in our direction, probably full of questions, and probably relieved. I escorted Courtney inside the locking outer door and said good night. As I turned to go out, she said, "You ought to go home and get some sleep."

"Yeah."

"Right. So what *will* you do?"

I gave it a quick smile.

"Ask a stupid question." She chewed her lip. "When I did my honors thesis on the Bread and Roses labor movement, I realized that a lot of people, right here in this city, women and men, did a lot of brave things . . . stood up for things."

"Don't be too quick to put me in their league. I just know myself, Courtney. If I roll over once, it's easier the next time."

"Suppose there isn't a next time? Maybe you need to weigh that in, too."

"There's always a next time. And knowing what you did—or didn't do—it sticks with you, and you feel dirty. I'm dirty enough as it is." She was studying me intently. I wasn't sure what her expression meant, and I wasn't going to try to find out. If she was looking for a mentor or a philosophy course, she'd do better back at Mount Holyoke. I gave her a gentle push toward the elevator. Then I drove off, my tires buzzing on the cobblestones, and headed toward where the late-night action was.

37

My last phone call had been as much a shot in the dark as poking redial on Fred Meecham's phone earlier. I'd copied the number off of the yellow legal pad on his library table. Twice and I'd probably have called it coincidence, but three made me wonder. The first mention of the nightclub had been on the book of matches on Flora Nuñez's little hallway shrine, and in the Polaroid I'd taken from her bureau drawer. At her funeral, her friend Lucy Colón had revealed that she and Flora and some others used to go there of a late evening for drinks. And now the number on the yellow pad had been answered against a background of voices by a woman saying, "Viva!" I'd listened long enough for her to repeat it and then hung up. Maybe it was still just coincidence, but I wanted to know.

Viva! had become a cause célèbre several years back when some of the citizenry, who had been after the club owners for years, trying to pull their license, citing public nuisance and affront to public morality, had written enough letters to editors that it became news around New England. But the owners held firm. Between payoffs and the Constitution, it's easy enough to do.

The area by the bar was packed deep with patrons so I had to worm through and then wait while the several bartenders set up drinks for the waitresses who jockeyed them out to tables. On the spotlighted stage, a slender Asian pole dancer was beginning her routine. When one of the barmen came my way, I asked him over the noise if Danielle Frampton was working tonight. He asked me why I wanted to know, and I said I wanted to see her. He sounded Greek or Albanian; he took me literally, glanced at a clock, nodded, and held up five fingers. If it had been more, I'd have tried to make myself clearer, but five minutes I could wait. In a shadowy corner I found a table the size of a pie plate. A fresh-faced young waitress wearing a black vest over a white blouse, black miniskirt, and fishnet stockings appeared, and over the noise I told her a Heineken. In a pocket of her apron was a microcassette recorder. When I asked about it, she tapped it with a finger. "The pad is for orders, this I use for ideas."

"What kind of ideas?"

"Stuff that occurs to me. Bits of conversation, characters I meet. Images. A Silly Putty face. That came to me the other night. See the assistant manager over there? By the office door? A Silly Putty face."

"Bingo."

She looked pleased. "Think so?"

"Nailed it. Writing your memoirs?"

"Screenplay. My mother thinks I'm nuts, a parochial school education and I'm walking around dressed like this. I quit Starbucks and came here because I wanted atmosphere." She shook her head. "I've got to move on."

"Don't let me keep you."

"No, I mean L.A. maybe, or Vancouver. It's the same old same old here. Nothing exciting ever goes down. I mean you're probably here tonight because you're bored, right? Tired of four walls."

"Pretty much," I said.

"I'll be twenty-one next month. It's like I'm in an Indigo Girls song. My options are running out."

"We're all being drawn down into the quicksand of time," I said.

"So true. Hey—is it okay if I use that?"

"Sure, if you want clichés."

"That's mostly what Hollywood stories are anymore. If you can retool them in just the right way, though, you've got a winner. Did you see *American Beauty*? You didn't miss much. It's nothing but clichés, with a quarter-turn twist. It won Oscars." She murmured the moldy chestnut about quicksand into her tape recorder. Then, to me, "What did you want to drink again?"

A few minutes later, another woman slid into the other chair. "Hello, Detective."

It took me a second to recognize Danielle Frampton. She was wearing a thin robe, her platinum wig picking up faint highlights, despite the dimness. At my questioning look, she nodded toward the barman, who was watching us with potential menace in his dark eyes. She gave him a wave, and he returned his attention to making drinks. "So . . . long time, Alex," she said over the ambient noise. "Are you slumming?"

"Business trip."

She pouted. "You didn't come to see me?"

"You're the first one I asked for. Drink?"

"Can't, I'm on next."

We did a quick catch-up, and I asked about her son, who stayed with her mom nights Danielle worked. The blond wig and the stage makeup aged her a bit past her twenty-five or so, but there was something slightly different, and I wondered if she'd had cosmetic surgery. The Asian dancer had finished up to whistles and scattered applause, and a tall redheaded dancer with meaty thighs took the stage. "So what's the business?" Danielle asked.

"Information. I'm interested in someone who used to come in here."

"His name?"

"Hers. Flora Nuñez."

"I've never heard. . . . Wait—the one in the paper? Killed at the carnival?" Her expression looked troubled, and slightly evasive. "What's that got to do with here?"

"Maybe nothing. Is there someplace where we don't need megaphones?"

"If you can wait ten more minutes or so, I've got a break." I gave the "OK" sign, and she tapped my arm and drifted away, dematerializing into the crowd. I was there, I might as well watch the show. I turned toward the strobe-lighted stage and nursed my beer.

Danielle was somewhere between acquaintance and friend. She'd evidently had her troubles with narcotics some years back but, as far as I knew, had gotten beyond them. She was a single mother, devoted to raising her young son. A year or so ago, a man had taken to turning up at the club every night and pestering her to go out with him. Then the phone calls began, and on a referral she asked me for advice—though she didn't want rough stuff, she insisted. I checked the guy out and learned he was a basically harmless sad sack who worked in a muffler repair shop and lived with his widowed mother and spent his spare time hanging around Comic Book Heaven. Maybe he'd confused Danielle with one of the tawny, tights-clad sexpots who passed for superheroines in the comic books and had fixated on her, I don't know. Getting him loose was a relatively easy job: I turned the game on him. I was reasonable with him and said, "You wouldn't want your mother to know where you go nights, would you?" That was all it took. As far as I knew, he was back in Metropolis. As for Danielle, I admired her spunk, her desire to be a good person.

When the redhead finally got down to her gold hoop earrings and belly button lint, the lights winked out to wolf whistles and lusty cheers. A steadier light bathed the stage, and Danielle Frampton came on with barely a pause, her platinum wig sparkling like spun sugar. She didn't need the distractions of strobe lights or a pole. She was actually a very good dancer; she had a lithe body—no need for cosmetic surgery there— and got away with a little more suggestion and less flesh. Still, by the time the set ended, there wasn't much I needed to imagine. I paid my tab, with a few extra bucks for the budding screenwriter. I waited by the door and soon saw Danielle coming my way, dressed in a faux leopard-fur coat and white stretch pants. We went outside and stood in the glow of the marquee lights.

I handed her the snapshot that I had found in Flora Nuñez's apartment. She looked at it and nodded. "I remember that. It was taken in the spring." She pointed out the other three women sitting with her around the table. "There's like a crew of us that got to know each other."

"And the guys?"

"They're off-duty cops."

"City cops?"

She didn't miss my surprise. "I think so. They come in sometimes on their nights off. They're okay."

"Do you know their names?"

"First names."

"How about this one?" I indicated the guy lifting his glass.

"Bob, maybe. Or Paul?"

"How about Paul Duross?"

"That sounds right. I haven't seen him in a while. Or any of them, actually."

I wanted time to think, to try to make sense of the details that were swarming like wet snow, but Danielle was restless to get back inside. She had begun to shiver in the cooling night. "What about Flora Nuñez? Did she come here often?"

"Only sometimes. I got to know her and some others when we took night classes. But this is the only other place I saw them. We weren't tight or anything."

"Did she ever mention someone named Troy Pepper?"

"The guy who killed her? No, I don't remember her ever mentioning him. The newspaper is the only place I ever heard of him. Why? What's this about? Are you working on that case?"

"I don't know. I guess I am slumming." I thanked her and touched her cheek. "Wrap up warm when you go home."

38

The wind gusted fitfully, as though uncertain of what it might become if it put its mind to it. Maybe it had heard about its big cousin Hurricane Gus and was getting ideas; but except for some scattered clouds, the sky was clear. Above the silhouetted buildings, the moon was a smoky cat's-eye.

Short of waking up people with phone calls, there wasn't much I could do to get answers. It was that time of night when the city's aching heart could rest for a little while, and I knew that I should rest, too. Courtney had been right. The thought train had been gathering speed, building momentum, rising toward some sharp blind drop-off, but now I discovered that some time in the past hour my energy had begun to run down. Try as I might, I couldn't coax out a single useful thought. If I didn't get some sleep soon, I was going to start hearing the streetlights talking to me. I remembered that I still had groceries in my trunk, too. Yet I didn't want to go home to cardboard boxes, my plastic-sheeted window, and the same nonanswers I had now.

A twenty-four-hour diner on Dutton drew me. I strolled past the high swivel chairs at the chrome counter to a booth in the back and slid in on ruby-colored Naugahyde, already stirred by the aromas of food.

"Hi, hon," the waitress greeted me, and though I knew I was one of a thousand, it still felt personal somehow. She had STEL stitched in pink above the breast of her white blouse. "Coffee?"

I dug a folded copy of the *Sun* from the corner of the booth and flopped it open and let my eye stray down the front page. There was an archive story on a demonstration from thirty-odd years ago, when university students had staged a peace march through downtown. Arriving in front of city hall, carrying Viet Cong flags and chanting "Ho . . . Ho . . . Ho Chi Minh," they had been met by construction workers. It was a working-class Democrat city, but when that old chestnut "patriotism" was in the fire, everything took two steps to the right. The beleaguered police chief had to call in the National Guard to keep hard hats from beating up the kids and torching their flags. I put the paper down. Stel sidled over on tired feet with my coffee and her pad. I ordered corn chowder. It came in a thick white mug, and as I was about to dip my spoon, I noticed there was a faint lipstick ring on the rim that the dishwasher had missed. I was about to complain, but I paused, wondering if I should keep quiet, if it might be the closest I got to a woman's lips that night. The point was moot. One spoonful told me the chowder was a lot better as an idea than a reality. I pushed it aside. In the lull, Stel came over and sat on the edge of the bench across the table from me. She unsnapped a little cloth cigarette case and took one out. She looked at me. "Mind?"

"You're the one smoking it."

"That seems to be a minority opinion these days. Lately I feel like a criminal, standing out there on the stoop." She took a light from the match I struck, drew smoke, and I saw her relax. She was a pretty, faded brunette with drooping eyes. She told me about Tom Waits sitting in there in the wee hours, nursing coffee and a club sandwich and sweet-talking her in his three-pack-a-day voice. I didn't know if it was for real, but it made a good listen, punctuated in the pauses with the wind pulsing against the big windows. A party of two middle-aged couples came in, noisily debating something or other, and trudged to a booth. I squinted their way. They might have been people I'd gone to high school with, though it was impossible they'd look that old. Stel let them get settled, stubbed the cigarette, and rose, exhaling a silvery strand of smoke. "Don't be a stranger, hon."

But wasn't that the appeal? A late-hours oasis where night travelers could be strangers: sufficient unto themselves, without history or a future, just there in the bright fluorescent and chrome heart of the urban wilderness . . . with lipstick on your cup. The city was full of waitresses on tired feet, looking for a snug harbor, however temporary, and some companionship to share the lonely stretches after a long shift, when they took off the uniform that still smelled of the foods cooked and eaten in the diner, someone there when they let her hair down, and a voice to sing them a lullaby till they dropped off to sleep. No one knew the night city better: not patrol cops, or the graveyard shift gas jockeys, or the hookers on Middlesex, those fallen sister-angels of the night. No one knew the empty sidewalks and the dim dawns as the waitresses did. Stel was pretty in a way that didn't hide the living, or feel it had to. Ah, Rasmussen, you're hopeless. When I pushed back into the night, the air had cooled considerably, and I was wide awake.

I was turning onto Market when I saw the flashers strobe on behind me. I flipped the rearview mirror tab to keep the cycling lights from frying my eyeballs and drew the Cougar to the curb. I opened the window and waited. A cop approached, taking his time, and I was startled to see Duross. If he recognized me, he showed no sign. Already the twitching colors washing across the brick facades of adjacent buildings were bringing curious faces to windows.

"Sir, I'd like you to come with us."

"Where? What's going on?"

"JFK Plaza." In the glare, his breath smoked. "Detective Cote has some questions for you."

And I've got one for you, I thought. *About your uncle Frank Droney.* But I let it lie. "Have him phone me in the morning, I get to the office at nine." I was irked at being late-night entertainment for insomniacs.

"Make it now."

Duross's face appeared to be set in concrete. I suppose I could've told him where to go, provoked him a little, which would have given us both some options. But I didn't need anyone informing me of Miranda-Escobedo, even if he could do it without reading it off a card, as I suspected Duross could. "We'll follow you," he said.

"I'll see you there." I trod on the gas before he could protest, forcing him to jump back. I didn't like wearing a leash.

Headquarters wasn't far. Duross caught up to me in the lobby, but maybe the presence of other people spared me a hassle. At the desk, as instructed, I unsnapped my belt holster and handed over the .38, which the desk officer made a note of in a log and passed to Duross. Wordlessly, we went through a steel door into an inner stairwell. Down one flight were the cell block and booking area. We went up to the next floor. Roland Cote was waiting in an interrogation room, perched on the edge of a long table. He was in shirtsleeves, with suspenders, his legs crossed at the ankles. He gave me an eyebrow flash for greeting. Duross laid my holstered weapon on the table near Cote, gave me a heavy look, and went out.

"Okay, you've got my attention," I said. "What gives?"

"What's your hurry? Take a load off."

"It's two o'clock in the morning. You want to sit and talk?"

"Unless you prefer to have a lawyer present."

I frowned and gave it a moment. "What for?"

"Interfering with an officer in the performance of his duties."

"Did Duross tell you that?"

"Have a seat, for God's sake."

I took one of the chairs at the table. Cote shifted position to face me. "I don't know why you're busting my balls on this," he said.

"What are you talking about?"

"You've got a good thing, you know it? I mean, think about it. You solve a case, or even just take a case, help someone out—the stuff I do routine—you're a hero. You get your name in the newspaper, maybe collect a bonus. I do it"—he shrugged—"it's just part of the job."

"Somebody call the twenty-four-hour diner on Dutton. I think I'm asleep in a booth there. I'm dreaming this."

"Keep being funny."

"Okay, sometimes I get kudos—not that often, but sometimes. But I'm also the one who gets my ass kicked. I'm here at this ridiculous hour on my own time, not on the clock, and I can't get an answer that's any straighter than what you're handing me? Forget funny. Now, what's this really about?"

"I ask the questions. You answer them to my satisfaction, you can call your little sweetie and tell her to fluff up the pillows. You can't fluff up a jail pillow."

"No," I mumbled, "they're as thin as your honor. Ask your questions."

Cote stood and walked around to the chair across from mine, his manner tougher now, as though he was determined to try another approach. The room was like rooms of its kind everywhere: as drab as a crow bar, nothing on the walls but paint. No clock. Time didn't matter in rooms like this. I couldn't tell if there was recording equipment in operation or not; I assumed there was. Cote said, "What were you doing out at the fairgrounds earlier tonight?"

"You seem to have the questions and the answers."

"I can turn this into a bust if I have to. Try again."

"This is beneath even you, Cote."

He moved a shoulder. Words didn't have much zing after midnight; we were jousting with rubber lances. There was a sound of footsteps moving in a quick march down the corridor. Frank Droney came in and shut the door. He had his shield on a flap on his sport coat pocket. I sat up straighter and glanced at Cote. He showed nothing.

Droney leaned against the door, arms crossed in an attitude that gave an impression of casualness, but it didn't fool me. I'd worked for him. Casual wasn't part of his makeup. Strip the muscle and hard fat off him and you'd find rebar and steel cables, with only just a tincture of rust on them. The system's failure was in elevating men like him to positions of authority; its wisdom was in not allowing them to get all the way to the top. He nodded for Cote to resume.

"What do you know about a trailer being burned at Regatta Field the night before last?"

"Only what I saw in the newspaper."

"You've been seen out there often lately. Why is that?"

"I'm working for the carnival owner," I said.

"Were you in any way responsible for acts of vandalism or criminal trespass there?"

"What would be the point?"

"To put us off the scent."

"That's me for you. Always trying to flummox the law."

Droney pushed away from the door. "Cut the crap."

"You cut it. You think I'd poison my own well?" I was angry now, fresh out of fun. "What's with the Hoover routine? I came in willingly. And how come I can't move without Duross stepping on my heels?"

Droney took a stride toward me. "I got it, Frank," Cote said, moving between us. When Droney moved back, Cote said, "Things are getting crazy around the city. We had several people beat up last night, and someone tossed a brick through a window at the cable TV station with a hate note attached."

"So now I'm responsible for the actions of other citizens of this town?" I flicked a glance at Droney. "Or are you looking to pin that on me?"

"Who says it was citizens? Maybe it was your carnival friends doing it." I sat back, awed by their logic.

"Did you discharge a weapon at the fairgrounds tonight?"

Was that what this was about? Was I being set up for something? Guardedly, I said I had.

"Is this the weapon?"

"Yes. It's the only one I own." A white lie; I wasn't about to cop to the sawed-off 12-gauge sitting on a ceiling joist in the cellar of my new house. "I shot it into the ground. There's empty brass in one chamber."

Cote drew the .38 partway from the holster and looked at it, maybe recalling a day when the Special had been the sidearm we'd all packed, or maybe we'd ramped up to a .357. No more; it was all semiautomatics now, which in my book missed the point. Some people preached the wisdom of carrying semiautos for the increased firepower and ammo load, but it also meant more working parts to jam in a tight situation. Besides, if you couldn't take someone down with six shots, it was probably too big a problem anyhow. "Why?" he asked.

"To make an impression." I told them the story.

"A torch? That's a pretty boneheaded move."

"I never said it was brilliant, but it was the best I could think of at the time. It seemed to work."

Droney reached and took the holstered weapon from Cote. "I'm tag-ging this and hanging on to it for now. Evidence. Discharging a firearm within city limits is a crime."

"So level a charge," I said.

When he got mad, Droney's heavy jaw grew lumpy, like a man with the mumps. "I may goddamned well do that."

"Hold on," I said, more reasonably. "I know the law, but I had to calculate the odds and take a risk. That friendly little band of citizens had already talked themselves into going out there in the first place, and they were hassling a young woman and an old man. I don't believe it would've ended there."

"It's against the law to fire a gun," Droney said doggedly.

"Sure," I mumbled, "unless it's an officer shooting an unarmed suspect running from an order to halt." As soon as I said it I felt the air in the room go frigid, but there was no taking the words back. And suddenly I didn't care. I was feeling the lateness of the hour, the fact that I hadn't slept in a long time, that my woman had dumped me, and that the lawyer who had hired me had quit. I was sick of being pushed around. "If you knew all this and you just got me in here to dance me around, bring a charge!"

Droney stepped forward, his sport coat flapping open. I caught a glint from the little tie bar clamped to his necktie: a pair of miniature gold handcuffs. There was nothing else cute about him. His eyes were electric with anger. A vein throbbed in his throat. His pointed finger was six inches from my face. "Fuck with me, mister," he said from a throat full of gravel, "I'll have so many cops on your ass you'll think you're leading a parade. I can tank you for interfering in a police investigation, for obstructing justice, withholding evidence. Firing a weapon, trespassing at a crime scene. I can jack you up for crossing the street, for zipping your fly!"

Cote looked at the floor; I think even he felt embarrassed by the outburst. But I couldn't shake the sudden question of how much they knew. Did they know, for instance, that I'd been inside Flora Nuñez's apartment? I was pretty sure I'd heard a cop come in there that night, was pretty sure I knew who, too. Did they know that I'd removed potential evidence? Sweat crawled under the sleeves of my shirt. Just then, a civilian employee stuck her head in, glanced around at the thick silence, then told Droney he had a phone call and ducked back out. Giving me a long, slow glare, Droney yanked his coat shut, buttoned it, and left. My head felt as if it had been released from a bench vise.

"There isn't much time," Cote said. "He'll be back. Level with me and I may be able to help you. Don't and he's going to bust you."

"Okay, he can mess with me," I said more measuredly. "None of it would stand up, but it would be a bigger hassle for me than for him. Yet he hasn't done it, so what is it you guys really want? For God's sake, we're working for the same end."

"You're just dragging things out. As long as that's going on, the case is news and things are staying stirred up."

"You overestimate my power in this."

He stepped back, shaking his head. He was growing impatient. "Pepper did her. It's simple. It's not the first time some dumb shit lost his head over a twitch, and it damn sure won't be the last. But maybe we can make people think twice. Gus Deemys is ready to trample him. Don't be in the way of that."

I didn't know if I could credit Droney with anything more than cynicism, but Cote, I realized, believed his spiel. His normal shift ran nine to five, yet here he was, long after, still plugging, as eager as I'd ever seen him. The case was getting press, and that's what Gus Deemys liked. Maybe things were exactly as Cote was presenting them. Was he right? All at once I was too tired to offer an alternate take; I had just enough energy to try one bluff. "Do I still get a phone call, or have you suspended all my rights under the Patriot Act?"

Cote sighed, and I realized he didn't have anything.

There was a rap at the door and I half-expected Droney to reappear, but it was Ed St. Onge. He looked as if he had been called out of bed. He glanced at me with bloodshot eyes, then at Cote. "Did you gooseneck him yet?"

"Cut it out, Ed."

"How about a fucking rubber hose?"

"We're just talking. Hey, Rasmussen, were we just talking?"

St. Onge shook his head disgustedly.

He walked me upstairs and along a corridor with framed portraits of police superintendents past and of the city officers who'd died in the line of duty. In his rumpled tweeds, he might have been heading for a weekend of partridge hunting at Lord Thrippleton's country estate. I didn't comment, though; I'd have welcomed him if he'd been in jodhpurs and a green sombrero. In his office he said, "Sit down."

"So people keep telling me. It's wearing thin."

"Sit down and quit being an asshole. And not one word about the crumby disposition! This time of night my filters are shut off." He went over, lifted a coffeepot off the warmer, and sniffed at what looked like brown paint in it. "Cup?"

"It'd keep me awake."

"That's why I need it."

"Yeah, well, I didn't just roll out of a cozy bed."

He spun, coffee sloshing in the pot he held. "You could've rolled into a cozy cell." He flung his free hand at the door. "Those guys are jumpy as hell, and I understand why. Things are starting to quake. There was graffiti on the steps of city hall this morning. 'Fry Pepper!' You like that? And some hapless longhair got stomped because a group of citizens thought he was a carny. Turns out he was a college student who'd thumbed down from Montreal to see Kerouac's hometown. We gave him bus fare back, but it's not exactly a PR coup for the city."

I'd had my nose too close to the ground lately to see the bigger picture, but I was getting it now. Shaken, I sank into the offered chair. "How'd you know I was here?"

"Got a phone call at home. Officer Loftis heard the dispatch call to pick you up. She took a chance I'd want to know."

That was a welcome surprise. "I appreciate it."

He poured himself a mug of coffee, black with a Sweet 'n Low. His MO hadn't changed a lot over the years, nor had his lair. The framed Sierra Club poster still hung facing the navy gray desk, though I doubted the choice had anything to do with his liking the tranquility of the wildflower meadow, its contrast to his world here in the criminal bureau. Most likely it was just there, like the tall cabinets of expired files on cases, where victim and perp (and probably arresting officer, convicting DA, defending attorney, deciding jury, and sentencing judge, for that matter) had gone as belly up as the flies in the overhead globes that cast their glare on the room. When Randy Nguyen had been a police intern, he'd put a lot of material into electronic databases, but bureaucracies hated to part with paper as much as Elizabeth Taylor did with the idea of marriage. Love has many forms. St. Onge parked a haunch on the corner of the desk and scratched at his mustache. "So tell me why you think Droney wants to screw you into the ground."

"Walk me out to my car," I said.

He glanced around. "What, you don't like your old home turf?"

"I'm a little short on nostalgia tonight."

My car was in front, and we got in. I opened my mouth to speak, but he stilled me and nodded across the square to where several cars were parked. "What?" I asked.

"Maybe nothing."

Or maybe watchdogs. I caught on. I thought I could make out the dark shapes of people inside one of the cars. "Hold your story for a bit," he said. "Let's find out."

39

Traffic was light at that hour, and easy flowing. At Ed St. Onge's instruction, I went down Arcand toward the central post office and Tsongas Arena and turned right onto French. No vehicle seemed to be particularly interested in us, but I cruised for another block or two. "Anyplace special," I asked, "or are you a 'journey, not the destination' type of guy?"

He navigated and we crossed the river, which lay wide and silent, illuminated with the reflected lights of the city. None of the cars lingering in City Hall Square had trailed us, which, St. Onge guessed, meant that they were protestors keeping vigil. On the west side of Christian Hill we parked and hoofed down an alley between nondescript yellow brick buildings. The only indication that they were anything but tenements was the industrial fan vent on one, exhaling a boozy smoke into the branches of an ailanthus tree. At the metal-sheathed door, a beefy guy in a black T-shirt that read THE KILLING HAND in blood red across his chest rose from a stool where he'd been reading a comic book, recognized St. Onge, and nodded us in. About a dozen people were sitting at tables around the edges of a room the size of my kitchen. At the center was a billiard table, with enough space for someone to make most shots without rapping your face with the butt end of the cue. A few of the patrons were familiar from around town, movers and shakers of one sort or another. I dug the irony. The narcotics squad was out busting kids for smoking pot, and here were city grandees, sopping up after-hours hooch, but that'd have to be someone else's cause; my plate was full. The rosy-nosed leprechaun behind the bar knew St. Onge. "What'll it be, lads?"

"Wild Turkey," I told him. "Got the one-oh-one?"

"Just eighty."

I nodded.

"Cola," Ed said. "Lots of ice."

"Cola?" I said when we'd seated ourselves in a corner.

"This arthritis stuff I've been on. Some kind of steroid. Alcohol is no go." He grunted. "Believe me, I wrestle, but Leona says she doesn't want to retire with some old stiff-leg."

"How many women make *that* complaint?"

The air was thick with cigarette smoke. Since legally the place didn't exist, neither did no-smoking laws. St. Onge hauled a deck of Camel lights from his coat pocket. He had quit for a while. I watched him tap one out, snap the filter off, and light up. "Why not just buy the plain old-fashioned cancer sticks?" I asked.

"Elementary. With a filter, you lose taste and potency, right?" He picked a speck of tobacco from the tip of his tongue. "I figure the companies spike up the nicotine in these brands even higher, so they'll keep selling. Break off the filter, you've got a nice strong smoke, the way nature intended."

"How did I miss that?"

He took a sip of cola. "One's about all of these I can handle. You going to get to it, or do I have to beg?"

Over the click of pool balls and the clunk of an occasional ball falling into a pocket, I laid out for him what I'd been spinning on my mental wheel, the fabric of vague suspicions about a conspiracy of silence. He was impatient before I got the third sentence out, but to his credit he listened all the way through, though from the way he crunched the ice from his cup, I could tell he wasn't happy. "That's it?" he said when I'd finished.

"What'd you expect? *The Big Sleep*?" I had to admit, at this hour it sounded pretty thin.

"A cop," he said simply. "That the theme?"

"Or cops."

"I'm still listening for all the proof—the eyewitness accounts and the smoking guns. That coming next? I can't believe you're feeding me this. Your story's got holes Brady could throw a football through blindfolded."

"What chance have I had to plug them? I can't move without cops getting in my face, Duross leading the charge."

"It's a reaction to frustration. Coping is easier if you've got a donkey to pin the tail on. But what do you expect? You're gunning for them."

"You're wrong. I haven't said this to anyone else but you."

"Your actions speak. The TV editorials keep spading up rumors, till the city is a tinderbox. The department's got a suspect in custody. They've been satisfied from the start, yet you give statements to the newspaper, show up at the crime scene trying to second-guess the professionals. It's a reasonable view that you keeping pushing the furniture around to keep your meter running."

"I haven't been on the clock since Meecham left the case."

"Okay, I hear that. Sounds like a loser all around, but that's your business. Now what's this about you firing a gun?"

I told him the story briefly. He shook his head. "So what are you, heading up the 'equal rights for circus tramps' movement?"

"I'm not joining the ACLU," I shot back. "I'm as mindful of vengeance as the next person, but we need to keep the justice system wobbling along until it comes up for overhaul. If we all leaned right when the thing went around a sudden curve, like some dimwits in this country want, it'd tip over and the wheels'd come off. And, for the record, I'm a professional, too."

He grunted but made no comment. I think that meant I'd made a point. Even so, I had to wonder how long it would be before Troy Pepper's remaining support vaporized. There wasn't much left. I said, "And I know that Duross is Frank Droney's nephew."

"You didn't hear that from him."

I agreed but didn't bring up Grady Stinson's name.

"He isn't using Droney's help. The kid is working hard to make detective, and he's determined to do it on his own merits."

"Yeah, I'm sure he's a bright pip of a lad. But back to the point. I've got a feeling about this one."

"Spare me."

I leaned nearer. "What happened to hunches, horse sense? Gut feelings?"

He frowned. "What happened to carburetors, spittoons, and typewriters?"

"I still have two of the above."

He forked smoke from his nostrils. "These days it's all probability theory and statistical analysis. You know that. DNA nails bad guys, not ESP. But suppose—I'm not making this a blanket endorsement—but in this particular case, suppose you're right. Suppose Pepper didn't kill the girl, and someone else did."

"Make it a cop," I said.

His face looked gray. Maybe it was the palls of smoke in the air, but he obviously didn't care for what I was saying. "All right. What's that have to do with the whole department? Because that's who you're going to be throwing dirt all over if you're not careful."

"Probably nothing, but it gives someone discretionary power over how other cops are going to react to the crime, what paper gets filed, what happens with evidence. If the victim was killed someplace else, a cruiser might even have been used to transport the body over to where it was found."

"Then how did her car get there?"

"I'm not sure of that. Somebody would have to have driven it there and left it."

"And then there's the crime scene evidence. Was that planted? You see where this is going? Nowhere. Now you listen. If there's a grain of truth to this theory, we'll find out. But I can almost guarantee you you're wrong."

"How?"

"How what?"

"You said we'll find out. How's that happen?"

"Let internal affairs work on it and discover what went down."

"And what's going to bring them into the picture?"

"I guess I'll have to," he said without enthusiasm.

"They won't take more than a few months. And how likely is it IA will push it that far? I've never been a big fan of one hand washing itself."

He butted his cigarette hard enough to make the big guy at the door look up from his comic. "You're wrong," St. Onge said in a warning growl. "Most cops are straight and law-abiding."

"Oh, come on, Ed."

"Come on yourself."

"I'm trying to spare you making a sappy speech. I never said all cops were bad. We agree in principle, okay? I'm still talking cases here, and in this case the uncovering will take time—all right, not as long as the Big Dig, but there are people to find, subpoenas, testimony to gather, witnesses to track down. You'll be eating cake at your retirement bash at the Club Passe-Temps before then, all your cronies cracking wise with Viagra jokes."

"I just don't want to see you end up in trouble, or. . . ." He broke off.

"Or what?"

"Worse."

"Flying the marble kite?"

"It's no joke," he said glumly. "You go after cops, you're crossing a line."

I kept quiet a moment. "It would get ugly," I admitted.

"Not really. No. This won't be the Hatfields and the McCoys, some long, bitter war of attrition. There's just you."

"And a lot of honest law, you said it yourself. Loftis seems okay."

"There's just *you*. For Christ's sake, cops don't have to be bent, or against you, to stand with other cops. It'll be just you and that popgun of yours. Where is it, by the way?"

"Droney drew my fangs."

"You'll go down hard, and that'll be that. The department will spin it any way it cares to—disgruntled ex-badge, probably. Resisting arrest. The TV and papers will buy it, dredge up old news clips, and that'll be your legacy."

"No 'Amazing Grace' on the bagpipes?"

"Fuck you. There'll be a short line of mourners, and snow on your grave by Christmas."

At a sharp *crack* I jumped. On the pool table, a break shot sent balls scattering. None clunked into pockets. The shooter caught my glance, shrugged, and grinned. In an odd way, I felt a sense of refuge being there. We were all in this together, safe from the bigger, more menacing world outside, transgressors with a mutual acceptance of each other's sins. To us.

I drank off my glass and asked St. Onge if he wanted another cola.

"Definitely no. Let's get out of here."

The cars were gone from the square when we got back to JFK Plaza, and along with them, I supposed, the imminent threat of civil disorder. As St. Onge got out, I told him to hold off speaking with internal affairs. I asked him if he'd look into getting my weapon back, and he said he would. "And, Raz, go home. Don't do anything stupid." It had a sound of finality, so I only nodded. "I'll call you first thing I hear," he said.

It didn't ring any tinnier than most of the other promises people made.

I did go home. I remembered the groceries in my trunk and brought them in and put things away. I locked the door and drew the shades. The phone message light was blinking. Someone named Frank from Walt's Getty had called seven hours ago. It was probably nothing, he said, but guessed that I could decide if I wanted to come by and speak with him. He was getting ready to close up, but he generally got there early, he said. I glanced at my watch: 3:57 A.M. I doubted he meant that early.

I was too wired to sleep. I should clean my gun, having fired it, but then I remembered it was downtown. So I found myself standing there in that cocktails-to-the-dregs, butts-in-the-ashtray time that Sinatra had put his mood indigo on, when even the musicians had packed up and split and there was nothing to do but brood. I took off my coat, and when I went to hang it in a closet, I saw clothes on the floor. Amid the chaos I'd been living in, nothing had jumped out at me, but it did now. Pockets hung out of slacks, jackets were turned inside out, having been gone through. My ties lay entangled like a nest of snakes. The cartons stacked in the living room were askew, the sealing tape torn open. I put on more lights. I went back to the kitchen and realized that the plastic sheeting over the broken window had been pried away and then reattached, but not securely. It flapped in the night wind.

My pulse throbbing, I tried to read method into the situation. Vandalism? A search? A threat?

I had no sense of what, if anything, might be missing. The intruder had been in a hurry. I had the thought to call St. Onge, but what was he going to do? Suppose it had been a cop? One name sprang to mind, but St. Onge had made his point: Cops would stand with cops.

After double-checking all the door and window locks, and stapling an extra sheet of plastic over the broken kitchen window, to keep out the wind if nothing else, I went into the living room and sat. I let the questions pile up.

Who had been here tonight in my absence? Who had violated my space? The police? Rag Tyme? The band of cowards I'd run off from the carnival site earlier? Someone from the carnival itself? The real killer—if that wasn't Troy Pepper? It could have been any one of a lot of people; God knows I'd made enemies enough over the years. And what had the invader been looking for? Evidence he believed I might have? Because I was getting close to discovering something? Maybe Jessica Fletcher, my sharp-eyed neighbor, had seen something; but I'd have to ask her tomorrow.

So what did I do now?

When you were under threat, you could sit and wait for it to come to you, to make itself known, and just hope that you saw it when it did. Or you could act first. In motion you became a moving target, but you had a chance. I went down to the basement. On top of a beam, swaddled in a towel amid the dust and cobwebs, was the antique sawed-off shotgun that I'd acquired when an old pizza maker named Vito had found it and laid it off on me. I'd had it cleaned up with a cockeyed notion to sell it, but I hadn't gotten around to that yet. And all at once, I was glad. Carrying the bundled weapon like a babe in arms, I brought it upstairs to the living room.

I found a box of cartridges left over from the one time I'd used the old 12-gauge. I loaded two and set the sawed-off on the floor beside the couch. I shoveled a handful of extra shells into the drawer of the end table. I looked around. What else needed to be done? The unpacked cartons gave me a thought. I opened one that stood in a closet and flipped through my collection of LPs until I found what I was after. I slid the disk from the sleeve, holding it between my spread hands, and blew across the surface—vestigial moves from an earlier day—set it on the turntable and activated the tone arm. I turned out lights except for a lamp in one corner and the ones outside. Without getting undressed, I stretched out on the couch to listen to the Moses Maxwell Quintet, thinking that maybe a barrelhouse blues would energize me, but the first cut was a moody number, faintly familiar as I listened, trying to put a name to it, but in the musicians' unique telling, and with my weary brain, I couldn't quite . . .

The telephone's ringing woke me, and I saw that the darkness beyond the windows was paling. I scrubbed at my face and sat up. I squinted at my watch. I'd been out for almost two hours. I picked up the phone.

"Mr. Rasmussen?"

The voice was low, familiar, but I was groggy. "Right here."

"This is Moses Maxwell."

" 'In My Solitude,' " I blurted. The song title had popped into my head.

"Say what?"

"What you were playing." I used the silence to knuckle cobwebs from my eyes. For a little while I had forgotten the world, but it all came back now. The police hustle at headquarters, the sawed-off shotgun next to the couch, the lingering presence of an invader in my space.

"Are you straight?" Maxwell asked.

"More than you want to know."

"Is Nicole with you?"

"Now?" I shook off the last of my weariness. "What's going on?"

A heavy sigh. "She got a phone call a couple hours ago. She didn't say who it was, and I didn't ask. I always give her a little leeway, 'cause with Nicole, you crowd her, she sometimes takes it wrong and gets emotional. Anyway, she left the hotel on kind of a tear. I thought she might be looking for you."

"Did you call the kennel? Maybe she went to visit the dogs."

"Tried it. The carnival, too—I'm here now. Nothing."

"How is Pop handling this?"

"He's still sleeping, so he doesn't know yet. I'm not eager to tell him."

I thought a moment, then told him to sit tight and I'd get back to him. I checked my service, thinking Nicole might have called while I was conked, but there was only the earlier message from Walt's Getty.

40

I'd have seen dawn through the east-facing kitchen window if it weren't sheathed with several layers of cloudy plastic. The only reason my stomach didn't feel empty was that the sidewalls were touching each other. Coffee was going to take too long to brew. I poured a glass of chilled tomato juice, tasted it, then fetched a bottle and tipped some whiskey into the juice. A "Hail Mary," they used to call it at the station house: tomato juice and anything you had handy. It went down smooth and warm as a zephyr. I wrapped the shotgun back in its towel and took it back down to the cellar. In my present state I was more likely to get caught with it than use it. As I unlocked my car, the corn moon was fading into the first pink glow of day, as pale as a ball of melting ice. Phoebe and I had missed it.

At the carnival site there were people up and about. They had unhooked the trailers from several of the tractors, which were running, the diesels burbling throatily in the cool air. I went to Pop's camper, tapped on the little porthole window, and went in. He was awake now, sunk in the chair, looking disheveled. No sign of Nicole. Moses said, "I had to tell him."

"What're you doing here?" Pop rasped. "Thought you were quits."

"What's going on out there?" I asked.

"Some of the crew found out about Nicole, too," said Moses. "It's the last straw for them. It's personal now. They figure to go into town for a confrontation."

"When?"

"I'm not sure."

"I tried to talk sense to 'em," Pop said. "I ain't got the energy to fight it."

"And there's this, too." Maxwell handed over the morning's *Herald*. "Page ten, I think."

It was page ten, but it wasn't a report about my discharging my weapon, or being rousted last night, or someone burglarizing my place; hardly big city news. Young Scoop Piazza had filed his story, which appeared under the headline "Sleuth at Odds With Cops in Carny Slay."

Great, that would stoke the fires. But my biggest concern at the moment was for Nicole. I put the paper aside. I motioned to Maxwell, and he and I walked outside together. The sun was fully up now, Friday morning traffic beginning to stream along both sides of the river, which reflected pink cotton-candy clouds. I said, "Can you talk to Pop again? Get him to delay signing the show over to Rag Tyme?"

"I don't know as I've got any bite. Seems like common sense doesn't matter no more. I tried it with them and got nowhere." He nodded at the dozen or so carnies gathered around the trucks.

"Tell you what—if you work on Pop, I'll give them a try."

He plucked at his little soul patch. "All right, let's give it a go."

Which I did, starting with my firsthand knowledge that the cops weren't in a jolly mood and that a clash with the locals wouldn't do Pop or any of them any good. It might result in jail or the hospital—*or even,* I thought but didn't say, *the morgue.* "If someone has taken Nicole, I'm going to try to get her back safely. But touching off a war isn't going to help her. It might put her deeper in hurt."

"Why?" Tito Alvarez said. "You know who's took her?"

"I can't say just yet, but I've got some ideas. It'd be a help if you could give me a few hours."

Alvarez and Red Fogarty exchanged a look, and Fogarty signed something to him. "Okay, man," Alvarez said, "we'll give it till three o'clock. After that, shit, if Nicole ain't here, I don't think we gonna be able to hold anyone back."

"And maybe we won't want to," I said.

Fogarty signed something else with his big, quick-moving hands. I looked at Alvarez for a translation, and he mustered a grin. "He says you said 'we.'"

I didn't have a lawyer's coattails to go in under, so I just gave my name to the woman who answered the phone at the courthouse. There was a delay, and the longer it went on, the less I believed it likely that I'd get to speak with the judge. Then a calm voice came on the line. "Yes, Mr. Rasmussen, this is Martin Travani. How can I help you?"

I explained that I wanted to speak with him and would have gone through proper channels, but Fred Meecham had left the case. "Yes, I know," he said. "Mr. Meecham informed me of his decision last evening. As for the rest, I'm pretty busy here today. You say this is important?"

"Yes, Your Honor."

"All right. Then perhaps sooner is better than later." He mentioned the name of a gentleman's club downtown and said that he was going to be there for a lunch meeting at noon. "Could we get together beforehand? Say eleven-thirty?"

I told him I'd be there. "And Mr. Rasmussen—it probably goes without saying"—he gave a small, apologetic-sounding laugh—"but the River Club requires a jacket and tie."

So what did I know? A key question still had to do with Paul Duross. And what about the other officers Danielle Frampton had said sometimes stopped by Viva! off duty? Were there links there? I couldn't very well go ask anyone at police headquarters. Or could I?

I called there and asked for Jill Loftis. All calls were recorded, so when she came on the line, I said, "Are you going to be away from your desk anytime soon?"

"What do—" She got it. "I have to go down to the motor pool to see if I left my gym bag in a cruiser. Figure I'll do that now, before I forget."

She was standing by the entrance to the motor pool garage when I arrived. "Thank you for calling Ed St. Onge last night," I said. "I appreciate it."

"It seemed to be in order."

Her gaze remained inquisitive, so I cut to the chase. "Do you think it's possible that a police officer, or officers, could be involved with the Flora Nuñez murder? Paul Duross, for instance?"

"You're still chewing on that?" She sent a quick look around, perhaps warning me that there were other people nearby. In a quiet voice, she asked, "Involved how?"

"I'm not sure. Covering up, possibly; suppressing evidence. Last night someone broke into my house when I wasn't there. They might've been looking for evidence they think I have."

She glanced around again. From inside the motor pool came the whir of a lug-nut drill. "You better be careful with this," she said. "People are already angry with you. Duross thinks you're harassing him."

"Or maybe he's nervous because I'm getting close to finding him out."

"What does that mean?"

"We'll have to see."

"Do you have evidence?"

I hesitated. "No. I have to admit that so far, everything is circumstantial."

She didn't look happy with any of this. I debated telling her that I was going to Judge Travani with my suspicions, but it would put her in the awkward position of having advance knowledge. She'd already stuck her neck out for me a lot farther than I had any right to expect. She turned toward police headquarters and stopped. "I can't help you. I'm sorry. All I can say is be damned careful where you go with this."

I said I would. "Do one more thing for me? And then I promise not to bug you again."

"What is it?"

"This conversation never happened."

She looked relieved. She even managed a faint smile. "Are you kidding?"

41

These days when someone invited you to a gentleman's club you weren't
sure whether you were going to sit in a paneled library full of old jaspers
rattling the pages of the *Financial Times* or have your porterhouse served
with a naked lap dancer on the side. The River Club was decidedly of the
former variety, occupying a three-story Georgian brick townhouse along
the Middlesex canal, with a lantern-lit entrance and granite hitching posts
in front, though all the horses were corralled under the hoods of Cadil-
lacs and Benzes in a side lot. I went through the coffered door into a
foyer lit with original long-stemmed gas sconces refitted with electric, the
light picking up the gleam of elegant old wood in the floor and wain-
scoting. A blond man wearing black slacks and a white shirt stood at a
greeter's podium. The nameplate pinned to his maroon-and-burnished-
gold brocade vest identified him as Duncan. He wasn't even born when
the damask silk wall coverings had been hung, but nevertheless he had the
snooty, inquisitional glance down pat. "May I help you, sir?"

I gave him my name. "I'm here to see Judge Travani."

He continued his appraisal of me a moment before he sniffed and
said, "If you'll wait here, please."

I had a feeling this would be a onetime visit for me, so I took in the sights. Beyond the foyer was a high-ceilinged room with a branching brass and crystal chandelier. To the left, a curved staircase rose to what was evidently a dining room. I could hear the low mutter of conversations over the muted clink of cutlery and smell the lavish aromas of gourmet cooking. On the wall to my right, big bwanas and grand poobahs of decades past gazed from gilt-framed portraits, including a younger Martin Travani, looking as dignified as a man wearing a sequined fez can. At least there weren't any stuffed caribou dangling their beards into the room.

Duncan returned. "If you could walk this way," he said unctuously.

The high-ceilinged room actually was a library, and there actually were people reading newspapers. It appeared as if someone had cleared out half the state forest for the wood paneling. Martin Travani rose from a reading table and extended his hand, which was soft, though he gripped mine as if it were a gavel. Lines formed in his broad forehead, and his eyes behind the steel frames of his glasses were inquisitive. I guessed my outfit passed muster, as he didn't say anything to the contrary. Duncan faded.

"Thank you for seeing me, Your Honor."

"I'd have suggested you come to the courthouse, but there's so little time there, and far too many distractions. I'm expecting lunch guests shortly, but I thought we could talk first."

I said the time was generous and I appreciated his making it for me. He buttoned his suit coat and gestured through a doorway on the right. "We can converse in here."

It was a smaller chamber, what once would've been called a drawing room. Underfoot was a deep blue carpet flecked with yellow and orange, as if someone had sprinkled it with gold dust and rusted iron filings. We took a pair of antique-looking wing chairs in a corner near a mullioned window that looked out upon the canal. At the judge's invitation I began to lay out my ideas. He listened with an expression that went slowly from concentration to concern, his small, even teeth nibbling at his lower lip. When I finished, he raised his eyebrows. "That's quite some assertion."

"I'd have spoken with Attorney Meecham first, but that wasn't an option."

"Do you know which police officers might be involved?"

I hesitated. "A patrolman named Duross, for one. Others, I'm not sure."

"Have you actual proof of any of this?"

"Not exactly, no, sir."

"Documentation?"

"No. But there are indications."

"I see." He turned his head to the window and sat silent for a time, his brow creased with thought, and I felt I'd done the right thing in coming to him. I was reassured by his wisdom and experience. Even his suit and the crisp white shirt and elegant silk tie conveyed a reasoned competence. He turned back to me. "Do you remember how the planet Pluto was discovered?" he asked. "Back in the last century?"

I shifted forward in the antique chair. "Astronomers guessed at its existence first, wasn't that it?"

"Yes, Percival Lowell, as a matter of fact. Before there were telescopes big enough to actually see it, he posited its existence from the movement of other objects. That seems to be what you're attempting to do here, isn't it?"

"I'm not sure I—"

"You've developed this theory of police involvement in a crime, and a possible cover-up, based on other things you perceive going on."

My shirt collar felt tight. I shifted again; the chair was as comfortable as a rock pile. "I think the indications call for a closer look."

"And how do you propose to do that?"

"Well, I haven't any jurisdiction. It's why I've come to you, Your Honor."

Travani curled a speculative finger under his lower lip. It was warm in the room, as if the overnight cold had activated the building's thermostat, set at a temperature sensitive to the creaky bones and gummy blood-flow of people for whom winter meant Palm Beach. If this and this chair were what the club-dues bought, I wasn't sorry not to be a member. "So you want me to be the big telescope," he said.

I cleared my throat softly. "I'm hoping that you'll know what to do next."

Duncan came in, escorting a prosperous-looking older couple. Judge Travani glanced at his watch and rose; I got up, too. "Vera," said the judge.

"Kostas." The woman kissed the air an inch from Travani's cheek. Kostas shook hands with him and gave me a faint glance. No introductions were made. Ignoring me altogether, Vera attempted a smile at the judge. Her face had been lifted too high, too often, so the effect was ghastly. "I've got a table—go right on up," said Travani. "Duncan will show you. I'll join you in a moment."

When they'd gone, Travani didn't resume his seat. "Mr. Rasmussen, I thank you for coming. Now, I really must go."

"I understand. Do you want to think about what we've just—"

"Oh, I've heard plenty," he interrupted. "You should hear yourself. Do you know how this sounds?"

"It's speculative, I know, but I think it warrants attention."

"You do, do you?"

"Judge—with due respect—you implied it yourself. When the astronomers actually looked, Pluto was there."

"You're standing on shaky legs. Even if you could fill the gaps, unlikely as that seems, jurisprudence imposes a burden of proof, of evidence, corroborating testimony. Those are the foundation stones of our legal system."

"Your Honor, I know. All I'm asking—"

"Enough!" I was surprised at how suddenly the anger had come. "I see now what you're pulling, criticizing the police, the criminal justice system. Well, you're not going to get away with it. How dare you barge in here making demands! You may leave."

He turned to go, and my own anger rose. I stepped to block him. His eyes widened with shock, and perhaps a tincture of fear. "Save the lecture for the bench," I said, my face hot. "I'm no court. It's why I can be quick on my feet, why I trust gut feelings."

He measured me with a look that was now just outrage. "Well, I feel sorry for you, then. You're a throwback. In your small shabby world of guts and . . . instincts, you're a sneaky little animal that steals in toward the fire and snatches crumbs and then darts back to the shadows." He moved his lips back from the small, neat teeth, which I was suddenly sure were a dental plate, into a sneer. "But you never get to bask in the warmth. You don't know the security and community where decent people live, and where the rule of law protects them." He pointed his finger. "I know all about you. You were a sworn officer at one time."

If he knew that, he knew the rest.

"Judge—wait." I was trying to rein in my frustration, to get us both back to a rational place. I needed him. "What I'm trying to say is—"

He swung his hands in a scissoring motion. "You violated the public trust, yet you want me to listen to you? There are men and women in this city who put the welfare of the public above their own—even above personal safety, and yet you're ready to malign them. Ridicule the system that protects you. No, I was wrong. I don't know you. I don't understand you. I'm trying very hard not to feel utter contempt for you, sir. Now, just go, while you're free to."

The desk man came over. "Judge," he said, but he was looking closely at me. "Is there a problem?"

"No, Duncan, it's fine."

"Do you want me to—"

"Beat it," I said.

The man straightened, tugged at his brocade vest, then about-faced, his blond mop wisping, his heels clicking determinedly across the parquet.

"That was rude," the judge said.

"He's rude. Everyone in here seems to be. You'd find better manners in any dive bar on Middlesex Street. But I guess that's what you pay the heavy dues for," I said, "a place to come and be as rude as you please."

"He'll be back."

"With people who can handle problems. Dues must also cover the salary of a former marine commando or two."

"Just get out. You repulse me."

Before you could say floorwalker, Duncan was back, escorting a medium-height fellow with a firm jaw and a bristling gray haircut. He wasn't large, but he looked like he'd be as adept at handling nonmembers as Kid Sligo was at expelling rowdy drunks from the Silverado Lounge. He wouldn't be rude; he'd be rough. Still, I might be able to take him, but it would involve busting up some antiques, and it would also mean charges being brought, maybe a lawsuit, and publicity, and I already had more than I wanted. We all stood there in silence a moment, like a museum diorama display.

"I have pity for you, sir," the judge told me, smoothing his tie. "And I find your presentation wanting. Frankly, I find *you* wanting. There's nothing more to say. Gentlemen, please see Mr. Rasmussen to the door."

In my car, I hermetically sealed myself inside, AC on full, radio loud. I drove with one hand and used the other to wipe sweat from my brow, which was hot as a baked brick. After a few miles I turned the music off, then the AC, and opened the windows. I used my cell phone and called the courthouse.

"Hello, Ms. Ouellette's line," said a brisk female voice.

"Is Ms. Ouellette there?"

"No, she's not. She didn't come in today."

"She's a no-show?"

"What?"

"Thanks for your time."

The way the state patronage system operated, Carly Ouellette could be gone from her desk six months before anyone thought to dock her pay or wonder why. I found a parking spot on Tenth and climbed out and looked for the woman's little gold Mazda but didn't see it. I crossed the street and went into her apartment building and rang the buzzer for her unit. Apparently she was a no-show here as well. I located the button for the building superintendent and pressed it. After a time, a mop-haired party in a tartan robe and bare feet appeared, looking like I'd dug him out of bin Laden's cave.

"I was hoping to talk with Ms. Ouellette in apartment seven," I said.

He yawned. "What about?"

"A routine inquiry." My PI license got his attention, but the twenty I dangled was the tongue-loosener.

"I seen her going out late last night with suitcases," he offered, pushing at his frizz. "Vacation, I gather."

"Any idea where she was headed?"

"La-La Land for all I care. I asked her did she want a hand loading them into that little rice burner she drives, and she told *me* where to go."

His face darkened with suspicions. "Why? You know something I don't?"

I gave him the twenty. "Do you have a key to her unit?"

The place didn't appear to have much beyond the furniture, which the super said belonged there, and trash tied in vinyl bags. He could choose to imagine she was on vacation, but I was pretty sure she wouldn't be back. Nothing personal had been left behind, nor anything that couldn't be more easily bought anew someplace else. The clincher was the telephone. When I picked it up, the line was dead, as though service had been cut off. Crumpled beside the phone was a three-by-five card with a phone number on it. The number had been lined out, but I recognized it as the general business line for police headquarters. I smoothed the card and put it in my pocket.

"She ain't a bad-looking head, but she's got this pissy personality," the super extemporized when we were back in the lobby, "like everything is out to annoy her personally. I'll see her in the hall and say hello, and it's a crap shoot whether I'm gonna get a scowl or be ignored altogether."

"Did she socialize with any of the neighbors?"

"What am I, a dorm mother?" He frowned, maybe testing to see if there was more green to be had. I gave him a stare, and after a few seconds he wilted. "Not that I ever seen. There was one guy used to come around. Big sorta good-looking guy. He maybe got wise that he could do better. Though come to think of it, he probably had a wife. It's like donuts, ain't it?"

"Come again?"

"Women on the side comes with being a fuzz."

From my car I called Danielle Frampton. Her answering machine came on, the out-going message about as clear as a subway PA announcement. I gave my name and was starting my spiel when she picked up, sounding groggy and disconcerted, as if she'd been dragged from a deep hole of sleep. "Alex?"

"You need to tell me the rest of the story," I said. "About your friends in the Polaroid." The silence went on just a little longer than it should have if I was wrong, and I knew I'd struck something.

"I told you last night," she said, recovering. "I think it was last night. I'm too fogged in to remember."

"Well, clear the fog, girl. This may be the most important conversation you'll have all day."

"I don't know what you mean."

I was looking at the crinkled three-by-five card I'd taken from Carly Ouellette's apartment—though not at the number; rather, at the reverse side. Coincidence, maybe (the woman *did* work at the courthouse, after all), and yet it was a juror ballot card, like the one I'd found in Flora Nuñez's apartment. When I'd pressed the superintendent at Carly Ouellette's building for more on the cop who used to visit, he sure sounded like Paul Duross. "The quicker you talk, the sooner you'll get back to dreamland."

"I'm going to hang up now. Good-bye."

"I'll be knocking on your door in fifteen minutes."

I heard a prolonged, cheek-puffing sigh that just as easily could have been a raspberry. "Let me get dressed. Fifteen minutes, no sooner."

42

The address was off Mammoth Road, a complex called Raleigh Court, one of those serviceable modern hives where several hundred people lived in relative privacy, though you were still aware of the opening of a door, a soft sigh of plumbing, the yip of a small dog—things suggestive of invisible lives beyond your own, like ghosts in the walls. Danielle appeared in a sherbet orange Danskin top and loose-fitting white stretch pants, her natural hair several shades darker than platinum, though even with the stage makeup scrubbed off, no one would've taken her for a secretary in a loan office. There were still sleep lines in her face. She led me into a small living room that was wall-to-wall carpeted and furnished with little beyond a sectional couch in guacamole green velour and a TV no bigger than a drive-in theater screen. A few scattered toys and children's CDs reminded me her son must be of school age—which was where he was now, she told me. Second grade. She yawned. "You want coffee or anything?" I declined. "I'm exhausted. I've danced six nights in a row." She stretched her arms high and then sank onto one length of couch and waved at the other end, which was heaped with newspapers. "Put that stuff anywhere."

I picked up the papers, under which was a textbook called *Take*

Charge of Your Writing. I glanced at her. "Don't tell me you want to write screenplays, too?"

"Huh? Oh. That was for an evening class at the community college. I never finished. I liked going to school, but it got in the way of work."

"Or vice versa," I said. It was my mantra of late.

"Whatever. A degree is nice, I guess, but it's like, all these years as a continuing ed student, trained for a job where I can earn four hundred bucks a week? On a good *night* now, I can take home six. Do the math."

I didn't ask her to do the math of passing years and wear and tear on body and soul. People could say the same about my choice of racket. She drew her long legs up under her. The cotton stretch pants showed her dancer's body to fine effect. She yawned again and tipped her head and gave me a long soft-eyed look. "How come you never hit on me?"

"Say again?"

"You heard me." She straightened up on the couch. "For real, I mean."

"I never have?"

"Not even close. You aren't married, like most of the guys who come on are. You're not gay. Maybe I don't light up your dials."

"Oh, come on. You look great."

"Do you prefer older women?"

"Depends on what they're older than."

"I'm serious. How come? Is it my son?"

"Your son's a peach, and so are you. But let me answer with a question."

"Am I a virgin?"

"Who played drums for the Moses Maxwell Quintet?"

She held my gaze for a moment, as though she were actually grappling with the answer, then her eyes glazed slightly and narrowed. "That's a lowball. I don't have a clue who that is."

I shrugged.

"Okay, mister smart-ass. Name the original guitar player for Dripping Squid."

I didn't make even a pretense of thinking. "If I knew that, I'd ask you to elope with me."

She stuck out her tongue. "Shaun Sullivan, later replaced by Steve Anthony. Anyway, they broke up."

"Well, there you go. Danielle, what I really need answers to has to do with this photo that I showed you." I offered it again and she took it. "You said that Flora Nuñez and the others would come to the club. Did you know them outside of that?"

"Well . . . a few of them I knew from night school. Flora. Her." She pointed to Lucy Colón. "We took a class together."

"What about the men in the picture? They're cops, right?"

"I told you that. They'd usually come by late, when they got off duty. With them it was just first names. Bob, Tom."

"How about Paul?"

"Maybe. Yeah, I think so. But only once or twice."

"Paul Duross?"

"I never knew last names."

"Why Viva!?"

"Because it's open late? I don't know." She shrugged. "Though now that I think of it, the way it got started is one night after class, we were talking and the teacher said how would we like to come to a party. I'm like, it's kind of an unusual question from your teacher, but there were the three of us, so we figured, well . . . it couldn't hurt our grade any."

"So you went with him?"

"Her. The teacher was a woman. We went, and from there we ended up at the club. After that, it just sort of became the place. There was one thing Flora told me, about how she had to go to court—for a lot of parking tickets, I think. And someone worked out a deal."

"Say more."

"She said he took her into a room and spanked her."

"You mean like . . ." I made a paddling motion with my hand.

"Yeah, like that. But according to Flora he looked pretty excited afterward, like he'd gotten off on it."

"Who was it, do you know?"

"No, I don't. But I believe it was a cop who set it up."

"Why not tell me this last night?"

"I guess I didn't think of it. It happened a while ago. And I don't want to mess with the court system. I've been there."

"Did she ever say anything else about the incident? Mention a name?"

She frowned. "You're not going to tell anyone what I just told you?"

"Danielle, this may connect to an innocent man about to be tried for murder."

This didn't seem to make her very happy. "Well, I haven't seen any of them in months. Probably since when that picture was taken. I dropped out of school, like I told you. I don't see myself as a paralegal. The teacher flunked me." She smiled. "Must've taken it personally. Good old Carly."

I looked at her. "Carly *Ouellette?*"

"Uh-oh. You know her, too?"

I had some other questions, but she was running out of answers, and she didn't bother to cap the yawns. I told her to get some sleep. I wished *I* could.

I sat in my car, panning for meanings in what Danielle had told me: off-duty cops, a secret courthouse spanker, and Carly Ouellette. It didn't yield gold, but it added facets to what I already knew. I needed to get access to Judge Travani again, to force him to listen. I couldn't try anything tricky. He'd see right through it; every day of the week people came before his bench and tried to con him. No, my best angle was a direct full frontal, with an element of surprise if I could swing it. I called the River Club, ready with a scam if Duncan answered, but fortunately he didn't. I asked the woman if the judge was still there. He wasn't. I tried the courthouse line, being sure to give my name. After a several-minute wait, Travani came on the line. "Rasmussen," he said, "if you persist—"

"Just one question, Your Honor. Who spanks the judge when *he's* been a bad boy?"

It was the blind gambit of a desperate and tired mind, a shot in the dark. At his angry *"What?"* I knew it had missed and zinged off into the void. I tried to recover with something contrite—forget witty—but my mind was empty. Then, in a lowered voice, he said, "I've got a hearing to get to. Call me here in an hour."

I was wide awake now. I called Fred Meecham's office and Courtney answered, as I'd hoped she would. "Can you confirm something for me?"

"Hello to you, too. How are you feeling?"

"Never better."

"Okay, I get it. Confirm what?"

She called me back in ten minutes. "Yes," she said, "Carly Ouellette taught an intro to paralegal studies for two semesters, the last being this past spring term. The evening division of the college likes to get working professionals to teach their courses. And just an FYI—I called her number at the courthouse and she hasn't been there at all today."

"You get a gold star on your forehead, girl."

At 2:30 I redialed the number that had reached Martin Travani an hour before. A woman with a pinched-sounding voice answered and I asked for him.

"I'm sorry, the judge has gone for the day."

"Could you check on that? He was expecting my call."

"Sir, he's gone. He left some while ago."

I had a sudden queasy feeling. "Do you know where he went?"

"Sir, the judge did not say, and that was sufficient enough for me. I did not ask." She spoke with slow, exaggerated patience, as subtle as a band saw.

"Would you have a number where I could reach him?"

"Let me reiterate that again. The judge is not here. I don't know where he is or when he'll return. I don't have a number, and I certainly don't know what this is in regards to." She was on a roll now, making no effort to mask her annoyance. "I answered this line because it rang, but this is not my desk, and I've got various mixed emotions about saying anything more. So please completely, totally understand me—there is no one here."

I was exasperated, too. "Are you there?"

"Formerly, in the old days I used to be," she said officiously. "Presently, at this time, I'm strictly an independent consultant."

"Not for the economy of words, I hope," I managed before she hung up in my ear.

I was floundering now, half-certain that something odd was going on, yet unable to see what it might be. I felt like I was in the old *New Yorker* drawing of a man in the desert, buzzards circling overhead as he's about to expire from thirst, while over the next dune, invisible to him, is

Las Vegas. For no obvious reason, perhaps other than it was close by, I remembered the phone call from Walt's Getty. How many hours ago had that been? I headed for the intersection where I knew the gas station was located. As I parked across the street, a man stepped from the gloom into one of the open bays, where he stood framed by festoons of fan belts and exhaust pipes, a ragged little cap on his head, one eye squinted against the rise of smoke from a butt hanging from his lips. Gasoline Gothic. I went over. "Are you Walt?"

"It's Waleed, actually. He's the owner. He should be back in an hour or so."

"What about Frank?"

He sucked the last puff out of his cigarette, dropped it, and killed it with a work boot. "The wife worries that all the fumes from pumping gas will give me cancer. I'm Frank."

"Sorry I didn't get back to you sooner, Frank. I'm Alex Rasmussen."

"Oh, yeah." He straightened his cap. "I seen your name in the newspaper and looked you up in the book." He motioned me and I followed him back into the garage, to a corner workbench cluttered with tools and greasy auto parts. He threw a switch and a flyblown fluorescent tube blinked once, twice, and came wearily to life. "Don't know if it means anything," he said, "in fact, the wife said it doesn't and I shouldn't get involved, but, well . . . this gal in the paper who got killed?"

"Flora Nuñez?"

"Uh-huh. I seen her photo and I realized she'd been in here earlier for gas."

"When was that?"

He poked a finger at a Pennzoil calendar, at the box for Sunday past. It was the last day she'd been seen alive. "Around noon, must've been. Driving a little green car. She seemed lost, looking for how to get to Tyler Park, for an address on Georgia Ave. I said I didn't know about that, but Tyler Park was easy enough to get to. I didn't think no more about it, till I read in the paper and saw the picture, and even then I wasn't sure, but I went through the charge slips and she'd paid with a credit card, which is how I matched the name."

"Would you happen to recall the number on Georgia Avenue?"

"Can't say I do. I thought . . . maid. You know, going over to clean one of them big houses. One thing I saw, there was a nun's habit lying on the passenger seat—though she didn't look like no nun I ever knew. Anyways, I directed her. Later, after I seen the paper, I told the wife. She said I should let well enough alone, the police already arrested the fellow who killed her, and they know what they're doing. She said, 'You watch all those TV shows and all of sudden you think you're a detective? Let it be, Frank.' But I don't know, I feel a citizen's got a duty. I remembered your name from the paper."

"Thank you," I said. "It may be important. When she asked about the address, did she say who she was looking for?"

"No name. I told her that's a pretty chi-chi neighborhood, there were probably a few living over there."

"A few?"

"Did I mention that? She said the guy was a judge."

43

Tyler Park was a lot farther from the Lower Highlands than the actual mile or so distance might suggest, so the gas station man's surprise at Flora Nuñez's interest in the neighborhood would have been real enough. This was old-moneyed Lowell, and if not as grand as Belmont Avenue in the lofty heights of Belvedere, it nevertheless could stand proud among the districts of the city. Martin Travani's home was a stately Tudor, one street back from the wooded park that gave the area its name. The grounds were neatly landscaped, the lawn beneath several ornamental fruit trees confettied with small bright leaves. I rang the bell.

As I waited, I stepped back from the brick stoop, still uncertain of what I would say if Travani opened the door. But he didn't, even after a second ring and a knock. No one did.

I wandered around to the side, where a stone path led between the house and a detached garage. I peered through one of the panes in the nearer of the two garage doors. A sea-foam green Continental was parked inside. Farther in was a second vehicle, partly concealed by the Lincoln, but I could see that it was gold, with a black vinyl bra on the front.

At a side entrance to the house I rapped on the storm door. The gold car, I realized, was Carly Ouellette's Mazda, last seen leaving her apartment by the building superintendent sometime last evening. Across the backyard, several young landscapers were mowing a neighbor's lawn, as they would need to do several more times before the killing frost. I thought of my own handkerchief-sized lawn. I knocked again.

Shortly after Lauren and I separated, and I was finally living in my own small apartment after several weeks on the sofa at my office, something happened to me one night. I was lying in bed sound asleep when for some reason I woke. As I sat up, rubbing my eyes, wondering vaguely why I was awake, a print of van Gogh's *Starry Night* in a heavy frame that I'd hung over my bed pulled the nail out of the wall and fell right onto my pillow. If I'd been lying there, it would have been a starry night, all right. The frame might have broken my jaw, or even decapitated me. Why had I awakened? Had I heard the faint sound a nail under stress makes and unconsciously become alert? Had the painting fallen *because* I'd sat up, perhaps making the bed vibrate? Or was there some primitive awareness at work, something at the farthest rim of perception? I've thought about that incident from time to time, and I never get any closer to understanding it. I have a professor acquaintance who insists that people don't have instincts, that any atavistic knowledge was left far behind in our animal past, that everything we know is a result of learning. I don't know about this, and maybe I use the word "instinct" imprecisely, but on occasion I have had odd perceptions, usually of something amiss.

I had one now. It passed along my spine as a tingle.

I knocked again: louder, more insistent.

The lawn mowers went on growling. I took out a credit card and tried using it to slip the lock, but I couldn't make it work. I looked around and in a bed of pachysandra I saw a stone rabbit. I hesitated, thinking of Frank Droney's threat—*I could tank you for interfering*—then picked up the rabbit and shoved it through a pane of glass. It was crude, but so was Mike Tyson's knockout punch. I didn't hear an alarm. I reached carefully past the jagged edges and unlocked the door.

"Judge," I called into the house. I listened for a voice. "Ms. Ouellette?"

I stepped into an entryway, anticipating someone frozen in fright, or a face squinched behind a trembling pistol. I saw only an array of coats hung on pegs and a pair of knee-high rubber boots, the kind that gourmet garden catalogs call wellies. I walked on soft feet down a short passageway, on the walls of which was a display of old-time photographs—photos, I realized, that mostly showed a stern, matronly woman and a boy. I went into a spacious and airy kitchen. On a tray on the counter were a china teapot and two cups and a plate of cookies. Comfort food. But what I smelled wasn't food or comforting. It was a faint, sour smell.

"Hey, Judge," I called again, louder, as though to scare away someone or something I didn't want to encounter. It was warm in the house, from the afternoon sun streaming through the windows, and a film of perspiration had formed on my brow, but cold prickled on the nape of my neck. On legs I had to coax along, I went through a set of sliding pocket doors into a large room with furniture that was a long way from new but whose elegance remained. I walked over carpets that oozed plushly under my hesitant footsteps. Photographs were a persistent theme, as was the presence of the pinch-faced woman in them, along with the sad boy/young man. Beyond was a dining room, with a big claw-foot oak table; a corner china closet held crystal and silver that hadn't felt elbow grease in many moons. Was this how the other class lived? It wasn't anything special. Maybe you only noticed the differences inside a bank vault.

I worked from room to room downstairs, opening and shutting doors. Beyond was a broad hallway, and the swoop of a banister and wide stairs to the upper floor.

In an upstairs bedroom, on a table was an array of framed photographs, many showing the same woman and boy as those downstairs, but moving the pair ahead through time, so that I recognized that the boy was Martin Travani. And I realized that no matter how much he aged in them, he was always the little boy.

Downstairs again, I began to breathe a little easier. I was headed for the exit when I spotted something I'd missed before when I'd been moving in the opposite direction. On the parquet, only partially visible, was what appeared to be a bloody footprint. It was man-sized, from a work boot, I judged from the sole pattern. What was puzzling, however, was the angle and its position facing out from the wall. Then I understood. The wall was constructed to conceal a door. It opened with a firm push.

I wrinkled my nose as the odor I'd smelled before became instant and pervasive. It was a scorched, vinegary, gunsmoke smell. The door had concealed a dark inner chamber. Breathing through my mouth, I felt for a light switch, and my fingers discovered that the walls were paneled in egg-crate foam, the kind used to baffle sound. Was I in a home music studio? I located a rheostat knob and gave it a slow twist.

In the gradually revealing light from spots set in the ceiling, details came into view. One wall was a mirror. Suspended from the ceiling were several knotted ropes, with velvet cuffs and Velcro fasteners. To the left, built into the corner, was what looked like a wardrobe cabinet with a drape-hung door and crisscrossing lattice on the side. I turned the dimmer knob all the way up.

On a pale beige leather couch set near the right wall lay a woman, her back turned to me so that all I could see was a disheveled mass of blond hair against her black ribbed-cotton sweater. Asleep? I had to bend across her and lean close to get a look at her face, and even then recognition came slowly. She didn't resemble the way she'd looked the last time I saw her, when she'd ducked into her apartment and slammed the door in my face. A gunshot to her head at close range had given her skull an odd, elliptical elongation, the way passage through the birth canal sometimes will a newborn's. Her jaw was wide open, locked in a silent scream. From the front edge of her cheek all the way back to behind her ear was a mess of erupted tissue, like the lobes of an overripe cauliflower. Curds of blood, like dark red smoke, had bubbled from her mouth to form a congealing pool on the bone-colored leather cushion.

My head swam. I fought an urge to flee . . . *might* have fled, but I wasn't sure my knees would hold. I braced on the sofa and shut my eyes. Tiny motes of light drifted before them. When I opened them, I saw the red spatter on a pillow wedged between her shoulder and the sofa back, its brocade fabric blackened around a burnt hole. I stood for a moment, trying to slow my heart for what I dreaded to find next.

The judge was behind the couch, underneath a sofa table, as if he'd crawled under there looking for safety. He was on his back, one leg curled and leaning against the wall. He was wearing the same suit he'd been wearing several hours ago at his club, but it was a mess. His starched shirt collar was blood-soaked. His mouth was collapsed inward, and the teeth, which indeed were in a dental plate, lay on the braided rug several feet away, evidently having been blown out by the impact of a gunshot. There was a thread of blood on them.

I looked around for an obvious explanation—for a gun that would make it play as a murder-suicide, but there wasn't one, as the footprint in the hall should already have told me. When I looked back at Travani, his eyes were on mine. He was alive.

I gripped his hand. "Hold on. I'm going to get help."

I rushed back to the kitchen, found a wall phone, and punched 911 and was amazed at the speed with which the call was answered. Ignoring the operator's request for my name, I told her two people had been shot, one still alive. I gave the address and hung up.

At the center of my fear and nausea, like the eye of a storm, was a cold calm. In a drawer by the sink I found several clean dish towels. I wet one under the tap and went back to the concealed chamber. Careful of where I stepped, I put the damp cloth on his forehead. I looked for the wound. It seemed to be behind his head. I didn't want to move him. He kept his eyes on mine. Perhaps he was speaking with them, though I didn't know what they might be saying. Maybe he had no idea who I was and was just trying to keep some link with the living.

I held his hand, and with my other hand I reached to the wardrobe cabinet and drew aside the drape. Instead of shelves or hanging clothes, I looked into an empty booth. For an instant I was confused, and then I realized what it was, or was meant to resemble. Lying on the floor in one corner was a costume—a nun's habit, and looped atop it a rosary. Thoughts were clustering at the back of my mind, like moths gathering around a faint light. I waved them away.

The judge's mouth twitched, an odd movement without teeth. Wanting to tell me something? I bent near. Instead of words, I heard a soft, clattery sigh, like a footfall in dry leaves. His eyes were still open, and there was still a pulse, but the light was fading from his eyes. What did judges dream of as they lay dying? A writ from on high? A full pardon? Conviction?

I heard the first siren. EMTs or the police. I wasn't there under any jurisdiction that I could invoke. The police would charge me. Criminal trespass, destruction of evidence, tampering with a crime scene . . . They might even try for two counts of murder, though that one wouldn't stick.

At the very least, they'd demand a full statement, which would have to be typed up, read, and signed. Not today.

As I stood up, it was as if I'd stepped off a still-moving carousel. For a moment, the world lurched under me, and then it steadied. Outside, from closer now, came an overlapping wail of sirens, approaching even faster than I'd imagined they would. Driving away, I had to force myself not to speed.

When you get overstressed, your mind starts to yammer. It begins to see things that may not be there. It can, says Poe, hear things in hell. Mine insisted on imagining stories. If the waitress from Viva! who wanted to write for the movies had been there, I'd have asked her if that was the way it happened, if the narrative suddenly took form in the mind, complete with characters doing their bits of business and action, speaking lines . . .

"Jesus. What happened?" The cop bends over the dead woman on the carpet. She's in the black-and-white costume of a nun. Cinched tight around her throat is a small beaded chain: a rosary. A rill of blood has run from one nostril, almost dry now. The cop draws back and turns to the judge. The judge sits on a bone-colored couch, bent forward, head in hands. He is having a difficult time of it. "Tell me exactly what happened," says the cop. "Everything."

I drove by rote through the afternoon traffic, the houses and buildings and bright trees blurring by. A weight of exhaustion was dragging hard behind the adrenaline, like a string of loaded boxcars hooked to a locomotive on a steep uphill climb. In those boxcars I could feel the freight shifting around.

The judge is hyperventilating, his face damp with sweat, his hair mussed. "She came here today and said she was going to stop this . . . not meet me any-more. I . . ." He swallows and regains some control. "I asked her to wear the habit one more time. Just once more. And go in there." He gestures at the booth in the corner. "To tell me her sins . . . ask me to absolve her, make her do penance. May . . . maybe I pulled too hard, I don't know. I thought the chain would snap. Oh, God, what have I done? What's going to happen now? I don't . . . I—"

"Shut up! Get hold of yourself. Tell me what happened!"

"There's a man who—"

"What man?"

"Huh? Who she was going to marry. A man she knew a long time . . ."

Grim-faced, the cop paces, leaving a space around the woman's body, glancing at the judge in disgust. "Did you spank her this time?"

At a stoplight, I saw a donut shop. Beyond the big windows, decorated with cutout paper leaves and cornstalks, people were sitting on stools, drinking coffee, reading newspapers, talking about the weather, and I had a powerful yen to go in there, to reenter that everyday world. But even as I thought this, I knew I was far beyond that. When the light changed, I sped past.

"Did you?" the cop demands.

"No, no. She was going to go to this man."

"Would she already have told him about any of this—about you and her?"

"She said she hadn't—wouldn't. She said he could never know."

"You believe her?"

"Yes. I do." The judge is in an agony of fright and remorse.

"Do you know the guy's name? Where he is?"

"He works . . . at the carnival."

The cop looks up. "The carnival that's here now?"

"Yes. She was with him there yesterday. He's the one she had a restraining order against. Carly would know his name."

The cop paces again. Stops. "All right. I'm going to need some help."

The judge grows attentive.

"That green car in the driveway. Hers?"

The judge nods.

"I'll take care of it. You'll need to clean up here. Take the rosary off and that damn costume. But don't touch her skin. Have you got some sheets? Better yet, a shower curtain. All right, get it. Let me make a call."

And that's what happens. Duross is going to the carnival anyway, for his paid detail. He'll get someone to help, to drive Flora Nuñez's car over to Regatta Field. He'll drive in from behind the meadow and dispose of her body. Why not? Since he has duty there a little later anyway, it'll be a simple enough thing to dump the body, park her car near the carnival, get into Pepper's trailer, and plant some evidence there.

Pieces were coming together. The juror ballot card that I'd found in the statuette at Flora Nuñez's apartment—had *T* stood not for Troy but for Travani? Were the dates appointments she had with the judge, to satisfy his kinky lusts? Set up by Carly Ouellette—who had first been a teacher and later procurer of her students? It would explain Lucy Colón's reluctance to speak with me; because perhaps she was one of the judge's women, too. Women from another country, who might have cause to fear the legal system and welcome a protector?

I puffed a shivery breath. It was one story. Another tale was more recent: *The judge and Carly Ouellette about to have tea, to discuss the crisis situation they find themselves in because of a nosy private investigator—and someone unexpected comes. Loose threads to be snipped . . .*

My cell phone chirped.

"Detective. You were quick."

The voice wasn't quick, though; it was ponderous and low and deeply distorted. *I have heard many things in hell.* "So were you," I managed.

"Not quick enough. You called nine-one-one from there."

The voice was electronically altered, giving it the guttural sound that the voices of evil entities in scary movies have. You saw devices for sale in the security management catalogs that enabled you to do that. I couldn't listen to it and drive. I drew sharply to the curb. "Okay, Duross," I said, taking a stab. "What do you want?"

There was a silence, and I was pretty sure I'd stabbed right, but the voice remained altered. "I want what you've got," it said. "Whatever you found at the judge's house."

And what you *must not have found,* I thought. "What makes you think I got anything?"

"Better pray that you did, or you have nothing to trade."

"Be specific."

Laughter that might have come from hell itself. "She keeps crying for her Pop."

44

I swallowed, wanting to loosen the Doric column my neck had become. I got enough breath into my throat to form words. "Nicole is with you?"

He gave an address. I scribbled it down on the only thing I had handy, the back of my new auto registration. "Forty minutes," he said. "Walk through the gate alone. If I see anything I don't like . . ."

"Wait! Let me—"

But the voice was gone, leaving only its echo in my head, like something pondering along the gloomy halls of a nightmare. I stared at the phone, willing it to ring again, to tell me what to do next. It didn't. So I fell back on what seemed logical. I called police headquarters. I asked for Paul Duross, but I was told he was off duty. For a moment I sat, feeling something moving in me, something dark like a fast-fading winter sky when it reminds you that death is waiting. I put down the phone. The woman setting up the Halloween display at the public library had spoken of breaching the barrier between the living and the dead. It was what I needed to do. I looked at the dashboard clock—I didn't have a lot of time—then raised the phone and made another call. It rang a long time before someone answered, coughing rust out, but at least it was a real voice. I steadied my own. "It's Rasmussen," I said.

45

I hadn't wanted to carry the sawed-off in my trunk for fear of getting caught, and lately it seemed as though being stopped was a daily thing, but now I was ready to take the risk. I had time enough to go home, get the shotgun, and still make the meeting. But one other thing first.

In my mind I replayed the voice on my cell phone—Duross's, I was convinced. It told me things: that he'd known I had been at Travani's house, that perhaps he'd come back and seen me. It told me that there was evidence, probably incriminating, or why risk going back? Most important, it told me that he had Nicole. He had no reason to kill her, but that didn't mean he wouldn't. He had to be feeling desperate right now. I needed to let him believe that I had found something before the cops came.

The video store was a little mom-and-pop operation on Westford Street. I asked the clerk, an Indian or Pakistani woman, if she had blank videocassettes. When she finally understood me, she said she didn't have any blanks. All right, I said, I wanted to buy one of her rentals.

"You don't have member card?"

"I want to *buy* one," I said. I had my wallet out and drew out a twenty.

After I made her understand, she took the money and asked me what I wanted. I said it didn't matter. "Do you want Tom Cruise? He is very popular. Or Julia Roberts?"

As I hurried toward my car, a black SUV with a stainless steel push bar rolled up onto the curb, cutting me off and almost pinning me against the adjacent building. Louis Hackett got out of the passenger side. "I thought that was your heap," he called. "Been looking for you."

"I don't have time right now."

"Wrong answer."

"I hope not. It's the only one I have. I'm in a rush."

"Yeah, to see me. I asked you nice, even warned you, but did you listen?"

The driver's door opened, and Squisher Spritzer climbed out and walked around the back of the Toyota. Hackett said, "You know, Rasmussen, maybe it isn't you, maybe you're just some dumb prick who wandered into the sound stage and ruined the whole shot, and the director's got to yell, 'Cut!' and waste a bunch of time getting everything set up again. Yeah, I really think that's what it is—you're a fuckup."

"Look, I'll meet with you—we'll huddle, we'll hondle, whatever you want—but it's got to be later."

He jabbed a finger into my chest. "You know, this is the kind of bullshit I hate."

My face grew hot and there was a thumping throb in my head. I felt time slipping away from me.

"But it's like that day on the river," he went on, "when the restaurant owner knew someone was skimming, only he didn't know who. Somebody's got to be an example." He looked at Squisher and made a sideways motion with his head. "I'm gonna cruise around the block."

I opened my mouth to speak, and Squisher punched me. It was a short, straight blow that hit my chest like a pickup truck. It emptied my lungs. I staggered a few steps back on the sidewalk, dropping the videotape. He locked his arms down against mine, pinning them to my sides. He head-butted me, which touched off a blitz of light. My legs went gimpy. He let go and stepped back, probably to let me drop. I didn't. He saw the cassette lying there and stomped it with a snapping crunch, as if it were Julia Roberts's fine-chiseled bones breaking—and mine next. I submarined a punch to his gut. It was like hitting a slab of butcher block. He knocked my next swing aside and hit me again. I got my hands up, but he chopped me in the throat. I gagged. He rammed me back across the sidewalk. My head and elbow cracked hard against the brick wall of a building.

Pain. I was treading in foggy water, trying to keep afloat. He was so close that his feet were bumping mine, like a clumsy dance partner's. I tried to raise an arm to push him back. My elbow felt like it had broken glass inside. He pressed nearer, squeezing with his thick arms. He was so close his face was a blur, pocked like a hazy moon. His cigar breath and cheap aftershave dizzied me. He could kill me. That quickly the thought came. There were no controls on the man; he would cripple me, or worse, as surely as he'd dropped a man into the Harlem River or mauled an opponent in the ring. Another moment and I'd have breathed my last. Already my vision was starting to speckle with light. I saw one chance to survive.

Bracing my shoulders on the wall, I jacked a knee up into his groin, hard as I could. His cheeks bulged bullfroglike and he gasped a chestful of breath into my face. I kneed him again. His eyes rolled and he shuffled back, a look of agony and surprise stamped on his face. He began to moan, as if the pain were starting to build. I'd have let it end there—I wasn't out for torture, only survival—but I knew that if he came around, it was going to go worse for me. Pushing past the hot ache in my left elbow, I gripped his lapels, both hands clutching hard on the slick polyester fabric. I swung him around. I dropped my shoulder and drove him against the building. He hit it and bellowed like a bull. I pulled him toward me, more pain in my elbow. He twisted in my grip as I started to slam him back. I missed the wall and we hit a plate glass window with a thump. A sign read MEMBERS ONLY: PLEASE SHOW ID. It was a health and fitness club, I saw. Beyond the reflection on the window, several women had quit whirling away on Exercycles and gaped out at us. Squisher reached for me, and I drove him back one more time. He went through the glass like a dump truck. There were screams. I reached in with my good arm and hauled Spritzer out. His coat was shredded, and there were speckles of blood staining the fabric.

My breath heaving, I eased him down on the sidewalk. "Can't you read? Members only."

46

Grady Stinson was on the sidewalk under the burgundy awning of the Ritz Manor, pacing, when I stood on the brakes. He pitched his cigarette into the gutter and climbed in, and I was rolling again before he had the door closed.

"You said ten minutes."

"I hit a snag. I'm here now."

He didn't bother with the seat belt; his generation of cops never had. His outfit was black chinos and windbreaker. I didn't ask if he was carrying a card with the image of a chess knight on it. I did wonder if he had a gun under there somewhere. He exhaled a strong peppermint smell that could have been mouthwash or schnapps, but I reserved judgment. He seemed sober, and that was all I could ask for.

"That from the snag you hit?"

I saw that my right hand, gripping the wheel, had several patches of blood congealing on the knuckles. "Yeah," I said and left it at that. They were just abrasions, but my left elbow was another story. It felt like something inside was on fire. Maybe, I hoped, we'd get this next bit over with quickly and I could get myself some rest. For now, I kept my eyes open for pedestrians as I zigzagged through the crisscrossing streets, heading north toward the river.

On the phone I'd told Stinson I was going to meet someone and wondered would he come along for the ride. He didn't ask a lot of questions, not even inquiring what he'd be paid, or if he'd be paid at all. He seemed happy just to be asked. My plan had been to have him at the wheel—he was good at that—but time was too short to switch. He said, "Where's the meet?"

"Not far. The address is there on the dashboard."

He looked at what I'd scrawled on the back of my registration, then at me. "This a joke?"

I glanced over. "It better not be."

"This address is bogus. I pulled patrols in this area." He flicked the registration with the backs of his fingers. "This is Nagasaki after the fireworks. It's Watts once the natives finished demoing it after the Rodney King verdict. Getting it?"

I wasn't.

"This is Dresden after the weenie roast. This address is desolation row."

But he didn't need to press the point. The long bulk of the Wannalancit mill, rehabbed and fitted to modern purposes, came into view, and I realized that I'd gotten the address right but had confused its location in my mind. The meeting spot was one street (and about fifty years) beyond what I'd imagined, and now I saw that Stinson's mental map was better than mine. The old Boston Hosiery building came into view, its tower rising from the five-story brick shell, bearded with ivy, windows blackened with time, and beyond it, hidden still, but there, was the one place in the city that I avoided the way Superman avoided Kryptonite.

A shiver clenched my shoulders and ran down my spine. Could Duross have known about that night? It was well before his time, and yet his uncle, Frank Droney, had been the one who'd made sure that my cop career was over. No, I couldn't buy that Duross knew that. It was coincidence. I refocused.

I slowed and drew into a vacant lot at an angle to the front of Boston Hosiery and facing it, 150 yards away. It seemed right: not obvious, commanding a view of the entrance. I shut off the engine. Stinson looked over.

"Okay, I want you to wait here and watch that gate."

"Sit and watch," he repeated, sifting it for deeper meaning.

"And one other thing."

I had to allow for the possibility that Duross was here ahead of me—he had obviously phoned from someplace nearby—but I didn't think he was. His call had made clear that he felt vulnerable, given that he believed Travani had files that he thought, rightly or wrongly, could expose him. Duross's goal would be survival. I found myself remembering Ed St. Onge's remark about my standing alone. Strictly speaking, I was a loose end. But among dogs you had to be too big to eat; or at least make them think you were. Power isn't only what you have but what your enemy thinks you have. What I had was Duross's belief that there was incriminating evidence, and that I possessed it. Nicole had no intrinsic value to him; she was simply his lever. He'd be sharp enough to see that there wasn't any reason to harm her, wouldn't he? I didn't pursue the logic of whether he'd feel the same about me.

"I'm going inside, into the courtyard," I said. "When the person I'm expecting shows up, let him get through the gate and then honk the horn." I gave a demonstration, which echoed forlornly off the vast brick relics beyond us. "One honk. And be ready to wheel if I signal you."

"This person you're expecting—a cop?"

I nodded. "Duross."

He blinked, taking this in. "You're heeled, right?"

"No."

Stinson screwed his face into something between a grimace and grin. "Shit, you always this well prepared?" He unzipped his coat, exposing what I realized was a shoulder rig and the checkered walnut grips of a handgun. He gripped it. It took a while to clear the holster. In a crisis situation, he could probably have hauled it out in time for the ME to arrive and pronounce him DOA. It was a Ruger Blackhawk, with a barrel about a foot long.

"What did you do, tell them to super-size it?"

"Forty-four Mag. Makes a statement, don't you think?"

"So does walking around naked."

"If all I'm supposed to do is sit here with my face hanging out, you should take it."

I was wrestling suddenly with my doubts about having dragged him along. Sure, he was a consenting adult, with his own badass fantasies, but this had nothing to do with him. Never mind that it would be impossible for me to conceal his cannon. Frankly, though I didn't tell him, I doubted I could hold it. My fingers were stiffening and my elbow felt hot and waxy, as if the joint were melting away. Besides, I rationalized, if things got tense, Stinson was the type to start throwing lead, and I had to think about Nicole. To his good, though, I remembered something about him that I had forgotten. Whereas a lot of cops hated having to wear a gun, couldn't hit a barn door with one, and hoped they never had to, Stinson had loved carrying, had love lighting it up when the situation warranted, or not. He went to the range on his own time and practiced. So, okay, maybe the risk/reward factor ran about even; but right now I needed him to stay put. "Hang on to your testosterone and sit tight."

With sweat oozing under my shirt, I left the keys in the ignition and got out. "Remember, when he goes through that entrance, honk." I started across the rutted vacant lot toward the empty street and the old mill.

47

I was winded when I reached the gate, from nerves more than exertion. I could feel my heartbeat in my palms as I gripped the vertical iron bars and peered through. Beyond was a passageway with an arched brick ceiling, a kind of tunnel about fifty feet long that led to an inner courtyard. I had a sick feeling in my core. Some of it could be laid to the beating I'd taken from Spritzer, and to the prospect of facing Duross, but I knew, too, that it was this place.

I had the wild thought that I'd been wrong about the address, that this wasn't where I was supposed to be. But it was. I knew that. And the gate wasn't locked. I lifted the heavy iron staple and dropped it over with a clank that echoed in the tunnel. I pushed the gate open on grating hinges and went into the brick-arched entryway.

I had been back here one other time since that long-ago night—on a March afternoon, with the members of an inquiry board: four men and a woman, moving around in a cold drizzle, hands in their coat pockets, expressions unreadable. I walked them through my version of what had happened. Only one of them, the woman, asked a question: "How does it feel to be here now?" A state trooper shot, a hit man killed, and me with a satchel of marked bills that no one seemed to be able or willing to account for. *How the hell do you think it feels?* I wanted to growl. But, no. Actually, it was a sensitive question, insightful even, and I'd answered it honestly, too naive to realize that the entire inquiry was for show, that in two flips of a fish's fin, as Phoebe might say, the matter had already been decided. Unbeknownst even to these five people, I'd been marked for occupational extinction. I hadn't come back since.

Now, with dread pooling in the pit of my stomach like seepage in a foul sink, I walked the rest of the way down the tunnel to the courtyard that opened beyond. As I stepped in, I faltered. I'd forgotten how large it was, almost imponderably vast, built to a scale that dwarfed people, even (the old brown-tint photographs showed) the thousands of workers who had gathered here to voice grievances that rang in feeble protest against the high enclosing walls.

A big dead sycamore rose from the weedy lot to the left, a scrap of black plastic bag skewered on one of the bare limbs and flapping in the wind like a pirate's flag. Below ran several rusted railroad spurs leading to long-defunct loading docks. Scattered about were piles of broken brick, and beyond that, cutting off a view of the river, the looming, neglected bulk of the Lawrence Manufacturing mill. To the right was an old canal, water moving in it even now, gushing past the rotted locks and down the long granite spillway to the river. The wind whined through the abandoned cloisters and tunnels of the mills in a melancholy hymn to another age.

At a sudden movement high on one of the walls, I turned and realized it was a security camera. It didn't do squat to reassure me. And just then I heard the car horn signal. Swallowing back a rising anxiety, I moved toward the entryway.

If I went down, the papers would have a field day with the implications. "Full Circle: Ex-Cop Returns to Scene of His Infamy." I wondered who'd play the part in the film. Outside of Mitchum, I could think of no one.

At the crunch of footsteps on the stones, I hurried to the edge of the wall. A moment later, a uniformed cop emerged. Jill Loftis. She looked just as surprised to see me.

"Whoa!" She spread empty hands.

"What are you doing here?"

She was slightly winded. "I'm glad I found you." She waved me back around the corner. "Duross is on his way here. You know that, don't you." Her words came fast, pushed along by adrenaline. "I've been watching him. I think you're right about him being involved in something."

"I know I am." I started telling her about the scene I'd walked into at Judge Travani's house. I had to. I'd been cute with the 911 call, but it was time to be level with what I'd done and what I knew. She listened with grim fascination, as if she were being presented with facts she'd prefer not to accept, but she no longer had that luxury.

"You think he'll have the girl from the carnival with him?" she asked.

"That's the purpose of this," I said. "Are you alone?"

"I couldn't involve others only on the basis of . . ." She paused.

"I know. On my say-so."

"Sorry. Plus, I have to wonder . . . what if there are others in it with Duross? No way can we handle a hostage situation." She was right. There were just the two of us, and only one gun. She drew the walkie-talkie from her belt. Her face tightened with concentration. She couldn't seem to make her hand unit work. She looked around, as if truly seeing the isolation of this place for the first time. "Damn it," she murmured, and I understood. She couldn't get a signal there in the enclosed yard. She looked momentarily helpless. "Maybe outside the walls I can try it. We have to let the department handle this. If you've got any physical evidence that ties Duross to what you've just told me, we have to bring it in."

Before I could tell her I didn't have any, the horn blew again, echoing along the tunnel. She glanced at me. "He's here," I said.

She hung the walkie-talkie on her belt. I ducked back, drawing her with me into the courtyard. We took cover behind a pile of bricks and faced the tunnel.

A moment later Duross appeared at the outer gate, backlighted by the afternoon sun, and peered down the arched tunnel. He was alone. He wore plainclothes, but he was holding a pistol at his side as he pushed open the iron gate and started slowly in.

Jill Loftis drew her sidearm.

"I'm sorry I got you into this," I said.

"I'm not crazy about it, either, but I'm here."

"Twice as hard for half the respect."

She managed a faint smile.

I told her I had to be the one to talk to Duross. He was expecting me. Just me. She didn't argue. "Get the girl," she said. "I'll try to cover you."

I moved forward, away from where she hid, not having any idea of what I was going to say to Duross, just hoping that something would come.

When he stepped out of the tunnel, he looked bulky in a dark blue sweatshirt, fade-washed jeans, and basketball shoes. He saw me, hesitated, then came my way.

"You've gone way too far, Rasmussen. I warned you." He was holding the pistol at his side though I couldn't see it well. "I'm bringing you in."

"That's funny," I said, barely able to find breath for the words, let alone ideas, "coming from you."

"Don't fool around."

"Don't *you* fool around. We had a deal. I've got what you're after."

He moved carefully, taking care as he stepped over the rusted tracks concealed in the weeds. His basketball shoes looked new. "A deal, huh? And what would that be?"

He wanted to hear me say it, to reveal what I knew. I said, "Where's the girl?" He was still holding the gun down, making no move to raise it. I kept my eyes on his, my hands where he could see them.

"You don't know what you're talking about. I'm taking you in."

Before we could joust any further, I saw motion off to my right, at the far end of the courtyard. A dark-haired man was running our way, making a reckless broken-field run over the weedy terrain. Stinson hadn't signaled any more arrivals. Duross saw him, too. As the runner got closer, I saw he was Asian. He had a shiny automatic in each hand, and a memory flickered spectrally past my mind.

Duross raised his gun, the motion lifting the bottom edge of his sweatshirt, and I was startled to see the blunt shape of his sidearm still

holstered on his belt. He had two guns, too? Before I could make anything of this, Jill Loftis stepped from her concealment behind the pile of
bricks, her gun drawn and held in both hands in front of her.

"Put it down, Paul!" she shouted. The words came back at us with a
flat echo.

"Jill—what the hell are—"

"Drop the goddamn gun!" Her voice was taut with alarm.

"Jill!"

She shot Duross twice. His knees sagged and he went down in the
weeds. I saw one sneaker-shod foot kick out to the side and go still. The
image stirred something in me, but I turned quickly half-deaf from her
gunfire. The Asian had quit running and now moved toward us, waving
the twin automatics. Instinctively I moved closer to Loftis; she was the
only firepower we had. The man wore a green sport coat, jeans, and work
boots. Work boots, not sneakers. I glanced toward where Duross lay, and
then back.

"He's the one who shot Travani and Ouellette," I warned her. "He's
Duross's man."

She was at my side now, watching him.

But she kicked *me*.

48

The blow wasn't as hard as Bud Spritzer packed, but it did the job. A sideways kick, with the thick-soled boot, it took my knee out. My leg buckled and I went down, falling hard on one of the rusted rails. Before I could rise, she stomped me down with her foot. I managed to turn my head sideways, my brain swarming with firefly light and bewildering questions, chief among them: *Just what the hell was going on?*

She stood over me, her gun pointed at my head. "I want the goods."

The goods? By some miracle, the ace I'd held before, I still held. My face was in the weeds, my body wracked with pain, and yet she believed I had taken evidence from Martin Travani's sex chamber—evidence that could implicate not Duross but her.

"We had an arrangement," I managed. "It stands. Where's Nicole?"

Neither her gun nor her cold expression wavered. "Sok!" she called.

Vanthan Sok came over. He had the weapon that Duross had been carrying, frowning at it, and I saw that I'd been mistaken in thinking it was a firearm. It was a Taser. Duross had been expecting that he might have to arrest me, nothing more. When he'd seemed bewildered by what I'd said to him, he wasn't acting.

I managed to change position slightly, turning onto my side, and looked at Loftis. "That was you on the phone?" I asked.

"Fooled you, huh? The department has a voice-altering machine we sometimes use for taking testimony from reluctant witnesses."

"And you called Duross and tipped him that I'd be here."

"I told him you were ranting about him, wanted to meet him." She shrugged. "It was your idea that Duross was dirty."

I looked at Vanthan Sok. "Is he dead?"

Sok paid no attention. He was still marveling at the Taser. "It's a fucking zap gun. Stupid fucker had his nine holstered the whole fucking time."

He stood over me, and I got my first close look at him. He was short, wiry, with high cheekbones and long dark hair. Under the green sport coat, which was made of some crinkly synthetic material, he wore a pink Polo shirt, with the crisscrossing straps of a double shoulder rig for his guns. He had one of his shiny automatics in his hand, a nickel-plated SIG-Sauer. St. Onge had called him a cowboy. His face was unmarked by anything he'd done—he could have been eighteen or eighty—none of it mattered to him.

"He's got what you couldn't find," Loftis told him. "I want you to get it."

He put his automatic into the double shoulder rig and stepped closer. He probably knew who I was. At least, he'd known enough to send gunfire through my kitchen window, no doubt at Loftis's suggestion. He kicked hard at the sole of my foot, and I saw his work boot and realized that the bloody print I'd seen in the judge's house most likely had been left by Sok, sent there to snip loose ends when Carly Ouellette had chickened and run.

Without warning, Sok pointed the Taser at me, worked the safety slide, and shot me.

I convulsed as the charge hit my chest. I fell back, limp. It was a non-lethal hit, the charge generated by a nine-volt battery, but it had the effect of knocking the body's electro-muscular system out of pulse—weakening an opponent enough to allow the shooter to apprehend even the most unruly combatant.

Loftis didn't seem to approve or disapprove. "Where is it?" she demanded.

I tried to get up, but I could barely move. I wasn't sure that I could even speak.

Sok tossed the Taser aside and with a fancy cross-armed move straight from DiNiro, drew his pair of SIGs. I had no doubt that he would shoot me where I lay. *This is it,* I thought. *This is how I'm going to die.* And I knew how it would play: "Blood Feud in the Mill Yard"—both Duross and me found dead. Loftis was likely thinking along the same lines, making strategy.

"No," she said. "Get Duross's nine."

I swallowed hard at the sick dread in my core and forced my gaze past Sok to Loftis. "You want the evidence I've got," I rasped. "Where's Nicole?"

"Close by. Your turn."

I propped myself onto an elbow. The effects of the shock were fading. "I've got Travani's files in my car."

Just then someone shouted, "Police!" It was followed by a boom.

The three of us looked toward the tunnel and there was Stinson, fifty feet away. He had his .44 pointed in the air, the barrel as long as his forearm. I didn't waste time noting anything else. Summoning strength I wasn't sure I had, I drew one leg up and kicked out hard, crashing the sole of my foot against Sok's shin with force enough to shatter the bone. He yelped a high, screeching cry and staggered back. But he didn't drop his SIGs. He pointed one at my head.

His chest broke apart like a watermelon kicked by a Clydesdale, the insides vaporizing in a pale red penumbra. The concussion from Stinson's .44 reached me an instant before Sok's corpse hit the ground.

Loftis didn't even turn. She bolted.

I rolled to my feet, not easy to do on a bad knee. I picked up the Taser, which lay beside Sok's body. I wasn't even sure it could be reused. But I didn't want Loftis dead. Waving Stinson off, I went after her.

She was a runner, and I felt dead-legged, but I gimped along after her. Although the courtyard was the size of the Roman Coliseum, there really wasn't anyplace she could get to that I couldn't reach, too, in my own time. She turned to look back, still running, and stumbled on some debris, but she didn't go down. I saw again how fit she was, how strong. Even after all the destruction and violent death, there was something strangely alluring about her. That didn't blind me to her danger.

She was running toward the far end of the courtyard, and it occurred to me that if she could reach the far wall of the Lawrence mill, she might get through a spillway gate, or scale a low fence, and be gone. I pushed myself harder—but so did she. I was too far away to use the Taser, which might work at twenty feet, though six or eight would be better.

All at once, she appeared to try to stop, skidding slightly in the weeds—and I realized that she had suddenly come upon the canal. Too late to stop, she changed her mind. She surged ahead, stepped on the granite sill of the canal, like a long jumper hitting the board, and launched herself into the air.

It wasn't too wide—twenty feet or a little more—but she wasn't Marion Jones. She would fall. She put her hands out, to try to break the impact or catch hold some way, but she was moving fast. She slammed into the granite wall on the other side with a sickening thud that I heard from ten paces away, a long whip of blood and broken teeth lashing away from her mouth and nose. But she hung on, clinging to the wall. I got there, totally winded.

"Where's Nicole?" I called.

She half turned, and the sight was ghastly. She appeared to be wearing a red mask. Her entire face was slick with blood, and one of her eyes had come out of the socket. Bits of shattered teeth flecked her chin.

"Hold on!" I cried, hoarse with panic. I looked around for some way to reach her. Or for something to extend for her to grab on to. Unlike many of the canals that crisscrossed the city, which were stagnant, this was flowing fast, rushing the final fifty or so yards to the Merrimack.

Her grip failed, or she simply let go. She dropped ten feet and hit the water with a clumsy splash. She disappeared for a moment, then reappeared. She may have been conscious, ready to struggle, but the current took her. She banged limply through the heavy, corroded timbers of the locks and was swept headfirst down a stone spillway, gathering speed as the water tore her toward the river. I lost sight of her.

Stinson's shout drew me back.

"This one's alive!"

He was crouched beside Duross. I limped back. "I'm calling for help," he said. He got the walkie-talkie from Duross's belt. I opened my mouth to instruct him, then shut up. Stinson had been a cop a lot more recently than I had. He activated the unit and said the right things—an officer down, a man dead, gave the locations . . .

"Tell them about Loftis, too," I said.

He did. He never offered his own name, or mine. When he'd finished, we stayed beside Duross awhile. He was unconscious and bleeding, but breathing. He'd been smart enough to wear his vest. In the weeds nearby, Vanthan Sok was already drawing flies. Stinson had made an amazing shot, and it had saved my life.

"Have you got paper for the howitzer?" I asked him.

"Kind of not. I think I'd better get myself gone."

We rose, both of us still adrenalized. "It'd be a good idea. Take my car. I'll catch a ride with someone."

He looked at me and tugged his black windbreaker down and pushed a hand through his hair, as if getting ready to meet his public. "Later, then." He started off.

"Stinson," I called. He turned. "Thanks."

He tipped a finger to his head, in an old cowboy salute, I guess, and headed for the tunnel, walking fast. In another minute, in the distance came the whining of sirens. I looked around, a sudden hollow feeling overcoming the pain I'd begun to feel, and I remembered that I didn't know what had happened to Nicole. Then a glint of light from the roof of one of the mill buildings gave me an idea.

Randy Nguyen was waiting as I opened the freight elevator and stepped into his world. "Holy smokes!" he exclaimed, waving excitedly at his bank of monitors. "What was that?"

It answered my first question, unasked. The old hosiery mill was one of the properties his company did security for. "You said these keep a taped record."

"Yeah, three days."

"The woman officer—"

"Jill Loftis. I checked her out in the PD files. There's a story there."

I cut him off. "I believe she brought someone with her."

"Yeah, the hoodie with the shiny bang-bangs."

"Earlier, back around three this morning." My God, that was how many hours ago?

He instructed the system with voice commands. "It won't take long," he told me.

Fifteen minutes later we hacked a padlock off an old storage shed at the north end of the mill yard. Nicole squinted into the light and saw me and started grinning like a bridesmaid who's just caught the bouquet. "I knew you'd find me," she said, plunging into my arms, the feather weight of her nearly buckling my left leg. "I just knew it."

49

I encountered Gus Deemys coming out of police headquarters as I was limping up the steps. The surgeon had promised the limp would be temporary, the result of arthroscopy to remove torn cartilage from my knee. The DA looked like he'd had a lot more taken out of him. His linen suit was wrinkled, his tie loose, and he had none of the cocky attitude that he liked to project. I had a brief temptation to needle him, the way he always did others, but you didn't prevail over your opponents by becoming them. Deemys couldn't let it be, though. He moved to block my path, keeping the upper step, so that in theory he'd be glaring down at me, but the extra inches it gained him only brought our eyes even. His were red with fury and fatigue. "Hear me, Rasmussen—if there's any way I can do it, I'm going to carve you in strips. I'm going to subpoena your records on this case. As of ten minutes ago I've requested a gag order be put on you. You can forget about grabbing headlines. You can't even talk on the record about this or you'll face charges. That's just for starters. I'm going to clamp you down hard."

"Okay if I scratch my ass once in a while?"

He scowled. "You really bitched things up. I hope you know that."

"An innocent man cleared? How do you figure?"

"The Pepper thing I can live with. But Loftis falling down? That's going to make one holy mess. The county is going to have to reexamine every collar she was part of, and reopen cases where Travani presided. You can bet your ass they'll all be appealed, and some of the guilty will walk."

"And you're here to add insight to injury."

His jaw lumped. "I'm holding you personally responsible."

I didn't point out that that was the system he had sworn to uphold. That Jill Loftis had, too. I clapped his shoulder. "Maybe it'll all turn out like tropical storm Gus in the end—just a lot of wind."

Ed St. Onge was in his office, copying words out of a book. An English-to-Khmer dictionary. I could see the curlicue scratches on the yellow pad. "That's ambitious," I said, "though I read that in California they've got these little handheld units that can read people Miranda in about forty languages."

"Yeah, they also elect old movie stars to public office." He set his pen aside. "I figure it can't hurt to try to meet some of these gang kids halfway. Though you didn't have that option with Vanthan Sok. Nobody would have."

I sat down.

"The weapon fired through your kitchen window was the same one used on Travani and the Ouellette woman. It was one of the SIGs recovered at the mill yard."

I gave it a sober nod. He did, too. One sure sign that summer was over was when he put away the heavy woolens for something breezy and light. I'd seen him wear seersucker in January. Today he had on a blazer in pale blue polyester—"powder blue" they would've called it in the decade it had been made—with brass coin buttons and darker blue piping on the lapels. Give him a glockenspiel and he'd have fit in at halftime over at Alumni Field. I didn't say boo. He seemed somber. "I'm surprised you'd want to see the inside of this place again," he said.

"It's not the place, it's the people." I told him about my encounter with the DA.

"He'll get over it. Even Deemys wouldn't find much joy in sending up an innocent man. Say what you want about the guy, once he cools down he'll work it hard and fair. He's here looking into whether any other officers were involved. So far it checks out as just the one." He grunted. "Sounds strange to say, but in a lot of ways, she was a damn good cop. Hardworking, smart. Tough."

"Just ask my knee."

"She had a way with the kids out running with the wolves, knew how to talk to them. They respected her. Which is most likely how she crossed paths with Sok. I figure he served her because she asked him to, and he'd have been glad to, wanting to stay on her good side. She kept him out of prison. Maybe he had the hots for her, too. My hunch about Travani is he once tried to proposition her, and she'd have told him not in this life, put him in his place. Which could've made her job hell anytime she appeared in his session, but they came to see advantages in being allies. When she went before his court, her collars stuck."

"And the judge got women for his private chamber, eager to atone for sins."

"Between Loftis and Carly Ouellette pimping, he was well supplied. We may never know the full story." He scratched at his mustache, which seemed to have grown grayer than I remembered. "There's still a matter of ballistics on some of the gunshots in the mill yard, but I imagine that'll get sorted out in due course. Your piece, at least, wasn't one of them." He opened his desk drawer and took out my .38. "Here."

I snapped the holster onto my belt.

"More perplexing, though," he went on, "is that nine-one-one call. It came from the judge's house, on his phone, but we haven't been able to identify the caller." Looking at me. "Maybe some civic-minded individual who was just passing by." I kept quiet. "Well. Not that big a deal, I guess." He gave it a wave of dismissal, wincing slightly as he moved his arm. "Damned arthritis." He took a pill, swallowing it with water. "I'll be off them soon. They don't want to keep you on those for too long or you end up with a face the size of a medicine ball." He capped the plastic vial and put it back in his desk drawer. I was ready to leave when he said, "You know how you sometimes wonder if things might've gone differently?" He'd been chewing on something since I came in, working it with his mind. I waited. "Like if maybe no one had talked O.J. out of shooting himself when he sat holed up in the Bronco after the chase. Saved everyone all that hassle."

"You're globalizing. Give the focus knob a twist."

"That kid died. The one who tried to quit the gang."

I hadn't heard it. "I'm sorry."

"Last night." He spread his hands. "What if he'd been able to come in here and tell us what he had in mind and maybe we'd been able to get him out of town till things cooled? Or if there was some way to meet with the rival gangs . . . a big conference room, coffee . . . talk things over before they . . . Ah, I'm just thinking. About Travani, too. What are we to make of him, spanking the bad girls who came before his bench? A judge, for God's sake."

He'd had a reputation as a man of probity, a sound and fair-minded jurist, yet he had elected to throw it down the toilet. He had abused my good will. Worse, he had abused his power. Worst, he had been willing to send two women to their graves and an innocent man to prison because, apparently, he never managed to bring to trial the adversary inside his own mind. Yet I could not get all the way past the thought that he'd been the boy in the old photographs I'd seen in his house, or that I had been there as he drew his final breaths this side of the void. Of course, I couldn't say that. Besides, what St. Onge was really asking was, what if the judge had realized he was messed up and had turned himself in before it went so far? I chose to put the question into the realm of metaphysics, and I left it there. No good could come of my wondering how things might've played out differently. I was happy to be right here, right now, because I almost hadn't been. "Dogs whose lives are lived on a short leash sometimes slip the collar and kick their heels up extra high," I said.

"I guess."

"How's Duross?"

"Still at All Saints, but not for much longer. He'll be out soon. He was wearing his vest, which probably saved him. Anyway," he said after a pause, "the city is safe for carnivals again. Maybe they'll give you free rides all day."

I glanced at my watch. "They're pulling out this afternoon." I rose.

"While I think of it . . ." From the floor underneath his desk he pulled out a cylindrical box, gift-wrapped in gold paper and topped with a shiny red ribbon. "Housewarming gift," he said. "Belated."

I judged it to be a fifth of something tasty. "Good for a cold night, when the frost is on the pumpkin?"

"Something to cheer you through the long winter."

"Much obliged. There're probably enough drinks in it for two."

"Don't be hasty."

"You won't be taking those steroids forever."

He grinned and shook his head.

I drove out the parkway, under a cloudless afternoon sky. The trees lining the riverbanks and distant hills blazed with furnace light. I had the window open, and the air carried a faint scent of burning leaves. It was illegal to burn them anymore, but somewhere leaves were burning anyway, and it was a magical smell that wanted to bring me back to childhood and happy times. On the calm water above the Pawtucket Falls dam, one of the National Park Service's tour boats was bumping slowly upriver, a fan of wake unfolding behind it. A ranger stood in the stern, declaiming through a bullhorn to a thinned crew of visitors, probably talking about how for centuries the spot had been a meeting place for the Indians, and how later the falls were the force behind the city's mills. It wouldn't be too long before the season would end and the boats would be hauled out and stored, the itchy woolen uniforms packed in mothballs, and a couple months from now, ice would begin to turn the river to clabber and there would be no smells at all in the air, only snow. But for now, golden autumn held sway.

Most of the carnival had pulled out already, the trailers and vans gone, leaving the big mowed meadow to a line of Portojohns awaiting pumping, and the duffers who'd be back soon, driving golf balls. Pop Sonders's motor home was still parked off to one side, though it was facing the boulevard now. Several bare-chested jacks were lashing the last of the amusement rides on a flatbed. Moses Maxwell was standing by a dusty blue Econoline van, his porkpie hat tilted back, his face tipped toward the sun.

"Howdy, Mr. Maxwell," I said.

He turned. "Hello, Mr. Rasmussen. I'm just waitin' on Nicole. Here she comes yonder." She was leading a troupe of dogs, the greyhound trotting along a little apart from the rest but looking healthy. Seeing me, Nicole waved. "Kind of like traveling with the band," Moses said, and laughed: a deep, throaty chuckle. It was a good sound to hear. I asked about Sonders, and he pointed. "Captain of the ship. He'll be the last man out."

We chatted a moment more, then shook hands, and I went over to where Pop Sonders was coiling a rope. Inside a red-and-black-checked hunting shirt, the collar turned up, he looked smaller than he once had. "Hoping I'd see you," he said. "Wanted to say good-bye before we pulled out." I appreciated that he didn't ask if I'd received payment (which I had). Farewells and money mix poorly.

"Where to?" I asked.

"We'll catch the last three days of what would've been a week in Providence, then on to a harvest fair in Bridgeport."

"Robert Mitchum's hometown."

"I didn't know that. I know the citizens there once elected P. T. Barnum mayor, and that's where John Ringling hooked up with him for their circus. From there we'll swing west through New York state— Utica, Rome . . ." He went on, mentioning destinations, like an old sailor naming ports of call. While he talked, I kept looking to see if Troy Pepper was around. I hadn't seen him since his release. Of course, there was no reason I had to; I'd done my job, collected a week's pay. Soon the remaining workers conferred with Pop, confirming that the caravan planned to gather at a food plaza on I-95 in a couple of hours and make the rest of the trip together from there.

I walked with Pop to his motor home, both of us moving at slower than our usual speed. Beyond, at the edge of the unmowed field, gold finches were darting among clumps of Canadian thistle, loosing little bursts of thistle down that drifted past like early snow. Sonders opened the driver's door and turned to me. "What I told you before about having a hometown—I meant it. Maybe if I'd had some place to go back to, a place to hang my hat, lick my wounds . . . I'd have gone. But I don't. *We* don't." He gestured at what remained of the caravan, waiting on him. He stuck out his hand. "I appreciate what you did, son."

I wanted to say to hell with that, wanted to tell him, *Stick awhile. In all the confusion of the past few days, we didn't get much chance to talk.* I'd like to have sat with him, and Moses Maxwell, in the mellowing autumn sun and hear their stories, learn from them. I'd been hung up on seeking facts and had gotten far too many of them. Now I wanted wisdom. But there's never a discount on that commodity, no closeouts or clearance sales; we all had to get it the same way, in installments, paying over time with the hard coin of experience. I shook his hand, then watched him and the others draw into the light afternoon traffic on the boulevard.

As I walked back toward my car, a black 4Runner with tinted windows climbed the curb and moved across the field to pull up five feet from me. Louis Hackett climbed out of the passenger side and looked around the vacant field. He cleared his throat and spat. "Sooner or later Pop'll get his ass in a sling again, and there won't be a bozo like you around to save it."

"And there you'll be."

"Time's on my side." He chased a bit of thistle fluff with his hand. "Squisher, though, that's another story. He never was a good loser. Not back in his wrestling days and not now. Only thing that'll make him feel better, he figures, is a little payback, for that busted store window."

I tried to see inside the Toyota but couldn't make out anything through the smoked glass. I hoped he didn't have a gun pointed at me. I shifted position slightly, to put Hackett between the SUV and me. "Tell him not to get his tights in a twist," I said. "I'll take care of the window."

Hackett reached and rapped on the hood, his gold pinky ring winking. The driver's door opened and Spritzer got out. "He says he's going to pay for that store window," Hackett told him. "He says he's insured." And to me, "You're cute, you know that? Isn't he cute, Bud?"

"Oh, he's a fuckin' cutie, all right."

"That again."

"Unfortunately it's a long ride home without the brass ring." Hackett lifted his shoulders. "Squisher's got another kind of payback in mind." The big man was flexing his fingers, his knuckles making a sound like corn being popped, and the pit of my gut churned.

"Look," I said reasonably, trying to ignore the churning, "climb back in and drift, and that's the end of it. We're clear."

"Hear that, Bud? He's gonna give us a chance."

"What's the point now?" I said.

"Hey. I said it ain't my idea. But partners got to stick together."

They weren't to be reasoned with. I could make a run for it, but on my knee I wouldn't get far. Or I could take my chances and hope to get in enough licks to keep things even. Maybe a passerby would get on her cell phone and the police would show up with a meat wagon in time to get whoever of us needed it most to a hospital. No, I would haul out my weapon, though I really didn't want to. I was sick of guns.

Behind the pair, a dusty gray pickup hauling a camper drew off the boulevard and came across the grass. We watched it draw to a stop twenty feet away. The driver's door opened.

Out of the bright county jumpsuit I didn't recognize him at first, but the long wooden mallet with the black friction-taped handle gave him away. Troy Pepper carried it lightly, letting it dangle from his good hand. He considered the two men for a moment, and then he walked over and stood beside me.

"These are the guys who wanted to kick Pop when he was down," I said, by way of introduction. "Gentlemen, Troy Pepper."

I didn't see it coming. The Rag Tyme boys didn't either. There was no buildup, no working himself into a frenzy, no wild karate cry. Pepper swung the hammer in a big looping arc and brought it down onto the hood of the 4Runner and rang a dent into the metal that splintered paint.

"*Holy shit!*" Spritzer said.

I jumped, too.

"That's your death warrant!" Hackett snarled.

The second blow smashed a headlight housing, spraying glass onto the ground. Pepper raised it for a third time and stopped, holding it overhead, ready.

I drew the gun then and cocked back the hammer, just to add a second vote. No one moved. "The offer stands," I said. "Breeze while your rig still runs."

Hackett looked as if he were calculating odds, wondering what the fight would be like now, then shook his head disgustedly. Spritzer just appeared bewildered, his big pocked face as barren as a distant moon. Hackett trudged to the 4Runner, and Spritzer followed. Climbing in seemed a labor. They wheeled a U-turn and drove off in a cloud of bitter dust. I holstered my gun.

The action over, Pepper seemed suddenly out of place, like an actor thrust onstage without any lines. He lowered the mallet. He'd been inside, what, less than a week? And yet he seemed changed. He still wore the expression of a man who'd just missed being hit by one falling piano but who fully expected there'd be another somewhere, it was only a matter of when. His eyes had a kind of stunned look, and the crows had trod deeper at the corners of them. I was glad to see him, and I said so.

"I was out to the cemetery," he said quietly. "She got a nice spot, Flora. The trees and all."

"It is nice."

"I wanted to say thank you."

Thank you. Words with as many meanings as "I'm sorry"—which phrase I had tried an hour ago at All Saints. I probably could have waited, but I owed Duross that. The three other officers standing in the private room let me in without a word. Duross sat in a high-backed padded chair, an IV stand beside him, with a single bottle suspended from it. He was pale, his shock of dark hair standing out starkly against a white bandage, his whiskers blue, but he looked only a little the worse for wear. He motioned for the officers to wait in the corridor. I fell back on small talk for a minute, and then I said, "I let some past get in my way. A past that had nothing to do with you. I was wrong."

"I'll be clear with you, Rasmussen," he said, his voice a dry whisper. "I'm not ready for that yet. What's between you and the department, you and Frank Droney, that's not for me."

"You're right."

"In time, after I get out of here . . . maybe we can sort this out."

I nodded. "You'll let me know."

And that was that.

"Thank you," Troy Pepper said, and it sounded right and set something straight for me.

"You're welcome."

For a moment we looked at each other, then his gaze slid away toward his vehicle and some horizon that perhaps only he saw. We walked across the yellowing grass, through the first fallen leaves, to the gray pickup, with its camper in tow, and I wondered if it would ever be possible to open the man up, to get him to turn some of his inside out for others to see. Maybe Flora Nuñez had done it and that was why he'd wanted to be with her, but her dying had sent him scurrying back inside, the way that groundhog is said to do when it sees its shadow. I didn't know. I stuck out my hand and he shook it. Then, with a shy, ducking motion, he reached into the truck and brought out a stuffed animal and handed it to me. A parti-colored teddy bear.

"I think it's the one your girl had her eye on that night." I didn't tell him she was my ex-girl; it was the thought that counted. I said that she'd appreciate it.

He drove back to the boulevard, and when there was a break in the traffic he pulled out. He'd be heading to join the others, all bound for southern New England and then points west. In my mind's eye I could see the painted wagons, and the whirling, lighted rides, could hear the barkers' cries and smell the cooking sausages and fried dough and the sweet scent of spun sugar. Carnivals were all the things Pop Sonders had said they were: throwbacks, reminders of something, their histories unfurling vividly behind them like pennons; endangered in some way, too. But carnivals weren't going to fade from the landscape anytime soon, any more than battered old cities were, or PIs, or people doing bad or good, either; or summer or fall. There's a rhythm to the flow of things, grand events and small, and each has its season and its reason, and that was about the extent of the wisdom I possessed. I watched Pepper's rig roll west along the river toward the last bridge, picking up speed and growing smaller, and for just one instant I wondered what that would be like, living on gypsy wheels, moving as part of a group, knit by struggles and bonds as complex as those of any family. Behind me I could hear the city, and feel it, too, tugging me with its own gravity. At the bridge, the camper turned, the sun winking on its windows, went around a corner, and was gone.

At the Registry of Deeds the teddy bear got through security without tripping any alarms or being eviscerated in a body cavity search. Phoebe was out, but her friend Janelle was there. She gave me a tender-eyed look. "I heard. It isn't you, you know. I think our girl needs time. She's not ready for a lot of yang in her life right now."

I asked her if she'd get the bear to Phoebe. "Of course. Good luck, Alex. It was nice to know you."

When I got home to my small house, which remained in serious need of a balancing touch of yin but would have to wait for it, I put Ed St. Onge's gift-wrapped housewarmer on the coffee table. Time for a wee dram. God knows I'd earned it. Moses Maxwell's LP was still on the turntable, which I switched on. In the kitchen, as the music began—"In My Solitude"—I got a glass, plonked in some ice cubes, and carried it into the living room and set it at the ready. Sitting on the couch, I listened for several moments to the young Mr. Maxwell's nimble fingers soulfully striding the piano keys, his bass man and drummer and horn player working, too, each musician telling his own story, yet weaving them into one larger tale. Finally I plucked the red bow off the tall box, peeled away the gold paper—and gawked.

Something to bring me cheer in the coming winter, St. Onge had said. The box held an amaryllis bulb, in its own decorative pot, with soil and growing instructions, and the promise of a beautiful, living companion. What was there to do but laugh?